PRIVACY

SETTINGS

ROANNE HASKIN

Kindle Direct Publishing

This paperback edition 2021

First published in Great Britain by Kindle Direct Publishing 2021

This book is dedicated to the fantastic strong women who have influenced us:

Our Mums, Mum in Law and Aunties.

You are simply the best.

Prologue

February

Bruce sat open mouthed, staring in disbelief at his laptop screen. When he had started his little 'project' to ensure he had oversight of the IT set up and security for his mates, he could never have envisaged what he would witness.

His addiction had started a few months back when he offered to install top of the range security systems in his best friends' homes. Due to his new business venture, Bruce had genuinely been able to source the best hi-tech system around for the domestic market at a fantastic, low price and his mates had all jumped at the offer. He had taken the opportunity to fit tiny spy cameras in all of their downstairs' rooms. He was no pervert, so he'd had the decency to leave the bedrooms and bathrooms alone. He had also set up speech recognition, echo devices, not to mention all sorts of spyware on various mobile devices, hard drives and the like. Total security 'peace of mind' for all of the gang. Or so they thought. It was certainly not difficult to listen in on conversations when you know all of your mates' login details.

At first, Bruce told himself it was just to 'check' all was working, as it should, but he soon became fixated on their private exchanges, or simply watching them go about their daily lives.   As his obsession grew, Bruce started to run pages and pages of weekly reports, detailing everything that had been said to each device and it made for scary reading. He hadn't stopped there; he had also obtained the internet router addresses for the entire gang. This meant it had been child's play to hack into their internet and run basic 'sniffing' software to acquire all manner of confidential information, dodgy internet searches and private accounts.

Over time, he had become consumed with his new 'hobby', taking every opportunity to watch or listen in through their various devices. He delighted in the notion that he could access any piece of technology in the home that relied on internet connection and not just the obvious mobile phones and security cameras. He had access to video door bells, PCs, laptops and TVs, even kitchen equipment and kids' toys. 'Internet of Things', it was called, something well known by data security geeks and hackers and it had meant that Bruce had carte blanche to take himself on his self-indulgent, voyeuristic journey.

Bruce knew he had seriously abused the trust his friends had placed in him, but he had somehow justified in his own mind that it was 'for their own protection'. He had revelled in the simplicity of how he could watch and listen whenever the mood took him.   He had even spied on his own wife and their children.

Today though, he felt far from happy. Slumped in his chair, Bruce was stunned and full of regret. Gazing at the images on the screen, the words of his beloved late

7

grandma sprang to mind, 'you never really know what goes on behind closed doors.'

Chapter 1

The Previous November

The heady aromas of cumin, turmeric and coriander mingled with the comforting tones of chicken and lamb encasing the group of friends in a reassuring warmth to fend off the icy November weather. Already two hours into the gathering, several members of the group had imbibed enthusiastically as usual and were keenly engaging in a range of conversations, which swirled and mingled to produce the general indecipherable hubbub of a gathering of close friends.

Bruce was in his element – a truly first class host. He surveyed the scene like a high class maître d', expertly distributing bottles of beer and directing Daisy, his gregarious wife, to where she needed to go next to keep the glasses of Prosecco topped up. The kitchen was high end designer and sophisticated, flowing into a generous conservatory from which a plethora of stylish fairy lights swathed the space in soft, magical twinkles. Ruby, a real party girl, had settled into the ample leather armchair and was engrossed in deep conversation with Frankie, who always regaled the group of friends with the latest development in her dysfunctional relationship with her partner, Adam.

Frankie and Adam had worked together at the local secondary school at the heart of the community. Frankie ran a successful business, a team of occupational and educational psychologists who did a lot of work in schools and colleges. Five years ago, she had taken on a major contract with Delvreton High School. At that time Adam had just joined the senior leadership team as an assistant headteacher. An affair soon bloomed and Frankie had played a major role in helping him to develop his career. When the post of headteacher became available a year ago, she had written his application and coached him for all aspects of the selection process including his final interview. Adam was now head of the school, a position he never would have attained without Frankie's constant support. Frankie's connections, her endless advice and guidance had essentially landed him the job; everyone knew he would never have been promoted otherwise.

The relationship between Frankie and Adam had raged on and off whilst Adam tried, not very hard, to extricate himself from his wife, churning out a torrent of empty promises. Frankie had always patiently waited, grateful for those snatched moments that any affair thrived on. For a successful, intelligent woman, she could be a real fool – that is what her loyal friends told her repeatedly. Ruby raised an eyebrow as she downed the last dregs of her Prosecco and Frankie started to laugh uncontrollably at her friend's characteristically irreverent advice.

'Fuckwit's only gone and done it again!' Ruby shrieked. 'Brooke, come over here and hear the latest saga', she instructed. Soon a flock of the girls were drawn like gulls in a feeding frenzy to Frankie and Ruby, the squawking exclamations punctuating the heady atmosphere. It was going to be a good evening.

'Starters are ready,' Bruce declared and proudly cast his eye over the large kitchen island, which was covered with homemade samosas, bhajis, kebabs, raita and pickles. Vincent, a relatively recent member of the group, loved nothing more than cooking massive quantities of food for his mates. Vincent was a talented chef and the group had got to know him since he had opened his restaurant in the centre of the town. He stood in the centre of the kitchen, tea towel tucked into his jeans, relishing his role as provider and beaming as the compliments flowed; the food really was delicious and the alcohol was enhancing everyone's appetite. Thoughts were eagerly focussed on the main course and more dishes were produced, in abundance and gratefully received: Chicken Korma, Lamb Rogan, Naans and a wealth of rice variations. The pleasure of eating, satisfying that most basic of instincts, dulled the noise for a while.

Suddenly, a loud burst of laughter broke out from a group surrounding Bruce as Ronnie, Frankie's brother, got into the groove of storytelling; he ran through the events at the wine tasting that Vincent had hosted the week before.

'Ah mate,' Ronnie addressed Stefan, a regular at the Otter's Head, who had not been at the tasting event. 'Arthur was battered! He just fell off his chair taking the table cloth with him and shit loads of red wine spilled all over Vincent's cream carpet!'

'No way!' Stefan was loving the tale, never disappointed by Arthur's antics and secretly pleased that he had been invited to Bruce's home for the first time. Stefan was starting to feel part of the gang, choosing the music for the group and taking requests. Everyone loved his DJ skills and this had earned him the nickname of 'DJ Stefan', which he secretly loved. He was enjoying the warm glow that a sense of belonging brought with it.

'Get some decent tunes on!' Stefan's wife, Cherrie hollered across the kitchen.

'Bloody hell, give me chance. Freebird up next!' Stefan bellowed back as he took control of the playlist.

Arthur beamed, sheepishly raising his beer 'How's the carpet mate?' he asked Vincent, 'I did offer to pay for the cleaning.'

'I just chucked loads of white wine over it,' Vincent said reassuringly. 'Always works, no worries mate. It was worth it for the entertainment!'

Ruby's gaze from across the room was not amused. She had been away for the weekend with the girls and this was the first she had heard of Arthur's latest misdemeanour.

'What's that?' she asked, her cold tone slicing through the heady atmosphere. 'How come you never told me this?'

Arthur grimaced slightly and squirmed on the high stool he sat on. 'I just didn't get round to it. Must have slipped my mind'.

Ronnie chuckled to himself as Brooke observed Ruby.

'Yeah, right!' laughed Bruce, joined by the rest of the crowd.

Ruby turned her back on the men, filled up her prosecco and stalked haughtily back into the conservatory. Brooke was watching this from her vantage point, noting that all was not quite as rosy as everyone was led to believe in the Harper household. Brooke's sharp intuition never failed her and she could sense that something was not quite right with Ruby and Arthur. She moved next to Ruby and uttered some quiet, calming words. 'You know what he's like. It was just a classic Arthur moment.'

'Yeah, he's a real knob-head, but he could have told me!' Ruby replied, looking thoughtfully into her glass before being pulled out of her reverie by the sound of music and the sight of Frankie trying to floss with Bruce and Daisy's daughter Rosie.

'Just follow me,' Rosie instructed as Frankie moved awkwardly, tongue lodged at the corner of her mouth indicating a high level of concentration. Despite being highly effective at work, she was hopeless at trying to master the latest dance move that every teenager, it seemed, could do naturally. Suddenly, Bruce burst in and began to floss effortlessly with Rosie.

'You're such a show off,' Frankie lamented and she strode into the kitchen. 'More Chardonnay for me. Maybe that will help me get my groove on!'

'I don't think so' laughed Brooke. 'But no harm trying.'

The hours passed, the drinks flowed and the group mellowed as the alcohol coursed gently through their veins. Talk roamed over the fertile ground of Christmas and New Year: plans for more get togethers, shopping trips and the prospect of days spent with elderly relatives. It was not long before the subject of Bruce's career plans came up; he was on the brink of pulling back from all the work his business was doing in the States and focussing more on the home market, certainly in terms of cutting back on the global travelling requirements. Daisy speculated on how this could affect Bruce who had, in the past, seemed to enjoy his frequent travels to America.

'Don't worry love; we'll take everything in our stride and there will be loads of benefits to you seeing a lot more of me', Bruce stated confidently. Daisy smiled as she knew nothing ever got in the way of Bruce's plans; he was the archetypal achiever, one of life's success stories and always in control of his destiny. She enjoyed the sense of security that brought as she looked at her lovely home and her great group of friends. The world's economy may not be the best ever but Daisy knew she and her family would always be more than alright. She continued to smile to herself and allowed her thoughts to wander to the perfect family day she would enjoy on Sunday. She and Bruce would stroll along to Otter's Head, the stylish gastro pub in the centre of Delvreton, they would laugh and joke with mates and then enjoy a long, relaxed late Sunday lunch with the kids.

Daisy's gaze fell on Frankie, her face pulled into a grimace as she sat alone up the corner, checking her phone once again, tapping frantically to reply, no doubt,

14

to Adam. Not everyone's life was sorted but no one understood why Frankie allowed herself to be treated like she was by him. She took a long slug of Chardonnay before standing a little unsteadily to hunt for her handbag and coat. Brooke and Ruby were following suit and exclamations about the late hour, of one thirty in the morning, signalled that it was time to accept the night was drawing to a close. Hugs and goodbyes, jokes and plans to meet up at the Otter's accompanied the exiting friends who drifted out into the darkness, navigating their journeys home. Delvreton was shrouded in a light fog as the group gradually dissipated. The couples linked arms and Frankie walked in between Brooke and Ronnie to ensure no slips, trips or falls. Once again, Frankie had drunk too much.

Bruce and Daisy quickly restored their beautiful kitchen to its pristine state and Vincent packed up the leftovers efficiently.

'Thanks mate. Great night', said Bruce. 'You've done it again, first class scran. You should do it professionally!'

'It really is my pleasure,' Vincent replied laughing. 'It was lovely to see everyone together again. Will I see you tomorrow at the Otter's? Think we'll all need hair of the dog,' he commented with a wry smile.

'Too right,' agreed Daisy.

With that, Vincent headed out into the darkness; the door closed behind him and the lights went off.

***

The sleety rain lashed the windows of the Otter's Head relentlessly. The smart pub provided a welcome haven from the elements. The Otter's was situated down a side street, just off the main square, at the centre of the market town of Delvreton. The Christmas lights swathed a row of bare trees, casting their festive glow onto the windows of the Otter's; they were already steamed up but any passers-by couldn't help but feel drawn to the scene within: a perfect scene of what a Sunday lunchtime experience should be, a scene epitomising what it means to be a fortunate member of a happy and content community.

What could be better than a cosy Sunday lunchtime in front of the wood burner fire that held pride of place in the open plan bar and lounge? Flames flickered and the glasses reflected shards of orange light that lit up the animated faces of the locals. The light grey, bleached panelled wood adorned the walls and covered the base of the bar that stretched at least three metres to give a sense of quiet, understated luxury. All bar stools were taken, which was the norm for any day or evening at the weekend. Five dogs of varying breeds, size and levels of excitement, lolled at their owners' feet or sat expectantly waiting for a doggy treat or the remnants of the tasty morsels on offer. Crispy roast potatoes, generous chunks of black pudding and prawn popcorn were set out along the bar: English tapas, a generous, complimentary offering to customers and now a traditional feature of the Sunday lunch experience. Shane, the host, liked to look after his locals although he often went a bit too far with the risqué comments he made to his female regulars.

An array of eclectic, well-chosen kitsch chairs were grouped around sturdy, solid wooden tables, which were for both diners and drinkers alike. There was not a free space anywhere and the huddled groups of friends and couples leaned in conspiratorially, laughing and exclaiming as the natural rhythm of the conversations ebbed and flowed through the popular lunchtime session.

At the far corner, about eight regulars crammed around one of the tables. Bruce and Daisy were at the centre, flanked by Arthur, Ronnie, Stefan and several others who were happy to attach themselves to whoever was in and looked like they were having the best time. This was typical of the Otter's: a truly friendly place where women regulars could confidently 'pop' in alone, secure in the knowledge that they would never be short of company. With the exception of the flirtatious bar owner Shane, no one would bother them.

'Get it down you!' Ronnie urged Daisy who confessed to a 'slight' headache but gratefully reached out to take the pint of cider on offer. Taking a sip, she smiled, relishing the apple tones. She sighed appreciatively and nodded.

'Yes, you are right, Ron. That is exactly what the doctor ordered'.

'Over here mate!' Arthur shouted, half rising from his seat and gesturing to the figure clad in stylish outdoor wear, complete with the Peaky Blinder in vogue cap and luxurious scarf. 'Vincent, mine's a pint of the Badgers while you're up there.'

Vincent waved and nodded happily, as he took his place in the queue and started some idle chatter with the other locals, waiting patiently to be served. The sense of bonhomie pervaded the Otter's and seemed to calm the customers who were happy to just bide their time and let the soothing warmth wash over them. In due course, Vincent deftly collected the four drinks he had ordered and picked his way through the tables and other customers as he made his way to his mates' table.

'Arthur, one for you and a cheeky little brandy chaser for the both of us,' Vincent chuckled, as he put the drinks down.

'Ah, just what I need, thanks a lot,' Arthur grinned appreciatively. 'That will chase the winter blues away and sort out the old head ache a treat.'

'Too right,' agreed Daisy as Bruce made a decent attempt at looking at her disapprovingly.

'What you looking at?' she asked, feigning an aggressive tone.

'Nothing, my sweet,' Bruce crooned.

'Where's Ruby and Brooke then?' Daisy asked.

'Still in bed!' Arthur laughed. 'Just like any Sunday and I bloody well got it in the neck when we left yours. Surprised you can't see any bruises.'

'Well, you should have told her about wine-gate!' said Ronnie

'Yeah, you never thought you'd keep that one quiet did you?' challenged Daisy. 'She's got a sixth sense where you're concerned, especially when you've been up to no good.'

'Which is all the bloody time,' added Ronnie, chuckling.

'Seriously, mate, I thought the girls were joining us. Thought Frankie was coming along too. It's good that she seems to be seeing a bit less of that dickhead Adam. She can do a lot better than him' said Ronnie. Although Ronnie's demeanour was that of a typical lad, underneath the jokes and the bravado, he really did have a soft, caring side and he always looked out for his sister, who was also one of his closest friends. With just three years between their ages, Frankie and Ronnie had grown up in a very close family environment. If Adam messed her around again, then Ron would be more than happy to step in and have a word.

'Oh my God!' Daisy shrieked, 'They're all here, look. Over here girls. Bruce will get your drinks in.' She gestured to Bruce who instantly jumped up, on his way to the bar already and signalling that his chair was free for one of the new arrivals.

Ruby, Brooke and Frankie pushed their way through the tables, saying hello to the locals as they passed and giving Bruce a peck on the cheek.

'Already on a chaser, knob head,' Ruby observed as she playfully slapped Arthur round the head before she slumped dramatically into the free chair left by Bruce.

Arthur grinned sheepishly at her.' You don't mind, really, my sweet, do you? I gave my darling wife a croissant in bed this morning and an extra special Sunday morning treat didn't I?' he grinned at his wife.

'Too much information!' exclaimed Brooke and Frankie nodded.

'I'm banishing those images from my mind,' Frankie laughed.

The friends certainly knew each other well and understood the undoubtedly passionate relationship that was the 'Ruby and Arthur' partnership. High octane all the way, whether they were loving or fighting. They were made for each other and the best fun you could ever have with a couple.

Chairs were chivalrously offered to the new arrivals and Bruce delivered the girls' drinks, signalling to the lads to join him at a rare gap at the bar that he had just spotted.

'Bloody hell, this prosecco is breakfast,' Ruby sighed. 'Don't think I've been up before three o'clock on a Sunday for ages.'

'I'm well ready for this,' Frankie added. 'Dragged myself out of bed at ten for a run with Adam and we ended up arguing again.'

'Why the hell don't you just ditch him once and for all?' Brooke asked with a concerned expression on her face.

'Look, you know I'm in a much better place since I stopped working with him. He just doesn't get to me any more like he did. He really can't control me anymore; in fact, I feel in control. So, I know you care but let's just forget shit-face and enjoy our Sunday... please.'

'Okay Bab,' said Brooke, looking towards the bar at the lads. 'Check out Vincent's Peaky get up! Is he after another woman at the moment or what?'

'Think so,' said Ruby. 'He'll be trying to impress some sophisticated woman, knowing him. He gave us another slap up nosh last night though. He's bloody amazing in the kitchen.'

'Too right,' Brooke and Frankie nodded in agreement.

'Anyway, mate,' said Ruby. 'Are we still on for that trip to the Mailbox on Friday Daisy?'

'Yeah, I'm up for that big time,' Daisy answered, stretching and yawning. 'Should just about be recovered and ready for a boozy lunch with you girl... but have mercy on me. I'm not in your league. I'm a lightweight really.'

'Who are you trying to kid?' Ruby exclaimed loudly.

The light had gradually faded and the winter evening was descending fast as the Otter's emptied. The friends said their farewells amidst confirmations of plans for the next weekend and the festive season ahead. Gradually, they drifted away into their homes, their lives, their worries, their hopes and dreams.

Bruce watched from a recess in the lounge area, savouring a quiet moment and surveying his friends. He felt good, he felt the warmth of belonging and he felt powerful. He looked at his phone and smiled as each friend was listed in turn on his unique App. He could switch on his lens into their lives whenever he wanted and his mind ignited over what he might discover. Not tonight though - he would carefully choose his moment to start his surveillance. This Sunday evening, he would simply enjoy the regular family time he so loved, knowing that whenever he chose, he could find out whatever he wanted to know about each and every one of the 'Delvreton crew'. It was going to be a very interesting Christmas; that was for sure.

Chapter 2

3 December

Daisy stepped out of Bruce's black Range Rover after having given him a hug and an extra sensual goodbye kiss, which took him a little by surprise but he certainly was not complaining. She waved to Bruce as she watched him drive away into the December mist and pulled her cashmere scarf tight, savouring a rare moment of calm. Mother to Rosie, a bright vivacious teenager and Iris, now a young woman of twenty two who had just set out on a career in teaching, Daisy was very much looking forward to her special day out with one of her dearest friends, Ruby. Daisy herself was a fitness instructor running her own successful local business. That, together with running her lovely home, left her with so little time for herself.

Today was her day and she smiled, looking forward to her first Christmas shopping trip. She anticipated a boozy lunch and bloody good fun. A table at Harvey Nicks was booked for one pm and she knew she would return home very much the worse for wear. Good thing was Bruce and Arthur really would not give a shit unlike that control freak Adam, Frankie's love interest. God knows why Frankie put up with him. Good thing was that her hubby Bruce and Ruby's hubby Arthur liked their women to have a good time and they would not be disappointed today.

Daisy looked at Ruby's elegant 1930s detached home, already boasting a beautiful Christmas wreath on the door, fairy lights stylishly twinkling away and banishing the cold and damp from this middle class street in the heart of Delvreton. Properties were snapped up within days when they went on the market and the close sense of community was viewed as a real bonus, a real selling point further enhanced by the popular oversubscribed school that Adam ran.

Daisy pressed the bell and smiled at the sound of Jingle Bells that alerted Ruby to her arrival. Arthur came to the door, beaming as he reached forward to hug Daisy and welcome her into his home.

'Your lucky day,' he proclaimed, 'I'm going into the city later so I will chauffeur you lovely ladies to your destination.'

'That's fab' smiled Daisy. 'We would've got a cab, but this is ace. Thanks mate.'

'Be down in a minute,' Ruby called from upstairs. 'Just deciding if I can risk my kitten heels. Don't think we'll be doing loads of walking will we?'

'Naah, we'll just hang out in the Mailbox,' Daisy replied.

'Bloody hell, that means my bank balance is going to take a beating,' Arthur complained, feigning extreme worry with his exaggerated hang dog expression.

'You're a property developer mate,' laughed Daisy, 'just get a few more of those apartments sold.

'Wow, you look hot!' Daisy exclaimed, as Ruby appeared in the hallway. 'Love the leather pants and those heels! Love that top too. Looks just like one I saw in a magazine and is way out of my price range. You sexy thing!'

Ruby beamed as did Arthur.

'You look pretty sassy yourself,' Ruby complimented her friend. 'I think we are ready to hit the big city of Birmingham. Driver please.' Ruby clicked her fingers, as she paraded out of the door, swinging her hips for effect to the delight of everyone.

***

'I just can't believe this!' Ruby exclaimed as she checked out a pair of beige slip on trainers from every angle in the shoe department of Harvey Nicholls. How can these possibly be three hundred and fifty quid? Who the fuck would buy these?'

'Yeah I know, Daisy agreed as she was drawn towards the Christian Louboutin shelf. 'I can understand it with these beauties though. I've always fancied a pair and thought Frankie looked ace in hers the other night round at ours but then she loves her shoes, doesn't she? I think she even wears them at work.'

'She needs some joy in her life, poor mare, having to put up with that dickhead Adam. Anyway, I think we are more than ready for a cocktail now before we have our posh lunch,' Ruby suggested with a broad grin and a glimmer in her eye.

'Now you are talking,' Daisy agreed as they made their way towards the escalator.

'Just look at all this designer gear,' Ruby said, as the escalator moved up through the floors and the friends stared at the glitz that was laid out before them, further enhanced by the large yet minimal white and silver Christmas decorations. It seemed that the world was bathed in a soothing richness of affluence and advantage. Just two miles down the road, families were crammed into high rise flats with no electricity and having to rely on foodbanks. These were the households where the kids went to the schools that Frankie and her colleagues worked with. When she shared the sad stories of the children and families that needed support from psychologists and social workers, the usual banter would cease for a few moments, as the friends realised just how lucky they were.

'Here we are!' Daisy announced as the escalator reached the top floor and the splendid bar and restaurant welcomed them. Grilled steak, subtle baked fish and a plethora of mild herbs and garlic scented the privileged air around them, as a beautiful young man minced towards them briskly, holding two large embossed menus. Ruby gave their names and they were escorted to their corner table. In a heavy French accent, Jean-Paul explained the specials and that he was delighted to be looking after them.

'So,' announced Ruby. 'I really think that a cocktail is in order.'

Daisy sighed happily and surveyed the Harvey Nick's cocktail list.

'Ooh, decisions decisions…. I think it's got to be a Sloe Gin Negroni,' announced Ruby. 'Had it last time and it was just delicious.' She smiled, anticipating the pleasure to come.

'Mine's got to be a Pornstar Martini,' giggled Daisy with a cheeky gleam in her eye.

'Go for it mate. We might have to try another as we're in no rush at all,' laughed Ruby as she surveyed the classy clientele and the beautiful interior design that flowed through the restaurant to the bar area. 'Yes, this is the life,' she sighed.

As they savoured their cocktails and had a mischievous exchange about Jean-Paul's ultra-pert buttocks but bemoaned the fact that he was clearly gay, they made their choices for lunch. A sharing plate of antipasti for starters, followed by the baked fillet of cod with whipped potato, asparagus and basil sauce for Ruby, a long time pescatarian and the dry aged rib eye steak for Daisy, a committed meat eater. She went for the fries and selected the béarnaise sauce.

'Aah, this is such a treat', Daisy pronounced as she drained her cocktail.

'Well, tis the season to be merry and we both work hard so we definitely deserve a bit of a treat,' Ruby stated. 'Now, that went down very easily. It would just be wrong not to have another! Same again, or shall we experiment?'

A second cocktail had been consumed and a bottle of the Pinot Grigio ordered, as the friends slowly and luxuriously worked their way through the delicious sharing plate. Their conversation roamed over the group of friends and paused for a while over their Christmas present list, some items selected for purchasing that afternoon.

The main course was stylishly presented to the two women by the flirtatious Jean-Paul. Even though his sexual preference was clear, like many gay men, he knew exactly how to make middle aged women laugh and swoon, even more so when the alcohol relaxed both their bodies and their inhibitions.

'Well, I am stuffed,' announced Daisy, her slightly pink cheeks betraying the pleasant, slightly inebriated sensation that she was clearly enjoying. 'I haven't had a good lunch time session since last summer,' she reflected. Running her fitness business kept her in very good shape and kept her on the straight and narrow in the normal working week, when she also ran her family home like a military operation. Similarly, Ruby was very diligent in her work, a labour of love, since she was passionate about the jewellery that she designed and made and loved the fact that she ran her own business. But today, they were free and they were definitely making the most of it.

'So, that was pretty damned bloody perfect,' Ruby announced. 'And just one little matter to clear up before we call over our pretty boy.'

Daisy smiled as Ruby scrunched the linen napkins and placed them at the centre of the table, as she deftly swept the stylish salt and pepper pots into her large tote bag.

'At these prices, I think I am owed these,' Ruby stated. 'They'll look good on the table this Christmas,' she smiled, with a satisfied look on her face.

'You can take the girl out of Delvreton...' Daisy chuckled. 'What are you like!'

'Don't knock it until you've tried it,' Ruby answered with a glint in her eye.

The bill was paid with a handsome tip for Jean-Paul and the girls tottered into the spacious, boutique powder room.

'Is that top you're wearing designer?' asked Daisy, who sat on the velvet chaise longue observing Ruby reapply her smoky pink lipstick.

'Yeah! It's a Maxmara. You were right earlier but I couldn't say that in front of Arthur. But as I love you, I'll let you into a little secret.' Ruby lowered her voice, glanced around and whispered. 'Are we on our own?'

Daisy felt a frisson of excitement. She had no idea what Ruby was going to say. 'Yeah, we are Bab,' she whispered back.

'Well, I've moved on from bar glasses and salt and pepper pots,' Ruby confessed, as she pulled the slate grey top out of her trousers turning round to reveal a hole at the back of her top, about five centimetres in diameter.

'What's that?' Daisy asked, not understanding what she was seeing.

Ruby tucked the beautiful top back in and proudly announced, 'three hundred quid for this. I wouldn't fork out that much even when I'm pissed, but it's a bloody great rush when you just help yourself from time to time.' Ruby reached into her large, nude leather tote bag to pull out a pair of nail scissors.

Daisy stared at her friend, seeing her in a slightly different light and gradually working out what she was being told.

'You don't mean... You don't mean that you went and nicked that, do you?' Daisy's blue eyes widened and she was not quite sure how she was feeling.

'What's the difference between a salt and pepper pot and a top, a jacket, a scarf, anything really? It's not about what it is, anyway; it's how it makes you feel, when you get away with it. I've done it loads of times. Mainly high end. The Mailbox is good but Selfridges also works and I make sure I frequent many snazzy shopping centres up and down the country when I travel for work, so I spread my sprees.' Ruby stopped abruptly, as the door opened and a mother and daughter walked in. 'Let's get shopping!' Ruby exclaimed, as a stunned Daisy followed her, her heels sinking into the plush carpet of the restaurant.

'So, shall we go and have some fun? Let's have a little look round and have a bit of a try on,' Ruby suggested, her eyes glinting in the soft golden light of the restaurant.

'Come on,' she pulled her friend along to the escalator and they descended to the womenswear floor.

'Just come over here.' Daisy pulled Ruby into a plush, discreet corner of a quiet area. 'Are you suggesting that we….that we…,' she hushed her voice. 'That we are going to nick something from here?' Her eyes were wide like saucers, as she looked expectantly at her friend Daisy's heart raced, but she was still experiencing the effects of the alcohol, so she managed to calm herself.

'It's no big deal and it really does feel fantastic,' Ruby said excitedly. 'Do you have any nail scissors? No problem, if not, as I have a spare pair, extra sharp… It's time to live a little mate.'

Daisy could feel her quickened heartbeat but she could not help feeling a surge of excitement. Could she? Could she really do it? Ruby surreptitiously passed the small steel scissors into her friend's palm, squeezing her hand as she did so.

'Good,' she said, as she looked at her friend's oversized handbag. 'That will do nicely. You can easily get a silk top in that. Let's go and try on and have a bit of an experience! That's what today is all about. Now, where shall we start? What about Joseph? We'll work round to Stella McCartney next.'

The next hour was a blur as Daisy followed her friend, running her hands over so many luxurious fabrics, gathering a range of clothing, handing them to the quietly solicitous, ultra-haughty shop assistants, more like models, who took the garments into the opulent fitting rooms, ready for the girls to start trying on. As the friends worked their way around the floor, Ruby gently guided and advised Daisy.

'Spend about ten minutes trying on. Show each other the garments. Make a lot of excited noises, then select just one – cut off the security tag and conceal it in the bottom of your handbag. Calmly leave the fitting room, leaving about six or seven hangers with the other clothes. Conceal the tag under the chair in the corner of the large spacious cubicle. Walk slowly, chatting to each other as normal. Leave the store and walk out of the Mailbox.'

'Mate!' Daisy's eyes gleamed at her friend, as they looked at each other across the table in the small bistro just round the corner from the Mailbox. 'What the fuck did we just do? I'm shaking! Just look at my hands.'

Ruby looked back at her friend, smiling serenely 'But did you enjoy it?'

'I don't know …. Yes…. I haven't felt like that ever. We took such a bloody risk,' Daisy let out a long sigh 'God, I need this.' She took a long drink from the large glass of Rose that had just been handed to her by the waitress. She waited until the teenager walked away.

'So, what did you get?' asked Ruby,

'I'm not getting it out here,' Daisy hissed. 'I went for that black sheer top from Joseph. It's really long, so I reckon I can hem it pretty easily, as the tag was low down. Oh my God! It's still sinking in.'

'Well, I got the gorgeous mink loungewear suit from Joseph - top and leggings. I'll just patch it up and the top covers the hole in the leggings. Five hundred quid's worth,' Ruby said, sipping her wine and looking very pleased with herself. 'I'll just tell Arthur it's from Primark or somewhere in the pre-Christmas sale. I don't even wear most of the clobber I 'acquire.' Ruby grinned, looking very pleased with herself.

'How much of this have you done?' Daisy leaned in, still talking in a hushed, shocked tone.

'I'll show you later, when we get back. I've got a cupboard full of the stuff. The rush is just amazing! I think I'm addicted,' she chuckled.

Daisy flopped back in her chair, suddenly feeling tired and not quite sure about what the hell just happened. What would Bruce think? What if she had got caught? What about Rosie and Iris? It did not bear thinking about. She just wanted to get home and sort out her head, which was feeling pretty fuzzy now with all the alcohol, the excitement and the shock.

***

Bruce had been concentrating intently for the past two hours on an evaluation document for one of his new contracts. He sighed and stretched, smiling to himself at the thought of a little more light relief. He had used his App earlier to connect with Daisy's phone and listen in on her lunchtime conversation with Ruby. He had to admit that he had experienced a real buzz from the fact that his tech developments were so successful and working so well. Bruce had also enjoyed the lunchtime conversation and he had genuinely felt happy that Daisy was having such a good time; she deserved it.

He decided to listen in on them again, to see how much money his wife was spending, he thought to himself with a wry smile. Bruce's smile was soon wiped from his face as he heard the exchange between Ruby and Daisy in the bistro bar. He shook his head in disbelief, as the reality of what they had been up to, dawned on him. How could they have done that? They had stolen from Harvey Nicholls. Yes, Daisy, Bruce thought. What if you had been caught? That could have ruined their reputation in one fell swoop. He just could not believe what he had heard and was devastated that his gorgeous wife, who he thought he knew so well, had behaved like that. Bruce sat and stared into the distance for some time, totally floored by this new insight.

***

The girls breezed through one of the nearby department stores in the new stylish New Street shopping complex that was part of the redeveloped train station. They quickly grabbed items to show they had done *some* Christmas shopping at least. They ran to make the five o'clock shuttle service then slumped into their seats for the short train journey back to Delvreton. As the train hurtled home, Daisy let her head rest against the window, lulled into a welcome daze, as the lights flickered in the high rise flats, which housed no end of poverty stricken single parents just trying to put food on the table. She could not get her head round what she had allowed herself to do that afternoon; stealing designer clothes, whilst unfortunate others had nothing to eat. She suddenly felt very ashamed of herself. She knew Ruby had a wild side, but she had allowed herself to be pulled into a world that she really should not have entered.

'Our stop sweet.' Daisy was shaken out of her reverie as Ruby grabbed her bags and led the way down the aisle and out onto the platform. Daisy followed obediently, a headache just starting to pulse on the right side of her forehead.

'The taxi should soon be here, my little partner in crime,' Ruby chuckled at her friend's forlorn expression. 'Smile! We've had a bloody great day and I can't wait to see you in that Joseph top. You can wear it for Saturday evening drinks at Frankie's place tomorrow night, if you get your act together. Get your sewing kit out sweet and I'll wear a little number from Selfridges. We can enjoy our guilty little secret! So exciting.'

Daisy nodded. She just wanted to curl up on her sofa, back in her safe, secure home and get what happened into perspective. It would be the one and only time she would stray like that but maybe she would hem and wear that top tomorrow evening. Lurking just below her sense of right and wrong was a tiny glimmer of excitement that she needed to suppress. She had certainly lived a little that afternoon. Who would have thought she would ever shop lift from Harvey Nicks? Who would ever have thought it?

Chapter 3

3 December

Arthur was in the kitchen diner preparing dinner for himself and Ruby. It was a Friday night ritual; he adored cookery and Ruby more than welcomed his culinary talents. Her idea of cookery was a charred fish finger sandwich. Arthur knew that Ruby had been out with Daisy. She would undoubtedly be a little sozzled, but no doubt content following a girlie day shopping and lunching. He loved her zest for life.

The steamed up black cab pulled up outside number seven.

'Thank you driver,' Ruby slurred and shoved a twenty pound note into his hand. 'Keep the change, Angel.'

The driver forced a smile, as his pocketed the 'change' for the nineteen pounds and ninety pence journey. He knew Ruby well though; she always paid £20 whatever the journey. Sometimes he won big time on her three pound trips to Frankie's house and sometimes he lost, like today. It would not stop him taking her business though.

Ruby had tried to persuade Daisy to come back to hers for another tipple, but Daisy had made it clear she was 'so done with alcohol' for the day and she jumped in her own cab. Just as well, as Ruby's plan to badger Arthur to drop

Daisy home would not have worked; he was already well over the limit.

Ruby rebounded off the taxi doors, various bags adorned with luxury brand logos in hand. She weaved her way down the driveway, one kitten heeled foot buckling momentarily. She hurled the unlocked front door open into the extra-large hallway and dumped her bags, as the warmth of the open log fire welcomed her, together with a frenzy of tails wagging, as her beloved chocolate coloured Spaniel, Murray, and her beautiful beagle-cross, Toby pounced on her. They had never quite been sure what other breed exactly Toby was crossed with, but he was handsome regardless. After they had finished kissing Ruby, both noses went straight into her bags.

'Murray! Toby! Get down! Get your snouts out, there are no doggie treats in there for you!' Ruby exclaimed, as they both bobbled off, jumping into their dog beds, tails still wagging and looking adoringly at Ruby.

'Alright Angel?' She cooed at Arthur, who was already very well oiled on various bottled beers and had moved onto a little tipple of brandy.

'Yes babe, moussaka for dinner,' he beamed as he handed her a glass of Prosecco. I know it's your favourite. 'Good day shopping?' he enquired, not really caring, but he thought he had better ask anyway.

'Oh yes, marvellous, thank you Angel and moussaka to boot, magnificent! I may have to treat you to a little favourite of your own later!' Ruby winked at Arthur as he made encouraging 'oh yes!' sexy noises.

Ruby sipped her prosecco contentedly, when she suddenly clocked the drink in Arthur's hand, or more to the point, her precious crystal brandy glass he was brandishing. The mood suddenly turned sour.

'What the hell are you drinking?' Ruby's warm tones plummeted from ninety degrees to minus ten.

'Brandy, why?' Arthur slurred his words.

'Not the drink, you dick-head. What is that glass?' Ruby gave him a very hard stare, any mood of hot passion killed off like a thunderstorm on a summer's day.

'You KNOW that is one of my grandpa's special crystal brandy glasses. They are NOT for using!' Ruby declared, with a stern look on her face that could curdle milk.

'Oh babe, they've just been sitting in the cupboard for years. Why can't we just use them? They're perfect for a tipple.'

'What if you broke it? You're already half-cut, you could drop it! Put it back NOW!' Ruby demanded.

'NO, I'm enjoying my brandy. I won't put it back.' Arthur goaded her, pretending to wobble the glass in his hand as if it was about to fall on the floor.

'PUT IT BACK NOW!' Ruby's temper was rising.

'Oh, oh, look I might drop it.' Arthur pretended to let the glass go. He really had no intention of dropping it; he knew only too well just how precious they were to Ruby. Unfortunately, he misjudged and the glass slid from his grasp, bounced onto the kitchen worktop and plunged, unceremoniously onto the flagstone tiles, brandy splattering across the floor, up the cupboard walls and even into the dog bowls. Ruby's precious glass detonated into smithereens.

'Oh my good God, you asshole! You know how sentimental I feel about those glasses,' Ruby hissed.

'Babe, I'm sorry, I...I didn't mean to...' Arthur stumbled for words. Feeling slightly woozy from the brandy and now very worried what was coming next. He knew there was no way Ruby was going to let this one go quietly.

'Save it.... you never MEAN to do anything do you Arthur? Like you never meant to snog that barmaid two years ago and you never meant to ruin my thirtieth birthday by turning up three hours late and you...' Ruby trailed off, drowned out by Arthur's louder retaliation.

'OH MY GOD, I cannot believe we're having this argument AGAIN! How many times do we have to dredge up this garbage? Why don't you just naff off back to the shops? You obviously forgot to get your Botox, you old trout.' Arthur's words were filled will venom.

At this, Ruby launched at Arthur, hands grabbing his throat. Unfortunately for Ruby, he was far stronger than her small frame. He pulled her wrists from around the grip on his neck and flung her backwards. Ruby staggered, mobilised and relaunched at him, eyes wide and red with anger and tears.

'Take that back, you cruel bastard TAKE THAT BACK!' Ruby was screaming now and both dogs' tails stopped wagging, ears back, worried looks on their faces.

'NO!' Arthur stood his ground, determined to hurt Ruby's feelings, even though he did not mean a word of it.

Ruby launched for his throat again, but Arthur grabbed her shoulders and pushed her away before she could strike. She fell backwards, landing undignified on the hard, flagstone floor. Arthur moved towards her, looming ominously above her. She saw her chance, a swift kick right between the legs.

'Take that!' A kitten heeled foot jabbed Arthur's crotch.

Arthur rolled into a ball onto the floor. 'Jesus Christ Ruby that was two millimetres short of my Misters!'

'Good,' she haughtily replied. 'And you won't be needing them tonight now anyway!' she declared triumphantly.

Arthur writhed around for a moment, but his pride was more bruised than anything.

Ruby picked herself up and dusted herself down, cooing to her frightened dogs. 'Come here babies, daddy's being a knob-head. Mommy loves you best.' Dogs' tails now wagging again, they snuggled up to Ruby. It really did seem to Arthur they were sneering smugly at him.

Arthur tentatively approached.

'Seriously Arthur, just get out of my face. I'm so goddam pissed at you. I can't replace that glass.' Ruby was not about to let him off the hook that easily.

'But babe,' he protested, as he took a tentative step closer. He was now looking Ruby square in the face, his lips an inch or two from hers. 'I'm sorry, truly I am.'

Ruby looked at his puppy dog eyes and suddenly felt sorry for him, even though she was still furious. She lifted her hand and struck Arthur round the face, a short sharp slap.

'Ow! You bloody... God that stung!' Arthur winced as he rubbed the raw skin, a red hand print now slowly revealing itself on his cheek. Then Ruby pulled him close and kissed him. He was about to pull away, but kissed her back. The kiss became frenzied as kitten heels were flung off feet, boots sprawling across the flag-stoned floor, with a fever of clothes following. Arthur's face was still smarting, but with his 'misters' fully intact he suddenly did not notice the pain. God, he loved her and just could not get enough of her. Ruby dug her freshly manicured, navy blue nails into his back.

'That's for breaking my glass, you knob,' she whispered as she bit his earlobe, pulling him closer and passionate love making ensued. One dog took the opportunity to lick brandy off the kitchen floor and the other, with a snout firmly into Ruby's shopping, helped himself to a silver pepper pot to chew on, whilst no-one was watching. At least, it appeared no one was watching.

***

Bruce was in his study, or his 'control room' as he preferred to think of it, his mind still spinning following the discovery of Daisy and Ruby's little shoplifting spree.

41

He was curious to find out more. It was Friday evening and he was just finishing off a conference call with American colleagues, as he heard Daisy stumble through the door, shopping bags dropped in a heap.

'Alright love?' he shouted. 'Good day with Ruby?' Bruce waited to see if Daisy would give anything away.

Daisy took a moment to answer, before shouting 'Yeah...thanks.'

Bruce thought her tone was a bit lack lustre, but nothing much else to give away her earlier pilfering.

Daisy would usually have been full of chatter, filling Bruce in on the day's events. She was desperate to sound 'normal', so added as an afterthought, 'I'm going straight in the hot tub, love,' trying to make her voice sound animated. She could not face Bruce asking questions about their day, what had she bought, did she have a nice lunch... she really needed to gather her thoughts first.

Bruce's heart sank a little, as he had half hoped she would come clean, maybe telling him she had made an awful mistake and was going to return the stolen item. Daisy said nothing.

'Okay,' Bruce replied and switched his teams chat off. He was done working for the evening, but he knew he would have at least an hour to kill before Daisy would tear herself away from the hot tub. He switched over to his security channels, immediately honing in on Arthur and Ruby. He was very keen to find out more about the day's events and in particular, what story Ruby would give to Arthur.

He could see Arthur and Ruby in their kitchen diner. Drinking brandy again Arthur, Bruce chuckled to himself. He could see Ruby chatting away and tuned into the sound. He knew it was an intrusion of privacy, but just lately he could not help himself. The more he found out about what people did in private, the more it horrified, but fascinated him. It was so very revealing what people actually said behind closed doors, compared to what they portrayed in public.

Bruce watched as Arthur teased Ruby with the brandy glass, then before he realised it Ruby was round his throat. Bloody hell, Bruce sat up a little surprised. That's a bit aggressive Rubes, he thought, but nothing compared to what he watched unfold: Arthur flinging his wife to the floor, Ruby's harsh kick and the slap, not to mention the passionate sex. Bruce was a bit dazed and impressed at the same time; they were so lovey-dovey in public. Yes, they teased, but to knock each other around like that and the passion!   Who on earth would think that two of his best mates could be so turbulent. He certainly had not experienced such physical aggression with Daisy, or any of his old girlfriends for that matter.   He was not impressed with Arthur shoving Ruby to the floor, but equally he decided he would never get on the wrong side of Ruby. Should he say something to Arthur about the shoplifting? No... he decided he couldn't, because then Arthur would question Bruce about how he knew. Reluctantly, he decided he would have to keep this information to himself, for now at least.

***

Arthur and Daisy, post-passion, were now chatting over dinner, the mood much calmer and the dogs much happier. Bruce's attention was re-ignited as he watched Ruby take her shopping bags to show Arthur her booty. Bruce waited to see what she would say to Arthur about her new acquisitions.

Bruce watched, as Ruby proudly showed off her 'new' salt and pepper pots to Arthur, pepper pot now rescued from Toby's chops.

'Like these Angel?' Ruby clucked, eyes sparkling.

'Err, yeah?' Arthur was not exactly sure what was to 'like' about silver salt and pepper pots. 'You buy them today?'

'No... I stole them,' Ruby replied smugly.

'Oh Jeez Rubes, you still doing that? I told you, you'll get caught out one day and I won't bail you out!'

'Yes you would!' she cooed, flicking Arthur a wink of her eye as she stood up, gathered her shopping bags and announced, 'I'm heading up for a bath and to put away my new clobber. I got myself some lovely new, sexy outfits too, just for you Angel,' she giggled.

Arthur laughed. 'I see. I'll look forward to a viewing although I'm pretty sure you bought them more for your own pleasure than mine,' he added, returning the wink.

'Who me?' Ruby replied, faked an indignant look, blew him a kiss, then pirouetted round and headed upstairs.

Bruce listened intently. So, Ruby had failed to mention her new outfits had also been 'acquired'. Bruce tutted to himself. Ruby, Ruby, Ruby... you are so wayward, he thought. It was well known amongst their friends that Ruby was the group's resident kleptomaniac, usually a beer glass from the Otter's Head, or the occasional bauble from a restaurant's Christmas display. However, silver salt and pepper pots were significantly more high-end than her usual swipes, not to mention the pricey clobber. It was far more risky to steal things so obviously expensive and from Harvey Nicholls of all places.

Bruce felt equally outraged and baffled. Why did someone like Ruby, with her own exceptionally successful jewellery business, need to resort to swiping from shops? Arthur was clearly less than bothered too. Ruby obviously had a track record and Arthur had seemed scarcely phased by the lifted posh condiments. It was becoming clear that Ruby and Arthur were not the picture of morality Bruce had imagined them to be and now his Daisy was caught up in this. Bruce had a sickness lurking in his stomach and had begun to feel very uneasy, but the uneasiness was accompanied by a compelling desire to find out more. He could not quite put his finger on it, but he was also feeling something else, something pleasing. Then it came to him, he was feeling a sense of power and to his surprise, he liked it.

***

The following evening arrived, the evening of Frankie's hotly anticipated party and Daisy was just putting some finishing touches to her make up as Bruce walked into the kitchen.

'Wow!' Bruce exclaimed, as he clocked Daisy. 'Is that the top you got yesterday?'

'Yeah. Do you like it? A bit more dressy than I usually go for but hey, it's the festive season and that Ruby is very bloody persuasive.'

'Especially when you're hammered,' Bruce laughed. 'It's lovely though, looks expensive. Did you splash out love?' Bruce waited expectantly for Daisy's response. He studied her face for a hint of a lie. Would she come clean that the top was stolen? Now was her chance.

'Would it matter if I had?' Daisy asked, a slight edge to her tone. Bruce earned a shed load of money, but he was careful and sometimes that irritated Daisy.

'Course not,' Bruce replied, thinking to himself how he knew it had not 'cost' her anything, in money at least, but maybe a different story if you counted the cost in lost morals.

'It does look expensive and I saw the designer version in Harvey Nicks for really silly money. You know me, I went and found this one, a pretty good copy in a little boutique just round the corner from the Mailbox.' As Daisy told her little white lie, she couldn't help smiling inside as she knew that this beautiful Joseph top had a price tag of three hundred and fifty pounds. Although she was very surprised at herself, she was getting a real buzz from the knowledge of what she had actually done yesterday afternoon. She was really looking forward to catching up with Ruby and having their own private chat to reminisce about their little spree. Bruce was staggered by the aptitude of Daisy's lying; he really didn't think Daisy had it in her to lie so bare faced to him.

'Taxi's here,' Daisy shouted from the hallway and Bruce dragged himself from his dark thoughts. 'Grab that bag of beers and Champagne love.'

Bruce decided to put his worries to the back of his mind for now; he was determined to try and enjoy Frankie's party.

Frankie's large, detached house nestled in a cul de sac on the outskirts of Delvreton. Just round the corner was a beautiful lake, a favourite spot of Frankie's for her morning runs and many a long walk with Brooke and their dogs. All of the homes were tastefully decorated with different shades of Christmas lights and Frankie's door, like all of the others, boasted a beautiful wreath. As Bruce and Daisy walked up the driveway, they could see into the sitting room, where groups of guests had already gathered and the party was clearly in full swing.

'Think some of Frankie's work colleagues are there as well as us lot,' said Daisy.

'Well, that should help to take the spotlight off Adam. I do want to see him though, as I've got that IT contract with the PFI facilities manager in his school,' Bruce replied.

'At least you'll have something to say to him then, as it's bloody hard to make conversation with him,' Daisy muttered.

Bruce was particularly keen to attend the party that evening, as he wanted to check out his new surveillance equipment, that he had installed in Frankie's study, opposite the sitting room. He knew that various guests would retreat to the quiet space in there to break away from the main groups - that always happened at parties - and he was very interested to listen in later, from the comfort of his home control room, to hear what was said in these private conversations. He could not help but feel a shiver of anticipation, knowing that he had this power and that no one had a clue about his capabilities.

Chapter 4

4 December

Frankie was ready. She had spent the whole day preparing for this party, the house and herself. She glided into the room, wearing her customary designer high heels and a chic little black dress. Her blonde hair was styled in a chignon and her make up slightly heavier than usual, but very much in keeping with the glamour of a pre-Christmas drinks and canapé evening. Earlier that day, Frankie had enjoyed some much needed pampering, spending the afternoon with Sienna, her hairdresser, who had decided to brave it alone by offering a mobile hairdressing service.

Sienna and Frankie went back years and, as is the case with many hairdresser/client relationships, friendships blossomed and the business side of the transaction encompassed a lot more than tending to hair. It very much flowed naturally into a confessional, therapy session as clients relaxed in their home environment, usually further enhanced by a glass or two of something sparkling and alcoholic.

'How come you are always so bloody glamorous?' Frankie asked Sienna, who expertly wove fronds of hair into foils, as she applied the honey, brown and blonde shades to Frankie's hair.

'Well, I can hardly turn up looking a sight can I?' Sienna chuckled. 'I owe it to my clients to make an effort.'

'I just don't know how you can apply those false lashes so easily, every morning, and your nails are always beautiful and you have gorgeous hair and you've also gone and lost even more weight! I really should hate you.' Frankie feigned a troubled tone, as she reached for her Champagne flute.

Sienna smiled. She had been so disciplined for the last month, dutifully following the 5:2 regime that Frankie had introduced her to, over a year ago now. Sienna was certainly beautiful but had not had much luck recently, especially where men were concerned, after a pretty acrimonious divorce. This was just one of the reasons Sienna had so much in common with her clients, many of whom became firm friends, who often confided their deepest secrets to her. Today was no exception. Frankie had brought Sienna up to speed on her latest frustrations with Adam, how he had been moaning about the money she had spent on the food and drink for her Christmas soiree later that evening.

'I just don't think he likes a good time,' Frankie reflected. 'Anyway, you can see for yourself later. It's great that you can come this evening but you will make us older women all look pretty dowdy. Please don't look too amazing tonight!' Frankie winked at Sienna. 'Which pair of your Louboutin's will you be selecting this evening then?'

'The silver, sparkly ones of course. It is Christmas and you just stop putting yourself down. You always look fab. You're a sophisticated lady, who can have her pick of loads of eligible men. Don't you take any shit from that

Adam.' Sienna paused. 'Look Frankie, you've always said you'd want me to be straight with you and, well... I don't want to upset you, but there is some talk going round the town about Adam. I wasn't sure about whether or not to tell you.'

'Go on,' Frankie encouraged Sienna, sitting up a bit straighter in her chair.

'Ok. I think you ought to know.' Sienna looked a little troubled as she spoke, nervously waiting for Frankie's reaction, as she took a very large glug of Champagne. 'Quite a few of my clients tell me that he's a bloody flirt when they go to parents' meetings. He's made a few inappropriate comments, apparently. It really sounds like he's on some sort of power trip but God knows why, as standards are starting to drop in that school. I haven't upset you have I?' Sienna felt a bolt of nerves, as she had never been quite so open with Frankie before.

'Not at all,' Frankie said making every effort to sound upbeat. 'I'm starting to realise that Adam really isn't the person I thought he was.' She sighed. 'But, you know what, I don't give a shit and we are going to have fun, big fun tonight girlfriend. I've had a God awful week and I am going to party.'

'Cheers to that!' Sienna raised her glass. 'And the chignon looks fab. Different for you, but it works. Anyway, I'd better get off so I can tart myself up.'

Frankie smiled as she saw her friend out. 'See you soon. I think I already feel a bit squiffy!' Frankie exclaimed, as she closed the door, Sienna's words rattling round in her mind.

Later that evening, Frankie really was ready to party. She had resolutely pushed the conversation with Sienna to the back of her mind. She glanced at herself in the mirror and smiled at her reflection, just as the doorbell rang and guests started to arrive. 'Not too shabby, if I do say so myself,' she said aloud.

***

Guests had already gathered, drinks in hands and full of chatter, when Bruce and Daisy arrived, clutching a huge magnum of Champagne and a bottle of bourbon.

'Great to see you guys!' Frankie hugged Bruce and Daisy as they arrived in the welcoming, festive hallway, handing their coats to their hostess. 'The gang are already in the sitting room and kitchen.' Frankie ushered them through. 'Tonight, we have Bonnie and Amber serving trays of drinks and food,' she declared proudly. Everyone knew the young women who often waitressed at the Otter's when they came back from university for the holidays. 'Anyway, Shane is here too somewhere, so at least he knows his top bar staff will keep his glass full all night!' Frankie laughed heartily and it was clear that she had already had a fair few glasses. 'Oh! And Sienna is here. She's already a hit and dying to meet you. Watch Bruce though Daisy, as Sienna is too gorgeous for words!' Frankie giggled as she saw a glimmer in Bruce's eye, just as Daisy elbowed him in the ribs.

'He knows he can look but never touch,' Daisy said, affecting a strict tone of voice.

Drawing in close to Daisy, Frankie whispered, 'Adam's just told me he's been looking at one of the townhouses on this development. I really think he's finally ready to commit. Maybe I will have a chance with him, after all.' She looked at Daisy expectantly who just smiled and squeezed her friend's shoulder sympathetically. Sienna's talk of Adam's flirting kept surfacing in Frankie's mind, conflicting with her desire to try to rekindle her faith in the man she wished would come good for her one day.

'Frankie,' a tall, burly athletic type appeared in the doorway of the kitchen. His shaved head and fashionable stubble was softened by arresting brown eyes and a wide smile. However, there was an undoubted arrogance about him. Something in his voice hinted at a desire to be listened to and noticed, especially where Frankie was concerned. 'Your brother is asking where the Moretti beers are and I'm damned if I know. You haven't put them in the cupboard, where they should be. Just typical.' He glanced at Brooke, who was also looking for Frankie. 'God only knows how she holds down that high flying job, when she can't even organise her own kitchen!' Adam said sarcastically. Brooke could not hide the disapproving look on her face as she once again bit her lip. She hated the way he spoke to Frankie.

'Okay, no problem. Think they're in the garage. I'll get them'. Frankie rushed off, eager to please her guests and close down Adam's negative comments, as she knew how much that annoyed her friends, especially Brooke and Ronnie.

'She's bloody hopeless,' Adam commented to no one in particular and then spotted Bruce and waved him over. Soon, Adam and Bruce were deep in conversation about network infrastructure, servers and the frustration of being bound by PFI contracts. Bruce's team would be at Delvreton High over the Christmas holiday, when the school shut down. As he talked, Bruce entertained the idea of a superb opportunity. He would install some of his spyware into Adam's office which would potentially provide some very helpful intel on Adam Pearson. Bruce was keen to get an insight into how Adam ran the school. It was his daughter Iris's second year in the PE department at Delvreton and some of the things she had let slip about Adam, inappropriate jokes with the pupils and student teachers, his throw away comments to staff, did not seem quite right, somehow. Bruce nodded and smiled to Adam as they spoke, all the time knowing that he had the capability to find out absolutely anything he wanted, about absolutely anybody. And that felt very good.

Ronnie looked on from the far side of the kitchen. He sipped his beer, with his gaze firmly fixed on Adam. Ronnie did not like him, not one bit, and the way Adam had just spoken to his sister made his blood boil. Ronnie would bide his time but he intended to intervene and save his sister from any more heartache.

Daisy broke away from Bruce and Adam, bored by 'work talk' and she scanned the rooms for Ruby, who she finally spotted up a cosy corner with Arthur.

'I'm not interrupting you two love birds am I?' Daisy asked as she squeezed into a gap next to Ruby.

'You know us, Love's young dream,' Arthur smiled.

'Don't know about the young,' said Ruby drily. 'Not sure about the love either!'

Arthur held his heart, a pained expression on his face. 'I'm so hurt. I need to find Ronnie to pour out my aching heart to a caring mate who will pour me a beer,' Arthur stated dramatically as he started to walk away, winking over his shoulder to Ruby.

'Knob-head!' Ruby shouted after him, the warmth in her eyes, a dead give-away for her true feelings.

'Look at you!' Ruby exclaimed, checking out her friend. 'You scrub up well and that designer top certainly helps!'

'Shush,' implored Daisy. 'I didn't know whether to wear it but I easily hemmed it, so I got rid of the hole completely. It feels wrong on the one hand and then oh so right! What a day we had mate,' she giggled.

Ruby noted the sparkle in Daisy's beautiful blue eyes and admired her thick blonde hair, cut in a short, elfin bob. Her toned slim body was perfect for that top and Ruby had noticed the appreciative looks Daisy got from some of the men as she had walked past them. A bit of sinning now and again never hurt anyone, Ruby thought to herself smiling.

'Can we go somewhere quieter to talk?' Daisy asked. 'I feel like I need a confessional and you're the only one I can talk to. Come on.' She pulled Ruby along, back through the open plan dining kitchen, along the hallway and into the study. Shutting the door behind her, she sat on the leather desk chair and gestured to Ruby to sit down on the smart, functional sofa opposite her.

'Phew!' she said, taking a long drink from her wine flute. 'This is good stuff!'

'Yes, and have you tried Vincent's crab cake canapés? Delicious!' Ruby commented. 'So, how do you feel the day after our escapades, my thieving buddy?'

'Don't say that,' Daisy said, breaking into a nervous smile. 'Bruce did notice the top though,' she chuckled. 'And I found myself lying, so easily. His eyes were burning into my soul; I could have sworn at one point he knew I was lying.'

'No way. That's just beginners' guilt! Can you now understand why I love my naughty, 'free' shopping trips so much then?' replied Ruby.

'How much stuff have you actually nicked? You said you'd show me when I come round.'

'Well, I have a big cupboard in our family room and it's full of my 'booty,' Ruby's eyes twinkled.

'Bloody hell!' Daisy exclaimed, with a look of admiration and slight shock. 'And you've never been caught?'

'That's right. I consider myself to be a female Robin Hood, as I only nick from super rich, high end shops that fleece us. They will never miss the odd item, profit they make. I just don't give to the poor. I just keep it all for me,' Ruby laughed heartily.

'I won't do it again, but I will have a look at your stash and I did enjoy being led astray. I have definitely surprised myself but I know Bruce would kill me if he knew,' Daisy pondered.

'No problem then,' said Ruby decisively. 'Because he will never know. Come on, I'm in the mood for a party. Let's see if we can go and wind up boring, tee total Adam.'

'You are so bloody naughty, but I like you!' giggled Daisy as she followed her friend, closing the study door behind her.

The festive party was in full swing. Frankie and Brooke were dancing in the centre of the makeshift dance floor in the sitting room, watched by a small group, including Adam, who was intently following Frankie's every move, with a fixed disapproving expression. Brooke was a great dancer and could even make Frankie look decent. Brooke's auburn hair shone, her blue eyes glistened and the beautiful full skirt of her party dress swirled. Brooke twisted and turned, leading Frankie expertly as they jived to the fast, rhythmic music. The copious amount of wine loosened their limbs and their eyes sparkled, as they were clearly having great fun. Frankie caught Adam's eye and smiled at him, suddenly taken aback by the hard, granite stare that he returned her.

Frankie slowed down the dance and suggested that she and Brooke get some food to 'soak up the wine, mate.'

Brooke was not really ready to stop but sensed something was not quite right with Frankie. She spotted Adam, gauged the look on his face and knew instantly that, once again, he was trying to curtail Frankie's fun. It always happened and Brooke was sick of it. She did not believe for one moment that he would ever commit properly to Frankie and move into the townhouse that he had 'supposedly' been to see.

Brooke watched as Frankie took a glass of wine from the tray that the lovely Bonnie offered her guests. 'This really is fantastic Prosecco,' she said appreciatively, as Adam came over to her.

'How many bloody glasses of wine have you actually had tonight?' Adam asked, looking at Frankie critically.

'Quite a few,' Frankie answered. 'It's a Christmas party,' she smiled up at him.

'I think you've had enough, you piss head.' Adam looked at her with disdain.

Brooke could not stand this any longer and stomped over. 'For God's sake Adam, give her a break and lighten up.'

Frankie smiled gratefully. 'Yeah Adam, just because you don't indulge, don't spoil our fun.' Frankie laughed but her smile slipped, as she caught Adam's stern expression.

'Come on,' said Brooke to Frankie. 'Let's go and get some gorgeous canapés and another glass to wash it all down.' She glared at Adam warningly as she guided Frankie into her kitchen.

'He's such a control freak,' Brooke hissed into Frankie's ear. 'Why can't you just see it?'

Frankie's eyes seemed to tear-up a little, before she collected herself and put on her customary brave face. 'He just doesn't like a drink. That's all.'

'Well, neither does Leah, but she's still the life and soul of the party but he's a boring controlling git.' Brooke muttered. Both thought of Leah fondly, whom they had not seen enough of recently but Brooke's point was very well made.

Frankie and Brooke enjoyed the food and quite a lot more wine, enjoying the joking around with their mates which was just the norm. Adam watched from a distance, stone cold sober, planning what he would say and do to Frankie, when everyone had left. The thought of some hard, rough sex was turning him on. At least, when Frankie was pissed, he really did have the upper hand and he could pretty much do as he liked to her. That definitely gave him a sense of control and it made him feel important, as he detested the fact she was more successful than him at work.

Sienna suddenly caught his eye as she threw her head back and laughed, a throaty laugh, responding to something Bruce had said. Adam's eye roved over Sienna's slim, lithe body, from top to toe. She was very fit, Adam thought to himself and decided that he would move in for a friendly chat, when the time was right. Adam just could not resist an attractive woman and this one was in the A class. He would enjoy flaunting his position as headteacher and wondered if Sienna would be loyal to Frankie or would enjoy his attention. Women were all bitches after all, and he relished the prospect of plying his charms on a new piece of flesh to see if he could reel in another one.

The evening was drawing to a close and almost everyone was worse for wear, so no one really noticed that Bruce was not in the thick of it, like he usually was. Bruce was sitting very quietly, all alone, in the dark study, staring at the App on his phone. He had listened to the recording at least three times as he heard his wife giggling with Ruby about stealing from Harvey Nicholls yesterday. Bruce was still reeling from the realisation that she had so easily lied to him, and now she was giggling about it frivolously with Ruby. He thought he knew Daisy but now recognised that he really did not know this side of her at all. Bruce stared into the distance, his world suddenly feeling a very different place indeed. The sinking, emptiness in the pit of his gut was getting deeper as he listened to the laughter of his wife and friends, friends that he thought he knew but he really did not know them at all.

In the taxi home, Daisy slumped onto Bruce's shoulder as he stared ahead, fixed on the darkness that intermingled with the optimistic lights of the festive season.

The taxi pulled up to Bruce's home. He paid with a tip, of course, and escorted his shattered wife up the path to the house; Bruce was always the gentleman. He just could not get the dark feeling out of his stomach as he dwelled on his wife's misdemeanours

As Bruce flicked on the hall light, Daisy perked up a bit.

'I just need to sort something,' Bruce said, smiling at his wife whilst a torrent of thoughts coursed uncontrollably through his troubled mind. 'You get to bed, love and I'll be up in a jiffy.'

Daisy was just desperate to get up to her sumptuous bed. She eagerly attacked the stairs, swerving from time to time, ricocheting off the beautiful, solid oak bannister which kept her on the right path, delivering her to her much needed oasis of peace.

***

Downstairs, Bruce stood still for a moment in the soothing darkness, before switching on the dimmer light in his kitchen and opening the large cupboard that housed a drinks collection, the envy of all who knew him.

He paused for a moment, before selecting the bottle of Bombo rum, that Frankie had bought him for his birthday the previous August. As he held the bottle, fondly caressing its contours, he remembered a great evening with his friends back then when everything was so simple, when he knew his wife, when he could trust her.

He poured a generous slug into a stubby, squat tumbler and made his way down the hallway to his study, his 'control room'. Hundreds of red, white and green lights welcomed him like old pals, surrounding an array of screens and so much high tech equipment.

Bruce flopped into the black leather chair at his desk, taking a swig of rum. Suddenly, he noticed an intermittent flashing of white light that meant there was activity from one of the cameras, the ones in Frankie's kitchen. Bruce saw that it was two thirty am, so why was the camera picking up anything? He flicked the switch and leaned forward, worried that he might see burglars, as Frankie and Adam slept upstairs.

Far from it. Bruce adjusted the lighting and then physically recoiled. There was an image, in sharp relief, an image that he did not want to see. He found himself looking straight at Frankie as her vacant stare met his eyes. It was as if she was imploring Bruce to help her, to save her in some way. Adam was behind her, looking triumphant as he stood upright and proud. Frankie was bent over the dining table, like a lifeless ragdoll, his hand pulling her hair back towards him roughly as he relentlessly drove into her like a piece of meat. Adam was definitely in control and it was as if he knew he was being watched. He looked almost victorious, like a conquering hunter or something worse.

Bruce shook his head, as if to banish what he had just seen. He just could not stand it. He flicked the switch and started hyper- ventilating before he gradually calmed himself. He had never put cameras into bedrooms or personal spaces – he had only ever wanted a peek into the lives of the group of friends, who he loved so much, to test out his new state of the art surveillance equipment. That was all it was ever meant to be. It really was not meant to be like this. Bruce realised, with a very heavy heart, that he did not even know his own wife let alone the others. He had never imagined what his cameras were revealing to him, all those terrible things he was seeing.

Chapter 5

5 December

Daisy was at Ruby's place. She sifted through hanger after hanger of clothes, from high end designer to bargain basement. All garments were neatly stacked in the 'secret cupboard' in Ruby's family room.

'Oh my God, Ruby, that's a hell of a lot of stuff. Hasn't Arthur ever asked you about this lot?' Daisy asked incredulously.

'No, he never even comes in here. None of us do really. We love the log fire and only ever stay in the kitchen diner since we did the extension and all the alterations. You know Arty, he only cares about his drinks cupboard and if that's full, then he's happy as Larry!'

63

'Bruce asked me about that top again this morning and he never talks about my clothes. Do you think he knows what we did?' Daisy turned to Ruby, a very worried look on her face.

'Don't be daft! How could he? That will always just be our little secret and we can do it any time you feel bored and fancy a rush. You just say the word.' Ruby's eyes gleamed devilishly.

'I just can't. Bruce is definitely different with me this morning and he's a bit off with the girls too. Not like him at all, so it can't just be the hangover. I think there's something else.'

'Well, who knows what goes on in anyone's head? It's probably just the pressure of switching his business over to the UK.'

'Yes, that must be it. He always seems so in control of work but yes, it's a really big change isn't it?' Daisy felt a lot better. It was always good to talk to a friend.

'Anyway, let me get you a Latte with Arthur's new coffee machine. That man loves a gadget. And Brooke should be round any minute for a dissection of last night.'

'Ooh yes,' Daisy said. 'God, it's nearly dark, look and it's only half three.'

'I'm up early again then! Ruby laughed, especially after all that Prosecco last night. I don't remember going to bed, just woke up with Toby lying on my head and that did nothing for the headache!'

'Delicious,' Daisy commented appreciatively, as she sipped her coffee, settling into the new, plush velvet sofa. 'I really like what you've done to this space and the log burner is wonderful. Hope Arthur and the lads stay at the Otter's for a while, because I am very happy sitting here.'

Jingle bells announced the arrival of Brooke who was welcomed enthusiastically by a cacophony of various pitches of barks, as Toby and Murray hurtled towards the door, legs slipping comically on the shiny, highly polished flooring.

'Hello guys,' Brooke greeted the hounds, as she entered the hallway. 'Is Daisy already here?'

'Yep, I'm all settled in,' Daisy laughed. 'It's well cosy through here.'

'Great. I'm ready for a sit down. I've braved the supermarket and it was bloody rammed.'

'Well, sit yourself down. Can I get you a coffee or a festive Bailey's maybe?' Ruby offered.

'A cheeky Baileys would be fab; it is the run up to Christmas now, after all,' Brooke sighed happily.

'So, who's up for a run next Saturday morning with me and Frankie? We're planning a decent few miles to try and burn off extra calories, before our over indulgence really kicks in.'

'Err, no thanks,' said Ruby quickly. 'I'll stick to my swimming.'

'Yes, you can count me in,' Daisy added. 'A nice bit of fresh air will be lovely, even if it's likely to be grey and wet.'

'Great, we'll get off road and run through the woods, past Squirrel's Nook then. We can have a good chat with Frankie as well. Can't believe she thinks fuckwit has any intention whatsoever of moving into one of those townhouses. He was on his typical form last night, watching her all the time and criticising her. Makes my blood boil. Ron's really mad too, and I think he's going round after the Otter's to see if he can talk some sense into her,' Brooke informed her friends.

'Must be bad for Ron to step in; he usually stays well out of relationship matters,' offered Ruby.

'He's just had enough and you know what he's like when he gets an idea in his head. Just a tad stubborn, but he has got a point and Frankie will listen to him. Oh, it's my phone. Hang on a minute guys. It's Ronnie. I'd better take this.' Brooke stood up and went out into the hallway. Some of her responses suggested that this was not a good call. She came back in, looking alarmed. 'I'd better get round to Frankie's, guys. Ron popped in on his way to the Otter's and he's pretty concerned about what she told him, something about what happened last night, after we all left. Ron said that Frankie really needs to talk to me, that it's 'women's stuff'. I think I should get round there. I was looking forward to a nice, quiet relaxing evening before facing my crazy schedule next week, but I can't leave Frankie, if she's upset.'

Brooke grabbed her bag, gave the girls a hug and reluctantly left.

***

Frankie looked pale and drawn, when she opened the door to Brooke, who gave her a long hug, then stood back to take a good look at her sister in law.

'So, what's the matter? It was a lovely night last night. You always throw a fantastic party and you've got us all in the mood for Christmas.' Brooke kept her tone light, but knew all was not well.

Frankie gestured to Brooke to follow her into the sitting room. The stylish tree lit up the room but Frankie's downcast expression was not in keeping with the festive atmosphere at all. Frankie pulled a throw around her and drew her knees in close, as if to give her some comfort as she curled up in the corner of the generous four seater sofa. She pulled Charlie, her beloved Hungarian Vizla hound, next to her. His long legs flopped over the edge of the sofa as he nuzzled into his 'mummy'.

'Come on then,' said Brooke. 'What's the matter? Ron phoned and there's clearly something up.'

Frankie sighed, then started to talk. 'I really tried with Adam and I foolishly thought he was going to make everything right and move into the townhouse round the corner. He's really changed since I first met him. I know you don't like him but, he really rocked my world and I would have done everything for him. Well I did do. I left Steve, got divorced and, you know,' Frankie paused. 'Me and Steve were done. I'd have left him at some point anyway.'

'We know all this,' Brooke said gently. 'So why has Ron asked me to come round? What's happened?'

'I've just had enough.' Frankie said, trying to muster some strength to sound convincing. 'It's a bit embarrassing, but he didn't treat me well last night and I can't let that happen again.'

'Yeah, Ron heard him putting you down again, just because the bloody beer wasn't in the right place. I mean, how pathetic. You know, we all get annoyed when we hear Adam talk down to you,' Brooke said gently.

'Well, it isn't just that and you know I don't really notice any of that which I guess is a worry in itself. Me of all people, no one ever talks to me with a lack of respect, yet I realise Adam does it all the time.' Frankie was clearly wrestling with her thoughts.

'It's a step forward, if you realise that now, mate. That's good,' Brooke said enthusiastically.

'There's something else.' Frankie faltered for a moment. 'When everyone had gone, I thought Adam had turned in. You know, he doesn't like parties or staying up late. Anyway, Bonnie and her pals did a great job clearing up, but I thought I'd get everything straight, so it would all be tidy for us to have breakfast.'

'Okay,' Brooke said, not sure where this was going.

'Well, I'd almost finished, when Adam appeared in the doorway. He said I'd woken him and that I needed to be punished.'

'What the fuck?' Brooke looked shocked.

'I thought he was joking. You know how it is with couples' cheeky little jokes. This time though, he sounded different. I feel embarrassed talking about it, but let's just say he was rough and he actually hurt me.

Frankie paused and wiped a tear away. 'Just look,' she said, starting to break down as she got up and pulled at the neck of her sweatshirt. 'I have marks.'

Brooke inspected Frankie's shoulders, with a horrified look on her face.

'Mate, this isn't funny at all. What the hell happened?'

Frankie coughed. 'Well, I'm sure we aren't the only ones to have intimate moments in the kitchen, but this wasn't like the normal routine. I really did feel that he wanted to hurt me.'

'What was he like this morning?' Brooke asked.

'A bit quiet, a bit moody and he left early to take his son to his football match.'

'Frankie,' Brooke waited a moment, before she asked the question she had to ask. 'You did consent last night, didn't you?'

'Oh my God! Yes, he didn't rape me, if that's what you mean!' Frankie wiped away the tears that were now streaming down her face. 'There's more.'

'What?' Brooke asked in disbelief.

'Sienna called me mid-morning, in a bit of a state. 'Oh God Brooke, Adam really is a low life. Apparently, he was flirting with her at the end of the night, after we'd been dancing. Sienna said it was more than just a joke and she felt really uncomfortable, and really bad for me. I know you don't know her very well, but she's a good friend and I do trust her. What the hell was Adam playing at? What's happening to him?' Frankie looked devastated.

'Look, this is all out of order and you must sort this. I think you've had a wake-up call mate. The time has come, and I think you know what you have to do. I'll stay here, while you call him. Come on, let's do it and you can move on with your life, once and for all.'

'What? Now?' Frankie looked distraught.

'Yes, or I can't vouch for what Ronnie might do,' Brooke stated assertively. She moved towards Frankie, who fell into her arms, slumped there for several minutes as Charlie looked on, ears back with a concerned look crumpled into his furry forehead.

'Come on. He must be back from football now,' Brooke urged. 'You need to call him. Just do it. This is all so wrong, on every level.'

'Okay.' Frankie pulled herself straight and reached for her phone, taking several long deep breaths. 'Here goes then.'

'Hi, it's me,' Frankie began. 'Are you okay? How was football?'

Brooke gave Frankie an encouraging smile as the conversation progressed. Frankie was clearly having a tough time, building up to the crescendo but she got there eventually, hung up the phone and fell back into the sofa.

'It's done,' she said quietly. 'I can't quite believe I just did that.'

'What did he say then?' Brooke asked.

'He said I'm an idiot. I drink too much and listen to my friends too much. He said I've made the biggest mistake of my life and that there is no going back.'

'Well, you've done the best thing ever. Stay strong because I don't believe for a minute that you've seen the last of him. Right, time for champers!' Brooke declared. 'This is the first day of the rest of your life. We are going to celebrate and we are going to have the best Christmas ever.'

Brooke came back from the kitchen and handed Frankie a beautiful, crystal flute. Frankie did not look convinced but took a gulp of the effervescent liquid, grateful that she had such loyal friends. She really needed them now.

Chapter 6

8 December

Frankie had been on Brooke's mind for the last couple of days. Brooke could not deny she was thrilled Frankie had finally ditched Adam, but knew this had been no easy task and was concerned that Frankie did not waiver and head straight back into Adam's bed. A psychotherapist, with her own practice, Brooke had evolved a sort of sixth sense about mental wellbeing and when it affected her family, she was even more on high alert. She and Frankie had a lot in common workwise and Brooke wished her sister in law could apply some helpful psychology to her own personal life. She made a mental note to make sure she called Frankie later, just to say hi and see how she was feeling. If she knew Adam's track record, he would not let Frankie go quietly.

Frankie was certainly one of the most generous people Brooke knew, whilst Adam was a total tight arse. Brooke could not even remember the last time he had paid for a round of drinks, let alone paid for a meal. His idea of 'treating' Frankie had been to book cheap hotel rooms, buy a sandwich and a bottle of plonk from the local petrol station that they would 'enjoy' in the hotel room.   Which of course was code for a shag. Brooke did not trust him as far as she could throw him, not least because he only ever drank one reluctant pint. Nothing wrong with that in principle, but Brooke suspected it was only because Adam was afraid his tongue might get too lose if he was inebriated and he might actually tell the truth; that he was low-down, lying, cheating dog. She was holding her breath that he would not come hunting Frankie down again, filled with false promises to treat her better, break her will and Brooke feared that she would go back to him. If he tried, Brooke had decided that this time, she would be one step ahead of him.

For now though, Brooke needed to tie up a few things with work. She was in her study which also doubled as her counselling suite. Walls were adorned with a mixture of Brooke's own artworks and various certificates of qualification. The room was decorated in a peaceful shade of green with two comfortable counselling chairs and there was a bookcase full of psychology and psychotherapy books. She had specialised in art therapy, blending her two great loves into her dream job. She was unashamedly proud of her achievements, which had not come easily. A past history of poorly paid jobs and bosses from hell, Brooke had had her fill of the eejits and egotists that she had to report to over the years.

Her last boss, Suki, had been a total bitch. Inadequate and incompetent, Brooke had quickly secretly diagnosed her with narcissistic personality disorder: a grandiose sense of self-importance, constant exaggerating of achievements and talents together with an expectation that all around her had to recognize her as superior. She had been so textbook, it was almost laughable. Suki had drained the life out of Brooke who had to navigate her constant unrealistic demands, whilst providing an endless source of excessive admiration to keep the peace, albeit totally fake. Suki had always been far too compelled by her own 'brilliance' to notice that Brooke was being spectacularly sarcastic. Brooke still shuddered when she recalled Suki's temper tantrums. Her eyes would fill with rage, spittle frothing at her mouth as she screamed at Brooke, her overly long hair whipping around her face, split ends and all. The only saving grace was knowing that Suki had been the biggest laughing stock of the entire company and had not long afterwards met her demise in the form of a dismissal.

Brooke pulled herself out of her rumination and finished off her mental health report. Her next client was not due for another hour. This would give her plenty of time to call Frankie.

Brooke dialled and Frankie's dainty face instantly popped up on screen.

'Hi Brooke! What you up to?' Frankie was really pleased to receive the call.

'Alright Bab, just calling in to say hi and see if you fancied a night out Saturday? Ron is away on a lads' weekend and I thought we could nip out for something to eat and maybe go down the local after? There's a Neil Diamond tribute singer on,' Brooke announced, with a sparkle in her voice.

Frankie and Brooke did not need any encouragement for a night out. They were always first up to dance, drank the most Prosecco and were inevitably the last to leave, usually carrying on the dancing back at either one of their places. Twirling round the room like a pair of teenagers, nineties indie usually being the music of choice. This was showing their age, but they did not care.

'Normally, I'd love to Brooke, but I'm just not feeling much in the party mood.'

Brooke's heart sank as she knew this would be Frankie mooning over her decision to dump Adam.

'Frankie, I know you must miss Adam, but getting out will cheer you up and you never know you might meet a sexy bloke!' Brooke was trying hard not to lecture, but equally really wanted Frankie to let her hair down and have some much needed fun.

'Oh Brooke, I'm just feeling a bit down. I know I've certainly done the right thing, as far as getting Adam out of my life, but I just need some time to lick my wounds before I can face a night on the tiles. You know what I mean right?' Frankie lamented.

'Well, okay Frank, if you're really certain, but you know where I am if you change your mind.' Brooke tried to disguise the disappointment in her voice.

Frankie was so strong in so many ways. Brooke utterly admired her, but for some inexplicable reason Frankie had been so intoxicated by Adam. What hold had he had on her? Brooke mused again for the hundredth time.

Subject swiftly changed, the pair chatted about the latest box set binges and the new season's line of shoes, then said their goodbyes.

With half an hour still to kill, Brooke glanced over to the tall, oak sliding doors in the corner of the room. Ronnie was great with DIY and had designed and built them for her. Brooke stretched and leant back in her chair, her ample bosoms rising like some sort of buoyancy aids, then sashayed over to the corner of the room and slowly teased open the doors. It revealed a rail of clothes, overly rammed with garments, all colours of the rainbow. Brooke pushed them aside revealing a small inset shelf. It was like her own personal Narnia as she pushed the clothes aside and grasped her secretly stashed tablet device that she kept well hidden from Ronnie. She had to be certain that he could never find out her internet history. The screen lit up and a thrill fired in her belly.

***

Bruce was bored. Daisy was out, busy looking for another fitness premises to add to her portfolio. He clicked his PC on. He knew it was wrong, but he just had to take a little peep at the latest goings on.

He continued to kid himself he was only looking in on folks, to make sure everyone was okay. However, the rather less savoury things he had recently uncovered were still nagging at him and he felt a compulsion, more than ever, to check in on the group. He could see straight away that Brooke was active. He sheepishly clicked the screen. Up popped an image of Brooke and Frankie; he listened as they chatted.

'God, fuckwit strikes again,' he thought, as he listened to the pair's discussion and plans. If only he could, he would smash that bastard's face in, but he knew it was

better to stay out of Frankie's business. His wife Daisy
would regularly gently remind him that Frankie will 'find
her own way out, when she's ready.' Bruce wished Adam
would find his way into a ditch, preferably unconscious.
Sipping his coffee, his eyes travelled around Brooke's
study. He had been impressed at the smart set up when
he had installed the IT security for her.

He continued to watch as Brooke ended her call with
Frankie and rose from her chair. He smiled as she twirled
over to the door of her wardrobe. Brooke had trained as
a dancer when she was a youngster, giving it up for boys
at age seventeen, but she still had the moves and he
laughed to himself that she even danced when she was
alone. He was a little mesmerised as Brooke tentatively
opened the wardrobe door.

'That girl needs a clear out,' Bruce chuckled as a red
strappy stiletto sprung onto the floor from its bolt hold of
various other shoes. He watched as Brooke pushed a rail
stuffed with garments aside and came back to her desk
clutching a tablet.

***

Brooke fired up the tablet. She was a little embarrassed,
ashamed even, but she could not stop. It's only once in a
while, this is the last go; she would regularly lie to herself.
But the truth was, she was addicted to pretty much every
casino and betting site. She had decided that today was a
roulette kind of day and she clicked the brightly lit, red
and green icon show casing a gold roulette wheel. Once
again, she became captivated by the
black...red...black....red of the spiralling wheel. Bet

placed, 'odds….odds….odds,' became the mantra in her head, as she fixated on the hundred pound virtual casino 'chip' on the virtual table…. or zero would do, because she would always stick a cheeky ten pounds on zero every time she had a go. The wheel slowed down and the fake little metal ball made a clink clonk sound as it bounced from number 27, to 13, to 36, finally settling on number 11. YES! Brooke enthusiastically yelled in her head. That was another hundred pounds profit in the bank.

No one really knew about Brooke's love of a flutter. It did not much matter what it was: blackjack, the dogs, poker, roulette and the slots, even bingo. But her absolute favourite was the horses. She had chased a few losses of course, but more recently the wins had kept coming and over the last twelve months, she had become more and more daring. Ron disapproved of her gambling, but he was sane enough to know better than to try and tell her not to do it. Furthermore, Ron had no idea of just how much she had actually got stashed in winnings.

Brooke switched to horses. She adored the names they gave them. She mused over the list: 'Langer Dan'; 'Dawson City'; 'Tiger Roll; 'Butterwick Brook… Definitely having a go on that one, she decided. Grey horses were Brooke's favourites. She liked the fact that there was often only one grey amongst the rich chestnut colours of the usual thoroughbreds and that the grey horses always stood out from the crowd. This was just like her choice of outfits, which were always bold, bright colours, never beiges or nudes. One hundred pounds down on Butterwick Brook. She knew the best trainers and always had a quick punt on anything trained by the Skeltons as well as scanning for her favourite jockeys: Rachel Blackmore and Jonjo O'Neill Jr, but in the end, she was always drawn to the horses' names. Butterwick Brook happened to be on at 9/1. They're off…. hooves thundered across the screen. 'Horse racing is just 'animated roulette', after all,' Brooke said out loud to herself, as she recalled an old quote that still resonated with her.

The commentators amused Brooke, with their excited but robotic sounding observations of the field. The commentary started. 'Runners stream towards the first fence… Tiger Roll is amongst the first to touch down. Grey Lion is out of it, making a shocking blunder at the first with Langer Dan jumping into the lead… Dawson's City moves towards the inside, followed by Butterwick Brook and Total Recall… Silvery Shuffle is well back and Dawson City's jockey is nearly unseated… Total Recall, just towards the rear of the field and oh, we've lost Total Recall at the third! Langer Dan, riding strong, has the advantage with Butterwick Brook on his tail… They head now towards the final turn, Oh! Tiger Roll has been pulled up! It's Langer Dan and Butterwick Brook, as they reach the final furlong… Butterwick Brook is gaining ground on Langer Dan and Butterwick Brooke overtakes. It's Butterwick Brook by three lengths, he's doing it easily. Butterwick Brook is now clear by five lengths and there's no coming back for Langer Dan. BUTTERWICK BROOK takes it! Brooke's heart skipped a beat and she squealed in joy. Another thousand pounds was bagged.

***

Before he had even realised it, Bruce was already running his sniffing software and was linked into Brooke's hidden tablet in moments. He sat agog as she placed bet after bet and not just a pound here or there, more like ten pounds, fifty pounds and one hundred pounds as the bets became more and more daring. Bloody hell... our Brookie's a little gambler, then he quickly corrected himself. No, a BIG gambler! At that moment, Bruce could hear Ronnie's voice calling up the stairs to Brooke.

'What do you fancy for tea, Brooke?' Ronnie shouted.

Brooke sat bolt upright, quickly switched off the tablet and frantically stuffed it back into its hiding place.

'Just a sec! I'll be there in a moment Bab. I thought we might have lamb tagine tonight.' Her voice was a little hysterical, as she desperately tried to stop Ronnie walking into the room, before the tablet was safely stashed back in the wardrobe.

Bruce watched as she headed out of the room. He could still see her Williams Lad's account on his screen, the numbers seeming to pop out like a 3D movie. Bruce gasped as he took in the balance of over twenty five thousand pounds.

Chapter 7

9 December

Arthur was on the move, but today he drove past his usual destination of the Otter's Head. He carried on to a less exclusive area of town where huge generic department stores sold pretty much everything, from designer perfume to pound shops that piled it high and sold it cheap. He was not sure what on earth to buy. He had never bought anything for a child in his life, without Ruby's advice. Where did he start? It did not help that it was for a little girl; he might have stood a chance of getting it right had it been a young boy – Action Man, Lego, Batman, or whatever was trendy these days. He would go for something in pink. That should work, shouldn't it? He hesitated, yes, pink, he was decided. He thought he would pick up some nice perfume too for the child's mother but what to get... no idea. He would ask the store assistant what designer brand was popular these days, maybe something by Chanel. He knew that was a good brand and he would throw in some flowers or chocolates. You can't go wrong with chocolate, he mused. The main thing though, was that Ruby could not find out, not yet. So, he furtively scoured the store, settled on his purchases and left. He promised himself he would tell Ruby, when the time was right.

**

Bruce was still reeling from his discovery about Brooke's secret habit when he clicked onto his screen and noticed that Arthur was on the move. He smiled to himself, thinking that Arthur must be on his way to the Otter's and Bruce really fancied a pint. He sat and watched, just to make sure. Bruce was surprised though, that today, Arthur was not heading in the direction of their beloved pub; he was heading towards a far less salubrious, neighbouring area. I wonder what takes him that way on, Bruce wondered. He could see that Arthur was heading for the large complex on the outskirts of the city where numerous department stores show cased gigantic outlets, filled with end of line or last season's offerings at more affordable prices. Probably buying more brandy, Bruce chuckled.

Bruce was just about to lose interest when he could see from the maps App on Arthur's phone, that Arthur had entered a children's wear store – now that is very strange, thought Bruce. Arthur and Ruby had a teenage daughter, who was more interested in buying online from 'Pretty Little Thing' or the like. There were no small children in any of their group; all sprogs were well into their late teens or twenties. Too old for kids' clothes and too young to be producing grandkids – well at least Bruce hoped so; he was definitely not ready to be a grandpa yet… his mind wandered. He watched, fascinated, as the tracker showed Arthur going from children's wear to a store best known for its make-up and perfume. Maybe for Ruby? Bruce thought, but then he paused. He was very confused now.

It was certainly well known that Arthur's 'go to' present was jewellery. Ruby was a successful jeweller, after all. She could always acquire various precious gems, platinum and gold rings, necklaces or bracelets and she always had her eye on a gorgeous piece that would not only be enjoyed, but also serve as an investment. Ruby just asked Arthur for the funds, whenever her birthday or Christmas rolled around and he was always more than happy to oblige. His wife had great taste and she knew far better than he did, what would suit her. Arthur was not really the romantic type; he never really needed to 'choose' anything for Ruby, and he never had a clue what to buy her. Ruby had made it very clear there had been but one occasion when he had actually bought her flowers.

Bruce's mind tried to make sense of what he was witnessing. The kids' clothes store - that did not add up at all. Why was Arthur in a kids' clothes shop? Maybe it was for a friend, but if it was that then that would have definitely been Ruby's domain. A perfume store... Bruce mulled it over, then it suddenly hit him. The dark horse! I bet he's buying perfume for another woman! Bruce was astonished, but slightly impressed. Arthur was the last person he would have placed a bet on to cheat on Ruby. Could he be wrong? Bruce was compelled.

***

Back at home, Arthur pulled onto the sweeping driveway. Ruby's mini clubman was not there, thankfully, so he was pretty certain she was out. Good, he thought. That would give him time to survey his purchases. Once inside,

Murray and Toby played out their obligatory, excited welcomes, jumping up for a 'kiss', or more of a head butt. Arthur calmed the dogs down with a bribe in the form of a leftover casserole. Tails wagged as both dogs tucked in contentedly.

Arthur carefully placed his purchases on the kitchen table. He unpeeled translucent pink tissue paper to reveal a velvet, smoky pink dress and matching shawl for a six year old, pink sequinned ballet pumps and a huge stuffed dog in the form of a staffie bullterrier, with a large pink bow around its neck. He then tentatively unwrapped a designer bag containing perfume, the bold gold lettering of the logo, unmistakably Chanel. He carefully lifted out an exquisitely wrapped bottle, together with a huge heart shaped box of luxury chocolates.

***

Bruce sat open mouthed as he stared at his screen. Visible from the security cams, placed in Ruby's and Arthur's home, Bruce could clearly see Arthur's haul from his shopping spree. Wow! Expensive stuff Arthur! Bruce let out a long whistle as he watched Arthur surveying his purchases.

Maybe Arthur was going to treat Ruby after all, Bruce contemplated, but the children's wear, that was just weird. Bruce watched Arthur take a roll of red and silver Christmas paper, laced with reindeers prancing through woodlands as he carefully wrapped the dress, shawl and pumps. Arthur topped it off with a large red bow and attached a handwritten tag. Arthur then took another sheet and tried to wrap the stuffed toy. This was much less successful as the paper became more like a scrunched up bit of loo roll, but Arthur persevered and, with a helpful hand from his overuse of sticky tape, he managed to 'wrap' the toy. Thank goodness he had the foresight to ask the shop assistant to wrap the perfume, Arthur reflected. Arthur did not even bother trying to wrap the heart shaped box; it was very pretty anyway, so he just stuck a huge gold bow and tag on top. Wrapped gifts in hand, Arthur piled himself back into his car, tentatively checking his watch to make sure Ruby was not likely to appear any moment soon.

He's on the move again! Bruce jolted himself upright and switched back to the App he was connected to via Arthur's phone. Bruce examined the tracking device as it blinked on the screen across various streets and roads on the map in areas unfamiliar to him. Bruce was intrigued, so he switched on sound to listen in on Arthur.

As Arthur drove, the streets looked so deprived. The houses were unkempt and shabby. Kids were running round outside without coats on a chilly December day, far too young to be unsupervised.   A few of the mothers were gathered in a huddle, babies in prams, on hips and in bellies. Most of the mothers were smoking and laughing. One screamed at her child to 'stop fecking about and get over here.' Nice parenting, not. Arthur shuddered and Bruce with him.

Arthur eventually pulled up at a dilapidated block of flats and a tiny framed, dark haired, milky skinned woman approached his car. She had a little girl with her. Arthur got out and embraced the woman. He gave her the chocolates, perfectly gift wrapped perfume and the stuffed terrier toy to the little girl who tore off the wrapping and was clearly overjoyed.

Bruce heard Arthur address the woman as Kerri.

'Thanks for meeting me. Kerri, you know we can't let Ruby find out, not yet anyway. I'll tell her when the time is right,' Arthur gabbled.

'You need to tell her soon,' she protested.

'I know. I know. I'll tell her when it's right, just not yet'. Arthur was feeling totally confused and could not even face the thought of what he was going to say to Ruby about the situation he had found himself in.

The pair spent a few moments talking and Bruce heard Arthur pause as he brushed a tear away from Kerri's eye.

'It won't be much longer, I promise,' Arthur said softly. He gave Kerri the wrapped outfit for the little girl and she beamed back at him.

'Thank you. We have so little money and this means the world,' Kerri said.

Arthur and Kerri chatted a bit about how chilly the weather had become and made a little more small talk as they said their goodbyes. He embraced Kerri once more and gently cuffed the little girl's cheek playfully.

'Now don't you forget to look after your new puppy,' he smiled as the little girl beamed back at him.

Arthur then got back into his car and drove away, leaving the image of a little girl staring at the back of his car with her new toy in hand and Kerri's sad face in the distance. He glanced in his rear view mirror, his heart was breaking but also searing with guilt.

**

Bruce sat in stunned silence. How on earth could he keep what he had just heard a secret, without telling Ruby? But equally, how could he betray Arthur? He simply had to intervene, but how? Bruce's head was spinning. What the hell, Arthur? No way. He was bumbling in his thoughts as he tried to make sense of this madness. I have to keep a very close eye on this one, he decided.

**

Ruby had known that Arthur had had a 'dalliance' seven years ago. She had been so furious with him, but he had begged her to take him back. Ruby loved him, so she did. They did the usual couples' counselling and it had actually helped them to sort out quite a few issues. The encounter had been brief and had not meant all that much to Arthur. He and Ruby had been going through a very rough patch and had momentarily separated when he had kicked off his involvement with a woman called Kerri. He had met her at a bar in the city when on a lads' night out. It was meant to be a distraction, a harmless flirtation, to give him an ego boost and some respite from his troubled marriage. His construction workmates had, however, encouraged him to 'go for it' with Kerri who had made it very clear that she fancied Arthur. Arthur had been very drunk and depressed, so he did. It was literally a one- month wonder and, when Arthur knew there was a chance for him and Ruby to make things work, he had ended it with Kerri and that had been it. He did not see Kerri again and things with Ruby took an upwards turn, after the counselling. So, after a lot of tears and heartache, they had both agreed to draw a line under it.

Only four months ago, Kerri had got in touch with Arthur via an old mate. He had ignored her texts at first, then after she had pestered him to please contact her, he had eventually texted back to say he was not interested and would certainly not be responding to any more of her messages. That is when she dropped the bombshell. She had a daughter, now six years old, and Kerri was absolutely adamant that she was Arthur's.

The initial meetings between Arthur and Kerri had been very awkward. Priority number one, he did not want to tell Ruby about the child, until he was certain this was not some sort of elaborate way to obtain money from him. However, after a few difficult and embarrassing conversations, followed by a DNA test, it had become obvious that the child was his and he actually started to feel very sorry for Kerri. She was from the wrong side of the tracks, penniless and had been living with a thug of a man who she had hooked up with not long after Arthur had left the scene. The man had provided a morsel of security for them, got them a council flat and he had paid for a lot of things for the little girl, despite him knowing she was not his. However, he also had a temper like a volcano and had been abusive to Kerri over the years. She had put up with it because she was so reliant on him for money. But, he was now in prison and she had been desperate and so she had had no choice but to track Arthur down and to tell him the truth.

Arthur and Ruby had one teenage daughter and he certainly had not bargained for another child, but he adored his daughter with Ruby and gave her the world. Arthur simply could not turn his back on this fragile and deprived child who was also his own flesh and blood. So, here he was and he was wondering when and how on earth he would tell Ruby.

Chapter 8

17 December

'Bloody hell! You were right. It's well spooky down here,' said Brooke, shivering a little as she nestled into the heated leather seat of Frankie's Q8. Frankie skilfully negotiated the long, pitch black driveway off a country lane that only the locals knew existed, dealing well with the poor visibility. 'There's fog and everything,' Brooke observed, a tinge of excitement in her voice.

This evening at Frankie's friend, Nancy's, had been planned for some time, viewed as a symbolic start to the festive holiday. Both Brooke and Frankie were really looking forward to two weeks off and both so relieved to leave work behind. Frankie needed cheering up after the ordeal with Adam, now no longer in her life. However, the fact that he was still hassling her with cruel texts was something she needed to deal with. Brooke was in good spirits, secretly revelling in her recent good fortune on the horses and at her virtual casino. A girlie evening at a beautiful house in the country was just what they needed.

'It's just like a scene from a Dickensian Christmas ghost story,' Frankie said, with a more positive tone of voice than had been heard since the break-up weekend. Frankie's tyres crunched on the gravel and the friends grabbed their overnight bags from the cavernous boot. They left the car and headed to the bright lights of the seventeenth century coach house, a most welcoming glow in the windows to fend off the chill from the ever densifying fog.

'Hello!' Nancy exclaimed, as she flung open the door. 'Come in, come in. Your Cosmopolitans are awaiting, beautiful ladies!'

Nancy's cheeks glowed as she greeted her guests. She was in her element, relishing the prospect of a cosy Christmassy evening stretching ahead. Nancy and Frankie had worked together for years and were great friends especially as both women had shared a similar experience of getting themselves entrenched with married men. Nancy seemed to be having a lot more luck than Frankie though, as her man had shown real commitment and up and left his wife only six months ago. Richard had set himself up very well in a small, but stylish apartment, so that he and Nancy could develop their relationship properly, how it should be. Tonight though, was female company only. Or so they all thought. Once Frankie and Brooke took their phones from their bags, Bruce was able to listen to their conversation. When Frankie held her phone high above their heads to take a selfie and then further photos of Nancy's beautiful home, Bruce also had a prime view. He was pleased that Daisy was out on a works do so he could settle in to his control room with a few beers and enjoy his entertainment. Rosie had a friend over for a sleepover, so he was totally free to listen and watch to his heart's content. His recent insight into Brooke's little secret made him even more curious to see how she acted when she was with the girls. Would she share anything with them about her gambling habit?

Brooke knew Nancy well, so the three friends quickly settled into the evening 'oohing' and 'aahing' at the tasteful way in which Nancy had decorated her beloved abode. Brooke had not been to the coach house before but had heard all about the many times Frankie had stayed there with Nancy, putting the world to rights and having some much needed time out from the rat race. Often, Frankie and Nancy had gone on long invigorating country walks to banish the irritation and pain that relationships with married men brought. They had also allowed the anaesthetizing effects of alcohol to wash over them on many occasions: at the coach house, on their many, infamous nights out in Birmingham and on a few cheeky trips abroad over the years too.

Brooke surveyed her accommodation appreciatively. The whole floor was open plan and covered in original oak wood panelling. The beams harked back to years gone by and Brooke tried to imagine what life might have been like back then. Tasteful, regular lighting was further enhanced by subtle Christmas twinkles, all set off perfectly by a large, cast iron log burner, proudly positioned against the original brickwork at the end of the large room. Old met minimal modernism perfectly in this beautiful and quirky home. Bruce had to admit that he was impressed. He had met Nancy a few times when she came out with Frankie and he could not help but find her attractive. Richard was a lucky man, he mused: a gorgeous woman with this fantastic home. Bruce settled into his plush office chair; he was enjoying his evening already.

Brooke looked forward to seeing the views of the vast countryside surrounding the tiny hamlet but breakfast was some time away and they had some good times ahead, before they even contemplated turning in for the night.

'Don't you ever feel frightened down here all alone?' Brooke asked, feeling a little shiver run down her spine.

'Not at all,' Nancy answered laughing. 'Who would ever find me? And there's a lovely group of us down here. There are four other houses – you'll see tomorrow when the fog lifts and we go for our walk.'

'Tell Brooke about the medium who came here last month,' Frankie urged her friend.

'What?' screeched Brooke. 'What the hell are you talking about?'

'Well, I decided to find out if Rich really is worth the effort, so I thought I'd seek some advice, from the other side.' Nancy and Frankie laughed at the shocked expression on Brooke's face.

'And?' asked Brooke tentatively, taking a long drink of her Cosmo.

'I got a pretty good response. Clare, that's my modern medium, also said this place has great spirit activity.'

Bruce sat up in his chair, clearly taken aback by what he was hearing. He was genuinely interested in the conversation. He smiled, shaking his head. Who would have thought that they would be talking about the spirit world and that Nancy had her own bloody medium? His surveillance project had thrown yet another surprise his way.

Brooke shuddered, eyes wide, clearly enjoying the sensation of being a tad unnerved and out of her comfort zone.

'And, even better, I have hedge witches from the sixteen hundreds looking out for me.' Nancy gave a satisfied sigh and sank back into her ample armchair next to the raging log fire.

'What are they when they are at home?' Brooke asked tentatively, looking around with a very worried expression on her face.

'Well,' Nancy began. 'Let me give you a little history lesson. Hundreds of years ago, witches lived along the fringes of a village behind the hedgerows. One side of the hedge was the village and civilisation and the other side lay the unknown and the wild.' Nancy took a sip of her cocktail, enjoying the rapt attention of her guests. 'So, these witches acted as healers or they were very cunning women spending their time gathering herbs and plants in the woods and fields and, yes, you've guessed it, the hedges. Apparently, the hedge witch usually practised alone and lived a magical life – just brewing a drink, or sweeping the floor were infused with magical ideas and intentions, making the home a safe and natural place. The witches practised herbal magic and were good witches. So, I like the thought of their spirits watching over me down here,' Nancy concluded, sighing contentedly.

Bloody hell, Bruce thought; there was much more to Nancy than he had ever realised. He sipped his beer thoughtfully and was looking forward to seeing where the conversation took them all next. He was really enjoying himself.

'You know a lot about all of this,' Brooke commented.

'I've really learnt a lot; my medium Clare has been an amazing source of knowledge and advice,' Nancy said, with a little pride in her voice.

'And consequently, Nancy's love life has taken a turn for the better, unlike mine,' Frankie added, looking slightly mournfully into the dregs of her cocktail.

'Stop that now!' Nancy instructed. 'Yes, I'm doing okay with Rich but I'm taking it slowly and you, my sweet, are well shot of that dickhead and you are going to look forward to many new and exciting opportunities in the new year. Enjoy life! Start dating and you will find someone who appreciates you and treats you right.' Nancy sprang up. 'Time to eat and time to drink a lot more!' she declared.

Plates of Italian meats, humus, dips, artisan bread and some delicious local cheeses were consumed, washed down with a couple of bottles of wine, as the friends relaxed into an idyllic Christmassy evening. Bruce was also getting into the festive spirit with them and he was savouring a particularly good bottle of red.

Frankie yawned and stretched. 'God! It's already eleven thirty.'

'Time for nightcaps then but we are not going to bed yet,' Nancy declared. 'We are going to have some fun. Let's just say it's not just the alcoholic spirits we are going to indulge in.'

'Ooh! I know what you mean,' said Frankie enthusiastically.

'I don't know,' added Brooke a little uncertainly, completely unaware, as were her friends that Bruce was in his element and even more interested in how the evening was developing.

'Time for a bit of Ouija,' Nancy said, taking a bottle of Calvados and three glasses over to the solid French oak dining table as she made a mischievous ghostly noise.

'Look out there at the fog,' Frankie said. 'It's so silent and...' she paused, as she walked behind Brooke's chair, then shouted in her ear 'SPOOKY!'

Brooke jumped then laughed. 'You bloody idiot! But it's good to see the old Frankie coming back. Anyway, I have done this before, you know. I'm not as timid about these things as you might think. When we were in our mid-thirties, me and Frankie did this. Remember, at that place in the Lakes with your parents. I remember your Dad went outside and tapped the windows whilst we were all in full- flow. We all jumped out of our bloody skin.'

'Yeah! We all love nothing more than being scared. Very happy days but, you know what, we're all still just as fascinated about the spirit world,' Frankie mused. 'The atmosphere is perfect here. You could feel pretty scared,

97

if you allowed yourself to. Mind you, remember when we were so pissed Nance that we went to bed and left the front door open! That's when you thought Rich's wife could have been stalking you. If she'd got in, it would have been just my luck for the crazy bitch to have come into my room, instead of yours!'

Brooke laughed. 'What are you like, you pair? You do get involved in some dodgy stuff with men.'

Bruce grimaced, his mind wandering to what he had discovered about his own wife and then those images of Frankie and Adam in her kitchen after the party came into his head again. He shuddered, focusing again on the here and now.

'But it's all working out now for Nancy. I think the mad bitch has moved away, hasn't she?'

Nancy nodded.

'And, I have finally seen the light and ditched Fuckwit. So, shall we see what's in store for us all in the new year?' Frankie rubbed her hands together and helped Nancy place the letters and numbers in a circle.

'Let's just have candle light now to really get us in the mood,' Nancy said as she turned off the lights, leaving the glow from the fire and the candle flames flickering gently.

'Okay, are we ready then?' Nancy began the ritual and the friends gently placed their forefingers on the shot glass in the centre of the circle. After a few nervous giggles, the glass stuttered to begin with, before gathering pace and swooping round the Ouija's circumference.

The glass whizzed round the board, spelling out 'WIN' and 'BEWARE'.

'Ooh, I wonder what on earth that could mean,' Frankie said inquisitively. The women giggled. Brooke knew exactly what these words meant.

'Beware the beast.' Nancy said, affecting a booming voice. 'Spirit world, what else can you tell us?' Nancy queried, with a fake 'Gypsy Rosie Lee' style voice.

A few further indecipherable phrases led to suppositions, then the atmosphere electrified when the words suddenly became a whole lot clearer.

'My God!' exclaimed Nancy. 'DEATH! Whose DEATH?' Bruce sat up a bit straighter in his chair and leaned forward to ensure he didn't miss anything; he was now totally enthralled.

'I'm not liking this,' whispered Brooke.

'Stay with it,' Frankie urged. 'Go on Nancy, ask again.'

'Whose death?' Nancy asked, clearly and calmly. 'Where's it going now then? What does it mean?'

The glass swept around the letters, before selecting B – A – D.

'BAD' - that's not a person,' said Brooke. 'Is someone ill, maybe? Do we know this person?'

Like lightning, the glass whizzed over to the 'Yes' tab, then stopped completely.

'Well,' Frankie said briskly. 'It doesn't make a lot of sense, does it? No one we know is 'bad'.' Frankie's expression belied her words as she reflected on her sad and sorry relationship with Adam. But, could you describe him as a 'bad person'? She shook herself and concentrated once again on the circle of letters.

'Let's just see if we can find out anything else about the situation before we turn in,' suggested Nancy.

Once more, fingers resumed their positions and the glass gradually moved again, swirling, picking up speed.

'It's spelling a word,' Brooke hissed, as the friends gazed intently at the glass 'N – O – O – L … it doesn't make any sense. Oh, hang on, I think it means the letter 'K'. Still not getting it. Oh, it must be 'Nook? Maybe 'Squirrel's Nook?' but I can't see how that links in with anything.'

'Spirit world, do you have any other messages?' Nancy asked softly, but the glass didn't budge as the three women momentarily stared at it. 'I think the spirits have run out of steam,' Nancy finally declared. 'A bit like me now. Let's call it a night and please don't dwell on this. It's only a bit of fun, and it doesn't make sense anyway.'

Lights were switched back on in a sudden bustle of activity, the glasses were placed in the dishwasher and plans were made for a walk, after breakfast the next morning. The three women went upstairs to their rooms. They wished each other a good night's sleep in bright chirpy tones, covering up a sense of unease that all of them felt and could not quite seem to shift as they gradually drifted off to sleep.

Bruce flopped back in his chair, exhausted. He shared his friends' unease as he contemplated what the spelt out words could mean. One of the women had commented that they did not know anyone 'Bad' but Bruce would beg to differ. From what he had seen of Adam's terrible behaviour towards Frankie, he would say that he was quite bad. Most unlikely though, that the 'Death' warning could be about Adam. Then there was the 'Nook' reference and that did resonate with him, just as it had with Brooke. 'Squirrel's Nook' was a well-known local beauty spot. Nevertheless, it was not impossible to connect these spelt out words into a coherent message. With a sigh, Bruce turned off the screens and left his control room for his bedroom.

As Bruce lay in bed, sleep evaded him for some time. His mind scrolled through images of Arthur with Kerri, stolen goods, gambling and the supernatural. As he eventually drifted off into a restless sleep, his dreams were filled with surreal images of casinos, witches and potions, all topped off with a mysterious dark haired gypsy woman. She held out her hands to Bruce. They were dripping in blood as her contorted face screamed warnings of murder. He sat bolt upright in a cold sweat, his heart thundering.

Chapter 9

18 December

Daisy finished drying her hair in the very smart changing room of Delvreton's hotel spa and gym. This was one of the main venues for her range of fitness classes and personal training programmes. She had finally finished a manic day with client after client, right from six thirty that morning until three in the afternoon. It was as if everyone was trying to burn off extra calories so that their over indulgence during the Christmas period would not register or get stored as fat. Apart from a few ten minute gaps between clients and a half hour lunch break, Daisy had been full on and she was relieved to have finished. That was her busiest day now before the holiday so she was looking forward to an afternoon drink with her girlfriends. She suspected that Brooke and Frankie would be a bit jaded from a night down at Nancy's place, but she knew that the gang fully intended to enjoy a few decadent afternoon drinks and luxuriate in the prospect of the holiday stretching out before them.

Daisy expertly tousled her blonde, choppy bob, applied some subtle eye make up to accentuate her deep, blue eyes and she chose her beloved red lipstick to add moisture and shade to her full lips. With a quick sweep of a mid-shade bronzer over her cheek bones, her makeup regime was complete. Daisy then checked her outfit in the full length mirror, liking her reflection: a gorgeous grey chenille track suit topped off by a trendy, long black and white animal print cardigan. Her silver Guess trainers finished off the look perfectly – just right for a winter afternoon's drink at her local. She heaved her large gym bag over her shoulder and picked up her handbag. Daisy waved goodbye to a couple of regulars in various stages of dressing or undressing and wished everyone a great Christmas as she departed the changing room.

When Daisy arrived at the Otter's she was not surprised that she was the first one there but she knew so many of the regulars that she instantly felt at home. It was just after three thirty and the lunchtime crowd of drinkers and diners were making an afternoon of it. Why not, with Christmas only a week away.

'Where are the others?' Shane asked, aware that it was a bit of a tradition for the girls to meet up on a Saturday afternoon. Sometimes their men joined them but they were all at the Wolves, West Bromwich match today, a massive local derby.

'They'll be here soon,' Daisy answered with a smile. 'Anyway, I'm leaving the car here so mine's a large Rose and go ahead and get what you want, Shane.'

'Thanks gorgeous. I'll have a vodka a bit later. You do look extra sexy today, by the way,' Shane winked at Daisy, very much aware of how attractive she looked, particularly with slightly flushed cheeks after her super active day. No doubt about it, Daisy was fit in every sense of the word.

'Flattery will get you everywhere,' Daisy joked, as she took her glass and paid.

'That's the plan,' Shane winked again. 'Hey, the rest of your crew are here, so do you want to order their drinks too?'

'That's great mate,' Daisy said as she waved her friends over and checked that they all wanted their usual tipples, which they did. We are all creatures of habit, Daisy smiled to herself.

Within a few minutes, the friends were settled at their table. They had all exclaimed at various items of clothing, giving special attention to Daisy's beautiful ensemble. Brooke was sporting a gorgeous new cape and she had that much coveted magenta leather designer bag on her arm again. Ruby was wearing her black leather trousers especially well and Frankie always looked great in skinny jeans and knee high leather boots.

Soon, the evening at Nancy's was being recounted by Brooke and Frankie. Everyone leaned in a bit closer when the subject of the Ouija board came up. The message was slowly analysed, word by word and there were some interesting interpretations.

'Well, Adam must be bad,' Ruby said straightaway. 'Who else do we know, who is bad?'

'Yes, it must be him,' Daisy agreed. 'I can't believe how he treated you the night of your party, Frankie. That was disgusting and I just can't get over what you told me,' she said, a concerned expression on her face.

Frankie shuddered slightly, allowing her mind to drift back to that awful experience, the final straw that led her to end it all. Except Adam hadn't left it there and she was receiving increasingly abusive texts from him.

'Look at these,' Frankie gave her phone to Brooke and nodded for her to pass it round to the others.

'Bloody hell,' said Brooke. 'What's wrong with the sod?'

'He just needs to leave you alone now,' agreed Ruby. 'It's not your bloody fault that his wife finally saw sense and chucked him out. And it's not your fault that his kids don't want to spend much time with him this Christmas. They're getting older now. They want to be with their mates not their sad father, who has to stay at his big brother's house for God sake.' Ruby looked disgusted as she handed the mobile back to Frankie.

'Just block him,' said Daisy.

'I will, but at least if I get his texts, it gives me an insight into his frame of mind. I'm sure I've seen his car driving past my place. It's like he's watching me.' Frankie shared this new information. 'At least I've been able to get out of Delvreton High. I miss the staff and some of the kids though.'

'Yes,' encouraged Brooke. 'But you were right to hand that contract to someone else in your team. You must distance yourself from Adam completely. He is a total sleaze ball,' she said, with genuine hatred in her voice. 'You have to stay strong now, Frankie. You must not give in to him, whatever he says. Promise us.'

'Course I will. He just gives me the creeps. Anyway, we have established that 'BAD' refers to him. So, were the spirits telling us that Adam is going to die?' Frankie asked with a smile.

'Let's hope so,' said Ruby. 'Let's all raise our glass to that beautiful thought.'

'Cheers!' The friends laughed as they toasted the demise of Adam.

'Where does bloody Squirrel's Nook fit in?' asked Brooke, enjoying the banter that was flowing, the more they drank.

'Fuck knows!' said Frankie, draining her glass. 'God, I needed that as we had a pretty big night at Nancy's, didn't we Brooke? Hair of the dog certainly works.'

Brooke smiled at her friend, once again enjoying the fact that she was getting stronger by the day.

'Seriously, though,' said Ruby. 'I don't think I'd fancy that Ouija board. What if you've gone and released some angry spirits, who come after you, or something.' She looked unnerved.

'What!' exclaimed Frankie? 'I just can't believe that you would be a scared of a few harmless spirits! You're a legend. You're fearless!'

'Not when it comes to stuff like that,' Ruby shivered. 'It gives me the heebie jeebies. I never realised your pretty mate Nancy was into weird shit like that.'

'It's just a bit of fun, but I think that there is actually something in it. That glass moves like lightning and it just feels really strange, like there is some force moving it,' Frankie reflected. 'You didn't push it, did you Brooke? I know I didn't and I've done this loads with Nancy, and I know she doesn't push either. So, maybe the prediction will come true.' Frankie smiled, pausing for dramatic effect. 'Maybe Adam, the 'BAD' man will get killed in Squirrel's Nook! Now there's a lovely thought!' Frankie laughed, so did her friends as she shook her empty wine glass.

'More drinks then!' proclaimed Ruby as she headed to the bar for another round. 'If the spirit world is right, then we definitely have something to celebrate!'

'So, what unearthly time did you start work today?' Frankie asked Daisy, as they waited for Ruby, aware that Saturday was her busiest day.

'Got to the hotel at about six, as usual, to get everything set up and started at six thirty with Paula, one of my most loyal customers.'

'Wow! I wouldn't fancy that on a Saturday,' Frankie commented.

'No, but I always have Friday off and I can pretty much call the shots all week. It's just that Saturday is a day when many of my PT clients want to really go for it. Paula's a surgeon so the six thirty start on a Saturday really suits her schedule.'

'Yeah, guess that makes sense,' said Brooke, but at least we can all just relax now. I must admit I'm feeling well mellow after the booze last night, all that country air on our walk this morning and now, more booze!' Brooke stretched contentedly, catching the eye of a group of young men at the next table, who were clearly admiring Brooke's marvellous bosom.

Frankie noticed and whispered to Brooke, 'I think you've pulled.'

Brooke laughed and told her 'not to be so bloody daft.'

A very pleasant couple of hours passed as the girls caught up on their news. Much was made of Daisy's discernibly more lean and muscly physique that all the friends admired. She was a much sought after personal trainer and always had a healthy waiting list.

'If fitness is your business, then you'd better look fit,' Daisy laughed as she responded to yet more admiring comments. 'And you know that I always indulge big time on Thursday and Saturday nights, so I just need to blast it in the gym to undo all the damage.'

'You look fab,' said Frankie. 'That military boot camp you do every two weeks with those dishy army guys has changed your shape. I love the way you look,' she complimented her friend.

'Lucky Bruce,' Ruby quipped.

Daisy paused for a moment and her smile slipped. 'We've been better, actually,' she said, her voice more serious than it had been all afternoon. 'He's in that bloody office, or 'control room' all the time and he's so preoccupied when he's not in there. He's also started to look at me, as if he's suspicious, or something. What really gets me though, is that when he's not in that sodding office, he seems to be staring at his bloody phone all the time, like some teenager. If I didn't know better, I'd think he was having an affair.' Daisy looked genuinely upset and took a long drink of her wine.

'No way! It must just be the new business. You two are so solid, the most solid couple I know,' observed Brooke, trying to reassure her friend. This was most unusual for Daisy to talk like this and Brooke felt a bit uneasy. Some things in life were meant to be, were constant and that was the case with Daisy and Bruce. They were the bedrock of the friendship group.

'Yeah, that must be it,' said Daisy doubtfully. 'I don't think it helped matters when Iris had all that trouble with her ex-boyfriend, Tom, not long ago. Bruce went into some sort of meltdown. Just so glad that's over but he's more protective than ever of the girls.'

'And you, too. That's all it is,' Brooke reassured her.

'You're not on your own,' Ruby chipped in. 'Arthur is staring at his bloody phone, a lot more than usual too, so I am definitely watching him,' she announced. 'Never trust a bloody man,' Ruby advised in a stern tone. 'Never trust them.'

The conversation stalled for a few moments before Frankie changed the subject. For the first time, she felt liberated. Yes, it felt good to be free at last from the controlling partner she had suffered for so very long. She also realised, listening to this conversation that not everyone's relationship was quite as perfect as you thought it was.

'How is Iris doing at the school?' Frankie asked, aware that Iris was in the PE department, the same department as Adam so she would probably see more of her headteacher than most recently qualified teachers would. Poor thing.

'She seems to love it,' said Daisy, a little uncomfortable, as she did not want to upset Frankie.

'That's great,' said Frankie. 'I'm so pleased for her. She's a lovely girl. I'm sure she will be fine. Just tell her to give Mr Adam Pearson a wide birth,' Frankie said, affecting a laugh to cover up the bitterness in her tone.

Her friends smiled back and it seemed a good time to bring their 'afternoon' drinks to an end. Before they knew it, it was six thirty and all of the friends felt a little jaded. They were all more than ready for their sofas to cuddle up with their beloved pooches, who would be waiting faithfully for them. Their partners were out somewhere in Wolverhampton after the big football match and they would be rowdy as hell when they got back. The girls' 'afternoon out' had been good but not quite as relaxed and comfortable as usual. There was certainly some tension in the air that afternoon. Despite the good humour, the quips and the in jokes, it was clear that all was not well. There was an underlying sense that some trouble was brewing in the town of Delvreton and, little did they know, but the four friends would find themselves slap bang in the middle of the eye of the storm, when it came.

Chapter 10

22 December

The next few days after the night down at Nancy's passed in a relative calm, as calm as the days can be leading up to Christmas. Bruce was keen to get his last job done, then he was really looking forward to taking a few days off from his hectic work schedule. He was also looking forward to devoting more time to his own personal surveillance project. This should be even more fascinating over the festive period.

The light was fading on the Wednesday before Christmas, the last day that the contractors were on site at Delvreton High. The lights on the beautiful Christmas tree, next to the main entrance, were already winking at anyone in the vicinity, as if they were on watch, guarding the building. Bruce once again thought that this school was a class act. That reassured him, as both of his daughters were entrusted to the school's care: Rosie was in year ten working so hard on her GCSE courses, bless her and his darling Iris was loving her teaching job. This gave Bruce more cause than ever to add just a little to the IT spec that he had agreed with Adam before the Christmas break. Yes, his additional 'special' spyware would enable him to see into Adam's inner sanctum, to listen in to his senior leadership meetings and to check that his girls were in the very best hands. Unfortunately, since he had witnessed that harrowing scene in Frankie's kitchen, he could not quite get his head around the fact that Adam held the post of headteacher at this fantastic school.

Bruce shivered a little, noticing the frost was already forming on the roof of the school. Would it really be a white Christmas like they seemed to be forecasting? He quickened his pace and entered the building through the automatic doors that welcomed him into the warmth of the foyer. He was immediately greeted by Sajid, the team supervisor, who quickly and competently talked Bruce through all the works that had been completed. Bruce nodded appreciatively; the job was all but done as he would have expected, since Sajid was the best in the business. Bruce informed his work colleague that he would just check the PC screen in Adam's office to ensure the CCTV was streamed effectively. Unknown to Sajid, Bruce also intended to install the microscopic cameras in the diagonal corners of Adam's office so that he could observe the running of Delvreton High at his leisure in the new-year, once the spring term resumed.

The office was overly swanky for a school, Bruce thought as he opened the door with his master key. He recalled Frankie telling them all about how Adam was spending too much money on making his office 'special' as part of the design process when the school rebuild was in its final stages. He had even had the audacity to amend the plans to add a fancy, adjoining shower room and high spec interior. Bruce remembered Frankie commenting on this being a step too far as the students ought to be the ones who should have all the perks, not Adam.

The furniture choices were certainly well over the top for a headteacher's office: a large glass conference table, modern sleek chairs and tan sofas placed in one corner of the stylish space. Yes, Adam was definitely on some sort of power trip. Bruce grimaced as he took in the scene before him. Adam had certainly landed on his feet at the expense of the students by the look of it. Bruce also recalled gossip about the female chair of governors having a soft spot for Adam, which had undoubtedly been associated with his premature rise to seniority. Frankie had stuck up for Adam when everyone expressed their surprise about his appointment but she had, at least, now admitted that he had been bloody lucky to land this prize job and probably was not up to it. At least, Frankie was seeing sense at last, now that her rose tinted glasses were well and truly discarded. The last headteacher had been amazing, apparently. She had transformed the place from a bland, coasting school to the best in the region and she could do no wrong. But she had been head hunted by the Department for Education leaving Adam to take up the reigns and Bruce fully intended to find out if Adam was up to the job.

Bruce worked fast and jumped down from the chair, which had enabled him to carefully place the cameras and adjust the settings. He double checked Adam's new CCTV system, wondering to what extent Adam sat in his big office chair in his big office just watching his staff and students. Bruce felt a thrill as he contemplated his ability to watch Adam watching… or whatever else this headteacher got up to.

Bruce checked in with Sajid, handed back the master key and invited him for a Christmas drink at the Otter's, where he had a cheeky little appointment with Ronnie in about ten minutes. As Bruce left the building, he had a spring in his step. Not only had he bugged Adam's office, but he had made a nice little profit from the work Sajid and the team had done for him. Bruce enjoyed the chill in the air and the festive scene of Delvreton's lights, twinkling in the distance, like a veritable Christmas card.

***

Adam stood in one of the upper level classrooms. He was carefully assessing Bruce from a distance as he definitely did not feel like speaking to him in person. Bruce was far too pally with Frankie for his liking, but he had been willing to let Bruce have the contract for the school's security since it was well known that Bruce was the best in the IT business. Adam watched Bruce leave before taking the stairs back down to the Admin block, where his ostentatious office held pride of place. Adam was clear about one thing though; he was the one in charge and he just wanted to be absolutely sure Bruce was the right person for the job. Adam knew everyone joked about him being a control freak but he did not care. He was firmly the boss now and he could throw his weight around as much as he liked.

Adam was still seething from the fact that Frankie had had the audacity to dump him. He fully intended to keep a very close eye on her. How dare she finish with him? Well, he would bide his time, but one day she would be sorry, very sorry indeed. The lights automatically went out as Adam left the building, skirting round the side to the service area where he had parked his distinctive, sleek silver Jaguar. He had not wanted Bruce to know that he had been in the building. Adam breathed a sigh of satisfaction as he settled into the ergonomic leather driver's seat, felt the purr of the engine and accelerated away from the building. A feeling of supremacy consumed him as he was reminded that Delvreton High was 'his' school, he was in charge of everything and everybody. Yes, he absolutely deserved to be in charge of the best school in the area. He allowed himself to relish the sense of power for a moment, feeling like he was invincible.

***

The Otter's was rammed when Bruce arrived, scanning the tables and bar area before he spotted Ronnie in the corner, pride of place, looking well at home and in deep conversation with Shane, the landlord. Bruce pushed his way through the throngs saying hello as he knew most of the regulars and noted that they had simply brought their friends and colleagues in for a festive drink or two. He would have to keep a sharp lookout for Sajid in a few minutes.

'Alright mate' Ronnie greeted Bruce. 'As it's Christmas, I took the liberty of getting you your first pint of Moonshine.' Ron handed the pint over to him, who admired the frothy head before taking a long slug of ale.

'I bloody needed that mate. Work is officially over,' Bruce declared as he placed his pint down on a well-positioned beer mat.

'Never!' scoffed Ronnie. 'Your Daisy says you're never out of that office of yours, or your control room as you call it. Unless of course, you're getting up to no good in there,' Ronnie laughed.

Bruce wished he had not felt a glimmer of guilt at Ron's words but he shrugged off the feeling. He wanted a night with his mate, with any of the lads who joined them, then he might share a few of his worries a little later on. He still had not managed to get to grips with Daisy's stealing and he was totally floored by what he had discovered Brooke was up to. Then there was what he saw at Frankie's, not to mention the bloody Ouija board evening. His insights into his friends' lives were not what he had expected at all. Ron was his mate, so he needed to try and alert him to Brooke's gambling but he could not give too much away or no one would ever trust him ever again.

'Bloody hell, penny for them,' Ronnie said loudly. 'Leave work alone now. Relax, drink and be merry. There's a bloke over there, looking at you.'

'It's Sajid! Come over here,' Bruce shouted jovially as he saw his friend gently push his way through the revellers.

Before he knew it, a couple of hours had passed very pleasantly. Sajid had bid his farewell and Bruce and Ronnie were now sitting in the far corner of the lounge area, with yet another pint of Moonshine.

'Mate, I'm done with the pints now,' Bruce sighed 'Think I'm gonna segue onto a nice, spiced rum.'

116

'Get you with your fancy lingo and your fancy drinks,' Ron laughed heartily. 'I'll stick to a good old glass of malt, if you're asking.'

'Be back soon,' Bruce said spotting a gap at the bar.

The friends were certainly feeling the Christmas spirit after a good four hours at the Otter's and they thought Arthur might be in soon. Bruce saw a moment to dull down the mood and take the chance to confide in his mate. Ron was always at the centre of the crowd, laughing, joking and beating everyone at racket ball, but he was also salt of the earth, someone who would never let you down. Bruce needed a bit of that now.

'Mate,' Bruce began.

'Yeah,' answered Ron, sensing a change in Bruce's tone of voice.

'Are you okay? That rum's not getting to you already is it?'

'Course not. Just wondered, if you ever think you don't really know people.'

'That's a bit heavy,' Ron pondered. 'I guess everyone is different when they are alone, not with mates, not with anyone.'

'That's a bit deep too.' Bruce observed.

'What's brought this on then?' Ron asked, looking earnestly at Bruce's expression.

'Well, Daisy seems different these days; it's since she went out for a day with Ruby, you know, just before Frankie's do.'

'Anyone would be different after a day boozing with Ruby,' Ron laughed. 'Mate, it's just women; we will never really understand them, will we? I know that we have a couple of good uns' though.'

Bruce was not quite ready to give up yet. 'Have you not noticed Brooke looking a bit different recently?'

'What do you mean?' Ronnie's interest suddenly piqued, not quite sure what Bruce was getting at.

'Well, did you see that dress she was wearing at Frankie's do? I'm not sure I would have clocked it but Daisy kept going on about it when, you know, she dissected the evening afterwards with the girls. Apparently, Brooke has loads of new gear and a really expensive new handbag. Thinking about it, there's something a bit different about her. Like Daisy, I mean – she's wearing different stuff. What's happening mate?'

Ronnie took a sip of his malt considering what Bruce had just said.

'I don't really notice what Brooke wears – she always looks nice and I haven't got a clue about fashion. She works hard like your Daisy so it's up to them really. The bottom line of our joint account is pretty much the same at the end of the month. So, she can't be spending more money.' Ronnie stared into the distance, clearly sorting out his response and his thoughts as he spoke.

Bruce wrestled with himself big time. How could he let on that he knew about Brooke's gambling problem, all the money in that bloody betting account? Thank God Frankie had dumped Adam, but he was still around – his daughters were both in his school. Then there were Daisy and Ruby, the 'Bonnie and Clyde' of the Mailbox. But what could he do? Truth was, Bruce just had to keep so much knowledge to himself. How could he influence his friends' lives knowing what he knew?

'Come on mate, get a grip. Arthur's just arrived with a few of his mates from work. Hold on tight!' Ronnie laughed.

Bruce shook himself out of his reverie and smiled although he felt like he'd had way too much to drink and would not last long with Arthur and his crew, especially as Vincent was with them; he must have just got back from that restaurant tour in London. He resolved to stay for about half an hour but he would have to make his rum last, or Daisy would kill him if he went home in a state.

Christmas music was in full swing and the Otter's emitted a perfect, festive atmosphere. Despite his earlier sense of positivity that had waned somewhat as, with the build-up of alcohol, certain phrases uttered by his friends, certain images and recollections bombarded Bruce's mind and he was feeling like a very troubled soul. Rather than the empowerment that knowledge brought, for Bruce, it was suddenly feeling like a millstone weighing him down.

'Whey hey!' Arthur proclaimed as he pulled over both a free table and several chairs. 'I have made my last phone call today to the contractors and I am officially on holiday. Lock up your daughters!'

'You're mad,' Bonnie, the waitress said with a smile as she briskly walked past Arthur.

'You wouldn't have me any other way, gorgeous wench!' Arthur retorted.

'She's young enough to be your daughter,' Ronnie advised laughing.

'I know! I just love our Bonnie Bon, don't I?' Arthur asked Bonnie, as she swept back with the empties.

'You do and you have to do exactly what Ruby tells you to. Just you remember that,' Bonnie countered with a twinkle in her eye. 'Seriously, Ron, am I serving at your do on New Year's Eve like I did at Frankie's?' Bonnie asked.

'Too right,' Ronnie confirmed. 'Only the best staff at our do. If you're good enough for our Frank, then you're good enough for us.'

'You betcha,' said Bonnie, as she flounced off, purposely camping it up to the appreciation of the group of mates.

'So much to look forward to. Cheers everyone!' Arthur raised his glass, joined by his work colleagues, as well as Ronnie and Bruce.

Ronnie had to admit that the edge had been taken off the evening slightly due to Bruce's odd comments about Brooke and the girls. He tried to recollect any changes he had seen in his wife but he just couldn't. No doubt about it, despite Arthur's arrival, Bruce had seemed to slump; he had lost his chirpy up-beat mood, that he had arrived with. Still, changing your business in the major way Bruce had, can't have been easy. Ron was so happy he had his skill of high end joinery and was so at home in his workshop and in renovating his beautiful Victorian townhouse – a real labour of love. Life was good, Ron confirmed to himself. He would make sure he was a really good mate and he would give Bruce an extra bit of attention, make sure he went to the Otter's, just the two of them, a few more times so he could check in with him. Ron certainly could not do the counselling that Brooke specialised in but it had rubbed off on him. He was getting a bit sensitive in his middle years. Ronnie smiled at this inward revelation and decided to do a good deed. He needed to get home for a curry with Brooke so he would rescue Bruce from the clutches of an alcohol fuelled Arthur. Bruce was definitely not up to dealing with that tonight.

After lots of back -slapping and promises to meet up loads over the Christmas break, Ronnie ensured that he and Bruce safely extricated themselves from Arthur and his gang. They eventually made it out of the Otter's after stopping to chat to all of the locals who had called them over as they passed.

'Bloody Hell, I'm pretty pissed,' Bruce declared, as he stood for a moment against the wall of the Otter's. The ice cold air hit him and helped somewhat in helping him to gather himself.

'I'm not surprised,' laughed Ron. 'That ended up as quite a session, but who cares? It's Christmas!'

The two mates walked off down the main street, the tall spindly, brightly lit trees elegantly lining their route and the friends eventually went their separate ways home. Both felt that something had shifted, just a little for Ronnie who could not help but dwell on some of the things Bruce had said in the latter part of the evening. The scale of the shift was much greater for Bruce and the fact that he was very much alone with his new knowledge was beginning to weigh heavy. Like an addiction though, he could not help fixating and speculating on what he might happen to listen in on and see over the Christmas period and beyond. It was tantalising and very worrying all at the same time. Bottom line, it was plain wrong but somehow Bruce thought that he might be able to do something right, to step into his friends' flawed lives and maybe save them, in some way.

He turned his key in the door to be met by the comforting aromas of cinnamon and mulled wine.

'I'm back love', he announced, as he staggered slightly through the front door into his home, into his kingdom. All would be fine, he reassured himself. Life was always good at Christmas.

Bruce threw his house keys into the ceramic bowl on the tall, elegant display table in the hallway of his beautiful home, now swathed in subtle golden light from an array of tastefully arranged Christmas lights, which seemed to be everywhere. Such was Daisy's sense of taste, that she always got it just right. All of her interior design touches were never too much and always added to the style that simply oozed from every crevice of this abode.

'Where's your Mum love?' Bruce addressed Iris who was sprawled on the large sofa transfixed on her iPad. She looked up. 'Last minute shopping for the dinner party tomorrow night, apparently.' Iris dragged her eyes from the screen and beamed at her Dad.

'Oh yeah, I forgot about that but you're here gorgeous and that's all that matters.' Bruce embraced his daughter, drinking in the vanilla scent from her long golden hair. 'This is the best bit about our family get together. Are you staying now right up to Christmas, then love?' Bruce asked hopefully.

'Just tonight and tomorrow Pops. I intend to get squiffy tonight! I'm knackered as the last few weeks have been bloody mental at work. But I'll stay at mine for the two days before Christmas as I need to recover here with some home comforts then I'm out with the girls for a wild Christmas Eve,' Iris grinned mischievously at her adoring father.

'Okay, I guess that makes sense,' said Bruce concentrating hard on not slurring his words. 'I was just up at your school this afternoon for one of my new contracts. Tree looks fab. Hey, weren't you the princess in the panto at the end of term?'

'Yep and I was a star!' Iris pronounced. 'Here, have a look at the pics.' She handed her IPad over and enjoyed seeing the pride on Bruce's face as he looked

123

appreciatively at his beautiful, talented and happy daughter. What more could a father want for his first-born? More the point, she was no longer with that prick Tom, who she had been so besotted with. Tom was a player and although Bruce saw that within minutes of meeting him, Iris had not shared her father's viewpoint at all. Tom was in sales and at thirty two, eight years older than his girl. That had worried the hell out of Bruce. He had found it so tough when Iris moved out into one of the bijou new apartments overlooking the river. In normal circumstances, he would have been delighted for her but the completion of the purchase coincided with Tom bursting onto the scene.

Bruce still hurt from the pain he saw his daughter experience because of that low life and how he had completely manipulated her. He had done the same thing, apparently to a number of other poor young beautiful women he had been seeing at the same time. Well, Iris was free now, back in the protective embrace of her family. Her protestation that she was 'done with men' suited Bruce down to the ground. Protect Iris he would; he swore he would even kill for her, and Rosie too of course, if he had to. Bruce knew Rosie's moves every minute of the day and he was ultra-relieved that Iris was now throwing herself into her teaching and enjoying her social time with a small group of lovely girlfriends whom she had known since infant school.

'Hey, who's that dressed as a genie? Isn't that your headteacher?' Bruce asked, still skimming over the photos of the panto.

'Yeah!' The kids loved him. 'Look, he's got a spray gold prosthetic fat stomach,' Iris giggled like a teenager. 'And all the staff ripped it out of him afterwards, when we had our 'panto wrap' drinks party at the Otter's last night.'

'I'm not surprised. It's not exactly the most flattering look,' Bruce said as he screwed his nose a little at the photo of the panto and pondered how appropriate it was for the headteacher to be on stage with all those attractive, young teachers. Iris seemed particularly enthusiastic as she went on a little too long about how Adam was actually 'very fit and a total gym addict'. Bruce started to switch off so he changed the subject.

'So, where did you lot end up last Friday night? Were you late back?'

'Not too bad. Got back at about eleven-ish. A few of the girls joined us which was lovely.'

Bruce hugged Iris again before heading for the kitchen in search of a cold beer. Having both of his girls home together was simply the best Christmas present ever.

'Don't let Mum know how many you've had tonight,' Iris advised. 'She'll be back soon and I can tell that you've had loads to drink, so she will too. Get me a wine while you're there please.'

'Okay cheeky and your mother won't mind me being merry, because it's my last day at work!' Bruce declared in a sing, song voice.

Whilst she waited for her Dad to sort out their drinks, Iris threw the IPad aside and picked up her phone, flicking

125

through an abundance of photos. She lingered a moment over the images in the Otter's last night, and one in particular. It was of her and Adam, both looking at each other and smiling warmly. He had his arm around her shoulders and she remembered that it had felt good to have some of his attention. Adam had said some lovely things to her about how well she was doing and that she should go for the new head of house leadership role that had just been advertised. Adam whispered that he thought she would be perfect and that the fact she was only in her second year of teaching did not matter at all. Adam joked that he had been watching her with interest; that she was very talented and he'd 'had his eye on her'. Yes, those were his exact words and she loved the fact that she had caught the attention of her boss.

Iris had overheard her parents talking a lot recently about how terribly Adam had treated Frankie but that did not change the fact that she thought he was doing a great job of running the school. Iris was also very much aware of the gossip about Adam and the new head of performing arts, Suzie. In fact, she had observed the two of them being very friendly at the Otter's, which would only fuel the gossip even more. That did not concern Iris. The fact was, she liked Adam as her boss and she was very keen to progress her career. She loved the fact that Adam clearly thought she had potential. Iris decided that she would definitely go for the leadership opportunity in the new-year. She would show Adam that he was right to single her out for career development. In her opinion, she could not have a better professional mentor, despite what her parents and their friends might think of him.

Chapter 11

Christmas Day

Christmas day finally dawned in Delvreton and a deep white frost threw a blanket over the town to give the impression of a magical, white Christmas. If just a few snowflakes were to fall then that would make it official and there was a very good chance of that according to the weather forecast.

Frankie opened the blind in her bedroom to savour the beautiful wintery scene before her, jumping back into bed to cuddle up with Charlie, her adoring Vizla. She contemplated the day ahead with her parents, Ronnie, Brooke and the four dogs between them all. It promised to be a lovely, traditional Christmas day and Brooke was hosting this year. That meant Frankie could enjoy a leisurely few hours until their parents arrived at hers to pick her before heading over to Brooke's at about one o'clock for presents, canapés and Champagne.

Frankie sighed as she allowed thoughts of Adam to drift into her mind and she checked her phone, almost a reflex action. Several texts had been sent yesterday that were harsh and threatening, which she had instantly deleted. Why couldn't he just leave her alone? As it was Christmas day, she hoped that she would not be bothered by him and reflected on the many Christmases she had spent feeling lonely and hurt that Adam could never be with her. It could have been different this year, 'but be careful what you wish for,' she said to herself. Quite simply, Adam was not the person she thought he was and she just did not need his miserable, controlling presence in her life. Pulling Charlie towards her, she nuzzled his neck, loving the satisfied noises he made in response to her. 'You're the only man in my life, my beautiful boy,' she crooned and felt at peace with herself and the world.

***

In all of the other households festive activities were already underway. Bruce had prepared a delicious breakfast of bacon and scrambled eggs with the bucks fizz on ice and was waiting impatiently for his girls to come down. Very different to when they were little, up at five and urging him and Daisy to get up to see if Santa had been.

'Come on girls!' he shouted again impatiently, feeling like the child in the family; how the roles had reversed. Where was Daisy? She should be out of the shower now, surely. Bruce was determined to have a lovely day with his family and put some of the worries he had about Daisy and his troubled friends out of his mind, at least for one day. He resolved to stay out of his office and to stay out of other people's lives. He smiled at the sound of several pairs of footsteps descending the stairs. 'I think he's been!' Bruce announced, 'You lot sound like a herd of elephants, by the way!'

***

In the Harper household, Ruby rolled over with a big smile on her face as she contemplated the beautiful diamond

ring adorning her finger. Arthur had redeemed himself
big time by coming up with some serious funds for her
present. He was now downstairs, rustling up breakfast
for her and their daughter, Lola. Yes, life was very good in
her home this Christmas morning. She snuggled up with
Toby and Murray as she planned to enjoy a few more
quiet moments before they both went down and tore the
paper off their presents like little kids.

Meanwhile, Arthur had the croissants in the oven and
the coffee machine was doing its job, filling the house
with a rich aroma. He sat for a moment on the sofa next
to the log burner, looking thoughtfully at his phone at a
picture of Poppy, already wearing the dress he had
bought her. A smile quickly slipped into a frown though
as he read the text from her mother, a desperate text
screaming out her sense of loneliness and fear that the
latest toe rag she had hooked up with was threatening to
turn up to 'enjoy' his Christmas dinner with her and
Poppy.

Arthur had a terrible sense of unease as he saw Ruby
enter the kitchen and he quickly shoved the phone behind
the cushion, adjusting his expression to hide the dark
thoughts in his head. How could he break away to go and
check on them both without Ruby suspecting anything?

***

'Are you nearly ready? What you doing up there?' Ronnie
anxiously shouted up to Brooke. 'I've done all the veg,
laid the table, put the turkey in and I've got the extra
Sauvignon Blanc chilled for you and your Aunty Sheena. I
know you'll both polish off a bottle in no time,' Ronnie

chortled. 'Plus your Mum and Dad will be over in less than an hour with about a thousand presents for us to open so get a jiffy on Brookie! I want to make sure I have time to take both our Dads to the Otter's for the traditional Christmas pint before dinner's ready!' Ronnie was in his usual 'hyper mode' that he adopted every time they had visitors for dinner.

'Down in a minute,' Brooke shouted back. She was nursing a slightly fuzzy head from too much Prosecco on Christmas Eve and was now glaring intently at her phone, not quite believing how little was left in her William Lad account. How had she managed to lose ten grand yesterday? Why had she moved onto those casino games? She must stick to the horses and she had big plans for the race meeting at Kempton on Boxing Day. Yes, she should get the money back tomorrow. Brooke gathered herself and fully intended to enjoy her day ahead, smiling at the prospect of a 'good day at the races' tomorrow, if only on the television.

***

Christmas day passed as it always did with its own natural rhythm, the gentle, yet assertive wave of tradition moving everyone through the present opening rituals, pre-meal drinks and canapés, the first course, the wine choices that elicited appreciative comments or critiques, the star of the show turkey and then rest... before anyone could possibly contemplate the prospect of Christmas pudding or the many other dessert choices.

Before they knew it, darkness had fallen on the friends and their families, heralding early evening as the first snowflakes gently wafted down from a silver, leaden sky to the sighs of genuine wonder as the inhabitants of Delvreton celebrated the monumental event of a genuine white Christmas. This provided a natural pause to the festivities, a brief moment of quiet, as each individual gazed wondrously at the falling snow, savouring the beauty of the natural world, amidst the onslaught of commercialism and the high expectations that typified the less pure side of the festival. Ronnie and Brooke naturally leaned into each other, as did all the couples in that household. Frankie knelt next to Charlie, who was also looking avidly at the snowflakes with the other three family dogs, all anticipating the rush of joy when they would soon cavort together in the rarity that was snow.

It was a similar scene in the other friends' households. Bruce was already outside, capturing the 'perfect Christmas' with his girls. Arthur and Ruby were also peering out from the warmth of their sitting room, Lola lying languorously on both sofas, not considering the snow enough of a 'big deal' to put down her new iPhone. Except Arthur was not as relaxed as he appeared. He had received yet more texts during the course of the day, each sounding more desperate as Kerri anticipated the arrival of her former, bastard boyfriend. All Arthur kept seeing was Poppy, the vision of pure innocence, in her beautiful party dress. What party would she have in a flat with no carpet, threadbare furniture and barely enough good food for a few days until reliance on the foodbank was the norm once more. And how much had Kerri had to drink? There was no way Arthur could get out to check on them today but he would have to get over there tomorrow and he knew he would be able to swing that. He laughed a bit too much at Ruby's latest quip but he wasn't laughing inside; more like weeping for his little girl.

In the neighbouring town, Adam sat alone staring fixatedly at his phone. He had managed a couple of hours with his kids when he had picked them up in the morning to take them over to his parents for present opening. He knew they did not want to stay long, much as they loved their grandparents. They just wanted to get back to their own home, their mother and the prospect of an afternoon with their mates as Fiona, Adams ex-wife had invited the neighbours round for a Christmas night party. He had bristled when Fiona's eyes glinted as she made a comment about his failed relationship with Frankie. Yes, that had made Fiona's Christmas. How could that bitch Frankie have done that to him?

Adam had just about managed to get through the Christmas meal with his brother and the new girlfriend, but could not wait to excuse himself and 'go to his room' like a bloody teenager. For Christ sake, he was the head of Delvreton High and look at him: sitting in a bedroom like a teenager on Christmas night with a bloody Baileys. Adam had never been one for drinking pints or any alcohol really, which was not a problem had he not frowned so much on those that enjoyed it. Even he needed something to dull the anxiety and annoyance that was accosting his emotional wellbeing. In the past he had managed to have it all. He would have been having a 'perfect' Christmas with his wife, his children, their friends but it had all gone badly wrong and he had got it so very wrong with that bitch, Frankie. He would show her. He sent a vicious text telling her what a 'sad cow' she was.

***

'What are you two so focused on?' Ronnie asked Brooke and Frankie who were peering intently at Frankie's phone. The two of them had broken away briefly from the main gathering and their parents, who were ready for some party games, had noted their absence.

'Just some pretty horrible texts from Adam. And he keeps phoning her,' Brooke updated Ronnie as Frankie stared at the phone, her brow furrowed with worry.

'What?' exclaimed Ronnie. 'Just switch that thing off. The man is a total git and not worth your attention. Come on, our parents are ready and in the mood for some fun. Just forget him; he's history and you are well shot of him at last.'

Frankie did as instructed, flinging her phone on the armchair and she dutifully followed Ronnie and Brooke back into the main sitting room.

'At last!' Frankie's and Ronnie's mum, Gloria, declared. 'We wondered where you'd got to. I hope you're not looking at that bloody phone again, Frankie. It's Christmas and you need to have a good time and focus on your family. So, what card game are we starting with? How much are we playing for?'

Brooke's ears pricked up at the mention of playing for money, albeit small amounts. The thrill of the gamble was still a thrill and she was very keen to play. As the games progressed, the wine and beer flowed and the shrieks of laughter from Gloria, got louder as her wins got bigger.

'Imagine we three at bingo next weekend with this lucky streak!' Gloria exclaimed as Mitch chastised her not to spend too much, with a cheeky grin on his face. Brooke slightly winced at the thought of how much she herself had spent on the casino over the last few days. A few quid at the Bingo was nothing in comparison.

***

Despite his resolve at the start of this very special day, Bruce had not been able to resist checking his phone and there were two streams of texts that bothered him greatly. This had, unfortunately, led him to snap at both Daisy and Iris, who had snapped right back at him and duly withdrawn to the snug along with Rosie and the dog. This left Bruce alone in his ample sitting room. He poured himself a very generous rum as he read through the texts again. The first set involved Arthur's big secret. Bruce recalled the images he had seen of Arthur wrapping the gifts for a little girl he now knew as Poppy. It seemed that Arthur was planning to check in on the girl and her mother the next day. All hell would break loose, he thought to himself, if Ruby got wind of any of this. He felt so helpless but he could hardly offer to help Arthur out, which was his natural instinct. That was what a best mate should do in normal circumstances. He would do anything for a normal life right now; turn back the clock to early November.

Then there was Adam. He was bothering Bruce more and more, having glimpsed into his world beneath the veneer of the fine, upstanding citizen, who was the head of the local high school and who made a speech at the start of the local carol concert every year. What a total fraud. Here was Bruce reading a torrent of threatening texts from Adam to Frankie; they were really spiteful and the venom was strong. He felt so sorry for Frankie on the receiving end of these, at Christmas as well, but what could he do? 'Absolutely nothing,' he said out loud as he stared into the flames of his minimalist gas fire, swirling his rum in the heavy tumbler.

Bruce turned his head to look out of the large picture window, transfixed by the heavy snow storm. Christmas day had started with such promise but the dead weight of the new knowledge Bruce had recently gleaned from his surveillance was changing everything. Except for Ronnie, none of his friends were who he thought they were and his wife had done something that had truly shocked him. Bruce took a long drink from his glass, staring at the thickening snow.

Chapter 12

Boxing Day

'Bye Love,' Arthur shouted up the stairs to Ruby as he left the house. 'Not sure when I'll be back as all the lads are at the Otter's and you know I've had that call out from the apartment worksite. Apparently, some bloody vandals got in so I need to check everything's okay and secure.'

'You can sort your own food then,' Ruby mumbled cuddling up to Toby and Murray. She had very little intention of doing anything much at all after the intensity of Christmas day and was very relieved that her daughter Lola was already round a mate's house. For once, she really did not care what time Arthur returned home.

Arthur slipped out, signalling to the Uber driver that just turned down his road. Yes, he would be at the Otter's but he had another visit to make first and it wasn't to his building site.

'Felstead Road and it's the flats mate,' Arthur instructed the driver as he scrolled through the texts he had received from Kerri, each one sounding more desperate and, very worryingly, more incoherent. She was obviously on the booze again so where did that leave poor little Poppy?

The landscape gradually changed from wide leafy suburban roads to the open expanse of wasteland on the deprived side of the city, the skyline dominated by the high rises, one of which housed Arthur's six year old girl. Arthur was experiencing levels of anxiety that he had not known existed as he realised that thoughts of Poppy seemed to invade his mind all the time now. He had no idea how he had managed to act normal at home and was concerned that he would be unable to keep up the pretence for much longer. How on earth would Ruby react if she had any idea about his situation? Arthur was sure that he knew exactly what her reaction would be and gave an involuntary shudder as he climbed out of the cab, momentarily looking up at the high-rise. The eighth floor loomed above him where he would soon see the reality of his little girl's existence. He set off, determined to tackle the stairs; he just could not face the stench of the lift.

**

Bruce was first to arrive at the Otter's and sat at a corner table transfixed to his phone and the several dramas that were unfolding. He knew exactly where Arthur was heading and knew pretty much what he was heading into, having read Kerri's texts to Arthur last night. He wished he could help but knew there was nothing he could possibly do to let his friend know he was aware of the troubles to come. He was also growing increasingly concerned about Brooke and Ronnie knowing what he knew about the Boxing Day race meeting at Kempton. After her loss on the casino App, Brooke had already placed at least four increasingly hefty bets, over a thousand pounds on just one race, the big one, the King George that Brooke always watched with Frankie and their parents. Yes, she had a decent stash of money in her William Lad account but if she carried on like this, it wouldn't last long.

'You're keen.' Ronnie laughed as he pulled up a chair. Bruce tore his gaze from his phone's screen.

'Alright mate.' He acknowledged his friend, forcing a smile. 'Just needed the fresh air and to get out of the house. You can go a bit stir crazy at this time of year.'

'Just needed a pint, more like,' Ronnie laughed. 'Any idea when Arthur's due in?'

'He won't be in for a while.' Bruce realised he had answered a bit too readily. 'Err, I seem to recall he mentioned he'd be in a bit later than the rest of us... for some reason.' Bruce tried to keep his tone upbeat, kicking himself for letting on that he knew anything more about Arthur's plans than the rest of them. He made a note to himself that he must be more careful; he could never let on what he was up to or he would undoubtedly lose his mates in an instant and probably face some sort of prosecution. Bruce shivered, shaking off his despondence then enthusiastically joined in welcoming the new arrivals in the 'gang', entering into the customary review of Christmas day and speculations about the big New Year's Eve party that was planned at Ronnie's place. Each of the friends took a turn at hosting the annual bash and they were particularly looking forward to this one as they were all keen to sample the recently added party basement room equipped with Ronnie's mega sound system.

By one thirty the Otter's was full and everyone appeared to be having a good time. Bruce surveyed the scene wondering what secrets each one of individuals making up the crowd had. What was happening behind the closed doors of each house on the streets of Delvreton?

'Penny for them?' Vincent asked as he slid into the spare chair beside Bruce. 'You alright mate?'

'Course!' Bruce answered slapping his pal on the back. 'Good to see you!'

'Blimey! Look at the time,' Ronnie exclaimed. 'Just time for a 'Captain's half' before I need to bid you all farewell and get round to Frankie's for the big race.' Ronnie always had to have just one more and his supposed 'half pint' was simply code for re-filling his pint glass that had less than one mouthful left in it. Ronnie got the round in, feeling slightly disappointed that it looked like he was going to miss Arthur. He felt sorry for his friend having to go into work on Boxing Day. That was tough luck, no doubt about it.

'The usual?' Ronnie gestured to Vincent.

'Please mate,' Vince answered, beaming as Ronnie managed to grab the barmaid, Bonnie's attention, who was holding two jugs of a Christmas cocktail concoction.

The landlord, Shane, was right on form as he guffawed 'Nice Jugs Bonnie!' like a character out of a 'Carry On' film. Bonnie rolled her eyes, passed the cocktail jugs over to a waiting punter and turned her attention to Ronnie.

'What can I get you chaps?'

'Captain's half of IPA please Bonnie,' Ron replied. Bonnie smirked, as she knew that meant 'fill the pint glass up please.'

Vince added, 'I need something a bit stronger after my morning, checking emails. No rest for the wicked! JD and coke please Bon Bon.'

'Well, you will go and take on your own restaurant mate. I guess that goes with the territory,' Ronnie teased. 'Sit yourself down, I'll bring the drinks over.'

Ronnie paused in his tracks, thinking about his life and how much he loved his work. Being his own boss was great and he was grateful that he did not need to deal with all the stress that so many of his friends had to put up with. He had noticed Brooke had been a bit more preoccupied with her laptop recently and he hoped she was not going overboard on work or worse, gambling again. He knew only too well she liked a flutter a bit too much; he decided to keep an eye on her. Thankfully, he did not have to deal with any problems this Boxing Day. He smiled to himself as he headed back to the table looking forward to a catch up with Vincent before his time was up.

'Looks like you lot could be in for a right session seeing as our Vincent has shown up,' Ronnie declared to the posse of male regulars who had now gathered at the table. 'A shame I can't stay for much longer.' Ronnie looked regretful as he gulped down the final dregs of his beer in one mouthful.

It was just before four o'clock when Arthur found himself back in the thick of it all, safe and content at his beloved Otter's unlike the world he had just had to walk out on. He would normally have been in his absolute element but he could not stop his mind wandering back over the scenes in Kerri's eighth floor flat, the scenes that had assaulted every one of his senses when the reality of the life of his poor child had dawned on him. It had hit him like a ton of bricks.

Bruce listened to the conversation between Arthur and Vincent as Arthur gave some cock and bull story as to why he had arrived so late on Boxing Day. Bruce reflected on how easily the lies seemed to flow out of his friends' mouths, including his own bloody wife too, conveniently forgetting his own recent lies. He grimaced for a moment before ensuring that he switched his expression to one of happiness to be with his mates at the festive time, just like any normal person. Bruce had begun to realise he was constantly playing a part in his own drama and that the days of being genuine and true to himself had long gone. There *must* be some way he could make the most of the situation he had found himself in. Bruce made a silent vow to himself that he would use his knowledge to do something good for his friends; there must be a way…

Earlier that day, when Arthur had arrived at Kerri's flat, he had been instantly alarmed to see the front door ajar. He had tentatively pushed it open, afraid of what awaited him. He realised that he had been acutely conscious of his quickening heartbeat as he shouted 'Kerri, Poppy, it's me, Arthur.' As soon as he saw Poppy running towards him into his arms, a surge of relief had swept over him like a tidal wave of paternal emotion. 'Thank God,' he whispered, picking her up and burying his face in her hair. He instantly noticed the unwashed aroma of Poppy's hair and body mingling with the acrid, stale smell of the dingy flat. There was not even a carpet on the floor for God's sake and it felt distinctly chilly.

'Let me have a look at you, my beauty,' Arthur said purposefully, keeping his tone light as he put Poppy down and appraised her. She was wearing the beautiful pink dress he had given her a week ago except it was far from beautiful now. It was filthy, with unidentifiable stains down the front and various bits of food. Poppy's hair was a tangled mess and the doll she pulled into herself had lost its clothes.

'I'm hungry,' Poppy implored, looking up pleadingly at Arthur who could not quite hide the concern on his face.

'Okay Angel,' Arthur said reassuringly. 'Let's see what we can find. Maybe some nice leftovers from yesterday?' Arthur thought of his fridge at home, bursting to the seams with gorgeous festive foods.

Arthur opened the fridge door and an unpleasant waft of stale food greeted him.

'What's that?' Poppy enquired, pointing at something wearing a coat of green mould. Her big brown eyes seemed to sear into his very soul.

'Tell you what poppet, I'll get us something from the take out in a bit yeah? Let's talk to Mummy first, shall we? Where is she?'

Poppy pointed to the hallway. Arthur guessed that there must be a bathroom and two bedrooms down there.

'Mummy's not still in bed, is she?' he asked, the question more to himself than Poppy.

'Yes, she was with that man and said I had to stay in here.' Poppy offered up the information readily.

'Is the man in there still?' Arthur asked, not wanting to believe what his poor daughter must be enduring in this sad little life. To think he was naïve enough to believe a pink party dress could have made any difference, could have made any of this better. Arthur felt stupid that he had believed Kerri when she had told him that everything was fine.

'The man went,' Poppy informed him and Arthur realised that was probably why the door had been left open. Whoever it was had not even bothered to shut the door, but why hadn't Kerri got up to check? He took a deep breath, put Poppy onto the threadbare sofa and instructed her to wait a minute whilst he went in search of her mother.

The bedroom was swathed in a dingy light, again bare floorboards and an old dressing table stood in the corner of the depressing room. Arthur noticed clothes had been randomly flung over it as his eyes roamed to the mound of bedclothes clearly covering Kerri, who had not yet sat up.

'Kerri, it's me Arthur,' he hissed desperately trying not to speak too loudly and upset Poppy.

'Why you here?' A sluggish voice sounded from under the covers.

'It's bloody twelve thirty and your little girl needs you,' Arthur hissed at her again, aware of the heightened sense of urgency coming through his utterance.

'You told me you had a nice little flat, you said everything was good for the two of you and you just needed a little bit of help from me. You're a bloody liar Kerri. This place is a fucking dump. Get out of that bloody bed. We need to talk.' Despite his efforts, Arthur could not help but raise his voice. He went over to the window, opening it to let in both some light and some fresh air.

'It stinks like a brewery in here,' he said, taking in a couple of empty bottles of cheap vodka and an overflowing ashtray. Just as he saw Kerri haul herself up, he took in the black eye, dishevelled hair and grimy bathrobe. Then he turned to see little Poppy in the doorway, sucking her thumb and despondently holding the doll in her other hand. Arthur was with her in moments, scooping Poppy into his arms and pulling her in closely towards him.

'I am taking this gorgeous little girl out for some food,' Arthur said again, trying to keep his tone light and cheerful for Poppy's sake. 'I can see you haven't checked that fridge of yours for weeks, have you?'

Kerri shook her head. Just as he thought. His stomach churned as he imagined what bacteria was lurking in there. He needed to get them both out of there fast.

'When we get back in about an hour, we are going to have a bit of a chat. Okay?' Arthur said cheerily, forcing every fibre of his being to prevent him from crumbling into a heap. Noticing a child's puffer jacket on the hook in the hallway, he grabbed it and left the flat, with Poppy safely ensconced in his protective arms.

Arthur had at least made sure that Poppy had a good meal inside her, if only fried chicken from the nearest fast food place. He could not risk being much longer and he was quickly formulating a plan to make sure that Poppy could have some time away from Kerri and that awful flat. Whilst Poppy ate her meal, he made a call to Barry or 'Bazzer' as he was affectionately known, a mate from the Jewellery quarter area of the city where Ruby worked. Salt of the earth, a real Black Country geezer and whose wife was a very experienced foster parent. Arthur had spun a tale about how he needed to help an old friend by finding a safe place for her child, whilst she sorted herself out and got away from an abusive partner.

Once he had gone back to the flat to have a word with Kerri, he would drop Poppy off at Bazzer's place; not that far from Delvreton as it happened.

Arthur had grabbed a few bits and pieces for Poppy, but he knew Bazzer's wife would have clean clothes and all Poppy would need. He had been chuffed to hear that there was another six year old girl being fostered by them at the moment, together with one other older girl. Bazzer's wife was used to having about four of the poor buggers on average.

Arthur's worst fears had also been confirmed about Kerri, when he'd had a quiet word with her, whilst Poppy had been instructed to wait in the sitting room, if that's what you could call it. Kerri had allowed an 'old flame' round Christmas night, once Poppy was in bed. They had got totally hammered, had a row and he had punched her in the face. He had left about ten minutes before Arthur had arrived, thank Christ, or who knows what could have happened. Arthur had suspected Kerri had a drink problem but he now realised how serious it was. He had to get Poppy away from this hell- hole to buy him a bit of time. Yes, he would give Kerri a few days to clean up her act then he would decide what was best to do.

***

It had been harsh walking away from the flat with Poppy but no Kerri. She had not liked his plan one bit and at first resisted the idea with an angry 'absolutely no fucking way are you taking Poppy anywhere without me.' Then, after some reasoning from Arthur, who made it clear it was in Poppy's best interest, together with a hangover from hell and her swollen and bruised face, Kerri had, reluctantly, relented on the condition that it was 'just for a week or so, while she got her act together.'

***

Arthur did not enjoy seeing Kerri in the state she was in and his heart broke as he heard her weeping, when she kissed Poppy goodbye. Despite this, Arthur knew he was doing the right thing by Poppy and had been pleased that Poppy had gone along with his 'adventure' story quite happily. She seemed to be genuinely excited and was looking forward to meeting her new friend, whose name was Connie. As predicted, Barry and his wife had met them with open arms. Arthur was reassured as Barry's wife ran Poppy a bath, sorted out some clean pyjamas for her and Connie took Poppy up to see her bedroom. Poppy was beaming with joy when she came back down the stairs, telling Arthur all about Connie's 'Frozen' themed bedroom that she would be sharing. Arthur knew he had to say goodbye and he knew that Poppy was safe and happy.

He slipped away and had sighed in relief as he made it back to the Otter's just before four which meant he should be back with Ruby by six at the latest and she would, thankfully, be none the wiser about this 'other life' he was dealing with. At some point though, Arthur anticipated that his two worlds would collide; he just was not at all ready to deal with it, not just yet.

***

Two miles away, Frankie's home was filled with shrieks of delight as both Brooke and Frankie had followed Frankie's and Ronnie's dad, Mitch's advice and backed the winner of the King George. Thistlecrack had stormed home, winning Frankie and her dad over a hundred quid. Brooke had done okay too, stating that she was very

148

happy with her seventy five pounds. Brooke was, in fact, ecstatic when she had a moment to check her William Lad account and the seven thousand five hundred pounds that had actually been deposited.

'Come on,' Brooke announced gleefully as she twirled around the room. 'What shall we have on the last race? Her eyes twinkled at Frankie, just as she clicked to place another thousand pounds at 9/1 odds.

***

At the Otter's, the group of friends were uncharacteristically quiet. Bruce and the lads were all engrossed in their phones for a few moments, as they checked on the latest football results, except Bruce was not checking the results. His eyes widened as he noted the latest deposit into Brooke's Williams Lad account and he raised his eyebrows even further when he read the desperate text from Kerri to Arthur about how she had made a hideous mistake and there was just no way she could cope without Poppy. She wanted to see Arthur urgently, she would not hesitate to find him, if necessary, and she was threatening to tell Ruby everything. What had Arthur gone and done?

Chapter 13

New Year's Eve Preparations

Brooke was in a rush. As usual, she had left everything until the eleventh hour and had a ton of organising to do for the New Year's Eve party that was to be hosted by herself and Ronnie this year. She had managed to hit the supermarket and purchased an abundance of goodies for the following evening. She just about had time to nip the dogs for a walk before she got stuck into her preparations. She had mulled over not bothering to take them out, but knew that would be counterproductive as they would follow her round all evening with expectant looks on their faces.

It was a bright day, cold and frosty, but with optimistic sunshine hanging low in the sky. One of those days that makes a person hope that spring is on its way, when of course it isn't. There was bound to be an excess of dingy grey days, damp days, scraping ice off windscreens days and scarves and gloves days to contend with first.

Smiling to herself as she strode purposefully across the frozen solid fields, Brooke was lost in a daydream of tomorrow's evening ahead. She had asked everyone to 'prepare a song', or at least prepare to lip sync along to a song and she was practising 'Don't Stop Believing' to herself. No-one was in ear shot, so who cared! Dogs bounded along at her side, tails high and noses low. She was enjoying the moment when the dogs abruptly came to a halt, pointing in that way dogs do, with a solid stance, one front paw lifted, head cocked to one side and ears pricked.

'What you seen Babbas?' Brooke enquired, addressing the dogs.

She stopped to listen, but could not hear anything other than the distant traffic. The dogs were not happy though and low growls ensued.

'Come on you daft bats, there's nothing,' she cajoled them along.

They headed on, but the dogs' behaviour was out of kilter, constantly returning to Brooke's feet, checking their 'pack' was still together; they were clearly apprehensive. Brooke stopped again to listen; she was starting to feel very ill at ease. She was alone, despite this being a popular dog walking spot. She held her breath... was that the sound of a twig breaking in the distance? She took in a sharp breath and flew around towards the noise. Nothing... she stood for a moment, swirls of her own ghostly breath surrounding her as her heart rate increased... probably a bird or something, she supposed. The trio started off again, Brooke no longer singing; instead, intently listening.

From out of nowhere, a flock of swifts emerged from the bushes, wings flapping and batting in a commotion of feathers. A startled Brooke jumped, eyes wide as saucers. Was there someone else there?

'HELLO?' she shouted out. 'Anybody there?' Nothing but eerie silence. She decided it was about time they headed home and she did so just about as fast as she could.

Relieved to be home, dogs content, Brooke started her various jobs: cleaning, baking and sorting Champagne glasses out. The incident was now fading from memory. Nonetheless, the experience had left her feeling like someone had been watching, following her even. She could not quite shake off the disconcerted sensation in her stomach. A hubbub of turmoil within her gut was totally at odds with the delicious cream cheese and whipped horseradish she was preparing for her signature smoked salmon blinis.

***

Everyone knew Ronnie was a man's man, loved a beer, sport and banter. He was also a skilled craftsman and always had some sort of carpentry, building or garden landscaping on the go. Brooke did not object. She adored the home he had created for them and she only had to barely mention something she would like in the house and it would appear: fitted wooden floors, wardrobes, a new bathroom or kitchen. The latest project had been the wine cellar/party basement. Brooke had the vision: all bare brick and rustic walls, chunky beams and homemade wine racks in oak, ambient lighting with amber and burnt orange fittings, a real wood floor and Ronnie's piece de resistance, a fully functioning bar and turntables, to rival any night club. Ronnie had been on it immediately. Now it was almost finished, just in time to invite guests for the New Year's Eve revelry.

Ron had been beavering away in the workshop all morning, completing the finishing touches for the basement he had built so carefully. The workshop comprised thousands of pounds worth of tools, equipment and a plethora of building materials. It resembled a DIY store. So very wisely, as Ronnie was most definitely the sensible type, he had asked Bruce to set up the security cameras. These had been linked to Ronnie's phone so he could check his screen at any point, to see that all was well. It even gave him an alarm if there was movement in the area and a suspected thief. So far, the 'thieves' had been an urban fox, a hedgehog and one of their beloved pet border terriers who had accidently been shut in the workshop, after following Ronnie in, when he had a giant sausage sandwich in his hand.

Ronnie downed tools and grabbed a coat. He had a choice of about forty different coats: 'summer breeze', 'blustery wind', 'light rain', 'heavy rain', 'slightly chilly', 'minus 30 degrees' the list went on. It drove Brooke to distraction, but it made Ronnie happy to know he had covered 'all eventualities'. Today was a 'light wind' day and he headed out to fetch the booze for the New Year's Eve party of all parties.

'I'm just popping out for beers Bab,' he shouted upstairs to Brooke.

'Okay, I'm just preparing the canapés for the party,' she replied. Both border terriers were at her feet, waiting expectantly for a morsel of smoked salmon to drop.

The scene was almost set in their stylish four-storey 1800s Victorian house that had been radically modernised. The ground floor comprised a cosy snug, a large orangery and a beautiful open plan kitchen diner with stairs that led down to the newly refurbished basement. Brooke was so excited for the party the next evening, that she could hardly contain herself. She was twirling around the kitchen to nineties' rock music, singing at the top of her voice, sporting her PJs whilst chopping, blending and blitzing.

The doorbell rang. It was one of those fancy bells when you can see who is at the door from your phone. The sound made Brooke jump out of her skin. She was still a little on edge after her experience earlier that day. She felt her cheeks flush with embarrassment, in case whoever it was had seen her 'shaking her stuff' through the window. She turned down the overly loud music and strode over to the entrance hall, stained glass throwing a rainbow of coloured beams across the floor. She could see the outline of a rather tall figure but could not make out who it was. It definitely wasn't Ronnie and anyway he had only left ten minutes ago and had his key. It could be Arthur, she pondered.   Where had she put her phone; she could have checked who it was. Ronnie would be sure to tick her off for not utilising the tech they had installed. He was way more security conscious than the overly trusting Brooke.   The figure thumped the door and her heart skipped a beat.

'Okay, Okay!! Hang on a second!' she hollered, trying to hide the irritation in her voice.

The two Border Terriers were now making low, unsettled growling noises, so she very tentatively opened the door. It was Adam.

'What do you want?' Brooke said coldly when she realised who it was.

'I want to talk to you. It's about Frankie.' Adam sombrely answered.

Brooke felt nervous, as she was alone and did not trust Adam, plus she was wearing PJs with no underwear and suddenly felt exceptionally vulnerable. Adam was the last person she wanted to see, PJ's or otherwise.

'Now isn't a good time Adam,' she stumbled over her words.

'Well, that might be so, but it's urgent.' Adam put a large size eleven foot over the entrance hall threshold.

'I didn't invite you in,' Brooke asserted.

Adam took a step back as she made him stand on the porch. Brooke's heart was now pounding.

'What the hell do you want Adam? You're not exactly welcome here.'

'I want to tell you what an interfering bitch you are. I know it was you who persuaded Frankie to dump me and don't think I'm going to let you get away with that, without any consequences.' Adam stepped closer as Brooke retreated backwards, barefoot and now very aware of her skimpy attire.

'Don't you dare threaten me, Adam Pearson. Any decision of Frankie's was hers, not mine and as far as I'm concerned it's the best decision she ever made!' Brooke's voice was more confident now, even though she was feeling far from self-assured.

Adam let out a foreboding laugh. If she had not been so scared, Brooke would have laughed too, as he sounded like a villain from a Disney film.

'I think you'll find it's the worst decision she ever made. I'll make sure of that,' he spat, his eyes full of menace. 'Seriously Brooke, you can't manipulate Frankie, filling her head with your psycho-babble garbage. Frankie is meant to be with me and I WILL get her back, mark my words and when I do, I'll make sure she never sees you again.' Adam's six foot frame loomed over Brooke's five feet two inches.

'Get the hell off my property Adam.' Brooke was not budging.

Adam laughed hollowly, pushing his face into Brooke's personal space.

'As if you could make me. I could knock you into next week,' he snarled.

'Get away from my house and out of our lives Adam. I'll call the police.' Brooke continued to stand her ground coolly.

'Alright, alright, no need to get nasty.' Adam's sneer had disappeared at the mention of police. Whatever he felt about Brooke's interfering, he had to uphold his position in the community as the goody two shoes headteacher and a respectable family man. The last thing he wanted was police sniffing around his business, especially in a small town like Delvreton where there were more gossipmongers than hot dinners served.

'I was leaving anyway.' Adam skulked backwards. 'Oh and by the way, nice outfit Brooke, *very* nice,' he smirked. 'Such a shame you're such a disagreeable witch,' he said, sarcastically as he turned on his heels and stomped back to his car, tyres screeching as he accelerated off the driveway.

Brooke stood in a daze on the doorstep, heart pounding. Her neighbours, Elly and Gillian, were just pulling onto their driveway and waved. Brooke held her forehead, now feeling a little dizzy.

'Hey Brooke, you Okay?' shouted Elly. 'You look like you've just seen a ghost!' Elly and Gillian, laden down with shopping bags, were both wearing concerned expressions.

'Oh, oh, I'm alright, just needed a breath of air. I'm madly planning for our big bash and think I've overdone it,' Brooke lied.

'Well, as long as you're sure Bab?' Gillian replied. 'We can't wait to see you tomorrow. Just let us know if you need a hand.'

Brooke waved and retreated indoors. Sitting alone in the kitchen, a little shell-shocked, she realised the incident had shaken her rather more than she would ever let onto Ronnie and she knew exactly who she was going to talk it through with. She picked up her mobile, scrolled her contacts to the welcoming icon that greeted her with Ruby's smiley face. Brooke pressed the key to dial her friend's number.

Ruby's phone was ringing; she could see instantly it was Brooke. Ruby was in the middle of painting a finger-nail, but answered anyway, whilst tentatively holding her pinkie finger at an angle so as not to smudge the varnish.

'What you doing Angel?' Ruby enquired.

'Oh Ruby, I've just had the fright of my life. That bloody bully boy Adam just rocked up at our place! You won't believe what he said!' Brooke garbled.

'What? What the heck was he doing round at your place? He must know he's not exactly flavour of the month!' Ruby sat upright.

'I know, I was as surprised to see him as you. Can you believe he actually threatened me Ruby? He told me not to be such an interfering witch and that he was going to get Frankie back, no matter what it takes. Oh Ruby, I'm so worried. She's taken him back so many times with his false promises. I know he might convince her to go back and he said he'd make sure Frankie would never see me again.' Brooke's voice started to crack.

'Not a chance! There is NO WAY on earth Frankie could be kept away from you and Ronnie,' Ruby reassured.

'What am I going to do Rubes? Should I tell Ronnie? I was thinking I might call the police, you know, just to go round and warn him not to trespass on our property again, or come anywhere near me.'

'Oh Angel, you don't want to mess around with the police. They'll take weeks to respond, and even if they did, they can't actually *do* anything unless he's physically violent.' Ruby's mind was now in overdrive.

'You know what Brooke, I know a few 'unsavoury characters' from the Jewellery quarter. I could make some enquires.' Ruby's voice lowered.

'What do you mean?' Brooke was not quite following.

'You know, to rough Adam up a bit, give him scare,' Ruby clarified.

'Oh my... bloody hell, do you think we could actually arrange that?' Brooke's interest was sparked. 'I hate him so much Rubes. I mean, I don't want him dead or anything, but someone to scare the bejesus out of him; give him a bit of a battering. That would certainly put him in his place. Nothing too over the top though, you know what I mean?'

'Leave it with me Babes, I know exactly who to call. Now, are you sure you're okay?'

'Oh God Ruby, do you really think we could?'

'I don't *think* we could Brooke, I *know* we could. I'll call you back. Ruby's mind was set as she ended the call with her friend.

At that moment, Brooke heard the familiar sound of Ronnie's key in the door. 'Got the beer Brookey,' Ronnie chimed. Brooke finally allowed herself to breathe.

***

Bruce was in his control room. He noticed that Fuckwit was heading towards Brooke's and Ronnie's place and he was immediately drawn in. Adam was ringing their door-bell and Bruce's set up allowed him to immediately gain control of the audio. He tuned into the conversation.

That bloody bastard needs to back off, Bruce thought. Anger was rising in his gut as he heard Adam's ominous tone with Brooke. His mind wandered back to the unsettling scene he had witnessed when Adam had been so rough with Frankie in the kitchen that night. Bruce shuddered, blotting out the memory but feeling concerned for Brooke's potential vulnerability.

He was now clear. Something needed to be done to get rid of Adam out of the group's lives, once and for all. Adam was not the upstanding citizen he so skilfully portrayed. Bruce wanted to let Ronnie know how sinister this had become. However, he knew that this could never be possible without fessing up to his undignified hobby of being the snooping spectator. If he did that, he knew that he would lose all of his friends forever.

***

Back on Delvreton High Street, Ronnie had just finished a few errands. The light had faded fast by the time he got back to the town's carpark. Just as he started the engine, he saw the distinctive silver Jaguar pulling off just several cars in front of him. Adam's car. What was he doing lurking round the town? Ronnie knew that Adam's brother's place was over ten miles away and the school was closed for the holiday. Adam had no business in Delvreton. Ronnie deferred to his gut feeling and followed the car, keeping a discreet distance behind him. His heart sank, but he was not surprised when he saw Adam drive in the direction of Frankie's estate. Just as he suspected, Ronnie's worst fears were confirmed when he saw the Jag turn off the main road into Frankie's development. Ronnie kept well back and slowly edged forward to the bend in Badgers Lane where he pulled to a halt. This gave him the chance to get out, take up cover behind a large oak tree and observe Adam.

Adam stopped about two houses away from Frankie's. He then got out of his car, crossed the wide tree lined road that her house stood on and slowly walked past Frankie's place, clearly taking his time to look closely at her house. He was dressed all in black and wore a baseball cap, so inconspicuous, especially as it was now dark. A few moments later, Adam came back and got back into his car. That was it. Ronnie shook his head, realising that Adam was simply keeping watch or more sinister, he was stalking Frankie. What a creep, he thought to himself. The relationship was done, over, so Adam needed to give up, once and for all. The fact that he kept sending Frankie those horrible, vindictive texts and was now watching her was so wrong on every level. Ronnie resolved to make sure that Frankie blocked Adam from her phone. He would not tell her that he had discovered Adam's penchant for driving by Frankie's place and watching her, as that would just freak her out. No, she did not need that, not after all the upset she had had to contend with. Ronnie would do right by his sister and keep a close eye on Adam for her. He did not think Adam would pose a direct physical threat to Frankie but he was certainly a control freak and clearly wanted to know what Frankie was up to with her life. Adam was, more than likely, checking to see whether Frankie had found another man to replace him. That would be the best outcome possible, Ronnie thought and maybe she might find someone at the party tomorrow, who knows.

As he was in the neighbourhood, Ronnie decided to call on his sister to enjoy a beer and a chat, before he headed home. Frankie was very pleased to see him as always.

'Hey, this is a lovely surprise,' she said, trying to calm Charlie down who was barking uncontrollably at the excitement of seeing Ronnie. 'Sit down quickly and he'll soon be quiet, once he can have a cuddle.'

Ronnie did as instructed and was soon sitting on the leather sofa in the kitchen with a beer in one hand, fussing Charlie with the other.

'Surprised you've got any time, what with all the preparations for tomorrow,' Frankie said, taking a sip from the white wine she had poured herself to keep Ronnie company.

'You know how organised I am,' Ronnie smiled. 'Brooke just sent me out for a last minute drinks order which is pretty big, as you can imagine,' he laughed.

'I can. I bet you'll have the equivalent of a bloody brewery at your place tomorrow!' Frankie said smiling and very much looking forward to the fabulous party, she knew it would be.

'Can't have any shortages for the biggest party of the year,' Ronnie said. 'We all need to have a good time, especially you now that you've finally seen the light and ousted that toe rag,' Ronnie said not wanting to reveal to Frankie that only a few moments ago, Adam was prowling around outside her home. Ronnie would definitely keep an eye on his sister and a closer eye on her ex. Truth was, Ronnie did not really think Adam would do anything to physically hurt Frankie. He was a nasty piece of work but he had a prominent role in the community and the bottom line was, Ronnie thought the headteacher of Delvreton High was a coward, underneath all that bravado. Ronnie prided himself on being a good judge of character. So, he would keep watch, without letting Frankie know that she had a guardian angel.

'Anyway, I'd better get off,' Ronnie said standing up. 'Just checking, you have blocked Adam's number now, haven't you? I really think the New Year should be a clean, fresh start for you. Why don't you just erase all trace of him and move on, okay?' Ronnie hugged Frankie and patted Charlie.

'Will do,' Frankie saluted her brother, smiling. 'I'm off to get a bit of pampering tomorrow morning then I will be ready to party! Get my favourite Primal Scream track ready on those new decks of yours,' she said as she waved Ronnie goodbye.

Chapter 14

New Year's Eve Party

The next morning, Frankie appraised her stylish manicure with a smile. Yes, just right. A gorgeous nude shade that she would be happy with when she returned to work in four days' time but would also serve her very well for the party later. She paid and added a healthy tip for Alex who had met Frankie's beauty needs for many years now. Having exchanged a few pleasantries, she left the local hotel and spa, Delvreton Lawns, which also provided the fantastic gym and pool that she and her friends regularly frequented.

Having checked her watch, Frankie was satisfied that she had more than enough time to pop into town to pick up wine and Champagne from Blakely's, the elegant wine shop that all the locals loved. She quickly parked her car in Delvreton centre and hurried along to the much-revered shop, pulling her scarf tighter round her neck to ward off the biting chill of the end of year day. An icy greyness seemed to shroud Delvreton, sending a chill through Frankie's body. She suddenly felt uneasy and whipped round to check no one was about to pounce on her.

The street was reasonably busy, as usual, with the well-heeled crowd of Delvreton doing their last minute New Year's Eve shopping, just as she was. She shuddered, happy to see the Blakely's sign just ahead of her as her phone pinged, alerting her to a new message. A sense of dread washed over her as she peered at the screen to see yet another text from Adam. His texts had been a steady stream since the fateful day when she had plucked up the courage to end it all. After five years, it was very raw and she understood that there would be fall out. After all, he had lost his 'perfect' family set up, albeit a total sham, but the fact that his precious kids knew what a cheating bastard he was had clearly hit him hard. Frankie knew, only too well, that Adam had a nasty, cruel streak and when he was wounded, this would obviously surface. She pondered whether to even read the message. Unfortunately, her eyes could not quite tear themselves away from the screen. She inhaled sharply as she read.

'You evil bitch. You don't ruin my life and get away with it. My kids don't want to see me this holiday and it's your fucking fault.'

That's it, Frankie resolved. She would do her chores and then block Adam's number when she got back home. She would follow Ronnie's advice.

Frankie glanced back once again, before opening the door of Blakely's. God, she was jumpy today. The reassuring old fashioned bell chimed as the door opened and the heady scent of mulled wine filled the air, accompanied by soft classical music. Frankie drank in the soothing atmosphere, instantly relaxing. A few customers were surveying the very well stocked shelves as Iban approached Frankie, arms outstretched to welcome her into a lovely hug. This was just what she needed.

166

'Hello stranger,' Iban announced. 'Where have you been hiding, gorgeous?'

Frankie leaned into Iban's hug gratefully before pulling back. 'Just mad busy with work,' she pronounced, 'but I'm here now and it's so lovely to see you. Is Bart here?'

'Course he is!' laughed Iban. 'Can't wait to tell him you're here.' Iban called out to his partner Bart who majestically appeared from the back of the store.

More pleasantries were exchanged and plans for the evening ahead shared. They all drank together regularly at the Otter's and they were very easy in each other's company. Iban and Bart were hosting a black and white themed cocktail evening at their loft apartment later that evening.

'Frankie you must come!' Bart exclaimed.

'Oh Bart, you know I'd love to, but I'm definitely earmarked for Ronnie and Brooke's do tonight. Maybe another time though?' She smiled.

Frankie chose several of bottles of her favourite Champagne and wine. Bart carefully wrapped the two golden Champagne bottles in stylish cellophane, finished off by extravagant metallic bows. After more hugs and air kisses, Frankie clasped her purchases tightly and left her friends' shop. She was still smiling, as she made her way to the carpark, before stopping dead in her tracks as she saw Adam's car pulling away about twenty yards up ahead.

Her heart beat quickened as she hastily rummaged in her bag, having placed her precious bottles on the ground next to the front tyre; she did not want to drop them. Frankie glanced across the car park as she opened the car door, placing the Champagne and wine on the back seat. Her breathing calmed as she gave herself a talking to. Adam had every right to be in Delvreton, she told herself. Still, he did not live there. His brother's house was a good thirty minutes away and there was another town that was much closer to him. However, he may just have popped into school to pick up some work, check on Bruce's IT update or use the gym. What did this matter to her anyway; Adam was free to go wherever he wanted. Nonetheless, Frankie just could not shake off the feeling that it was a little too coincidental that he happened to be there at the same time she was. Had he been following her? she pondered. The harsh, threatening text message from him was at the forefront of her mind. Blocking his contact would likely wind him up even more but he would have to understand and just let her move on with her life, into a brand new year.

Back at home, chores completed, Frankie picked up her phone. Her finger hesitated for a nanosecond, but with a swift flick, Adam's number was blocked. Frankie was determined to enjoy New Year's Eve with her very close friends. Her beloved Charlie was having a 'sleep over' as she had dropped him at her parents so she could stay out as late as she liked. Then she turned her attention to some rare pampering time: a long bubble bath with the obligatory glass of pink Champagne, of course. She then assessed her wardrobe and decided to

168

resurrect her 'rock chick' look. Black leather trousers, which thankfully still fitted perfectly, a sheer black top and fake fur cream jacket to soften the look, all rounded off with her new sparkly Christian Louboutin's. As she waited for the Uber, she felt a much- needed sense of optimism and was, finally, actually looking forward to the evening ahead.

***

Throughout Delvreton, similar preparations were happening at Ruby's and Arthur's, Daisy's and Bruce's and, of course, Ronnie and Brooke were particularly busy, making the final arrangements for the big night ahead. Bruce was trying to be extra positive and solicitous to Daisy and the girls as they ummed and ahhed over prospective outfits. He was also making a point of staying out of his office but still managing to keep a surreptitious track on the abundance of various devices he possessed. He had noticed that Frankie had finally blocked Adam's number which must be a good thing given the increasing level of threat that his texts held. Brooke was literally riding high on her Boxing Day wins at the races so her secret account was back to a healthy twenty five thousand.

The most worrying development was the awful stream of desperate texts from Kerri to Arthur, no doubt exacerbated by the looming end of year. Bruce mulled that, when all was not well with life, problems always seemed amplified over the festive and New Year period. Bruce had no idea how Arthur was managing to cope with it all, especially how he was keeping things normal for him, Ruby and Lola, whilst knowing what big trouble inevitably lay ahead for them all, sadly.

***

Twenty minutes away, Adam was livid that Frankie had blocked his number. He was also still reeling that his own kids preferred to stay with their mother to attend a neighbour's party than spend the evening with him. He'd had to resort to another dull evening in with his brother, who was pathetically 'loved up' with his new woman. Adam was not relishing the idea of watching them coo at each other all night. Snatching his keys, he shouted goodbye and left his brother's place.

He needed to clear his head and he planned to have a drive around Delvreton to see who exactly was going to the big party at Frankie's brothers. He would not be surprised if Frankie had her eye on someone there, the bitch. He should have been there tonight. Of course, he had plenty of other woman on his radar, but he had never really been at the receiving end of being dumped before and he was not going to let this one go quietly. Frankie had better realise he still had some unfinished business with her.

Earlier that morning, Adam had spent a good hour stalking Frankie on Google, scrolling through numerous photographs and posts. His stomach instantly filled with jealously as he read a news feature about her. There she was in a large photo spread, smiling with a group of secondary school pupils. They were celebrating yet another success story about a mentoring programme Frankie had introduced. 'Why the fuck should she get all the accolades?' he said out loud to himself. He had certainly taken advantage of her connections, when it had suited his own career desires, but he could literally taste the bile in his mouth at this latest accomplishment. He was still seething about it as he drove round Delvreton, desperately trying to fend off his own sense of insecurity and failures. If Frankie was going to be some sort of local celebrity, he had been certain he would have had a piece of it too. Now there was no chance of that. How dare she fucking dump him? His tyres screeched as he took a corner too fast, almost veering off the road. As he managed to regain control of the car, he was far from in control of his own toxic bitterness.

**

Ronnie's and Brooke's street was lit with sparkling lights, piercing through the light fog as guests started arriving at the party. All of this was observed by the lone figure, dressed from head to toe in black, standing discreetly in the shadows across the road. His car was parked round the corner, well out of sight. Light chatter, exclamations of delight as old friends were reunited, drifted through the cold air and mingled with the dull throb of music emanating from the majestic Victorian house.

Bonnie, Amber and a couple of their student friends had been enlisted once again by Brooke and Ronnie to provide a first class service to their guests. The team of bright, attractive young things expertly worked the room, dressed in sophisticated black and white attire to add a touch of elegance to proceedings, effortlessly offering trays of delicate, colourful canapés. Guests mingled in the large high ceilinged open plan sitting room and dining room that flowed into a beautiful orangery built by Ronnie. No guest was left with an empty glass for even a moment, not even the Landlord, Shane, from the Otter's Head, who had rocked up. He smiled as Amber teased him that he was her 'boss' so she could not serve him too much alcohol. Other guests spilled into the new basement party room, delighting in Ronnie's audio set up, enjoying their chosen drinks in crystal Champagne glasses, beer bottles or extra-large gin balloon glasses.

**

It was about nine o'clock, when the figure across the road blew on his hands, gradually relinquishing his resolve and surrendering to the freezing temperatures; he reluctantly made his way back to his car on the next street. He had observed many familiar faces happily entering the house, party central, including Frankie in her tarty leather trouser get up. God, what was she thinking? Adam muttered to himself, the bitter cold biting into his face, and the bitter jealousy taking hold of his heart.

'She's far too past it and should know better than to dress like a twenty year old,' his face contorted as he wittered to himself. Even though she actually looked amazing.

Adam blasted his car's heating system on high and considered what to do. Should he stay here like a sad loser or get back to his brother's place and start cultivating potential possibilities for his own personal life in the New Year? His mind drifted to Suzie, the new head of performing arts. He remembered how keen she had been to flirt with him at the Otter's Head after the panto. That night seemed like much longer than just two weeks ago. He could always come back to Delvreton later, to see what was developing. He had no desire to drink any alcohol and he was keen to find out whether Frankie left on her own. He put the car into 'Drive' and accelerated away. Clouds of vapour from the car's exhaust swirled into the cold night air, as his mind relentlessly spun in circles, contemplating the unthinkable possibilities of Frankie with another man.

***

The party was now in full swing. Sienna was jiving with Vincent as a group gathered round them, egging them on. This included Nancy and Richard who was renowned for 'not being the dancing type', but even he found himself starting to move his hips to the rhythm much to Nancy's delight as she pulled him into the centre of the circle. Brooke was in the thick of the dancing as usual, twirling and smiling with her old friends she had not seen in an age. Tommy, an old school chum, was rifling through records with Ronnie, trying to find some Lynyrd Skynyrd.

'Looking for the obligatory 'Sweet Home Alabama' Tommy?' Tommy's partner Leah, squealed, bluffing her way through some line dance moves.

The group burst out laughing, observing Leah, sporting one hand on hip whilst she pretended she was cracking a whip with the other. Brooke's heart melted a little as she felt blessed to be with such great mates, the altercation with Adam now a distant memory. She gazed around the room at the happy faces, new and old friends alike. A particular warmth filled her heart as she observed Frankie chatting and smiling. She certainly didn't appear to be missing Adam, thank God.

Frankie seemed at ease as she chatted with her neighbours Georgie and Dermot. Further delight was expressed as Damien and Jeanie arrived in their usual flourish. The group had lived next door to Frankie when she had rented a beautiful barn conversion after her divorce and they were all saying how wonderful it was to see her again. Brooke beamed as she mused that Delvreton was such a close community where friendships quickly blossomed. Yes, there was definitely life after a break up.

Most of the guests were now in the new basement, where Stefan had taken up his obligatory role as DJ and was doing a sterling job of choosing just the right play list from Ronnie's fantastic vinyl collection. Bonnie, Amber and their mates, now free from their duties, had joined in the party and the booze was flowing, as guests readily helped themselves to drinks. Laughter and chatter filled the air. Frankie decided she'd had enough fizz and opted for her old reliable Chardonnay. She made her way up to the kitchen and rifled through the fridge, empty wine glass poised. As she closed the fridge door, glass filled, she virtually collided with a tall, sturdy figure and nearly spilt her drink.

'Nearly!' he exclaimed, as Frankie looked up into his handsome face. She found herself giggling, a bit like a teenager as she realised that she had come face to face with Dexter, who was a bit of a local legend. About twenty years ago, Frankie, Ronnie and Brooke had enjoyed a wild Christmas Eve at a local hotel where 'Dexter and the Dudes' had headlined, a tongue in cheek local glam rock band, made up of the local rich kids, who were all known for their crazy, drink and drug fuelled lifestyles. Frankie had to admit that she'd had a crush on Dexter, like many of the young women in Delvreton at that time, but it had been years ago. She had never given him a second thought since those cheesy rock band gigs but now here she was, standing in front of him, staring into his ruggedly handsome face. No doubt about it, those deep green eyes were definitely glinting back at her, an arresting slightly crooked smile showing off his straight white teeth.

'We look like twins,' Dexter laughed, taking in Frankie's leather trousers and markedly glancing at his own with a very wicked grin.

'Yeah,' she said smiling. 'Haven't worn these for some time, but I knew the party would end up as a rock fest, given Ronnie's and Brooke's taste in music.'

'You should wear them more often,' he said grinning. 'You wear them very well indeed.'

'Oh stop it!' Frankie responded, play hitting him on the shoulder, emboldened already from the several glasses of wine she had consumed, on top of the Champagne. 'I know I'm probably well past my time for wearing these but what the hell. It's New Year's Eve and I've had a pretty crap time lately.'

Frankie found herself confiding in Dexter about her disastrous relationship with Adam, the edited highlights only, of course. The more she talked, the more she was becoming enthralled by the personality of this attractive man. She liked the fact that he had a pretty laissez faire attitude to life, as he dabbled in a variety of business ventures enjoying the financial security that his wealthy family provided. He had a number of property interests and closest to his heart, was the opportunity he had to fuel the local music business by managing a promising new rock band. His life was the polar opposite of hers and it sounded captivating. The evening had become very interesting indeed; she smiled to herself.

***

Bruce had just come up for air from the basement, where he had enjoyed dancing with Daisy, both of them relaxed by the heady party atmosphere and the abundance of alcohol, both of them much more at ease with each other than they had been for weeks. Bruce slipped into an empty armchair in the dimly lit orangery, offering a perfect vantage point for a spot of 'people watching'. This time it was real and not through hidden cameras or hacked texts and Whatsapp messages. This was the old fashioned, pure way of watching others without the aid of technology, but just as fascinating.

Bruce sipped his drink as his eyes roved over people in twos, peoples in threes and fours dotted around the large space before he alighted on a striking couple standing in the corner of the lounge area. There was something edgy about them, in the way they dressed and the way they were standing. He suddenly realised that the woman was Frankie and it gradually dawned on him that the man she was gazing adoringly at was Dexter Croft; he had not seen him for ages but was very much aware of his wide boy reputation. Dexter trod that fine line between respectable entrepreneurial endeavours and some highly questionable 'projects'. He also had a reputation for being a real cad with the ladies. He had never settled down and seemed to have no intention of ever doing so. Bruce could not quite decide whether this emerging alliance would be good or bad. Frankie needed some fun that was for sure, but with Dexter Croft? A lot more trouble could be brewing and Bruce could not help but look forward to seeing what his surveillance would present to him via this latest development in his friends' lives. One thing was certain; it would seriously piss Adam off. He watched the new couple leave the room, no doubt headed for the basement.

***

The steamy basement was now in full throttle and the party panned out exactly as anyone would have predicted. Brooke and her gym buddy Samuel's obligatory duet of 'Don't Go Breaking My Heart' was appreciated by everyone, as usual. There were numerous (failed) attempts at break dancing, air guitars were played and Ronnie's old school mate 'fireman Tony' hurled himself around the makeshift dancefloor to 'The Liquidator'.

'Bloody bostin' party our kid!' Tony slurred as he helped himself to another beer, then flung himself back onto the dance floor, grabbing Samuel's wife, Juliet, to join him just as the first bar of 'fat bottomed girls' filled the air. Juliet, who was often a little shy, looked slightly horrified, but the rum and coke gave her enough Dutch courage to strut her stuff too, much to Samuel's delight. Ronnie chuckled at Tony's boldness.

As Auld Lang Syne sealed the evening, the following few hours passed like mere minutes leaving the revellers, now very much the worse for wear, exclaiming at the time and how much everyone loved everyone else. All of the guests gradually left, some swaying, some giggling and some shouting 'tara a bit', the local expression for farewell, far too loudly for the late hour as they stumbled into taxis.

Brooke and Ronnie agreed to undertake the big clear up operation the next day, when they eventually surfaced. They smiled as they climbed the stairs, safe in the knowledge that their party would be talked about and dissected for many days to come, the welcome aftermath of a truly great bash.

***

Two hours earlier the lone figure, clad in black, had returned, sitting in his car this time, parked just across the road. He grimaced at the late hour – one thirty and the party still in full swing. He would not hang about any longer and at least he had received a very positive and keen text from Suzie, when he had wished her a 'fun and exciting new year ahead'. Yes, Adam needed to move on to greener and younger pastures; he just needed to put Frankie in her place first, Frankie who had the audacity to end it with him. As he drove away, Adam's mood was darker than the black, wintery sky.

Chapter 15

2 January

It was the second day of January. Bare branches dominated the horizon, the sky a dreary grey, a light mist chilling the air with a clagging layer of sadness. The reality was sinking in that the festivities were finally over. Christmas lights were being prematurely taken down, jaded Christmas trees with slightly dusty baubles and dried up brown pine needles stood valiantly in hallways and lounges. Heavier stomachs and bathroom scales revealed the results of overindulgence to many horrified individuals, young and old.

Brooke was staring at the numbers on her scales. Oh for God's sake, five pounds gained. How the heck did that happen? She cogitated, then remembered the daily handfuls of cashews, extra- large dinners, the Boxing Day buffet, the take aways on the quiet days in between Christmas and New Year, the boxes of chocolates in front of cheesy Christmas films, that cheeky tipple of Baileys on more than one occasion, a couple of cheese boards and that was without all the canapés and copious amounts of Prosecco. Oh yeah, that'll be what happened, she remembered. Brooke dressed, donning her track suit with gusto, the obligatory new pair of Christmas trainers, a woolly hat and gloves, then headed outside.

The girls had arranged to do a run around the woodlands at Squirrel's Nook, which offered a decent ten kilometre route. Brooke clearly needed to attend the gathering, even though she was not much feeling the love at that present moment in time. Ruby had declined; she was certainly never going to be the running type and her lean body meant she did not much have to care. 'No thanks chickas. I'm nursing a hangover from hell and I have a date with a box of Thorntons,' Ruby had laughed when they had invited her.

Daisy was certainly the fittest of the group and was excellent at encouraging them all along, looping round so she could chivvy up the hangers back. She could clearly run rings round Brooke, but Brooke was just glad to be able to manage the run at all. Frankie was in good shape too. She had run a few marathons in her past and she was ahead of the pack today. Brooke was holding her own for once, determined to keep up with them, even though she was slightly more out of puff than they were. She took an extra deep breath as her cheeks reddened.

Clouds of silver vapour emitted from the group as they panted their way towards the woods. Four dogs were in tow, mud flying off paws and the occasional excited yap pronounced their excitement.

The three friends chatted as they ran, recounting the New Year's Eve merriments.

'Brooke, totally class party again mate,' Daisy declared.

'Thanks Daise. You know me, I love a good do and any excuse for a dance and a drink!' Brooke replied, beaming. 'What were we three like doing our 'Rocksasize' with Ruby,' Brooke giggled.

'Rocksa-what?' Daisy looked puzzled.

'Rocksasize! You know, our drunken Zumba class, but to full on rock tunes, where we were all taking it in turns to bust our moves!' Brooke recollected with glee.

'Oh, that's what that was! Now I know what you're on about!' Daisy was now laughing at the memory of the four of them, one behind the other in a chain reaction of their 'best dance moves'. In reality, they had not actually been half as good as they had all believed two nights before, given they were all drunk as skunks at the time. Daisy cringed a little at the memory.

'Oh my God! How bloomin' hilarious was your Bruce in that 'I want to break free' get up! My apron certainly suited him!' Brooke giggled to Daisy.

'He's so much fun and such a good sport but I have to commend you and Ronnie for getting out the obligatory air guitars and treating us to a bit of AC/DC,' Daisy chuckled. 'Your work mates Leah and Tommy are good singers aren't they? Tommy really does a good rendition of Frank Sinatra.' she added, rather impressed.

'Hey Frankie, what about your mate Sienna getting off with Vincent? He's a dark horse, all sweetness and light with his culinary skills, but he obviously loves the ladies! I have to say he's definitely got the moves of a soul man and I can see why Sienna fancied a bit!' Daisy was laughing, 'Quite fancy a bit myself, he looks like Luther! And don't mind if I do!' she said, increasing the pace a little more.

Frankie chuckled. 'Well I can imagine Luther would go for a bit of you Daisy. What you like with that sexy bum of yours! Daisy, Daisy, Daisy, who knew you could do such a good rendition of a lap dance! I bet Bruce was well chuffed!'

Daisy laughed heartily. 'He's seen it all before mate!'

'Soo…. talking of sexy bums,' Daisy started. 'What occurred with you and Dexter after the New Year's party was drawing to a close? We saw you both duck off into the snug by yourselves, after two in the morning.'

'Oh my,' Frankie replied. 'He's a dish. I totally fancy him and the fact that he's edgy is even more attractive. Don't get me wrong, he certainly isn't a keeper but he's definitely Mr Right Now!' Frankie laughed. 'And before you ask, yes, I did sleep with him and it was ace,' she declared wryly.

Daisy and Brooke 'whooped' in unison. 'Go Frankie! I hope it proved you can get that fuckwit out of your system,' Brooke managed to pant out her words as she recalled with unease Adam's unwelcome visit just before New Year's Eve. She was certain it would not be the last time Adam reared his ugly head, unfortunately. They all had to be vigilant, where he was concerned.

Frankie was not even out of breath and she spoke without the slightest hint of exhaustion. 'I really don't have feelings for Adam any more. Dexter is helping me to look ahead and forget all the rubbish I used to put up with. I honestly think this year is going to be a game changer and I'm definite about one thing: there is no

183

going back to Adam, ever. I'm glad I've blocked his number as I dread to think about the poisonous texts he would have sent me on New Year's Eve. You all know that he thinks you lot 'don't get him' and are trying to poison me against him, or something.'

'The only reason we don't like him is because of his behaviour. He's a controlling, philandering bully.' Brooke was now on a rant.

'He's also a boring old git. I don't trust anyone who never has a drink. I reckon he's scared he'll give away too much, if he's inebriated,' Daisy added. 'It's like dragging a dead donkey round with you! Anyway, let's have no more mention of his name. Tell us all about Dexter,' she pleaded with Frankie.

It turned out Dexter was a work mate of Ronnie's. Ronnie had given him a very casual invitation before Christmas and never dreamt he would actually turn up. However, he had, much to Frankie's delight. He was certainly a bit of a player, but also very much the smouldering, sexy type. Many women found him irresistible, even though they knew he was out and out bad news on the relationship front. He had turned up in a very sharp jacket with some rock band tee underneath, leather trousers and was sporting a pair of trendy trainers. Dexter was all dishevelled hair and clutching a bottle of Jim Beam, on his arrival. Very rock and roll and utterly attractive.

'Well, there's not much more to tell, apart from I fancy him, but he did tell me he manages local bands in his spare time and he's doing quite well out of it, by all accounts. We've also arranged another date for Friday night and I've asked him to stay over at my place.' Frankie shot Brooke a sideways glance, to check out her reaction but she needn't have worried. Brooke was delighted and let out a little 'Wit Woo!'

'Hey you two, enough with your chat. Come on let's pick up the pace,' Daisy spurred them on. Brooke was just about managing to keep up, her cheeks glowing and now totally out of puff.

Daisy was now ahead of the pack, followed by Frankie then Brooke a few yards behind, four dogs out in front, tails high, tongues long. Squirrel's Nook was a local beauty spot and it was not unusual to see numerous couples, families flying kites, youngsters playing footie or dog walkers, but Daisy had not bargained for what she saw next as she turned the corner into a wooded glade.

Before them, plain as day, were three middle aged men, jeans down, bare bottoms exposed and three proud penises right on show, as they appeared to be fondling each other. Daisy screamed and as Frankie caught up, her jaw dropped in total and utter disbelief.

'Oh my good God! You dirty pervs!' Daisy spluttered.

By now, the men were scrambling to pull up their trousers. Brooke, who caught up a minute behind them, surveyed the spectacle as one of the men fell forwards into a bramble, his foot now tangled round his jeans, bare bottom a full moon. Brooke burst out laughing. Frankie's dog Charlie, decided this was really fun and pounced on the bare buttocks. The man yelped. His two accomplices

185

had managed to cover their modesty and had made a dash for it, closely followed by Brooke's Border terriers who thought this was a great game of chase.

'Call your dog off! A muffled voice appeared to come from the bare bum.

'Charlie, get down,' Frankie managed to splurt through her laughter. The man's face, bright red, appeared from the brambles, his leg now untangled from his jeans. He quickly did up his flies and scrambled to his feet.

'Oh that reminds me, I need to chuck those leftover cocktail sausages!' Frankie exclaimed to the man as she wiggled her little finger in the air at him.

By now Frankie and Daisy were in total hysterics.

'Last time I cook Coq au vin!' Brooke added.

'Or spotted Dick!' Daisy snorted, who was now bent double, completely helpless with laughter.

The man made a dash, Charlie the Vizla following, leaping playfully up his torso, at which moment Brooke's border terriers re-appeared. One of them was proudly sporting one of the men's trainers in his jaws.

'Oh my God, ladies. What the hell just happened?' Frankie had just about composed herself.

'Well, if you go down to woods today you're in for a big surprise!' Daisy snorted again.

Brooke rescued the trainer and flung it into the direction that the errant ramblers ran away.

The three of them were in bits and in no fit state to run any further. They linked arms and walked back towards home, each taking it in turns to come up with the best euphemism they could manage. 'Wang', no, no... 'Trouser Snake!'

'I've got one... Gearstick!'

So, it went on as they rebounded between composing themselves and falling into fits of hysterics again.

Frankie suddenly recalled the Ouija board evening, the warnings of someone 'BAD' and Brooke's observation that 'Nook' could mean Squirrel's Nook.

'Hey,' Frankie began. 'Do you reckon those three musketeers were the Ouija's warning?

'Could be?' replied Brooke. 'But I reckon it was more sinister, it spelt out 'death' too, remember?' Brooke shuddered as she recalled the evening at Nancy's place.

'What a thought for us all to savour,' Frankie continued. 'That this could be the very spot where Adam meets the end of his days. Just can't for the life of me think how that could happen,' she pondered. 'What a shame!'

'Yes, it's a delicious thought,' said Brooke. 'Probably the result of too much of Nancy's Calvados, someone's wishful thinking and a responsive glass, whizzing round that board guided by one of our fingers.'

Although the spirit's prediction was giving rise to some gleeful banter, the friends gave a little tremble as they walked away from the beauty spot in the fading light of the afternoon. Squirrel's Nook would, indeed be the perfect scene for a dramatic death.

Chapter 16

3 January

The gradual acceptance of January meant that life steadily got back to normal and resumed its natural rhythm. Everyone resigned themselves to the fact that the party season was well and truly over and turned their attention to work and the regularity of normal life.

Ronnie had some rare time to himself and he was definitely going to use it for a game of racquetball. He jumped in his car and headed towards the centre of town where the local cricket club housed all manner of sporting facilities, including courts. He knew 'Bez', 'Humpo' and 'Shezza' would already be there having a knock about. Brooke never ceased to be amused by the fact that none of the racket ball crowd called one another by their actual names.

Ronnie was just about to pull into the car park, when he spotted a familiar figure, driving his pretentious silver Jaguar. Adam. What's he doing hanging about Delvreton again? Ronnie wondered. Ronnie was on red alert after Adam had, eerily, sat watching Frankie before New Year and he knew Adam would never give up his precious free time to hang about the school when it had been closed for the holiday season. Ronnie was certainly not one to give up a racket ball game, but instead of pulling into the car park of the sports club, he switched direction and followed Adam's car. He had to be certain Adam was not going to stalk Frankie again, and if he did, Ronnie was ready to call him out this time.

Ron's concerns were realised as Adam headed off in the direction of Frankie's place. Making sure he kept a decent enough distance not to be spotted, Ronnie followed Adam's car and sure enough, he, once again, pulled into Badgers Lane. His car was far enough away not to be too obvious, but close enough to see Frankie's front door.

Ronnie also pulled up and quietly took up his position behind the oak tree once more. Well out of Adam's view. A moment later Frankie appeared; she was dressed to impress and intently chatting on her phone to one of the girls no doubt.

Frankie gracefully glided into the driver's seat of her Q8 and headed out of her driveway back towards the town centre. A few moments later, Adam's car engine started and he was on her tail. Bloody lowlife, Ronnie thought to himself; he really is stalking our Frankie. What is wrong with him? Frankie has made it very clear she is not interested in rekindling their relationship.

Ronnie sprinted back to his car and started after Adam. Like some sort of farce, the three cars were in tow. Frankie was unaware that Adam was on her tail, and Adam was unaware that Ronnie was on his. Ronnie, now a few cars back, could still clearly see the silver Jag amongst the sea of functional family cars. Frankie landed at Delvreton's high street delicatessen, a place that Ronnie had always found 'a bit too swanky,' but was a firm favourite with the girls. He could now also see that

Dexter was waving to Frankie from the pavement. She had obviously hit it off with Dexter at the New Year's party a few days before and it looked like they were on a date of some sort. Frankie was now settling in, Dexter, chivalrously taking her coat. A waitress placed a bottle of bubbles with two Champagne flutes in front of the couple. It was clear to see that Dexter and Frankie were pretty into each other. Ronnie smiled; it was about time she had some fun, but what would Adam make of this, Ronnie wondered. He decided to stick around for a while longer to find out. If Adam was about to make a scene, Ronnie would most definitely be right in there to stop any harm coming to Frankie.

***

Adam sat in his car seething. He had been sure that Frankie had left Ronnie's and Brooke's on New Year's Eve with another bloke in tow, and now here was the proof. He felt physically sick as he watched Dexter brush her cheek, hold her hand and lean over to kiss her. Frankie was obviously enjoying Dexter's company as she threw her head back and laughed heartily at something her date was saying.

Adam was consumed with jealousy. How dare she move on so quickly? He had thought he had a good hold over her. It had been so easy to draw her back to him, whenever the whim took him but that was in the past. Now he was not so sure. She looked so... happy. He was just about ready to smash that bastard's face in. Adam got out of the car and started to head towards the high street deli, his face etched with disdain and anger, his fists

191

clenched.   Suddenly, he stopped and changed his mind.
No, now was not a good time, he thought. Despite every
jealous fibre in his body willing him to charge into the
deli, grab Dexter by the scruff of his neck and knock him
into next week, he somehow managed to reign himself in.
Adam knew that if he caused such a scene, his reputation
would undoubtedly be tarnished forever. He could even
lose his job and he was not about to risk that. No, he had
to find another time and place. Reluctantly, he skulked
back toward his car, sat down and leant back in the seat,
theatrically placing his head in his hands. Mind now in
overdrive, he decided he would wait until Frankie was
alone with that man. Yes, that is what he would do, then
he would make sure Frankie got what was coming to her.

***

Ronnie watched with interest, taking in the scene of
Frankie with Dexter, Adam's obvious rage and his strange
behaviour, approaching the deli, then retreating to his
car. He had obviously thought better than to approach
Frankie, Ronnie thought. However, the scene left a bitter
taste in Ronnie's mouth. Adam stalking his sister was not
something he was going to ignore and if he found out that
Adam did it again, Ronnie would definitely be having a
few words with Frankie's ex himself. Ronnie could not
care less that Adam was viewed as some sort of
upstanding citizen and he hated Adam's pseudo sense of
morality and respectfulness. At that moment, Adam's car
pulled off away from the high street. Ronnie watched the
Jag disappear off into the distance, then turned his car
around and headed back for his game of racket ball,
unsure if he was still in the mood. He had made his mind

up about one thing though. Ronnie had decided, there and then, that if Adam ever dared touch a hair on Frankie's head, he would make him pay for it big time.

* * *

Frankie and Dexter jumped a cab back to her place. After a very enjoyable afternoon tea and Champagne, both of them were feeling pleasurably inebriated and decided it was best not to drive Frankie's Q8 back home. Frankie had really enjoyed his company and a sleep over would be the icing on the cake. She had also spotted Adam's car driving off into the distance earlier, during her date with Dexter. She had not mentioned it to Dexter, but if Adam was going to be the jealous type, she would really give him something to be jealous about. He must be stupid if he thought she had not spotted him walking across the road towards the deli, albeit that he had obviously decided better than to interrupt their date.

'Bring it on,' Frankie said out loud to herself as she freshened up in her en-suite.

'Bring what on?' Dexter enquired. She jumped, as she had not realised he had entered the bedroom.

'Oh! I… Bring on more Champagne darling,' she quickly replied, a little flummoxed.

'Oh, most definitely,' he replied. 'But let's take a little break from the booze first,' he said as he took her in his arms and they both tumbled onto her king size silk sheets.

Chapter 17

7 January

The first day back at work in January was tinged with a greater sense of optimism than normal. Like many people, Frankie usually struggled with the January blues as the world seemed very stark, stripped from the bright lights of the festive period. Frankie always joked that she was heavier and 'financially challenged' at the start of a new year. Not only did Frankie face an exciting new prospect in her professional life as she was taking on a contract with a big retailer focussing on workforce wellbeing but her personal life had also taken a turn for the better now that Dexter was a regular feature. She felt liberated and vibrant and allowed herself a few moments to reflect that she had more than managed to 'move on', leaving her toxic, dysfunctional relationship with Adam behind. Having blocked his number, she'd had no idea that she would meet a tall, dark, handsome new man that very same evening, in fact. She was not looking for anything long term after what she had endured with Adam, but Dexter Croft was exactly what she needed for now: some excitement and some pure, unadulterated fun.

With a spring in her step, Frankie walked the short distance to the Otter's Head at the end of her working day. This time, she was not meeting girlfriends; she had a date with Dexter or 'Dex' as she had very quickly got in the habit of calling him. Butterflies fluttered in her stomach as she anticipated seeing him again.

Conversation with Dexter just seemed to flow so easily, whenever they were together and Frankie was very much enjoying making plans for the next big day out with the gang – a fabulous day at the races, especially since Dexter was now also invited. The plans had just got even better, when Dexter offered up a VIP viewing box, which his mate had a deal on hiring out for all the main race meetings. It just so happened that his mate was away in the Caribbean, so happy days all round. Yes, this was going to be a good year, Frankie smiled to herself.

***

Bruce had his mobile app set to audio. He was sitting at home, listening to his friends' conversations in the background, a cosy habit he had taken to, so he did not miss any vital information.   He became drawn to Frankie's and Dexter's plan for the races. He smiled to himself as he revelled once again in knowing this news before any of the other members of the group. He felt the familiar sensation of power and omnipotence, an electrifying force coursing through him. Little did Frankie know, but it was not just Bruce who had stumbled upon them. Adam had entered the pub to meet a few colleagues and from the other end of the bar he had spotted Frankie. Adam's eyes were on stalks, as he scrutinised Frankie in a cosy huddle with this mystery man yet again. Who the hell was he? Adam resolved to find out as he quickly acted out an emergency call on his mobile, hastily informed his colleagues that an urgent family matter meant his plans had abruptly changed and he had to immediately leave.

There was no way Adam wanted to bump into Frankie like this; when he met her and her new man it would very much be on his terms, he resolved, as he jogged down the street to his parked car. He would definitely bide his time and pounce, when Frankie was least expecting it. She might think it was all over but he would be the one to make that decision. A plot was forming in Adam's mind, a small flicker of a flame that quickly escalated into a burning desire to wreak his revenge and to cause chaos in Frankie's life.

***

Frankie reluctantly decided to call it a night. She did not want the date to end, but it was a 'school night' and time was ticking. With Dexter in tow, she spotted the Delvreton High crew who she had grown to know so well as the school's resident psychologist. They hollered over to her.

'Hey Frankie, come and say hello!' One of the group actually knew Dexter so the conversation instantly flowed. Frankie felt warm, fuzzy and utterly relaxed as Dexter chatted to the group with ease. She savoured the feeling and pondered for a second on how Adam had made her feel so uncomfortable in the company of her friends, so many times over the past years. Thank God he was not with his colleagues tonight and she was thankful that no one even mentioned him. Life was certainly looking up and confirmed to Frankie that ending it with Adam could be shaping up to be one of the best decisions she had ever made.

***

Back in his office, Bruce was scrolling through several pieces of CCTV footage from Delvreton High that had been captured that first day back. It all looked pretty routine until he honed in on Adam's office. At first, everything seemed quite mundane: Adam at his ridiculously large desk, a brief meeting with his PA, Patricia, then he was clearly working through his emails. At about one o'clock, Patricia announced his line management appointment and an attractive young woman was ushered into his office. His PA retreated into her adjoining, significantly smaller work space, shutting the door firmly behind her. Bruce sat up a bit straighter, as he noticed a discernible change in Adam's demeanour and he could almost feel the sexual chemistry in the room. Bruce soon worked out that the young woman was Suzie Frazer, a relatively new middle leader, who led performing arts and had directed the Christmas panto. Bruce judged her to be about thirty, about five foot six in height and certainly very attractive. As they chatted, it transpired that she and Adam had shared a gym session earlier that morning. Bruce listened intently as they both joked about 'getting the new year off to a good start', and he could not help but notice the blush on Suzie's cheeks when Adam commented on how 'fit' she looked. A bit overfamiliar Adam, Bruce thought to himself. HR will be on your back, if you don't watch it.

The pair worked through an agenda of sorts, but the conversation became increasingly laced with cheeky innuendo as Adam took great pleasure in emphasising key words such as 'performance', how he would have to set Suzie's 'performance targets' and with a cheeky grin, 'what they could possibly be...' Adam was certainly the most animated he had been so far that day and as he stood up at the end of the meeting to see Suzie out of the office, Bruce saw Adam place his hand gently on the small of her back. Suzie slowly stopped, flicked her mane of blonde hair over her shoulder and confidently made eye contact with her boss.

'I'll certainly think about what those performance targets might be then,' she smiled flirtatiously as Adam smiled back, clearly taking in all the features of the attractive young woman before him.

'We could maybe discuss them over a drink at the Otter's one evening after work,' Adam suggested. 'As you're still pretty new round here, it would give me more time to give you the low down on this place and for me to invest in your development,' he continued, still smiling and holding eye contact with Suzie.

'Well, I can't say no to an offer like that from my boss can I?' Suzie answered, with a cheeky giggle. 'Especially if I need him to perform again for me.' She lingered for a moment, before adding, 'you know, in the summer drama production that we're planning.' Bruce was certain he saw Suzie wiggle her butt as she walked away from Adam to the door, certain that he was watching her every move. This young woman was as bad as he was, Bruce concluded, frowning deeply.

When Suzie eventually left the office, Bruce did a double take. He watched Adam recline on his leather sofa for a few moments, stroking his crotch, head flung back with a very satisfied expression on his face. Much to

Bruce's relief, the office phone rang and Adam composed himself quickly. Bruce suddenly felt like a voyeur and exceptionally uncomfortable, but nonetheless, witnessing such lewd behaviour further justified his motivation for further surveillance of Adam. This man was the headteacher, for God's sake, in charge of almost eighteen hundred young people, including Bruce's own daughter Rosie, not to mention that his gorgeous Iris had to work for this unprofessional prick.

The exciting prospect of slap up hospitality at the races that had cheered him up earlier had suddenly disappeared as Bruce was once again tormented by the burden of this new knowledge he carried. The more he saw, the more he realised that nobody appeared to be what they seemed, including his close friends. Bruce's head filled with dark thoughts of the unsavoury sexual encounter he had witnessed in Frankie's kitchen. Adam may present himself as the fine, upstanding headteacher but it was clear that he was a power crazy predator and to Bruce's mind, this made him very dangerous.

As the week wore on, Bruce took some solace from the fact that at least he could keep a close eye on Adam. Once again, his obsession grew as he observed him at every opportunity. During meetings, Adam had to be centre of attention. He skilfully played the role of joker, all too often taking it too far with his sexist and inappropriate jokes. Adam's male colleagues seemed to enjoy the banter and were content to go along with him. However, Adam's PA, Patricia, frequently looked mortified and Bruce started to really feel for her, having to put up with her boss's inappropriateness, his unreasonable demands and his abuse of power but still remain at his beck and call, with a smile on her face. Many of the female colleagues in Adam's team had clearly started to give him a wide berth. Patricia was understandably worried that she could lose her job if she did not meet Adam's requests and turn a blind eye to the unprofessionalism that typified this headteacher's behaviour.

Watching Adam's interactions with the students at Delvreton High further confirmed Bruce's suspicions. Adam regularly preened like a peacock as he supervised students, welcomed them in the morning or took up his break and lunchtime duty slots. Bruce physically recoiled as Adam 'strutted' his stuff around the place, swaggering with overconfidence, especially when he wore his PE kit. Jokes with students started to go over the top far too often, some students laughing along with him, but some clearly fearing what would happen if they didn't; how could they not? When Adam shouted, he did so with gusto, frightening the life out of many. Bruce shuddered at some of the humiliating phrases Adam used to chastise, but what really disturbed Bruce was the way Adam's body language changed, when he spoke to attractive year eleven and sixth form girls.

Bruce definitely agreed with Frankie that standards of uniform had dropped off recently. He saw teenage girls in very short skirts, 'modest makeup only' rules no longer enforced. Bruce was disgusted as he observed Adam enjoying the views. Yes, something was very amiss, but it was all so subtle. Apart from the conversation Bruce had witnessed between Adam and Suzie, there was nothing concrete to justify him acting on his concerns. As in most of the situations he found himself, there was absolutely nothing that he could do.

Reluctantly, Bruce resolved to seek a bit more information from Rosie and Iris, in a low key way of course. His anxiety levels were peaking and he was keen to hear their views of Adam to try to quell his fears. He would get a student's perspective from Rosie and a teacher's perspective from Iris. He mainly wanted assurances that they did not have much to do with this so called 'headteacher'.

***

Bruce's attempt at gleaning information from Iris had not gone at all well. He had popped into her apartment one evening as he was allegedly on his way to the Otter's. It was a dull, cold Wednesday in January and he found Iris immersed in assessing 'A' level PE coursework. Over a beer, they passed the time of day, but it was blatantly obvious that Iris just wanted her Dad to leave. When Bruce mentioned Adam's name, her expression said it all – she was not at all keen to talk about him.

'I don't know much about him,' Iris shrugged, showing her clear irritation. 'I hardly ever see him. What would I have to do with him? Iris begrudgingly stated that Adam was okay but she had a lot of marking to do. To some extent, this was exactly what Bruce needed to hear. At least one daughter seemed well out of that scumbag's inner circle. He would try to persuade her of the benefits of finding another school that would be better for her career development. Yes, that would ensure that he fully protected one of his daughters. Bruce felt pleased about that at least as he bade his rather sullen elder daughter farewell, on his way for a quick one at the Otter's. Maybe he would broach the subject with Rosie tomorrow. For now, although distracted, he would try to enjoy his beer with Ron and Arthur.

After dinner the next evening, Bruce retired to his office to give Rosie a chance to tackle her physics homework, whilst Daisy was still out taking a couple of fitness classes at the new gym in town. Nothing of major concern had turned up on the Delvreton CCTV cameras. In fact, Bruce could not help smiling, as he saw Iris leave by the main entrance at about four thirty, with three other young teachers. They all looked happy and he pondered what it must feel like to have your whole professional and adult life stretching out before you, full of options and opportunity. Make the most of it my darling, he urged Iris in his thoughts. Before you know it, you are approaching fifty and that old pyramid of choices has narrowed so much. His beautiful girl looked radiant and content and Adam was nowhere to be seen, so all good.

Bruce grabbed a beer and sauntered upstairs to Rosie's room. He tentatively knocked on the bedroom door, aware of the soothing music playing within. Typical, Rosie had it all sorted. She had most likely researched the best music to play in order to optimise brain capacity and the soft lighting seemed equally conducive to engendering productive thought processes. He swelled with pride as he saw his beautiful girl pouring over her textbooks with a confident air of academic prowess.

202

Rosie pushed her glasses up the bridge of her nose as she looked up at him.

'What's up Pa?' she asked, smiling.

That melted Bruce's heart. 'Have you got a minute sweetheart for your old man to sit down and have a bit of a chat?' Seeing the positive expression on his daughter's face, Bruce dramatically flopped onto Rosie's pristinely made bed, careful not to spill any of his beer.

'So, shoot,' said Rosie. 'What's new in your world?'

Bruce genuinely enjoyed a pleasurable catch up with his girl. Long overdue, the two of them had not had the chance to converse like this for a long time. It was incredible how every day, mundane life got in the way of the most important things: time for a parent and child to connect, to chat and to enjoy each other's company.

Much as this was turning out to be a special evening, Bruce could not help himself. He desperately needed his bright, innocent daughter to give her verdict on Adam. The conversation centred on Delvreton High and Rosie's opinion of her teachers. This led naturally into Bruce asking her about her headteacher.

'He's okay,' Rosie said, eyes raised as she considered her response. 'More than okay, really. You can have a laugh with him and the PE lads in his A-level group think he's a legend.'

When pressed further by Bruce, Rosie's answers became more interesting, starting to stack up with the conclusions he had drawn from a range of his observations recently.

'He used to go out with Frankie, yeah?' Rosie looked at her Dad for affirmation, then continued 'I always wondered why, cos Frankie's so clever. They don't seem to go together somehow. Mr Pearce jokes around all the time and some of us wish he'd be more serious and talk to us about stuff like Oxbridge. He spends way too long with the 'in crowd' kids if you ask me and everyone says you get way more attention if you're female, blonde, have orange skin and wear your skirt shorter than your blazer. Doesn't bother me though and I'm glad Frankie's not with him anymore 'cause I really like her. I think it's amazing what she's doing now, with the mentoring programmes she's leading in so many schools and she's really helped me with planning my UCAS application to Uni.

Bruce listened intently, marvelling at his daughter's intelligence and wisdom for one so young.

'And another thing,' Rosie continued, clearly on a roll now. 'Everyone has started gossiping about him, saying he fancies the new drama teacher. What's her name? Oh yeah, Miss Frazer. A lot of the boys fancy her too but there's all sorts of gossip about her going into Mr Pearson's office, after parents' evenings and stuff. When they're on duty together, they stand dead close and she's always swinging her hair about, laughing at his jokes and looking into his eyes. And he encourages her too.'

Bruce could not help but laugh at Rosie's accurate impression of Suzie. It would even be quite funny if he had not witnessed the darker side to Adam's character.

Bruce's mind wandered to Adam's encounter with Suzie in his office and Adam touching himself, in school of all things. Bruce finished his beer with a heavy heart from the knowledge that weighed him down like a ship's anchor. He hugged his precious girl and left her in peace to finish her science homework. He just about had time for one more look at the Delvreton High camera footage in his control room before Daisy got back.

Chapter 18

8 January

The bar of the Rockin' Robin was already three deep when Ronnie arrived to meet Dexter to watch the new band he was managing. Ron had been on the new apartment site all afternoon on the salubrious outskirts of the city, pricing up what promised to be a lucrative job for his business. He had met Dexter's brother Jake there, as Dex was 'somewhere or other,' according to his younger sibling. Ronnie knew better than to ask about Dexter's whereabouts, as he was well aware of the many 'projects' Dexter usually had on the go. One of the projects he did know about though was this new band. 'Lockdown' was getting a lot of local attention and Ronnie was really looking forward to seeing them right at the start of their story. He had been planning to attend this gig for some time but when he rekindled his friendship with Dexter at the New Year's Eve party, Ronnie had been delighted when Dexter had insisted that he must join him at the Robin as his guest. Ronnie quite rightly anticipated that he would be in for a good night.

'Over here mate!' Dexter was making his way towards Ron as best he could as most of the people in the popular music venue knew him and were keen to engage him in some banter. Dexter resisted their approach, as he was firmly focused on attracting Ronnie's attention, so that they could both get to the small stage and hang out with Dexter's talented lads. There was also a table laden with every bottled beer imaginable and a selection of bottles of spirits. Dexter was always an excellent, very generous host, one of the many reasons he was so popular. Ronnie eventually made it over to his friend. He was soon immersed in discussion with a few more of Dexter's mates as they watched the band members tuning up their guitars. A group of four twenty somethings were certainly rocking the grungy Nirvana style look to great effect - shoulder length locks, lithe, rangy bodies and the essential brooding expressions. The lead singer certainly caught the eye of the female fans. In a recent tweet about this up and coming band, he had been compared to a swarthy, Heathcliff type character. The baggy white cotton shirt was open to the waist and his tight, ripped black jeans and biker boots completed this very sexy outfit. A throng of young, gorgeous women were strategically positioned at the front of the crowd and were already gazing adoringly at their icon, desperate for his performance to begin.

'Hey Jus,' Dexter called out. 'Are we ready?' he asked the lead singer, pointing at his watch. It was already twenty past seven and they were running late.

A few moments later, the bar was full of raucous sound as the deep timbre of the bass sent vibrations through the bodies of the clamouring crowd. The distorted power guitar chords and the skilfully placed heavy rhythms created a superb background to Justin's deep, guttural voice, sending a few young women into delighted swoons. The lyrics of 'shattered glass,' were original; they somehow managed to create a haunting effect and an overall, highly effective discordance from the deep, grinding rock and the poetic, strangely beautiful words. This was all perfectly enhanced by the vision of the lead singer and his handsome band members, all moving seductively as they seemed to be totally immersed in their music.

Ronnie nodded appreciatively and raised his beer bottle to Dexter, who was clearly proud of his latest discovery. His avuncular protectiveness would ensure that Justin and the lads would be very well looked after, as they went on to navigate their way through the thriving rock scene of the Midlands, following the likes of Black Sabbath, Slade and Led Zepplin, the trailblazers of past. Being managed by Dexter would serve them very well indeed.

The band was a great success with the Rockin' Robin's loyal clientele, who knew a hell of a lot about music. In Dexter's opinion, this first gig at a decent venue could not have been better. Ronnie was really enjoying himself, especially when he found himself laughing and joking with Justin, well aware that a group of young, very attractive women were not taking their eyes off them. It felt good to be in this 'in crowd'. Dexter was always great to spend time with, especially when the beer was flowing and classic rock played all night. Having to shout a bit to be heard was well worth it.

It transpired that quite an eminent music critic was in attendance and Geoff Prescott soon made himself known. The group moved into a smallish snug area of the traditional pub so everyone could be heard. Geoff recorded Dexter first, as the manager of this up and coming group, talking eloquently about possible plans to play at Glastonbury, as well as the festival scene in general as the summer music calendar beckoned seductively. Dexter was just so bloody good at this, Ronnie thought. Then attention turned to Justin who was more than happy to share his blues influences and to explain his song writing process. Ronnie listened intently, genuinely enjoying being a part of this inner sanctum. He felt pleased that Dexter afforded him this opportunity, as Ronnie had always been an avid music fan since his early teenage years. After a good twenty minutes, Geoff seemed more than satisfied that he had enough for his story that would feature in a prominent music blog. Dexter high fived Geoff as a farewell gesture and talk quickly turned to plans for the rest of the evening. Justin was understandably keen to re-join his band members, his doting fans and particularly those adoring young women, desperate to make his acquaintance. Dexter and Ron entered into some lively banter with Justin on the subject of his female fan base before patting him on the back and pushing him back into the throngs of the main lounge and performance area.

Dexter signalled for Ron to stay with him in the quieter space to discuss his grumbling stomach.

'I'm so ravenous, man,' Dexter declared, rubbing his stomach for dramatic effect. 'Do you fancy some top scran with some quality wine and then even more beers?' He laughed heartily.

Ronnie was also feeling peckish and he had already cleared it with Brooke that he would be out until late.

This Lockdown gig had been marked on the calendar on their kitchen wall for some time now. In normal circumstances, Brooke would have come along too but she had a hectic schedule at the moment so midweek gallivanting was out of the question. Had it been the weekend, then Brooke would not have missed seeing this band.

'Too right mate. Some great live music, washed down with a few ales always gets my appetite going. What do you suggest?'

'I know just the place, my man,' Dexter answered.

Ronnie was not surprised, as Dexter always seemed to know the best places to go, wherever you happened to be with him.

'A good mate of mine is this top Spanish geezer, who is ace at the old tapas. He actually cut his teeth at his parents' restaurant in San Sebastian, in the Basque country, so he is the real deal. You'll love him, I know you will.'

'Lead on then mate.' Ron laughed, marvelling at the endless stream of contacts that Dexter seemed to be able to call on, whatever the situation you were in. He always seemed to know someone who could further eek out the good times.

As they both pushed through the ever more animated drinkers towards the exit, one in particular suddenly careered into Ron, knocking him into the wall.

'Sorry mate,' the tall, slightly dishevelled rocker apologised. 'I'm well wasted,' he admitted with a crooked smile as he staggered off into the distance.

'No problem at all mate,' Ron replied, noticing the Kurt Cobain vibe and the scar on his cheek. The Robin was a pretty edgy venue, Ron thought to himself and that was what made it the perfect place to come and appreciate some quality, live rock. Ron tapped the errant drinker on the arm as he walked away from him, following Dexter onto the street outside.

'Come on,' Dexter urged. 'Only a few minutes from here. It's on Vittoria street, named after some battle in Spain as it happens.' Dexter gave Ronnie a running commentary on some historic moments, as they walked briskly to ward off the winter chill, a stark contrast to the boiling hot Rockin' Robin.

'Nice one,' Dexter announced as he pushed open the door of the Vittoria tapas bar, the perfect location for the stylish eatery in this historic part of Birmingham. A tasteful renovation of an old traditional boozer, the new hotspot for gastronomes was only three weeks into its journey.

'Dexter!' A flamboyant, stylish character greeted both Dexter and Ronnie with enthusiastic hugs and kisses on both cheeks.

'Mateo!' Dexter replied with equal gusto. 'This place looks the dogs.' Dexter held Mateo in a lingering embrace, much to Ron's amusement who was happy to extricate himself from Mateo, as soon as it felt polite to do so.

'You look good, my man!' Dexter continued, attracting the attention of a group of four attractive women who seemed happy to take in the vision of the handsome men so ostentatiously greeting each other. They were like two peacocks proudly showing off their plumage. Ron recoiled a little from the excessive show from both Dexter and Mateo but steeled himself and went with the flow. Ronnie had never been keen on demonstrations of affection, even with his closest family. He was relieved once the drama abated and he and Dexter were shown to a prime table in the understated, yet classy eating area.

'Let me present you with some of our finest wine, whilst you peruse the tapas,' Mateo offered. 'A little white to begin, then we move to the red.'

'We are in your hands, mi amigo,' Dexter smiled, hamming up the Spanish accent.

'This looks pretty good,' Ronnie said as he appraised the tapas menu. He glanced around, registering that the majority of the tables were full. The other diners were well heeled and discerning; news of this authentic restaurant had already whetted the appetites of a knowledgeable, foody crowd, always on the lookout for a new, high quality eatery. Not bad for a place that had just opened and on a mid-week night. The venue was clearly going to be a success. He settled back in his chair and looked forward to the second part of this great evening so far. Ronnie would certainly enjoy recounting his experience to his mates at the Otter's this weekend. This little liaison between Dexter and his sister was quickly shaping up to be a very good thing. It had already rekindled his friendship with Dexter and the deal on the apartments earlier was clearly linked to this. And, icing on the cake was that Frankie had finally ditched Fuckwit!

'You know what,' Dexter said raising a stylish wine glass full of amber nectar. 'Let Mateo surprise us with whatever his protégé suggests for us. We are in his very capable hands. God, that's fucking spectacular,' Dexter stated as he took another long drink from the wine glass. 'Life is good, my friend.' Dexter raised his empty glass to Ronnie, as he signalled his appreciation to Mateo.

'I thought you'd like that,' Mateo smiled. 'This is the famous young white wine of the Basque region. It is an excellent start to the evening's delights. Mateo replenished glasses as he theatrically placed bread, salt fish croquettes, lightly fried calamari and thick slices of tortilla before Ronnie and Dexter. He then went back to the bar and brought over a lush tomato salad.

'After this, I will bring you our finest red to accompany your second round of tapas. Pasar bien, mi amigos.' With a flourish, Mateo swept away from the table, leaving Ronnie conscious of the fact that the other diners were looking, eager to see who the guests were that were attracting so much special attention from the flamboyant patron.

'Yes!' Dexter exclaimed, as he pierced a couple of delicious pieces of squid and spooned a croquette onto his plate. 'I knew Mateo would nail this. I visited his family's restaurant in San Sebastien two years ago. The food was just off the scale. Never tasted anything like it, you know what I mean mate?'

Ronnie nodded, himself very much savouring the feast before him. He and Brooke frequently ate out and in all of the best local haunts, so he definitely knew quality when he encountered it. He would look forward to telling Brooke all about it and knew that he would definitely be making a booking at this tapas bar very soon indeed.

'It's one of the gastronomic centres of the world. Not many people know that,' Dexter continued. 'Maybe we should go over there as a foursome sometime. The girls would bloody love it. Mind you, we all would. Eating and drinking the best there is, and admiring spectacular scenery. What's not to like?' Dexter was in his element and genuinely liked the idea of a short break abroad with his latest woman and the good company that Ronnie and Brooke would certainly provide.

'You just name the time and we are in,' Ronnie replied enthusiastically, but secretly thought that this was probably wishful thinking, fuelled by too much to drink. He was no fool and realised that what many people discussed as plans late at night, seldom materialised or stood the test of the cold light of day.

As more food was consumed and a beautiful bottle of the red was adored, conversation flowed easily over a wide range of topics. Not surprisingly, Frankie figured quite a few times. She was 'classy' in Dexter's view and he enjoyed her company. He had not managed to progress from 'A' levels to University but he had benefited from a very good public school education and was widely travelled. Dexter, like Ronnie, was appreciative of culture and the finer things in life, which in their minds, encompassed the world of rock and great music. It was all part of the same thing. Dexter was not quite so keen on the fact that Frankie worked such ridiculous hours, but recognised that their relationship was in its early days and its casual nature seemed to suit them both. In direct contrast to uptight Adam, Dexter was cool and laid back, which brought significant advantages to this relationship; just what Frankie needed right now, Ronnie thought to himself.

'That was ace,' Ronnie said, leaning back in his chair and wiping his mouth with the napkin. He sighed contentedly and once again complimented the truly great wine, one of the finest from the North of Spain.

'It certainly was,' agreed Dexter. 'That was a top evening all round, my good mate, Ronnie. A bit too early to turn in though. What about we have a final nightcap?'

'Don't mind if I do,' sighed Ronnie. 'As I thought this could end up as a late one, I took the liberty of booking tomorrow off.' He smiled, relishing the thought of making the most of what remained of the evening and enjoying a rare midweek lie in.'

'Great minds, and all that,' agreed Dexter. 'I have always tried to organise my days so that I never have to start too early.' He smiled at Ronnie, before catching the ever- attentive Mateo's eye once again to order some rather large malt whiskeys. The bar was gradually emptying and a sense of pleasant peacefulness washed over the lingering diners. Ronnie felt that this atmosphere presented the perfect opportunity to share his anxiety about Adam; he had to talk to someone, as he just could not bring himself to worry Brooke with it all. She was not quite herself now, so there was no way he wanted to burden her with his concerns about Frankie's safety.

Ronnie launched in and started to tell Dexter about his observations of Adam's recent behaviour. It just wasn't right, was it? Dexter listened contemplatively, slowly sipping the amber liquid and swirling it in his glass as he gathered his thoughts.

'That is out of order mate,' Dexter commented. 'No doubt about it. Her ex sounds like a total fucking moron. He wants to watch himself, as well, or he'll lose his job. But that would make a lot of people happy by the sound of it.'

'Yeah,' said Ron. 'How the hell can he fool everyone at that school and the bloody parents of Delvreton that they can trust their kids with that wanker? He's just not wired up right, in my view.'

'Yeah, Frankie gave me some of the lowdown on him, but I could tell she was keeping a lot back. He sounds like one sick fuck. Snooping around her home is just not on. At least you know that I'll be keeping an eye out for her too. If you have any more worries, let me know and I can make sure that I am around.' Dexter paused, clearly thinking for a moment about the direction the conversation could take. He seemed to make his mind up and continued. 'I think I can trust you, right?'

Ronnie nodded. 'You can, goes without saying.'

Dexter continued. 'I know you are well aware of what goes on around our local area. You know that I like the variety of life and that I like to dabble, shall we say?'

'I know that,' Ronnie affirmed.

'Well, I know a lot of people who can sort things out, you know? It would be very easy for me to call in a few favours and make sure that we keep an eye on our Adam, as well as watching over Frankie. That should take some pressure off you and reassure us both,' Dexter concluded.

Ronnie thought for a moment and then responded. 'That would be great mate. That would mean a lot.' In truth, it would genuinely take a weight of Ronnie's mind.

Dexter raised his glass, downed the remains of his whisky in one and gestured for Mateo to charge their glasses once more. Talk turned to plans for the weekend's race meeting bash and Ronnie felt happy with this new dimension to his life; a life with Dexter in it certainly added some richness and also some reassurance. Ronnie was definitely feeling on the wrong side of drunk. He glanced at his watch and was not too surprised that it was well past one o'clock, and a week night! It had been a great evening and Ronnie felt relieved that he had been able to share his worries. Having Dexter as an ally in his mission to protect Frankie against Adam was a real result. Ron knew that he would sleep very well that night.

Chapter 19

10 January

The next week passed relatively uneventfully but the build up to the Warwick race meeting mounted and a sense of excitement grew. The group of friends were more animated than ever, as the women planned their outfits, choosing bright vivacious colours to ward off the grey winter days. The men talked about likely bets and the best method for pacing their alcohol intake throughout the day when the prospect of a free bar would undoubtedly tantalise them all.

The icy winter day posed no barrier to the friends' plans to have a thoroughly good time together. Two races into the card and everyone was at least three drinks into the endless possibilities of the very well stocked free bar. The constant flow of food to the buffet table was thankfully ensuring that stomachs stayed well lined in order to stand up to the onslaught of the constant flow of alcohol.

'Bloody hell, mate! Look at you; you're glowing,' Ruby whispered into Frankie's ear as they stood on the balcony of the box, looking down on the parade ring where the statuesque, prancing horses for the next race were making their entrance. Beautiful, fine limbed animals trotted and skittered, their tendons and muscles almost bursting at the seams of their burnished bodies. Frankie was in a trance, as was Brooke, before Ruby literally burst in on their deep thoughts.

'What's happening out here with you two?' Ruby asked.

'Just admiring the gorgeous horses and feeling the pleasant effects of those Champagne cocktails,' Frankie smiled, with a wistful look that Ruby instantly registered.

'You have a gorgeous new animal in your life now, my girl!' Ruby giggled, squeezing Frankie's arm as they both looked appreciatively at the pure hunk of charming flesh that was Dexter. He was effortlessly entertaining the lads with an account of his boozy night out with Ronnie, earlier that week.

'Hey,' Brooke shouted animatedly. 'The horses are going down to the start. Get your bets placed and come out here onto the balcony to watch. It's fantastic being right at the finishing post.' Brooke was glowing, in her element and more of an expert in this domain than anyone would ever guess, although Bruce knew everything about Brooke's gambling addiction, of course. He would certainly keep a very close eye on the funds in her 'secret' betting account today.

Brooke looked great in her stylish purple overcoat and classy bejewelled vintage look fascinator, finished off with a much coveted pair of plum, velvet block heeled shoes. All of the girls had made an effort: Frankie in her black and white animal print fur coat, a gorgeous matching hat and a pair of beautiful white knee length boots. Tight black trousers showed off her long, toned legs, which

219

clearly met with Dexter's satisfaction. After much thought, Daisy had elected to wear a tight fitting emerald green velvet midi dress, a silver grey long overcoat and black patent boots, whilst Ruby was rocking a gold trouser suit like only Ruby could, topped off with a classy camel coat and nude stilettos. She too was sporting a chic gold fascinator to keep Brooke company. The men were booted and suited appropriately with an array of bright shirts and ties to bring some colour to their get ups. All in all, they were an attractive, affluent looking group, very much at home in the private box that Dexter had arranged for them.

Suddenly, the third race was off and the group of friends were silent for a few moments. They had to squint through the mist to make out the horses and riders that were on the far side of the course, where they had started. The large screen opposite was a great help to ensure that none of the race action was missed until the spectators could enjoy seeing the horses up close as they thundered down the home straight, before heading out for the final circuit. Shrieks of excitement pierced the winter's day and mingled with the noise from the crowds in the main grandstand.

'Go on, Double Shuffle,' Brooke shouted. 'He's in a great position,' she observed excitedly to everyone. 'Go on my boy! Do your stuff Nico,' she urged her horse's jockey, as if he was a close friend.

'Where's mine?' Asked Ruby.

'He's there, number 6. Look, he's mid pack,' Arthur said helpfully, moving to stand next to his wife.

220

Frankie was also watching intently. She loved the races and loved horses, having started riding at the tender age of four. One of her secret plans was to have a horse of her own one day again. Once work was a bit more settled, she made a promise to herself. For now, though, she was happier and more content than she had been for a very long time. She looked over to Dexter who caught her eye and gave her a lovely smile. He moved along the balcony, standing behind Frankie so she could lean into him and enjoy the feeling of his strong body. She, like the others, started shouting for their horses, as they rounded the bend for the last time, took the last hurdle and raced for the finish, mud splattering the jockey's jodhpurs, silks and faces. The ground was heavy and some of the horses were exhausted from battling through these challenging conditions.

'Yees!' Brooke shrieked, as Double Shuffle got the better of Gold Sovereign, Arthur's choice. He had to have that one as Ruby worked with gold every day of her life. An each way bet ensured he was not disappointed. Brooke skipped along the balcony.

'Champagne for me,' she sang out, beaming with joy as Ronnie watched her, an eyebrow slightly raised. 'Come and join me girls.'

'How much have you won then?' asked Ronnie.

'Sixty quid Bab! We are in the money,' Brooke said delightedly.

Bruce took a quick look at his phone, not realising that Daisy was watching him. 'Oi, you're not meant to take any work messages today,' she shouted, making Bruce jump.

'I know love. I'm only checking out the next race.' Bruce was really checking out Brooke's betting app. Just like Boxing Day, her sixty quid win turned out to be a six hundred pounds win. She needed that, he thought to himself, as she had taken some hard losses over the past few days. Bruce knew that Brooke would be going for it today. He hoped that her luck would last for the next three races, although he also knew that she was placing bets at all of the other race meetings that were on for that day too. Daisy was suddenly beside him, asking for his selection for the one thirty. They both poured over the race card and Bruce enjoyed the feeling of being close to his wife. Their relationship had been so up and down recently and he knew that he had been giving off some real stress vibes, given all the things he had seen. Thank God Daisy always put it down to the pressure of his new business. He would try not to think about anything today other than having a much needed good time with his wife and his best mates. He would try hard not to let his mind wander into their secret lives, just for today.

'Come on everyone. Come and get some Champagne,' Brooke called. 'Dexter has put a case of something pretty special behind the bar for us. It's LPR!' She exclaimed. 'Totally delicious!'

'Not for me mate,' said Ronnie to his wife. 'I'll stick to the ale, thanks. You know me and I'm going to have some of that beef that has just arrived,' he announced with a smile. The others were also starting to salivate as the aroma of the beef pervaded the box and the group took some time to eat, to savour the first class buffet and to simply enjoy the luxury around them. Today was a real treat and they were all determined to indulge in every moment of it.

Everyone was succumbing to the alcohol now and the noise level had risen significantly.

'Come on,' Frankie urged Dexter. 'Let's go down to the parade ring and pick our next horses based on their conformation. I need some fresh air too to sober up a bit.'

Frankie and Dexter grabbed their coats, explained their plan to the others and made their way to the lift down to the main area outside.

The harsh, cold wind hit them full force, as soon as they left the warmth of the vestibule. Dexter put his arm round Frankie and she found herself leaning into him once again and enjoying the sense of security this brought her. Always fiercely independent and formerly, always distrusting of Adam, she had built a protective fortress around herself, which she had needed throughout her previous relationship. It felt good to let her guard down, just a little bit. They spotted a gap at the fence of the parade ring and Frankie started to give a running commentary on the conformation of all ten horses, as they paraded. She loved being so close to them, seeing their finely tuned bodies and hearing the snorts as they emitted steam into the winter's air from their flailing nostrils.

Just as Frankie was explaining her selection to Dexter, she spotted a couple of familiar faces opposite. Yes, it was Patricia, Adam's PA at Delvreton High and her husband, Andrew. It seemed that Patricia had spotted Frankie at exactly the same time and she waved enthusiastically, already starting to make her way around the perimeter of the ring. Frankie and Dexter did the same and they were soon standing as a happy foursome. Introductions were swiftly made. Patricia had got to know Frankie really well in the five years she had worked at Delvreton High and she had been devastated when Frankie recently left, sending in another member of her team. Patricia had been party to all the drama of Frankie's relationship with Adam, often wishing she had not known all about it. She had never really adjusted to being Adam's PA; she much preferred the former headteacher but she had just about managed to reconcile herself to her professional fate.

'Look at your outfit!' Patricia exclaimed. 'You look like you have stepped off the set of Dr Zhivago, or something! You look great! Wait 'til I tell the girls in the office that I've seen you.'

Frankie smiled and happily exchanged news for about five minutes, as they all wanted to take up their positions to watch the next race. They moved to a raised bank, which offered a decent vantage point. Dexter fell into a natural conversation with Andrew and Frankie continued to catch up on any gossip from school and she was not disappointed

'I'm only telling you this because you seem so happy and it does look like you have managed to move on from Adam.' Patricia looked a little uncomfortable but Frankie urged her to continue.

'Well, everyone's talking about Adam and the new drama teacher, Suzie Frazer. She always seems to be in his office. They are always laughing and joking around the place when they are on duty together and all the kids are gossiping about them, as well as the staff. She's only thirty, if that and this is her first middle leader role. You wouldn't think it, how bloody confident she is.'

'What a bloody idiot!' Frankie commented. 'He should know better by now, or at least know that he needs to be a lot more discreet than that. He's the head of the school – reputation matters.'

'Yes, but it's as if he thinks he can do exactly as he pleases and he loves the fact that Suzie seems to absolutely adore him. What's worse – get ready for this.' Patricia leaned into Frankie and lowered her voice a little. 'He is apparently advertising another Assistant Head post to oversee all the extra-curricular stuff, and you can bet who he's lining it up for.'

'What?' Frankie was genuinely shocked. 'But there are already enough members of the leadership team. And anyway, if he was going to have another senior role then what about Tim, Gemma and Martin? They've had middle leader roles for years. Bloody hell, he is going to seriously piss off a lot of his staff, if he appoints Suzie.'

'Well, watch this space,' Patricia replied, 'because I'm almost certain it'll be her.'

Frankie had played a major role in designing and delivering a management development programme at the school so she knew many of the staff and their career aspirations. She also knew that Adam's behaviour would upset a lot of good people.

Frankie sighed at Adam's questionable ethics as she gazed into the distance, noticing the horses lined up and ready to lunge forward as they waited for the starter to give his signal.

'Surely the governors won't let him do that?' Frankie looked at Patricia.

'Don't be so sure. You hardly ever see one of the governors. Standards have dropped since he's been in charge. You've only got to look at the inappropriate length of the girls' skirts! Anyway, I've had it with him and I'm actively looking for other jobs now, like a lot of the admin staff.'

'Oh Trish, that's awful,' Frankie sighed.

'It's time for me to move on. I can't work for someone so unethical. Tell you what though,' Patricia chuckled mischievously. 'I'll really enjoy telling Adam that I saw you today with Dexter. Quite a few people know of him, you know – he's a bit of a celeb round Delvreton and I bet Adam will want to find out all about him too. He'll be jealous as hell.' Patricia laughed heartily.

Frankie shivered a little. She knew how controlling and cruel Adam could sometimes be and she really hoped he would leave her alone, especially as he seemed to have a new young thing to occupy his time. It had been a good two weeks now since she had blocked his number, so maybe she was home and dry. She had definitely moved on from him and she really hoped that he finally felt the same way.

Plans were made to meet up soon as the two couples went their separate ways at the end of the race. Frankie and Adam were in extra high spirits as Frankie's selection had gone on to win comfortably and Dexter was clearly impressed by her equine knowledge. He had splashed out fifty quid too so at 7 – 1 that gave him a very nice four hundred pounds return. That would pay for the champers at least, but money really was not an issue for Dexter. He did well from his property ventures and he got a buzz from a few deals that were not always completely above board. He loved having a foothold in the underworld of Birmingham but he would make sure that he kept that side of his life away from Frankie. Her job was too high profile and respectable, so there were certain aspects of his life that she did not need to worry her pretty little head about. Keep it simple, was his motto and it served him very well.

Frankie and Dexter re-joined the group and noticed a change in the atmosphere. Ronnie and Brooke were huddled up a corner. It looked like Ronnie was almost lecturing Brooke, which was unusual for them. Brooke pushed his arm away and seemed to stumble as she made her way to the bar area. 'Brooke!' Ronnie shouted after her. 'Be careful, love.'

Brooke took a glass of Champagne, sat herself down at an empty table and peered fixedly at her phone screen. Daisy flopped down next to her, berating Bruce for being too preoccupied and both could not help but notice that Arthur was uncharacteristically quiet, staring into the distance as he stood alone on the balcony, away from his group of mates.

'Something doesn't feel right,' Frankie whispered to Dexter, who said that a couple of drinks would sort everything out. He headed off to the bar with a spring in his step. She was not so sure though as she scoured the box for Ruby but could not see her. What had happened whilst they had been away?

Quite a lot.

After a strong start, Brooke had lost heavily and drunk heavily, much to Ronnie's disappointment. It just was not like her to hammer the Champagne so quickly as if she was determined to get off her face. Yes, Brooke liked a good time, but she never behaved like this. Bruce and Daisy had had words out on the balcony as Daisy once again accused him of being 'obsessed with that bloody phone,' and told him 'to use the race card! For once, just give the technology a fucking rest!'

Meanwhile, Ruby had picked up Arthur's phone, having seen a text alert, promptly thrown it at him, grabbed her coat and left the box in a major huff.

The last race came and went and the whole tone of the day changed completely. A silent group left the box, took two lifts down to the vestibule and headed out into the bitter, cold, dark Saturday evening. Thankfully, the minibus awaited them in the carpark. There were a few attempts at light hearted conversation on the hour long journey back to Delvreton but the conversation was clearly strained. Everyone got dropped off at their respective homes, hugged each other farewell and there was a mention of plans to meet up soon, but the mood was sombre, all things considered.

Too much alcohol, too much excitement. That is what must have happened. That was the natural, understandable conclusion to draw, but Bruce knew exactly why the day had ended like it did.

Soon after Bruce and Daisy got home, they welcomed Rosie back, who had enjoyed a sleepover with her best pal, Jade. Bruce could safely spend a few moments checking his phone in the snug, as Daisy seemed to have thawed a little, buoyed up as ever by the sheer effervescence of Rosie's natural demeanour. She also knew that Bruce would be genuinely checking in on Iris. They knew that she usually met up with the girls on Saturdays and the group of best friends were trying out a trendy new bar, just on the outskirts of Lichfield.

'She's having a great time!' Bruce declared brightly as he came into the kitchen.

'Yes, she does text me as well,' Daisy commented. 'She's my gorgeous daughter too, you know!'

'We get some things right together, don't we love?' Bruce was encouraged by the softer look on Daisy's face, as he knew she was thinking about their beautiful children.

Truth was, Iris was having a great time but for more reasons than her parents were party to. She sat surrounded by her very attractive group of friends on one of those new large, raised round tables to enhance the party atmosphere in the bustling bar that was rammed to the rafters. All of the girls had agreed to 'glam up' and Iris was enjoying the attention she was attracting. A deep cobalt blue sequined mini dress accentuated her long lean body and those much admired legs were perfectly complemented by a pair of beautiful navy, suede stilettos, which showed off her subtle self-tan a treat. Iris had, by now, carefully swapped her phones, placing her 'main' iPhone into the zip pocket within her silver, oversized clutch bag. She had deftly replaced it with her 'party' phone and was loving looking at the stream of photos that had been taken of her in various poses; she was in the centre of the shot, flanked by an array of lovely young women.

'Whoo!' shouted one the friends, Aimee, over the noise of the bar. 'Iris has her party phone out everyone, so we can get up to anything now!'

It was common knowledge among the girls that Bruce could be somewhat overprotective and had overstepped the mark on several occasions in the past when he seemed to know too much about Iris' evenings out. They knew his line of work, so they had hatched a plan with Iris to adopt the 'two phone' approach to life and it had worked beautifully. Iris always made sure that she used her main iPhone to text friends with a slight degree of risqué comments so that she did not arouse her father's suspicions. She also took a range of photos on it too, as she knew he could definitely hack into those. However, her 'secret' phone was used for the serious communications she needed to have with her 'gang'. It was on this phone that a torrent of texts appeared which made Iris beam from ear to ear, attracting a flurry of attention from her mates.

'You look like the cat that got the cream,' commented Fleur. 'What are you looking at?'

Iris grinned, with a smug look on her face. 'Wouldn't you like to know?' she teased.

Fleur moved to stand next to Iris. 'Come on, the others are ogling that footballer by the bar. You can tell your best friend about who's making you look so happy!' Fleur knew that Iris had taken a sensible break from men since Tom had been such a prick but she had sensed that someone new had recently come onto the scene.

'It's nothing really,' Iris confided. 'I'm just communicating with my head of department about some opportunities about work.'

'Okay,' Fleur agreed with a smile and a hug for her friend. She was aware of how badly hurt Iris had been and was pleased to see her friend looking genuinely happy again. 'I'll leave you to your texting then. You need to forget about work now. I'm off to see if there are any more footballers available!'

Iris smiled and settled into her comfy, oversize padded bar chair. She had received a few texts over the weekend so far and there was definitely a familiar edge to them. She particularly liked the one in response to the photo that she had sent of her and the girls, posing at the start of the evening. She knew that was a bit over the top of her to send that photo but she felt tipsy and she got a very positive response back. A warm feeling washed over her as she vowed to be careful. Iris was no fool and knew that there was an element of risk, if she decided to continue this communication. However, she really wanted to get that leadership job that she had recently applied for. A few friendly texts with a colleague from her own department could not hurt anyone, surely.

Chapter 20

15 January

Kevin Smith was leaning up against a display cabinet at his local boozer in the Jewellery Quarter, nursing a Jack Daniels. He had arranged to meet a friend of Ruby's, who he vaguely recalled meeting once at one of the Christmas parties Ruby liked to throw for the Jewellery Quarter gang each year. Brooke, or something, her name was; he seemed to recall she was top totty.

At fifteen years of age he had decided that 'Kevin Smith' was not a name that was going places. 'Kevin Smith' was far too safe, like magnolia walls or vanilla flavour. Why stick with vanilla when there is rum and raisin on offer? So, as a teenager, he had made his mind up to ditch 'Kevin' to the room 101 vaults forever. Now, he went by the name of Blaze. Blaze was a perfect name for the kind of guy he wanted to be. Blaze was a name that was going places. Blaze would be the sort of guy sporting a red Ferrari, driving to his private jet. 'Kevin Smith' was probably still waiting in a wet bus shelter in Tipton. Blaze was definitely not magnolia. A blaze of fire, a blaze of glory. He let his mum off for calling him Kevin though, since she still did his washing and ironing.

Blaze knew that Ruby and her friend needed a bit of assistance and he was exactly the sort of guy to provide it. However, he never took on a 'job' until he had fully surveyed the client. He propped himself up, tried his best to look like a disinterested and brooding rock star and waited for them to arrive.

About ten minutes earlier than arranged, an attractive woman in her early forties appeared. She was wearing a leather coat and dark purple velvet dress with knee high, black boots. She had a subtle air of 'Goth-rock-chick' about her but in a middle aged, sophisticated kind of way. Blaze had despised the Goth scene, as he was much more of a grunge type. He especially hated those desperate EMOs that had crawled onto the rock scene in the late 1990s, trying to look like characters from the Matrix movie. Blaze watched the woman as she tentatively glanced around the room, before she moseyed towards the bar tender, ordered a white wine spritzer and found herself a seat alone, at a table set up for two.

White wine, Blaze contemplated to himself. She was not your regular vodka swigging totty then; she was classier. He studied her sapphire blue eyes, her slightly ruffled, layered hair cascading gently onto her shoulders, just above her very ample breasts. Nice rack, he thought to himself. She was also wearing trendy glasses and looked a bit of an intellectual type to him. Not that he was interested in her mind. Bit of a newscaster type, he thought, the sort you see on breakfast news shows. A MILF for sure, he smirked to himself. He watched her nervously surveying the room, her wrist watch, the other customers, and then her watch again. He would not approach her yet though. He would make her wait for a while longer. In the meantime, he was certainly going to enjoy the view.

Brooke was sitting, apprehensively sipping her Sauvignon Blanc. She glanced at her watch, then round the room, then at her watch again. She was uncharacteristically ten minutes early. She had agreed to meet Ruby and 'Blaze' at the Rockin' Robin Brew House. Brooke was quite sure that Blaze was not his given birth name. Anyway, Ruby knew him through a friend of a friend of one of Arthur's colleagues, or someone or other. It had been made clear that Blaze was 'their man', if they needed a bit of 'assistance' to give Adam a scare. Brooke was praying Ruby would arrive before Blaze turned up.

Brooke gazed around at the clientele and décor. She was fascinated by the brew house. It was like a rock and roll museum and she was transfixed by the endless rock memorabilia adorning the walls and the glass display cabinets. There were signed album covers, guitars, drums, keyboards and outfits with a plethora of posters of every rock and roll genre. These ranged from Buddy Holly to Rush, AC/DC, Nirvana and the Foo Fighters, with a homage to just about every rock band in between. The customers were dressed in amazing retro get ups, women with vintage victory rolls in their hair wearing 1950s rockabilly circle skirts. Many of the guys were dressed like characters out of the film Quadrophenia, Paul Weller types, in Harrington jackets with cool hairstyles and winkle pickers, most of them sporting out of this world artwork tattoos.

Brooke caught the eye of a thirty something man, languishing against a display cabinet. He threw her a wry smile and she instantly looked away, moving the angle of her chair slightly so that her back was turned towards him. The last thing she wanted was to get hit on. She needed to be available to make her arrangements with Blaze, when he arrived, pay him and leave as soon as she could. She definitely did not want to have to answer any awkward questions from an enamoured local wanting to know if she 'came here often' and 'what brought her here?'

Brooke fixed her attention on a woman sitting at the next table instead. Brooke was staring, a little too long, at the woman's leg completely covered in a Japanese style tattoo of a dragon, just as Ruby breezed in.

'Brooke! You're here. Not like you to be early,' Ruby jibed.

'Bloomin' heck Rubes, I am such a bag of nerves. I wanted to get here as early as possible and get this over and done with,' Brooke declared, relieved to finally have her friend here with her.

'Be cool, Brooke. Blaze is okay. He's been to a few of my Christmas parties. He's a bit of a rough diamond, but he's a cuddly bear really,' Ruby assured Brooke.

Brooke was not convinced that anyone who went by the name of Blaze could be all that cuddly.

'Oh, he's over there,' Ruby directed her gaze to a cabinet full of David Bowie collectables.

Brooke turned towards Ruby's stare, then recoiled as she realised this was the same guy who had been eyeing her up from when she had first arrived. Since Brooke had had no idea who he was, she had done her utmost to avoid eye contact with him. It then dawned on her that she had been rather standoffish with him. She began to feel a touch of panic about what he might do, if she had pissed him off.

'Oh shit! Is that him? I think I gave him the cold shoulder earlier. I hope he doesn't think I'm a high maintenance bitch,' Brooke said nervously.

'Shush your chatter,' Ruby chastised. 'It'll be fine. Be cool; he's coming over.'

A muscular, blond haired man who had been standing in front of a 'Glass Spiders Tour' concert poster was approaching their table. Blaze was not what Brooke had expected at all. She had imagined an overweight, heavy metal type, with a shaved head, overgrown beard, patched up jeans, Doc Martins and a slightly too small leather waistcoat, whiffing of patchouli oil. Instead, Blaze was unassuming. He was tall, slim, wearing a boot cut jean, black tee and a dark green military style jacket. He had a long fringe and was somewhat of a throwback to a 1990s rock star. He reminded Brooke of Kurt Cobain or Michael Hutchence. And he certainly had a swagger when he walked.

'Ladies,' he greeted them.

'Hi,' Ruby smiled at him and pushed a glass of bourbon his way.

'Thanks ladies,' he smiled and took the glass.

Brooke studied his face. He was a bit older than she had first thought; early forties, she reckoned. Tanned skin that was slightly leathery, steely blue eyes and couple of broken teeth. He was actually probably not bad looking in his day; the only sign of his less than wholesome lifestyle was a faded scar across his lower left cheek. Looked like he had been glassed in the face, or something in his youth, Brooke supposed.

'So, I hear you have a little bully boy throwing his weight around?' Blaze commented.

'Yes,' Ruby replied. 'He dated our friend for a number of years, messed her around good and proper. She dumped him a few weeks back, but he won't go away. He's been sniffing round Brooke's house and he really frightened her.' Ruby gave a brief overview of their 'problem'.

'So, you want him out of the picture, right?' Blaze held a steely azure, blue- eyed stare at Brooke.

Brooke was thinking that she felt a bit funny. This situation was exciting, but she was also scared half to death. She was trying hard to manage a mixture of feelings: exhilaration and trepidation. She realised Blaze was waiting for her to respond, as her mind came back into the room.

'Oh, yes. I mean, well, I don't want him to die or anything. But he's bad news and thinks he's so perfect. He projects himself as this well to do respectable type, when he's got loads of women on the go, treats them like dirt and bullies his way through life. He's a real control freak type, you know?' Brooke babbled.

'Oh yes… I know the type,' Blaze's silky voice permeated through Brooke's skin. 'Think the world owes them. They take what they want with total disregard for others. Charming type, I bet?' He enquired.

'He is,' Ruby agreed enthusiastically. 'Charms the pants off, quite literally!' She giggled, then stopped herself. This was no laughing matter. She continued. 'But he's dark, you know, treats women rough and he scared the life out of poor Brooke here, because she dared to challenge him about his little games,' Ruby explained.

'I see,' Blaze agreed. 'You saw right through him, girl, eh? And he didn't like being told, I can bet?' He addressed Brooke.

'Well, yes, I guess I did. He was making Frank, I mean our friend, so miserable and he came round to my house and threatened me to back off. I'd just like someone big and experienced in these matters to make him feel like I did that day and… well you know… just scare him?' Brooke said hesitantly.

'It'll cost.' Blaze was cool.

'Oh yes, yes. We've got the money,' Ruby explained, as Brooke pushed a brown envelope, containing £2000, over the table to him. Brooke had hesitated in her choice of a brown envelope. It was so clichéd, something out of a drug movie or something, but when she put the money in her purple Radley purse, adorned with West Highland terriers and balloons, it had felt rather glib.

Blaze calmly checked the contents of the envelope.

'It's done then. Good doing business with you, ladies.'
Blaze swigged back his Jack Daniels and was out of the
door, before Brooke and Ruby even had time to answer.

'Oh God Ruby. What have we done?' Brooke
suddenly felt sick.

'It's okay. Adam needs knocking off his perch, and he
won't get hurt. He will just get a bit of a scare.'

'Really?' Brooke's head was swimming.

'Really,' Ruby assured her friend. 'Now, what do you
want to drink? We might as well enjoy this place, now
we're here.' Ruby was up at the bar before she had
finished her sentence, such was the need for a drink to
settle their frayed nerves.

Brooke sat, stomach churning, but she also felt a sense
of relief. If Blaze, or whomever he might hire, could give
Adam the fright she intended, he might crawl back into
his hole and stay away from their lives for good. She
could only hope as she sunk back into her chair and took a
massive gulp of wine, as soon as Ruby placed the glass in
front of her.

The friends indulged in more drinks and caught up
generally, as they had not seen each other since the
eventful weekend at the races. They laughed as they
recalled the way the day had ended with everyone ending
up pretty pissed, as anticipated. No wonder, since there
had been a free bar. Life had soon got back to normal
and Brooke and Ruby were enjoying the sense of relief
now Blaze had departed. As the wine flowed, they even

started to relish a sense of satisfaction, as they contemplated what Adam had coming to him.

***

Bruce was occupying his usual spot in his control room. He had been spending more and more time surveying Ruby, since he had uncovered the little shoplifting game she had shared with Daisy. He had noticed Ruby and Brooke were out and about and he had decided to tune in. Maybe they were out thieving, he thought.

'Wow, the Rockin' Robin Brew House!' he declared to himself, leaning back in his leather chair. That's a bit young and edgy for you pair, Bruce thought as he mulled over the fact that his edgier days had been sent packing with the arrival of his first daughter Iris, twenty three years ago. He could hear they were talking to a male voice. Bruce concentrated hard to take in the conversation.

Bruce could not be sure who they were talking about, but he was pretty convinced it was Adam, and it sounded like they had just paid some reprobate to rough him up a bit. He was definitely not going to get too upset about the thought of Adam with a broken nose, but he was horrified that Brooke and Ruby were somehow, mixed up in this. What if it backfired? What if this individual did more harm than intended? These kind of people would not hesitate to point the finger directly back at Brooke and Ruby, if it would save their own skin. Bruce held his head in his hands. What the hell was going on with his mates? Had he really been that naïve? Did Ronnie and Arthur know? He was worried for the women, but also worried for himself. Once again, Bruce felt like he was in a world where he simply did not belong.

Chapter 21

18 January

Bruce had now been tracking Arthur's covert meetings with the dark haired woman, who he now knew was Kerri, for a number of weeks. He had spent days pondering what he was going to do about it all. He had finally resolved to take some direct action. He was going to engineer it so that Ruby could 'bump' into them. Bruce was too worried to tell Ruby himself and that course of action felt far too risky, as she would demand to know how he knew. That simply could not happen.

This way, it would all be out in the open, but no one would find out about Bruce's little invasion of their privacy. Bruce was not exactly sure what Ruby knowing about this woman would achieve, but he knew he could not look Ruby in the eye for much longer and continue to live with the amount of guilt that was boring into his very soul.

The plan had been easy to engineer. A spa day for Ruby and Daisy always went down well. Bruce was picking them up but on the way home he would 'have to' drop some hardware off in the neighbouring area – he would do this to coincide with one of Arthur's little liaisons. After tracking Arthur for a number of weeks, he knew exactly the time and the place. It had been so easy to persuade Daisy and Ruby to go on the spa day, a treat for Daisy's birthday and she could choose any friend to take along. Daisy had been torn about who to take, but Bruce had 'suggested' that Ruby needed the break, as she had been working so hard recently. Daisy had agreed, of course, and it was all set up.

The women were all giggles and mellow as Bruce picked them up from the spa hotel at the end of the day. It was in a beautiful rural setting with an abundance of luxurious features: aqua therapy pools, saunas, steam rooms, hot tubs and every treatment imaginable. They had both had manicures, pedicures and massages, together with a very leisurely lunch and rather too much to drink, of course.

'Hello love, thanks so much for picking us up. We've had the most marvellous relaxing day,' Daisy chimed, her cheeks glowing attractively.

'Oh yes, thank you Bruce, much appreciated. I don't think I'm fit to drive anywhere, after all that pampering and Prosecco!' Ruby added.

Bruce smiled but he was feeling nervous. Would his little plan work out? Would Arthur be where he usually was? Would Kerri be there with him? Would Ruby even notice them? His heart was pounding but he was doing his very best to appear normal. This was the first time he was taking some direct action based on his insights and he hoped it would turn out to be the right decision.

'I just need to make a bit of a detour to drop some stuff off on the way. Is that okay, love?' Bruce enquired.

'Yes love, no probs. We're very chilled and happy to wait in the car,' Daisy answered amiably.

244

Daisy and Ruby continued chatting away about the wine on offer in M&S amongst other things and Bruce was relieved that he did not have to make any more small talk.

Fifteen minutes later, they were in another world, an unfamiliar area of run down streets and high rises. Bruce turned onto the high street that was lined with a plethora of tanning salons, vaping shops, kebab houses, tattoo parlours and pound shops. Then there was the café, a modest affair: 'Dina's Diner' was adorned in 1950s style American diner décor, plastic tables and chairs. A Wurlitzer took pride of place in the corner, with old fashioned vinyl singles from a bygone rock and roll era. Waitresses, in red gingham dresses with matching scarfs in their hair, did their best to look cheerful.

Bruce parked up and pretended to rummage in the boot of the car for the hardware he needed to drop off to an 'old mate' in the cut price repair shop. The words 'Len's Den 2' adorned the slightly worn out sign. It looked to Daisy like it sold pretty much every type of hardware and re-conditioned appliance imaginable as she pondered there must be a 'Len's Den 1' somewhere. She shook her head and smiled.

Right on cue, Arthur and the woman appeared from inside the diner. He had his arm gently round her back, guiding her and the little girl, who was holding his hand.

Ruby and Daisy were still chatting, then Daisy looked up. 'Hey, isn't that Arthur over there?' She squinted, puzzled, surely not? 'Yes, yes it is. What's he doing here!'

Ruby sat up and looked over in the direction of Daisy's stare.

Daisy shouted out the window, 'Arthur! What you doing this side of the tracks?'

Arthur looked over to the car and the colour drained from his face. 'Mate…Daisy… Mate….What you doing round here? Arthur gabbled.

'Bruce is just dropping some stuff off to an old mate. We've been to the spa! Bloody brilliant, it was,' Daisy chattered on.

But Ruby had already fully assessed the scene. She had immediately recognised Kerri, who was quietly standing, watching the exchange. Ruby flew out of the car, tears streaming down her face as she pounded over to Arthur, who was now physically shaking, his face an off-white, greyish colour.

'You low life, lying, cheating… what… I just knew… I KNEW IT! You're seeing her again!' she screamed.

'Angel, Angel I'm not…I need to talk to you… I need….' Arthur was trying to find the words but no words came. No words could save him now.

Kerri's little girl was in tears. Kerri was trying to explain, but nothing was making sense to Ruby anymore. Her head was spinning due to a mixture of Prosecco, spa treatments and the shock of the terrible scene unfolding before her. She felt like she was on a spiralling merry-go-round, getting faster and faster and making her feel extremely sick. Ruby suddenly threw up in the gutter.

Daisy sat, open mouthed, watching this totally unforeseen turn of events from the back seat of her plush car. Bruce was back inside at the wheel, saying nothing, but watching the drama play out. He contemplated the series of events that he had orchestrated, the way he had cleverly manipulated the situation due to the special body of knowledge that he possessed. There was something else, a darker, stronger feeling was creeping up on him. What was it? His sphere of influence, a sense of being in control was intoxicating. Yes, that was it. It was the sense of power that he felt. He had engineered this happening. Ruby had needed to know what had been going on with Arthur and Kerri. This was right and proper, what he had done; he convinced himself. Bruce saw himself as a guardian angel and he smiled as he realised that he was really enjoying how his deity like act had made him feel.

***

Back at Delvreton, Ruby sat curled up on Daisy's sofa with tear- streaked cheeks. She cradled a cup of coffee in her hands. 'What am I going to do, Daisy? What the hell am I going to do?'

Chapter 22

24 January

Ruby had spent the last five nights at Daisy's house; she knew it was now time to face the music. Arthur had been texting her non-stop since the incident of Ruby discovering him with Kerri. Ruby did not want to see Arthur at all, but she was missing her dogs Toby and Murray with all her heart and she knew that whatever happened next, she had to have a proper conversation with Arthur at some point. Her daughter Lola was also distraught and even though Lola was a capable, independent young woman, Ruby at least owed it to her to go home and try and sort things out. These reasons were all in addition to Daisy's compassionate hospitality, which Ruby knew she could not take advantage of for much longer. She had already taken liberties staying for so long, but would be eternally grateful.

Ruby took a deep breath as she stared at herself in the mirror. She barely recognised the forlorn face that looked back: sunken, tired eyes from lack of sleep and hours of crying, pallid skin and unwashed hair, scraped back into a loose pony tail. Ruby did not care though. The last thing she felt like doing was dolling herself up.

Ruby sipped the coffee Daisy had kindly left by her bedside, before she had headed out to work. She threw on the track- suit she had been wearing at the spa day. It was the only clothing she had with her, when she insisted on going back to Daisy's house, after the altercation with Arthur in the street. Daisy had kindly given her a new toothbrush and washed through her underwear, so at least she had some standards, she thought, and tried to muster a smile, but she could not even manage a flicker of the lips. What on earth had she become? She sighed to herself. Ruby picked up her bag and phone and, with a heart heavier than a hundred jewellery quarter gold bullions, she painstakingly dialled a taxi.

***

Arthur was already waiting at the front door when Ruby's taxi pulled up. She stepped out into the cold January day. It was minus two, with a wind chill of minus five, the weather presenter had helpfully indicated on the news earlier that morning. Ruby did not even have a coat with her. If she had not been so utterly freezing cold, she may well have just walked in the opposite direction of her home.

Ruby barged past Arthur, dumped her stuff in the hall and went straight over to cuddle Toby and Murray. Their tails were going ten to the dozen with absolutely no comprehension of why Ruby had been away for so long.

Lola peered round the corner of the landing stairs. 'Mum! Thank God you're back. Mum, I know you're so angry right now, but you have to work things through with Dad. Please talk to him.' Lola had tears in her eyes.

'Lola, my angel, I'm sorry I've been away for so long, but I had to get my head straight. You're a grown up now. You understand, right?' Ruby's voice was trembling.

'I know mum, I know. I'm going to nip out. You two need some space.' Lola grabbed her purple, cashmere winter coat and matching bag and headed out in her matching purple fiat 500.

'She's such a considerate young woman,' Arthur stammered.

'Arthur.' Ruby's voice was cold and unemotional.

Arthur wanted to hold his wife in his arms, but knew better than to choose this moment.

'Babe, please come into the kitchen. We need to talk,' he said, trying to keep the pleading tone from his voice.

'We do.' Ruby then managed to utter the fateful words: 'Arthur, I want a divorce.'

***

Tears were forming in Arthur's eyes. 'Ruby, honestly that isn't the answer. You need to understand, Kerri and I are not having an affair. You *have* to believe me.'

'Well, you haven't exactly had the best track record and I know for a fact you had a fling with her years ago, when we separated. What's to say it hasn't been going on all along?' Ruby's voice faltered, as she held back her tears.

'I haven't seen her since we got back together,' Arthur stammered. 'I promise you on Lola's life.'

'Prove it!' Ruby had more conviction in her voice now, still fighting back the tears.

'Well, I guess, I can't prove it, but I can explain why I was with her. Please at least hear me out,' Arthur implored.

'Go on.' Ruby pulled up a chair and sat back expectantly. 'This had better be good,' she threatened.

'Ruby, I don't know how to tell you this but Kerri's daughter Poppy, well...' he paused, taking in a deep breath. 'Well...I'm her father.'

There was a very long silence as the words reverberated around the room, like a pinball bouncing around its glass cabinet. Ruby sat voiceless, totally stunned.

'Ruby, I didn't know about Poppy, until a few weeks ago. Kerri never told me and at first I didn't believe her, but I did the right thing and got a DNA test, after she insisted I was the father. Basically, you and I had already got back together when she found out she was pregnant and by that point, she knew she didn't want me in her life.'

Arthur went on to tell Ruby about Kerri's string of disastrous relationships, settling for an abusive man purely to put food on the table, a relationship which had seen Kerri take countless beatings and psychological abuse. Kerri had eventually managed to escape this man, but skint, starving and desperate, she had contacted Arthur and told him the truth about his status as Poppy's father. Kerri had promised she did not want anything from him long term, just a little bit of help to get her through this rough patch and if he did not want her to, she would not tell Poppy he was her dad. Arthur, had of course, immediately assured Kerri that he would do the right thing by Poppy and that, in time, if Poppy wanted to, he would like to be in her life.

'So, Ruby, that's why I was with Kerri. There is nothing romantic going on at all. I just needed to do the right thing for Poppy.' Arthur sat sullen, waiting for a response.

Ruby's mind was whirring as she took this in. 'Arthur, I, I don't know what to say'. She was feeling devastated by this news, but equally, as the mother of Lola, she could not begin to imagine that any child could be left to starve. In the end, she just about managed to mumble, 'Arthur, I just need some time to process this.'

'Yes, of course, of course, I understand.' he said. 'But please, can you just think about us before you do anything drastic. This doesn't change how I feel about you Rubes. I love you. I have always loved only you and this situation with Kerri should never have happened. But it has, and it turns out I have another daughter and I can't turn my back on her, Rubes.'

Ruby nodded slowly, then dragged herself out of the chair. 'I'm taking a bath Arthur. You can sleep in the spare room tonight.'

Arthur accepted his fate. 'Thank you for hearing me out Ruby. I promise we can work this thing out.'

***

Over the following days, Ruby exchanged only a few curt words with Arthur. He kept trying to talk, but she needed to think. Ruby had also decided to take some time off work, as she could not concentrate on anything much, least of all creating magnificent, diamond jewellery for happily just- engaged couples, brides, grooms and lovers.

Ruby had watched Arthur's every move, since she had been back home. She had checked his phone, his emails, followed him to the supermarket without his awareness, sat on the landing listening to his phone calls, but there was no evidence he was liaising with Kerri. This particular morning she was watching him making breakfast from behind a crack in the door. She eventually entered the kitchen and sat down.

'Was Poppy the little girl with Kerri that day I found you in the street together?' Ruby asked.

Arthur turned to look at Ruby, grateful she was eventually engaging him in conversation.

'Yes, that's her,' he replied quietly, stopping what he was doing and pulling up a chair next to Ruby.

'She looks a bit like you,' Ruby said, with a sadness in her voice. 'You do know this means Lola has a sister she knew nothing about, well a half-sister at least.'

'Yes,' Arthur replied.

'What's she like?' Ruby asked.

'She's cute, you know, but she's not had a good start in life. I am really worried for her Rubes. Kerri isn't a reliable mother. As much as she clearly loves Poppy, she's not really capable of looking after her properly. She has no money to provide the basics and often doesn't even manage to get her to attend school. The first time I met her, Poppy was in a rag of a dress, unwashed and hungry. Her bedroom was a state Ruby, no sheets on a filthy, bare mattress, which it turned out was full of lice. Kerri told me Poppy was sent home from school because she was so filthy at one point. But, that's really no surprise. Kerri can't get it together to get out of bed some days, let alone clean the flat.

Ruby looked horrified. 'How could you leave her in that hell hole?' she asked, shaking her head.

Arthur explained everything that had happened on Boxing Day, and that Poppy was now with Barry and his wife under their foster care. Ruby looked relieved.

Arthur continued to tell Ruby what awful conditions Poppy had endured, before he saved her. 'There was never any food to speak of. I think the only meal Poppy had was when she was at school, when she actually attended. Otherwise, it was just take out burgers and fries at the weekends and holidays. Once, I saw Poppy taking a piece of stale cake out of the bin. Poor lamb must have been desperate to eat out of the trash. After that, I regularly went round with supplies. Often, Kerri was no-where to be seen, most likely down the pub, but God knows how long she'd left Poppy alone for, long enough for Poppy to be starving. It's heart breaking Rubes.' A tear rolled down Arthur's face.

'Another thing Rubes, Kerri drinks, and I don't mean like we do at parties and the weekends. She drinks vodka at ten in the morning, stacks of it and I've found her

254

comatose on the sofa, more times than I can count. Kerri has very questionable taste in men and I know Poppy has seen and heard things no six year old should see. Kerri's last suitor was a right idiot, the wife beater type. I'm sure he knocked Kerri about. I think he's in prison now for GBH.'

Ruby had listened intently and was clearly drawn into Poppy's story. 'I honestly don't know what to say, Arthur. I don't think I can get involved in this. This is your mess, your responsibility.' However, as she spoke, her heart was breaking for this little girl, despite the circumstances of her existence. Ruby knew she needed to be strong and help somehow. But could she really open up her heart to this child, without seeing a reminder of Arthur with Kerri, every time she looked into Poppy's eyes?

***

Bruce was in the kitchen with Daisy.

'How's Ruby?' He tentatively enquired.

'Oh, not so good,' Daisy replied, staring Bruce right in the eyes. He suddenly felt a pang of guilt. 'Bruce,' she cautiously asked. Did you know Arthur was going to be with Kerri that day you drove us from the Spa? I mean, I just can't get my head around how coincidental it all was, us bumping into him with Kerri like that.'

'Err, no love. How could I have possibly known?' Bruce lied. He was beginning to realise the magnitude of what he had engineered that day. Seeing Ruby so utterly desolate had been tough to watch and he certainly had not bargained for her staying at their place for almost a week. Should he have left well alone? He was starting to think that maybe he should have. Was he as bad as his lying wife, who steals, his gambling friend Brooke who hides her winnings, or indeed, Arthur, who has a secret child he was keeping from Ruby?

'Well, okay then,' Daisy replied, still watching him. 'I suppose there was no way you could've possibly known, right Bruce?' She paused, as her eyes burrowed into his soul. Silence. 'Well, I've got a few errands to run. I'll be back in about half an hour. I thought we could have Thai take out tonight.'

'Sounds good love,' Bruce answered, studying his wife's eyes. For a moment, he felt almost like she was onto his secret game. Could she have found out that he had been spying on her and their friends? Of course not, he reassured himself and quickly brushed the thought away.

Bruce sat, quietly contemplating his recent actions, whilst Daisy ran her errands. Maybe Daisy did know what he was up to. Maybe it was just his guilty conscience. He had so been enjoying the new- found knowledge about his friends and family, but right now he was feeling a certain sadness. What joy could he possibly find in contributing to the potential split of two of his closest mates? He felt utterly wretched and thoroughly ashamed. 'Dear God, what have I become?' He said aloud, shaking his head and sighing deeply.

**

Ruby was sitting at the kitchen table, staring into space. Arthur was at work and Lola at college. But even though Ruby had the place to herself, she simply had to get out. Since finding out about Poppy, it had felt like the walls were closing in on her, her life spiralling out of control. She grabbed her coat and bag and headed into town.

Ruby toured around a few of her favourite shopping haunts, but just could not muster the energy to try anything on. She wandered around aimlessly for half an hour or so, her mind whizzing with images: Poppy, Arthur, Kerri, Arthur with Kerri and back to Poppy and her desperate situation. She tried to blank the thoughts out. She found herself wandering into her favourite department store, and stood looking at the Dior Couture lipsticks. There was literally every shade, from the brightest red to the palest pink. She picked up a sample and swiped the bright red across the back of her hand. The assistant was serving another customer and totally wrapped up in demonstrating the latest concealer. Ruby ran her fingers over the rainbow of colours, then gently picked up a colour called 'Paris' and dropped it into her handbag. She lingered a while, picking up a few other lip colours, before gently placing them back on the display and moving along to the perfumes.

A display of Penhaligon's perfumes caught her eye. She had not seen them before and the packaging lured her in. There were dozens of subtly different coloured scents in vintage style bottles, each adorned with a unique gold cap in the shape of a different animal or bird: a cat, an owl, a puma, a bull, a stag, to name but a few. Ruby stopped at a rose coloured bottle, brandishing the head of a wolf as the cap. 'The Coveted Duchess Rose', the label proudly declared. She carefully undid the cap and spritzed a couple of times onto her wrist. It smelt divine. Just for that split second, her troubles were forgotten. She looked at the price tag: two hundred and four pounds for seventy- five millilitres. 'Jeez,' she said under her breath. Then, with a covert glance around the room, she furtively pushed a film wrapped, boxed bottle into her tote bag. Maybe she was feeling a little extra cocky today, or maybe she was just downright depressed, but something compelled her to stay a while longer. She caught the assistant's eye.

'Excuse me,' Ruby said as she approached a stunning looking perfume assistant, who was sporting an amazing 1970's retro, weave hairstyle. 'I'd like some advice on these wonderful perfumes please, Sarah.' Ruby was feeling extra bold and addressed the assistant by her name as she noticed the golden, embellished name- tag.

The assistant beamed at Ruby.

'Of course madam. Do you have a particular scent type you're seeking? Floral, fresh or more musk? Our Yasmine is very popular,' she paused, holding a tester bottle with a cat's head over a tiny slip of paper.

'Oh, yes please. I'd like to smell the musky one,' Ruby grinned.

The assistant went on spraying and spritzing onto various test papers, with just about every scent on the stand. Ruby was enjoying the attention and continued to 'ooh and aah,' as each scent diffused into her nostrils.

Sarah, the assistant, did the usual hard sell, about how unique these fragrances were, how she adored and used them herself and how many positive reviews they had received. This was despite the fact that the display area was now so heavily perfumed with all the mixed scents, Ruby thought it smelt like a monkey's wedding.

Ruby opted for something called 'Clandestine Clara' that proudly sported an embellished golden peacock's head. An 'exotic spicy' choice, the assistant assured Ruby as she added two hundred and four pounds onto her credit card. It felt delicious that she had purchased the perfume, knowing full- well that the second rose scent had already made its way into her bag, along with the designer lipstick. Ruby watched the assistant carefully tissue wrap and bow the box, placing it into a designer paper bag and adding yet another bow to secure the handles, before passing it to Ruby and wishing her a good evening.

Ruby proudly strolled towards the exit. Just as she was about to leave through the revolving doors, a security guard appeared.

'Excuse me madam, I'm afraid you'll need to come with me. We have reason to believe you have goods on your person that have not been paid for. Step this way please.'

Ruby's body turned to ice.

***

Two and a half hours later Ruby was sitting on a cold, plastic chair, in a small, grey room at the back of the store. The security guard and Sarah, the shop assistant from the perfume counter, together with two police officers were with her. Sarah was no longer beaming. They were reviewing the CCTV footage of Ruby stealing the lipstick and the perfume. This had been utterly pointless in Ruby's mind, since they had already searched her bag and retrieved both items, with no receipts or evidence of payment. Why were they torturing her with this footage?

'Madam, we need to make it very clear that this store is now at liberty to press charges for shoplifting.' A police-woman was talking. 'From our records, we can see that this is your first offence. However, as the items in question were of significant value, the worst case scenario is that you could end up with a prison sentence.'

'What?' Ruby's voice trembled. She had never, ever thought for a second she would get caught, but even if she had, she had assumed it would be a ticking off by a security guard. She would simply give the items back and that would be it. But here she was, listening to a police woman talking about prison! At that moment Ruby burst into tears. Through long sobs, she told her entire sorry story about how she had just found out about Poppy, that she had not been thinking straight and most of all, that she was so sorry. She just didn't know what had come over her.

After another hour of mortifying questioning, a very stern caution and the realisation that she almost landed herself with a criminal record, Ruby had, finally, been free to go home. She left the grey room, feeling utterly humiliated but eternally grateful that she had not ended up at the police station, or worse, incarcerated in a police cell overnight.

Tear stained streaks across her face, Ruby had woefully headed home. When she arrived, she gratefully fell into Arthur's arms as she retold him the entire, sorry story. Or at least, she just about managed to tell him, when her sobbing abated, enough to permit her to talk through all of the details of her dreadful experience. Finally, it seemed that Ruby was ready to tame some of her wilder predilections. The thought of Poppy entering her life was certainly part of this, but she was also very much aware of having crossed a line, when she suggested entering into that dark, ominous deal with Blaze. She had a very bad feeling and really wished that she and Brooke had left Blaze's 'services' well alone.

Chapter 23

25 January

It was just before nine, when Frankie checked the time and realised she needed to make a move. She had managed to clear the bulk of her emails so she was good to go. She spent a few moments discussing her diary with Sam her PA, before leaving the head office to attend an appointment at one of the primary schools she worked with on the Felstead estate.

Frankie gave all of the schools she worked with a great service and she was a 'hands on' educational psychologist. She was highly visible, often working closely alongside the support staff, teachers, middle and senior leaders. She was frequently in classrooms and regularly observed the children at lunchtime and break times, checking the way they interacted with each other, the lunchtime supervisors and their teachers. She had a particularly keen eye for those children who were well behind in their learning, the loners, those subjected to bullying and the bullies themselves. She treated them all with the compassion and discipline they needed to succeed. As Frankie watched the staff, she smiled as she could clearly see how much they also cared for these pupils. 'Tough loving', was what Frankie called her approach and that is what was happening here with incredible results. She genuinely cared for these children and made a point of meeting and greeting them on the gate in the morning and saying goodbye at the end of the day – knowing as many names as possible, their achievements, their interests, their ambitions and their struggles.

Frankie's mind wandered back to the last board meeting she had been invited to attend and smiled as the progress of the new safeguarding plans was acknowledged. As chief psychologist, she had led on plans to support school leaders in addressing some major safeguarding concerns. The Chair, Martin, who had managed a deluge of challenging questions with great aptitude, focused the committee's attention on a sad glut of cases in two primary schools on the East side of the city. This was a particularly tough area and it was clear that social services' capacity was stretched to the limit. Five cases of extreme neglect were cited and Frankie had been tasked with bringing back a full report on these to the next meeting.

Frankie had sat at her desk, absorbing each heart breaking case in minute detail. Her eyes scrolled down the names, trying to picture the pupils: Elijah aged five, Poppy aged six, Liam aged seven, Roman, aged four and Miracle, aged eight. The case notes were truly shocking and Frankie was determined to ensure that these children got the very best service from her. Today, she was checking in on Elijah and Poppy; she would drop by the other school to see the other three pupils the next day.

Frankie pulled up at Park Hill School, a few minutes before the time she had arranged to meet the headteacher. She shivered as she got out of the car and felt the onslaught of the harsh January weather. As she walked to the school's main entrance, she scanned the area, noting the high rise flats that dominated the skyline. Their slit like windows were like hostile eyes, glowering at the school, the squat building that provided a much needed sanctuary for the four hundred and fifty children that attended there. Most of the children lived in these flats, so there shouldn't be any attendance or punctuality problems, Frankie mused. However, that was not the case, as many of the parents could not even manage to get themselves dressed, let alone ensure that their children were up and ready to start the school day. This was the situation for one of the children she was checking on today. Poppy's mother had serious issues with alcohol and domestic abuse but at least the child was currently in foster care, apparently.

Elijah was a different case. His mother had learning difficulties, but she was coping well now it seemed, now that the right level of support was being provided by social services to enhance the school's excellent provision.

Frankie was soon walking the school with Ted, the young headteacher, who was so passionate about providing the very best education and care for all of the children in his school. Recently appointed, Ted was exactly the sort of head that this school and community needed. Frankie complimented Ted on how great the school looked. Bold colours typified the beautiful wall art that told captivating stories about key historical figures down one corridor. Another wall was full of quotes from children's books, brought to life by vibrant illustrations. Ted beamed with pride. Frankie and Ted clearly shared the same values and they chatted, as they walked, about how these children needed a leg up in life. They needed the best education possible to set them on the right path, a path that would lead them off this estate, one day. Frankie felt privileged that she could play such a valuable part in this mission.

First stop was a year one class for Frankie to observe Elijah. The experienced middle- aged teacher oozed care for all of the children in her class. She had untamed, curly hair, was a little plump and had an arresting smile. It was clear that the children loved her and were clamouring to answer her questions to receive a merit stamp in their planners. It was also clear that Elijah was well on her radar for some extra care and attention. He sat on a table at the front of the classroom, under her watchful eye. As the stood at the side of the room, Ted explained that Elijah was gradually growing in confidence and that he did not seem to have any learning difficulties. His progress had just been delayed because his mother had not been able to stimulate him properly. Now, both Elijah and his mother were really benefitting from help from the school's parent liaison officer and from the right level of family support from the designated social worker. Frankie looked forward to her first session with this little chap.

Ted and Frankie thanked Mrs Sullivan, who beamed back at them and they set off across the school to find the year two class, where Poppy resided. Like Elijah, Poppy now seemed much happier since the foster placement with Mr and Mrs McGrath. Prior to this, Poppy had been quiet and withdrawn. Attendance had been a major issue and when she had made it in, she had been late. What had really concerned Ted and the designated safeguarding lead, was Poppy's dishevelled appearance, which had sadly led to some spiteful treatment from some of the other children. It was not surprising that Poppy had not wanted to go to school, which tied in well with her mother's agenda of staying in bed, most of the day.

The year two class was just as bright, cheerful and welcoming as the previous classroom. A young newly qualified teacher was reading a story animatedly. Each one of the children was enthralled as Mr Jones moderated his voice skilfully to build up to the climax of the witch swooping down on her broomstick. The tension was then released by a well-placed funny moment and all of the children shrieked in pure delight. Following Ted's whispered guidance, Frankie's eyes alighted on a little girl sitting on the front row in the carpeted 'story area'. Her thick auburn hair was neatly tied back and her uniform was perfect. Suddenly, her hand shot up in response to Mr Jones' question and she confidently told him that 'enchanted' was an adjective. Poppy beamed as Mr Jones praised her and promised to award her a merit stamp when they all went back to their tables before lunch.

As they walked back to Ted's office, the headteacher told Frankie about the transformation Poppy was experiencing into the happy little girl that she appeared to be. This had happened in a short amount of time, but everyone knew how skilful and experienced the foster mother was. Ted was sure that Poppy's confidence would continue to grow. He knew that there was a full social services review taking place on Poppy's mother. His main concern was about what might happen, if Poppy was placed back with her mother. It would be so sad to see her regress considering the great strides forward that she had made. Ted hoped that Frankie's formal assessment of Poppy would confirm his views of this child's rapid development.

Frankie checked on a few other matters and then she left Ted's office, feeling reassured from her visit. This school was rapidly improving under Ted's leadership and the children in his care were all the better for it. She resolved to do everything possible to ensure that she could apply her expertise to support this passionate and committed headteacher.

Frankie drove back to the office well in time for her afternoon meetings. As she drove, she listened to the weather report and, as suspected, it seemed that heavy snow was forecast. She wasn't surprised, given the searing cold wind she had just experienced. Frankie resolved to make some contingency plans with her colleagues as it would be sensible for them all to work from home, if the weather worsened. Frankie smiled to herself, contemplating a 'snow day' and the possibility of a snowy walk with Dexter maybe? Stop it, she thought to herself, still smiling. If there was a snow day, she would have loads of work to get through at home and she should not entertain such frivolous ideas. She continued to smile though, as thoughts of her new relationship always had that effect on her.

Chapter 24

4 February

The next day, true to the weather report, snow had fallen heavily, with no let up and more was forecast. Frankie drove home extremely carefully from her Birmingham office. She was a highly experienced and competent driver, further supported by her top of the range Audi Q8 but she was still relieved to pull onto her driveway as you never knew if other, less well equipped cars might just stop dead and block the roads. She smiled to herself as she had also enjoyed taking a cheeky call from Dexter suggesting that he should come over on a 'school night' and get totally 'shitfaced' with her since she did not need to get up at her crazy normal get up time, just for once. Why not? She thought to herself. Work was really tough at the moment, dealing with a range of new contracts, new clients and a heap of new 'key performance indicators'. She stretched her arms above her head and took a moment to savour the warm luxury of her car, before braving the elements and she could not help but smile at her good fortune. She was looking forward to being a bit 'naughty' mid-week as this was never normally an option.

Frankie had sensibly changed into her Hunter wellies just before leaving the office and she pulled up the fur-lined hood of her parka, all ready to make a run for it to the front door. Charlie was staying with her parents that evening; she would normally pick him up on her way home but her mum had advised that she should not worry about that tonight in view of the shocking conditions. At least, Dexter would take her mind off missing her gorgeous boy; she smiled. All of her family and friends were totally dog mad, so she knew Charlie would enjoy a night with his Granny and Grandpa, where he would be treated just as well as the most spoilt of kids.

As soon as she walked into her hallway, Frankie sighed. The house was a perfect temperature and the lights were stylishly dimmed thanks to the high tech Apps technology everyone seemed to have these days. She was particularly grateful to Bruce for setting this up for her with his super high tech know how that she readily admitted she knew nothing about.

Frankie checked her watch and was pleased that she had time for a quick shower and change before she rustled up some supper for her special mid-week encounter. She was not quite sure what Dexter had meant, when he had said he felt like pushing the boundaries a bit and showing her a bit more of his real self. Sex had been very good in their short time together but refreshingly straightforward so she hoped he wasn't a secret '50 shades' devotee. No, Dexter was a caring, thoughtful lover so she was not sure what he had meant. Maybe some dodgy cocktails and some wild dancing perhaps as they let go of their inhibitions on a 'school night'. He was certainly a great mover, she remembered from the New Year's do and his stint as lead singer with 'Dexter and the Dudes' gave him that sexy rock star swagger that she and many other women clearly appreciated.

Within twenty minutes, Frankie was ready for the evening ahead. In her beloved skinny jeans and black sweatshirt, she was feeling relaxed as she set to work on prepping a seafood linguine for later, tossing some salad and slicing some of the delicious artisan bread from town. She took a glug of her favourite white wine and found herself dancing happily to the soft rhythms of 'Nirvana unplugged', a particular favourite of hers. Everything was now prepped and the heavy snowfall provided a calming, tranquil effect as Frankie was momentarily mesmerised by the thick flakes she observed, cascading gently, in balletic grace outside her kitchen windows. It looked so beautiful out there serving to heighten the sanctuary of her warm home. Just perfect for her evening in with Dex. This New Year had started so well and Frankie felt a strong feeling of positivity wash over her.

Little did she know that Adam would set off from school in about an hour, but instead of heading out of Delvreton, he would point his car in the other direction and head across town towards Frankie's place. His Jaguar was four wheel drive so the snowy conditions posed no barrier to his plans. Little did Frankie know that Adam frequently drove past her place, so he could keep an eye on her.

At exactly the time he had said, Dexter arrived in his Range Rover Velar and came into the house like a whirlwind, shattering the calm ambience Frankie had been savouring. He deposited a Waitrose bag of Champagne onto the granite worktop and handed Frankie an expensive box of chocolates and a lavish bouquet of flowers. He was more animated than usual but Frankie put that down to the excitement of the snow and the midweek rendezvous. She was also absolutely delighted with her gifts.

Frankie and Dexter quickly knocked back a couple of glasses of Champagne and they were soon dancing vigorously to AC/DC like a couple of giddy teenagers.

'Bloody hell!' Frankie exclaimed, 'I can't believe I'm doing this on a Wednesday night.' She poured two more glasses of Champagne and she found herself being swept up by Dexter into a fast- paced jive. He turned the music up, even louder and started an over exaggerated impression of Angus Young, seizing a broom from the utility to use as a guitar, much to Frankie's delight. As he did so, he drank even more Champagne, straight from the bottle, further enhancing the rock star, errant image.

'That's brilliant,' she laughed as he was still doing his impression. 'But if we don't get some food inside us soon, we will be totally smashed...and the night is still young,' she laughed. 'Be back in a few moments. I'm desperate for the loo.'

Whilst Frankie was away, Dexter quickly took out a packet of white powder from his jeans pocket. He deftly cut a line of coke on the kitchen table and snorted greedily, sighing appreciatively as the drug instantly hit home. Frankie appeared just a moment later.

'Forget the food, I want you first,' Dexter said huskily, pulling Frankie towards him and kissing her passionately, pushing her against the kitchen wall. 'I want to be inside you.' Before she could say a word, he had removed her sweatshirt and had unhooked her bra. He started kissing her breasts frantically, before dropping to his knees in front of her, pulling down her jeans and thong, instructing her to cast her jeans aside and he pushed his tongue inside her. He then did truly incredible things that Frankie had never experienced before. Dexter stopped for a second and smiled up at her, then continued his mission as waves of pure physical delight washed over her entire body.

Frankie groaned, her head flung back, her eyes closed as her hands raked through Dexter's thick, dark hair pushing his head into her groin. So engrossed were they that neither of them noticed a shadow pass in front of the kitchen window, followed by several flashes in quick succession. The snow had been so captivating that Frankie had not closed the blinds as she normally would have done; this could have been the biggest mistake of her life.

Faster and faster, Dexter worked his magic. Frankie gasped as a surge of ecstasy overcame her. Within seconds, Dexter was on his feet, trousers round his ankles, lifting Frankie slightly against the wall as he entered her and moved rhythmically. Frankie grabbed his buttocks, screaming as he too reached his climax of extreme pleasure, ramped up considerably by the cocaine in his bloodstream.

'Fuck,' Frankie said, sliding down the wall. 'What was that?' she gasped as she took a moment before getting up to collect her discarded clothes and pulled on her jeans.

'If you don't know that, you need to attend some of your kids' sex education lessons,' Dexter laughed. 'God, that shit is good and I need more. I'm comfortable with you now,' he said, heading for the table and removing a wrapper from his jeans' pocket.

Frankie could not quite process what she was seeing for a few moments, her thinking dulled somewhat from the alcohol. Then she realised that Dexter was actually snorting a line of coke, right in front of her from her kitchen table and she didn't like what she was witnessing. A plethora of conflicting, confusing thoughts crowded her head as the realisation of what was happening hit her like a juggernaut.

Just as she was about to say something, there were four loud, insistent knocks at the front door.

'Shit!' Dexter exclaimed, hurriedly hiding the evidence.

'Is everything out of the way?' Frankie hissed, her eyes darting round the room, images of a police raid and the end to her career in one fell swoop. She walked tentatively to the door as the knocking recommenced and then a forceful kick followed.

'Who's there?' she shouted, her heart hammering.

'Who do you think?' shouted Adam. 'Let me in. I think you need to because I've seen it all,' he shouted again. 'You don't want the neighbours hearing me, do you?'

'Oh no! Why are you here?' Frankie simply could not believe that Adam would show up and at the worst possible moment imaginable.

' I came to make sure you were okay, now I've found out all about that low life you're shagging and I've seen more than I ever wanted to see!' Adam shouted. 'Let me in or I'll raise merry hell, I swear.'

Dexter came to join Frankie. He was clearly wired now and unsteady on his feet, as he had necked nearly two bottles of Champagne – good coke had that effect on him.

'Let him in, or he'll attract too much attention and we don't want the filth here,' he urged Frankie.

She opened the door and Adam burst in.

'I knew you needed looking after,' Adam almost shouted at Frankie. 'You left me for him! This low life. I thought you had more sense and taste than this.' Adam gestured towards Dexter, a derisory, angry expression distorting his features. You're the stone head everyone said you are. I've been watching you,' he said, lunging towards Dexter and pushing him hard on his shoulder.

Dexter stumbled backwards. 'Don't fucking touch me, you mad fuck,' he slurred, as he tried to stabilise himself, before lunging back at Adam, but the alcohol and the drugs made him far from stable on his feet. Adam came back at him again and punched Dexter in the face.

Time seemed to slow down for several moments as Frankie watched the scene before her. It was as if everything was happening in slow motion, events unfolding that were so incongruous in her decent, civilised world. She just could not accept what was taking place in her beautiful home, in her orderly life. She was disconnected somehow from it all, just for a matter of seconds and found herself fixating on the falling snow, so white, quiet and pure as if offering her some sort of solace. Then she snapped back into her terrible reality as she tried to find some sense in the ranting and shouting.

Dexter was holding his nose and oh God, there was blood. Adam was still firing out his threats to both of them it seemed as he was now, thankfully, heading for the front door, muttering something about evidence – she wasn't sure what he meant by that. Then there was silence for what seemed like an age but was probably only a matter of seconds. Frankie found herself taking deep, sharp breaths as she realised that she was shaking uncontrollably.

'Are you okay?' she asked Dexter tentatively and was a little surprised to see him on his phone.

'Yeah, just get the fucking car round here now!' he shouted.

'God, what are you going to do?' Frankie pleaded, so worried that he would go after Adam; her world was already in tatters and she just could not bear to contemplate anything else tonight, a night that she would never forget.

'I'm getting out of this madness. I'll tell you something though. That prick is lucky I was out of it, or I'd have killed him. The pathetic, little twat. He has stepped way over the mark and he will have it coming to him, just you wait.' Dexter spat out the words as he noticed the headlights lighting up Frankie's drive.

'It's our kid, Jake, and I need to get out of here. I'll call you.' Dexter did a quick sweep of the kitchen table, and ran out of the house, still a little unsteady on his feet.

With that, Dexter had gone, quick as a flash. His younger brother picked him up and whisked him away from the mess of that night.

Frankie was stuck though, right in the middle of a whole heap of trouble. She waited for the sound of the powerful engine to die away and then slumped into a kitchen chair looking at the three empty Champagne bottles, the only evidence of the disastrous events that had just taken place. Despite having consumed about a bottle of wine, she felt so alert, so sober; it was unreal, that overwhelming feeling of dread as she tried to stop her hands from shaking and to calm her breathing, which had quickened again.

Meanwhile, Adam had just pulled up outside his brother's house. He had somehow managed to calm his breathing down too – Frankie was not the only one. He was so relieved that he was back safe now as he couldn't recall his journey back and the snow was still driving down hard. That meant the roads were deserted. He'd had no idea the evening could have turned out like it had. When he decided to drive past Frankie's place, a regular occurrence, he had not really expected to see the black Range Rover on her drive. He had just got into the habit of keeping an eye on her as old habits die hard and he wasn't really sure where his surveillance of her might lead. Maybe it was the haunting atmosphere of the snow that had led him to park his car up the street, double back and decide to take a peep through the kitchen window. He had been drawn to it by the loud rock music, so out of place on a mid-week evening in a house on this very respectable middle class estate. He was curious to see just what was taking place inside and what he had seen had taken his breath away.

After the drama that had unfolded, Adam had sprinted out of Frankie's place, unsure whether Dexter would have come after him as he had a reputation for being a thug. Adam smiled, pleased that he had thumped the bastard and safe in the knowledge that Dexter would have to stay away from him given what he had on him. He scrolled through the photos on his phone grimacing at the ones of Frankie and Dexter against the kitchen wall but he smiled at the image of the kitchen table in the foreground. It was clear to see: a small plastic bag of white powder on the kitchen table, clear as day. The Champagne bottles added perfectly to the scene of debauchery. He had so many options for how he could use this to his advantage and he knew he would enjoy the days to come. Once again, he had absolute control over that bitch Frankie, and that was a very good feeling indeed.

Frankie had no idea she had sat in that kitchen chair for so long, the whole evening in fact, but the sharp chill suddenly roused her from her very deep and dark thoughts. She realised the heating had gone off and for the first time since the debacle, she looked at her watch and saw that it was past eleven. She could not be bothered to move. Her mind had explored all the nooks and crannies of her current situation and she concluded that it was not a good place to be. How could everything change in an instant? How could life go from being pretty damned good to bloody terrible? It had all turned on a moment; life really was on a knife- edge, she mused and she had just crashed and burned. Clichés were helpful at such times for a reason.

Her mind was still racing, going back over events: before Adam had arrived it had started to go wrong. She would never allow drugs into her home and there she was having passionate sex with a man who was drunk and high! And Adam saw it all! This was the stuff of nightmares. God knows what Adam would do, but she knew that her future was not looking at all rosy. It was so bad that she had not even picked up the phone to call Brooke, Ruby or Daisy. She wouldn't know where to start if she tried to share her experience. It was all too raw at the moment.

Frankie heaved herself up from the chair, her teeth chattering. She grabbed a glass and a bottle and headed upstairs to bed. There was no way she would get a wink of sleep without the help of a trusted bottle of quality brandy. This bottle was the only friend she could confide in right now; she did not even have her beloved Charlie to snuggle up to.

Sleep she did, eventually, and Frankie woke to the sound of the buzzing of her phone. Shit! It was her PA who had called and it was ten thirty in the morning. Panic seized her as she registered a very thick head, sandpaper dry mouth and a leaden heart as the evening before played back to her like a series of larger than life stills in a film. This film was a thriller and a tragedy wrapped up in one and she really did not want the starring role that she had. Frankie dragged herself out of bed and pulled up the blind. Good, at least Dexter's Range Rover was gone. She assumed Dexter's brother had driven him back at some point that morning to pick up the car. At least Dexter hadn't knocked on the door, as she definitely did not want to see him.

All members of her team were working from home for the day due to the snow. Therefore, no one would know that she had got up so late, thank God. Frankie called Sam back and lied about having been on work calls since first thing and just missing Sam's call as she had gone to get a much needed mid-morning coffee... if only Sam knew. Frankie shuddered. Sam had no reason whatsoever to doubt Frankie's story as, until last night, Frankie was the perfect boss and the consummate professional. What if it all came crashing down because of just one crazy night? These thoughts bombarded Frankie as she tried to keep calm and converse with Sam as normal about the likelihood of the Executive Team meeting taking place that evening given the weather conditions.

Frankie was managing quite well considering and then she froze as Sam ended the conversation with an after-thought... Something about a client of hers at Delvreton High needing to talk to her urgently. Frankie kept her tone calm and reassured Sam that she would return the call that morning. The conversation was over and Frankie fell back on her bed, staring up at the ceiling and wishing she could wind the clock back, just twenty four hours would do.

Reluctantly and with a heavy heart, Frankie reached for her phone and dialled the direct line number for Patricia, Adam's PA and Frankie's friend. She had to find out what Adam was planning for her; at least, she would know her fate then. Frankie could not bring herself to call Dexter and was not really surprised that he had made no contact with her. She was still reeling from the fact that he had brought a class 'A' drug into her house and that she had had depraved sex with him, when he was high. How could she have been so stupid? How could she have failed to see the signs? She should have sent him packing.

***

After a hectic morning sorting out the final technical details of a new contract, Bruce sipped his coffee and decided that he deserved a bit of a break. He did a cursory check of his surveillance system, quickly scanning the footage from his friends' home security cameras. Even on a weeknight, it was amazing what you could happen upon. He certainly was not disappointed when he alighted on the footage from Frankie's home. Open mouthed, he watched the events unfold and did a double take on several occasions. Alcohol, drugs, sex and a fight. Bloody hell, Frankie, Bruce thought to himself. What have you gone and done now? He looked at the live camera feed but realised that she was not in any of the downstairs rooms. He was not surprised as she must have a hangover from hell and probably not at all keen to face the day, after what had happened. He switched on his listening app, curious to hear any of her conversations, following the aftermath. He was enthralled by what he heard.

***

Patricia was clearly surprised to hear from Frankie as she was not expecting to hear from her that day. Frankie had, of course, been in contact with Adam during the working day but she had always used his personal, mobile number until the relationship had ended last month. Frankie made up some lame reason for the call but it was clear that Patricia did not believe her. Nevertheless, she put the call through to her boss.

'Good morning!' Adam's chirpy up-beat tone signalled the trouble she was expecting. 'Wondered when you would call. It's almost midday but then you must have one hell of a headache,' he laughed, clearly enjoying himself. 'Thought you'd have been at your office, when I called earlier. Our school is shut but most of the staff managed to get in. Ah, but you had a really heavy night didn't you?'

'Just cut to the chase,' Frankie said curtly. 'Why do you want to talk to me?'

'What?' Adam said, hamming up his surprise. 'After what I've seen! The crime I saw take place! Well, don't you think I have a responsibility to make sure you are fit to work with children and young people?'

'You total bastard,' Frankie said quietly, her heart racing, as she saw her whole career flash before her.

'I think you need to be a whole lot nicer and more respectful to me, if you know what's good for you.' Adam's tone had changed; it was now sharp and tinged with threat. 'Unblock my number now so that I can contact you whenever I need to and you had better answer my calls. I haven't quite decided what to do for the best. I need to think about it but, rest assured, you will be the first to know.'

'Okay,' Frankie said quietly, trying to sound strong but Adam could detect a sense of desperation in her voice and he was enjoying himself.

'Bye for now. Have a lovely day and I'll call you later,' Adam said in a sing- song, sarcastic voice as he hung up.

Frankie hung up too, putting her head in her hands. Less than twenty- four hours after that dreadful night and Adam was already making her suffer. She had no idea what to do but knew she needed some help. Her hand trembling, she dialled Brooke.

Chapter 25

5 February

The day after the heavy snowfall, Daisy decided to head out for a run, as far as the conditions would allow, of course. She had managed quite well on the Squirrel's Nook circuit as the temperature had started to rise and the path was no longer icy, just slushy and very muddy. As she headed back on to the streets, she decided she would swing by to say hi to Brooke. On arrival, Ronnie was in his garage working up the latest new creation for their home.

'Hi Daise, how you doing?' Ronnie smiled.

'I'm good thanks, slightly hungover. The snow got us in the mood for some of Bruce's spiced rum and I always have to refrain on a Friday evening because of work. So, we had an impromptu, cheeky little session,' Daisy chuckled. 'Is Brooke in? Not that I don't adore your company Ron, but I wanted to talk to her about plans for our next weekend treat. We all need something else to focus on, now that we've been to the races.'

'She's actually nipped to her parents, so you've just got me. Sorry Daisy, second prize,' Ron laughed. 'Come in, out of the cold. Fancy a cuppa while you wait? She'll be back soon.'

Ron drifted into the adjoining kitchen leaving Daisy for a moment in his 'man cave'. She scanned the rows of tools, equipment and boxes of kit: saws, hammers, chisels and screwdrivers, boxes and boxes of tiny nails, large nails, screws, washers, nuts and bolts. She couldn't even name most of the objects. She ran her hand over the panel of chisels, from a tiny nail file size to one that looked like it was for elephant toes. There were paint pots in all manner of colours, brushes, rollers, drawers full of tapes, wires, sealants and grout. Ronnie certainly catered for every eventuality! She hovered over a box containing mallets and hammers and she picked one up. It weighed a ton, far more than she had expected. She wielded it like a lumberjack, just as Ronnie reappeared.

'Suits you Daise!' he laughed. 'Have hammer, will travel!' he teased her.

'Oops, sorry Ronnie, I was just fascinated by all this kit!' Daisy carefully placed the hammer back in its box.

Ronnie ushered Daisy into the kitchen breakfast bar after she had taken off her muddy trainers. With coffee and tea in hands, the conversation started to flow. Talk of the kids, holiday plans, Daisy's fitness business and the conversation naturally turned to Bruce.

'How is Bruce anyway? I haven't seen him at the Otter's for a bit,' Ronnie enquired.

'Oh, you know, he's always bloomin' working these days, I feel like I hardly ever see him.' Unexpectedly, Daisy started to well up.

'Hey, hey, what's the matter?' Ronnie put a hand on Daisy's shoulder.

'Oh Ron, I don't think Bruce is all that well, you know. He's just obsessed with work and constantly in his office. He seems distracted and God, I can't even believe I'm telling you this, but I even started to worry he was having an affair at one point.'

'Not a chance!' Ronnie's reply was full of conviction. 'You and Bruce are just perfect.'

'Well, hardly,' she forced a smile. 'You know, we are in many ways, I suppose. I've always been so happy and so has Bruce, as far as I know, but just lately he's on those bloody computer screens, none stop.' As Daisy started to share her concerns, she actually felt better and at the same time, she made a mental note to make sure she booked them a date night in the diary, away from home and kids at a posh restaurant or somewhere nice, maybe even a weekend away. Yes, that's what they needed, some quality time together.

'What the heck does he do in there all the time?' Ron asked.

'He has a lot of conference calls, meetings, resolution of IT issues and dozens of emails. I just think maybe this new direction for his business is causing so much more pressure than he ever imagined. We both thought that pulling out of the US business would make life so much easier, but the opposite seems to be happening. The hours he's been putting in has just got ridiculous.'

'Well Daisy, since we're sharing, you know none of us are perfect,' Ron added. Brooke is spending way too much time on her betting sites. I know she loves the horses, but I do think she spends too much money on it. You know me, Mr Sensible,' he smiled. 'So you see, not everyone can be perfect all the time.'

'I'm pretty sure Brooke has it under control,' Daisy urged, but in all honesty Daisy had been rather surprised by the amounts Brooke seemed to bet at race days they had shared in the past. She decided now was not the time to be totally honest about that.

'I also chatted to Bruce, you know, and he did mention he'd had a few work things weighing his mind down. Maybe he's trying to protect you from it Daisy, but I say a problem shared is a problem halved. Maybe you could broach it with him?' Ronnie was trying to be helpful, but wasn't at all sure he was giving the right advice. He started to wish Brooke would hurry up home.

'Thanks Ron, you really are a good 'un',' Daisy smiled gratefully.

At that moment Brooke came bustling through the door.

'Uh oh, looks like the boss is back. I'll leave you two to your planning,' Ronnie laughed.

He headed back into his man cave, affectionately clipping Brooke on the bottom as he passed. 'Alright Buggerlugs. Daisy's in the kitchen.'

'Oh, great, I need to discuss plans for our next weekend treat!' Brooke said, feigning eagerness but weighed down badly by her deep concerns about the mess Frankie was in. She still couldn't get her head round what Frankie had told her about Wednesday night.

The two friends were soon engrossed in conversation but not about ideas for the next weekend getaway. Daisy had instantly realised something was wrong with Brooke and she had urged her to share her problem, which she did. Both agreed that Frankie was enmeshed in a whole lot of trouble. Adam was back in control with a body of evidence that could bring her world crashing down. If Adam decided to share those photos, then Frankie's career was vulnerable. Dexter had revealed a side of him that had shocked Frankie and she was not keen to see him again. The fact that he had stayed away after that fateful evening must be a good thing then, but what if he decided to go after Adam? That was a distinct possibility and Frankie actually seemed to view this as a positive course of action – she hated Adam more than anything now. However, if Dexter went and roughed up Adam, it could all land back at Frankie's door.

The only thing to do was to sit tight, the friends concluded. They needed to be there for Frankie; that went without saying. One thing was certain: Frankie had no luck with men, none whatsoever.

***

Later that evening, Daisy mulled over the conversations she'd had with both Ronnie and Brooke. It was such a shame that everything was going so wrong for Frankie and that bloody Adam was back on the scene, giving her hell. The girls would stick together and do everything possible to support their friend through this; that was for

287

sure. Then Ron's words echoed through her mind: 'few work things weighing his mind down'. Bruce was at the Otter's and before she knew it, she was making her way along the hallway into his office.

Daisy tentatively sat down in the plush leather chair. She pressed a few buttons and PCs pinged to life. Password protected. Damn it, she thought. Then she tried a few of the obvious possibilities: kids' names, birthdays, her name, dogs' names…Nothing… then she had a brainwave and entered the letters carefully: 'Otter's Head' 'BINGO! She was in. Trust Bruce to have a password that was something to do with his beloved pub. All of the screens came to life. There was nothing much of interest: reams of data, emails, boring spreadsheets and a few unflattering jokes about Donald Trump. Then, a particular icon caught her eye. She clicked it and found herself looking into an office. God! It was Adam's office. Daisy recognised it because she had been there, when she'd been invited to a meeting with Adam about Rosie being selected for one of the top gifted students' projects.

 Suddenly, Daisy heard Bruce's key in the front door. She jumped out of her skin, quickly closed the screens down, turned off the light in the room and rushed down the hall into the kitchen. She picked up a knife and started chopping vegetables.

'Alright love?' she said, her heart still beating fast.

'Yes Bab, you? Bruce kissed her cheek.

'Dinner will be ready in about half hour,' Daisy said breathlessly, her heart still pounding. Why could Bruce see into Adam's office? Maybe it was just part of the work he was doing at the school. Still, this did not make any sense. Her mind was racing.

'Great, I'm so hungry! Just need to check on a couple of work things. I'll be back in a jiffy.' And with that, he was off down the hallway to his office.

Daisy let out a long breath. There had been nothing of particular concern she could see in Bruce's emails, albeit she had only had a few moments. She decided she would broach the subject of what could be troubling her husband later. For now, she was determined they were going to have a relaxing meal together and try to reconnect, somehow. She would bide her time and, when the opportunity presented itself, she would go back to Bruce's room. That view of Adam's office was troubling her for some reason. Daisy was now totally convinced that her husband's inner sanctum was where all the answers to her questions would be found.

Chapter 26

6 February

Brooke, Ruby and Frankie were huddled round Daisy's kitchen bar. Snacks were spread out invitingly and wine glasses filled. Ruby had been feeling so low with all the drama of the Kerri and Poppy revelations that she really needed this evening with her girlfriends more than ever. The four women chatted about the usual topics: work, outfits and men, then inevitably, the conversation turned to Ruby's latest situation with Arthur.

'Hey Rubes, how's things'? Brooke tentatively asked. 'You're back at home now right? Have you worked things out with Arthur?

Ruby had regaled the gang with the latest on the Kerri situation a few nights before, but had yet to mention the subject of Poppy. She had spent so many sleepless nights thinking of the desperate situation, her anger at Kerri for getting knocked up, her disdain for Arthur for getting involved with Kerri in the first place, but most of all her anguish for the innocent little girl Poppy, who was, after all, Arthur's daughter.

'Oh, where do I start?' Ruby sighed deeply. 'Well, you know how bloody hard it hit me when I found out Arthur had shacked up with Kerri all those years ago. When I saw him with her the other week it all came flooding back. We were so on the rocks at the time, and I really had thought it had been the end of us when we separated all those years ago. But you know, well, we're meant to be and we worked things out. Seeing them together the other week, I was so bloody furious with him! For one thing, why was he hiding his little visits to Kerri from me? I mean, what was I supposed to think? He was meeting up in secret with another woman! But it turns out, they're not having an affair, as hard as that might be to believe.'

'What do you mean? Brooke asked confused. 'How can you be so sure?'

'I'm pretty certain he's not with Kerri,' Ruby sighed.

'Then what?' The three friends looked intently at Ruby for an answer.

'It turns out Arthur is the father to Kerri's little girl. Poppy, her name is.'

There was an audible gasp from Brooke.

'Oh Rubes. How you feeling about this? Frankie asked gently.

'Well, at first shocked, then bloody angry, but now, well... I feel sorry for her. The poor thing has been taken from Kerri, who's a total alcoholic, according to Arthur, and the worst bit is she hooks up with all sorts of unsavoury blokes who take advantage of her, beat her up even. She has no money, no possible prospect of getting a job, let alone getting her act together to look after Poppy properly. She lives in those dilapidated rental flats on the east side of the city. Felstead, it's called, I think. Honestly, I could cry to think that the little girl had to live there with all the drugs, prostitution, beatings and stabbings that go on at that estate.'

'Hang on a minute.' A jigsaw was falling into place in Frankie's mind. How old is Poppy and what's her surname?

'Err, she's six. I think her surname is Baker?'

'Poppy Baker goes to one of the schools I work with!' Frankie exclaimed. 'Oh my God, Ruby, I know her. She's a sorry state. She's currently under special safeguarding. We're in the process of trying to put a plan in place to assist her mother too. I can't believe it Ruby. Poppy is Arthur's?' Frankie was dazed.

Brooke and Daisy sat speechless, totally agog at this latest revelation.

'Ruby, the school was trying get Poppy put into urgent foster care, when we found out that someone, we had presumed Kerri's estranged partner or perhaps a grandparent, had put Poppy into the care of a foster family, Barry and Daksha McGrath. They've been fostering for years, but whoever put Poppy in their care completely bypassed social services, and we were drafted in to provide evidence of her schooling, her attendance and so on. We're in process of formalising the arrangement as the McGraths are excellent foster parents,' Frankie explained.

'Oh my God! Frankie, I'm so relived, as that little girl's desperate situation has been keeping me awake at nights and Arthur is so worried about her.'

'Ruby...' Brooke slowly formed a question in her mind, and even more slowly spoke it aloud to Ruby.

Ruby gazed at Brooke. 'Yes?'

'Ruby, if Poppy is in foster care that means she'll likely be put forward for adoption, or the courts will seek to place her with the biological father, Arthur...' Brooke's words trailed off.

Ruby went ashen as Brooke's words crystallised in her mind. 'Oh my God, I am going to be a step mother to a six year old.'

The three friends sat in a stunned silence as they contemplated Ruby's predicament.

Chapter 27

7 February

Seven am Saturday morning and Adam was well into his early morning run, before he headed into school to pick up some 'A' level marking he had forgotten. The wet earth squelched and splattered up his legs like a Jackson Pollock painting as he ran through the wooded section of his route for the first time. He breathed heavily but felt good and was certainly feeling much fitter since starting the ninety- day programme to get back in shape after the Christmas excess. These days, he was ever more conscious of encroaching middle age and that did not sit easily with him. When he had been with Frankie, age was less of an issue, as she was four years older than him. Adam had enjoyed reminding her of that all too frequently and that she was lucky to have her 'toy boy'.

Adam found his thoughts roaming to the terrible night when he had found that low life Dexter round at Frankie's place. What was she thinking, hitching up with the local wide boy? It had come as a real bolt out of the blue, when Frankie went and dumped him before Christmas, just because those bloody friends of hers were getting at her. Then, when he went round to make a play to get her back, he was with her. The images of Frankie up against the kitchen wall, whilst Dexter had his way with her made him shudder. Then the thought of those photos that he had on his phone, made him smile. He was really enjoying being able to taunt Frankie and threaten her.

Yes, life was good again, as he was in total control once more. He fully intended to make Frankie's life a living hell.

Adam did not like failing at anything but he now had two major disasters in his wake; his marriage had looked ideal to those looking in from the outside: a 'perfect' wife, home and two lovely kids. Adam doted on them both and it was really rough that his children had witnessed their mother's pain as the realisation gradually dawned on her that her worst fears about her husband were indeed true; that he had been seeing his associate at work, that bitch Frankie, for nearly five years. The truth, when it had hit her like a sledgehammer, had really hurt and she had thrown Adam out. For once, she had not cared about the neighbours, when she had flung his clothes and belongings out of the window, onto the front garden. Adam had been forced to move in with his brother, who was recently divorced, so they had more in common than ever before. The searing guilt Adam felt, when he saw the look in his children's eyes, was tough. Still, he was starting to feel the benefits of being viewed as a very successful man, a powerful man, who was now free to have some fun with quite few adoring females in the school that he lead.

Adam was relishing the sense of power that engulfed him in his role as headteacher of Delvreton High. He was getting used to Frankie no longer being the resident psychologist and enjoying the attention of a number of other doting females on his staff body. He did have to admit though that Frankie was much cleverer than he was: she had a natural flair with words, being an eminent psychologist who frequently gave formal presentations so skilfully, never looking at notes and captivating her audience so easily. She had done that many times, both in training sessions with staff and in motivational assemblies. Adam had always suspected that Frankie looked down on his lack of academic prowess. So, he had made up for that by literally flexing his muscles by overly promoting his past sporting success in the local league football team.

Adam picked up his speed as he headed towards Squirrel's Nook, a light misty rain soaking through his tracksuit and a slight chill starting to mingle with his perspiration. He looked at his watch; it was still only seven thirty. Always an early riser, Adam never liked to waste his day even at the weekend. He would get back to school, take a shower in the gym, grab the marking he had forgotten yesterday and then pick up his kids for brunch.

What was that? The woods looked deserted. Who would be out so early on a Saturday morning in February? There it was again. It sounded like someone was behind him. The rain was heavy now and Squirrel's Nook was shrouded in a light fog that had descended out of nowhere. Adam suddenly stumbled over a gnarled tree root and was flung forward, losing his footing completely. The moss covered earth came up to greet him and he slammed into the ground. At that moment, a dark figure lunged forward from behind one of the majestic oak trees that Squirrel's Nook was renowned for. A heavy boot smashed into the back of Adam's head then relentlessly and mercilessly kicked him again and again, the black leather boot repeatedly, forcefully connecting with Adam's back, despite the guttural groans that emitted from him. Then a hammer came down and cracked his skull. Darkness washed over Adam as he fell into unconsciousness. The non-distinct figure agilely sprinted away, into the gloom of the dawning day.

A good hour must have passed, before the throngs of dog walkers ventured out into the gloom of the February winter's day. A particularly lively springer spaniel suddenly made a series of high pitched yelps from the epicentre of the woods.

'Burt, get back here,' a woman's voice shouted urgently. 'I don't want to have to come in there to get you. Bloody dog,' she huffed as she clambered along the muddy path, slipping and sliding. 'What?' The woman stopped in her tracks, as she saw her dog, tail wagging ten to the dozen, circling the mass on the floor, barking excitedly. His owner, a middle aged woman, who worked in the local artisan bread shop, cautiously approached what clearly was a body. Images of crime TV shows swirled through her mind, when bodies were discovered, often by dog walkers. No, not here, not in Delvreton; this could not be happening to her. Breathing heavily now and clearly in a highly stressed state, the woman grabbed her dog. She could not touch the body; she had to find someone who could help. Running, as best she could, with the excited Burt pulling her forward, she came out into the open. The strangled screams for help, piercing through the heavy fog were hers, she realised. Thankfully, two very fit runners were soon by her side, a man and a woman, urging her to keep calm and tell them what was wrong. The woman runner put her arm round the dog walker, as her partner ran into the woods. 'He's a physio at the hospital,' she explained, a tinge of pride in her voice. 'Don't worry, Dan will know what to do.'

'I just feel so helpless,' the other woman spluttered.

'Not at all. You discovered the poor man and you did the right thing to get help. Thank God we came by at that moment. It's Nicola, by the way.'

'Thanks,' sighed the dog walker. 'I'm Sally. What do you think happened?'

Dan shouted to Nicola, who checked Sally was okay and sped off into the woods. Dan had quickly assessed the situation, called 999 and an ambulance was on its way. He confirmed that there was a pulse but it was slight and intermittent.

'Bloody hell,' Dan confided to Nicola. 'He's in really bad shape but he was clearly on his morning run, so he can't have been left here long. For Christ sake, who would do something like this to a bloke out on his weekend, early morning run? Someone has done a really terrible thing, Nicky.' Dan's face was ashen.

'Oh no!' Nicola clasped her hand over her mouth in shock. 'I thought maybe someone had collapsed but,' she paused, as she visibly gathered her thoughts. 'You're saying someone has purposely hurt him?'

Dan looked up. 'I'm saying, it looks like someone has pretty much beaten the poor bugger half to death.'

A flurry of activity ensued as the ambulance hurled across the field, blue lights flashing and a team of paramedics doing what they did best, everything in their power to save a flagging life.

By now, a small crowd of the good citizens of Delvreton had gathered, emitting genuine concern for one of their own. No one knew who at this stage and there was a palpable sense of shock and disbelief that any foul play could have happened in this area. Delvreton was a safe place, an area where fathers did not get too stressed about their daughters walking home after dark. Already, that sense of security had been badly shaken and everyone's world rested on slightly less secure foundations. The crowd watched as the stretcher was expertly loaded into the ambulance and it sped away, lights flashing, cutting through the miserable grey day, sirens declaring the fragility of human life.

In the ambulance there was a hive of activity but it was clearly going to be touch and go for the patient.

'He looks like he's kept himself in shape,' the paramedic commented to his colleague.

'He'll need to be,' she stated, shaking her head as she tried to process the ferocity of this attack. Nothing she had not seen before, but usually down a back alley in a dodgy part of Brum, never in the lovely 'safe' middle class town of Delvreton.

Nicola and Dan half-heartedly jogged away from the scene they would never forget. Dan was determined to find out all he could about the victim he hoped he had done a little towards saving. The crowd gradually dispersed, back to the warmth of their homes, knowing that everyone would be glued to the mid-day news, desperate to find out what had happened. Who was the jogger who someone had so badly beaten up? More to the point, why? How could anything like this take place in their beautiful town? There were so many unanswered questions.

***

Just a mile down the road, Iris lay in bed in her cosy apartment, but she was not enjoying the lazy, indulgent lie in she had looked forward to all week. It was only nine thirty but she could not understand why she had not received a text on her secret phone. She was agitated and worried that she had maybe made a fool of herself, by seeming too eager to show her gratitude for being able to progress her career. Why had there been no response to the texts she had sent back to her boss, about how delighted she was to have secured her first leadership post? It just did not make sense that there had been no reply. The gloom of the day seemed to infiltrate the stylish soft tones of the young woman's bedroom. Iris sighed and buried her face in her plump pillow, not quite sure why she had a nagging feeling that something was wrong.

News of the early morning drama had spread fast through Delvreton and no walkers, joggers or dog walkers had the desire to frequent their normal, beloved woods. A hush fell over Squirrel's Nook, still shrouded in fog; the quietness and the greyness of the morning certainly seemed fitting for the terrible events that had taken place there.

Chapter 28

8 February

News of the assault on the jogger in the woods ricocheted around the community like a tornado, stopping everyone in their tracks on that fateful Saturday morning. No one talked about anything else as they all speculated on what could have happened and who the victim was.

By midday on Sunday, the identity of the jogger had been revealed. Phone calls, texts and messages flew around the town. It did not take long until the dreadful news had reached Frankie and her friends.

Frankie took a deep breath as she tried to process what had happened. She had just taken a call from the police to check that she would be available to talk to them later that afternoon; she was grateful that a couple of officers had arranged to visit her at home and that she had not been required to go to the station. She poured herself a very large glass of Chardonnay and sat down on the sofa, pulling Charlie in close to her for a much needed cuddle. She decided that she had to call Dexter, just to gauge his response. After the awful encounter with Adam a few nights before and the threats she had received at work from him, she had to reassure herself that Dexter was not in the frame. She was not naïve and knew that not all of Dexter's acquaintances in the world of property development were fine, upstanding citizens. But, could he possibly be involved in the attack? She sincerely hoped not. She also hoped that the police had not included her in their suspect list.

'Hi, Dex; it's me,' Frankie announced as Dexter answered his mobile. She had not actually managed to see him since the Wednesday evening, when the dreadful fight occurred and she felt a tad awkward. She was not exactly avoiding him as she had genuinely had a late meeting on Thursday and she had a longstanding dinner date with Ronnie and their parents on Friday for their Dad's birthday. She could not help but sense that things had changed between her and Dexter though and the recent realisation that Dexter had a penchant for the odd line of coke was not sitting easily with her either.

'Hi,' Dexter answered and Frankie thought she detected a certain coolness in his tone, unnerving her a little.

'How are you?' she tentatively enquired.

'Not bad, considering your ex-boyfriend's a bloody lunatic,' he answered. 'I don't take kindly to being punched, at least when it's the last thing I was expecting, and completely off guard. Fucking good job I wasn't expecting it because he would have been in big trouble otherwise. He's very lucky.'

'I know. I couldn't believe how he behaved. Is your face okay?'

'I'll live, but I've got a bit of a bruise still.'

'Have you seen the news?' Frankie asked cautiously.

'No, I had a meeting with the old man on site of the new apartment development just out of town. I took the pushbike to blow away a few cobwebs, so not heard any news yet. Why?'

'You're not going to believe this.' Frankie paused, before she updated Dexter. 'Adam was badly attacked yesterday morning, when he was running first thing in Squirrel's Nook.' She waited, listening intently for any trace of a clue in his response.

'What?' Dexter genuinely sounded surprised, then she felt a chill as he uttered the next words. 'Well, that's only what the fucking loser deserves. My day is just taking a turn for the better,' he laughed cruelly.

'I don't think you realise.' Frankie paused again. 'The beating was so bad that he's been hospitalised. I just can't believe it and I've got the police round here soon. Dex, you do have an alibi, don't you?'

Dexter laughed again. 'You really think it could be me?'

'No, course not but I guess you do have a motive.' Frankie paused again, not comfortable at all with how this conversation was shaping up.

'I can't believe you think it could be me!' Dexter replied. 'Bleedin' hell Frankie, what do you take me for? You really don't know me at all, do you? He was maybe a little too indignant for Frankie's liking. He paused, then added, 'Frankie, of course it wasn't me, but better all-round though, that you don't mention that little altercation on Wednesday or that I was at yours. Trust me, it's better for you too if you want to get rid of the boys in blue and prevent them from bothering you too much.'

'I'm sorry, Dexter, I… I just don't know what to think anymore,' Frankie lamented.

'Look, Frankie, I really like you, but I can't get involved in this sort of crap right now. I think that maybe you and me need a bit of space for a while,' Dexter asserted, with a hint of that hard edged tone, clearly apparent again. 'If you know what's good for you, do not tell the police about Wednesday night. I know a lot more about this stuff than you do.' His tone was clipped now and to the point.

'Whatever,' Frankie said and ended the call abruptly. Steadying her breathing, she took a long gulp of her wine. She did not feel confident about Dexter at all and she was not quite sure what she should say to the police about her relationship with him. The revelation about his drug taking had certainly muddied the water. You don't really know what people are truly like, she reflected. That certainly applied to both of the recent relationships in her life, and she was realised that she was fed up with men in general. 'Shit, shit, shit,' she repeated to herself, her mind whirling.

Frankie considered calling Brooke, but then decided it would be better to leave it, until after the police visit when she had something more concrete to tell her. The last thing she needed was Brooke in a spin. She sighed, as she desperately wondered what on earth was she going to say to the police. She could not quite compute the fact that she knew of a possible suspect for Adam's attack and she would have to keep that hidden, at all costs.

Frankie found her level of anxiety mounting as she tried to patch together her strategy for meeting the police. It was the weekend, so at least she had more time than usual to reflect on recent events. She stared despondently out of the window of her study, the ice cold grey day somehow fitting for the chill that ran went right to the core of her being. Was Dexter *really* capable of violently beating up Adam? On the one hand, Adam had it coming given how brutal he had been recently, the way he had pounded Dexter not to mention the trail of threatening emails sent to her, filled with slanderous gossip. If Dexter *had* gone after him, then it really did make her own position precarious in terms of her professional reputation for starters, as well as making her a bloody suspect for a serious assault, simply because she had been dating Dexter. Tears started to roll down her face as she realised a whole heap of trouble could be in store. She reached once again for her faithful wine glass, burying her head in her even more faithful dog's fur.

***

Later that evening, it transpired Frankie's tears had been in vain. The visit from the police turned out to be a straightforward formality. A female detective and a young male officer, who were very personable, were only there for a matter of minutes.

'Just a routine visit madam, nothing to worry about,' the friendly faced, female detective had reassured.

They had been informed by a number of Adam's work colleagues, including Patricia, that Frankie had been in a relationship with Adam but that it had recently ended. They were actually more interested in her involvement with Dexter Croft, who was already on their records for a series of drug offences, for starters. Frankie had looked suitably shocked at this revelation and she decided not to disclose the fight that had taken place the previous Wednesday evening. She emphasised the fact that she had not seen Adam since early December, which had been easy to corroborate. Yes, it would be better all-round if she did not need to have much to do with the police, so omitting to tell them about Dexter and Adam's debacle had felt the right thing to do. The truth was, Frankie actually relished the fact that Adam had been beaten. He deserved it, after his behaviour and the misery he had given her for so many years. She assured herself that the police would surely realise that she had nothing to do with him anymore and, after a few days, Adam would be on the mend and all of this worry would soon be a distant memory.

Frankie also managed to do an Oscar winning performance of playing down her involvement with Dexter, reinforcing the fact that she had only known him since New Year's Eve and only on a casual basis. Thank God, there was a good distance between her home and her neighbours and that Georgia and Dermot, whose home was closest to hers, had been away when it had all kicked off that Wednesday night. Frankie was feeling confident about her ability to keep that horrible event under wraps. Only her best girlfriends knew about it and she intended to keep it like that. She could only pray that the heavy blanket of snow had covered up the events of that evening and kept them covered.

***

Twelve noon and Brooke had just watched the local news with abject horror.

'Oh my God, oh my God,' Brooke was reciting, as she dialled Ruby with a trembling finger. Ruby answered immediately.

'Ruby, OH MY GOD!' Brooke babbled.

'Brooke, I know, I know, I've just seen the news. They've found Fuckwit's body in Squirrel's Nook He was half dead, but apparently he's in hospital in a pretty serious condition. He might need to go on life support. A fucking life support, Brooke! This isn't what we asked Blaze to do!' Ruby was also in a complete state of shock.

'What the hell are we going to do? Should we call the police? I didn't want the bugger to be hospitalised, just shaken up a bit with maybe a black eye or two,' Brooke stammered.

'Look, I think we need to just stay calm and work this through.' Ruby's mind was searching for an answer, but nothing was forthcoming.

'It had to be Blaze, Ruby,' Brooke implored. 'Who else would do this and it might get traced back to us. Oh Jesus Christ Ruby, I can't go to prison!'

'No one is going to prison! He's not dead and besides, how could anyone ever trace this to us? Look, we've just got to stay quiet and keep our heads down. If you hear anyone say anything, act shocked and no one will suspect a thing.' Ruby said with uncertainty, as she did not actually believe a word she was saying. The last thing they needed was Brooke going to the Police in a panic.

'You're right, you're right. I'll keep my head down.' Does anyone know if Frankie's heard yet?

'I don't know. I'll call her.' And with that Ruby abruptly ended the call, leaving Brooke holding her phone in disbelief. As the panic subsided a little, Brooke's mind wandered to the possibility that there could be a few people, who were keen to see Adam get what he deserved. She knew that Dexter had to figure in the frame and she felt concern mounting for Frankie.

***

Frankie saw Ruby's number pop up on her mobile.

'Frankie, its Ruby. Have you seen the news?'

'Yes, of course,' Frankie replied slowly and calmly.

'Are you okay?' Ruby enquired.

'Yes, I'm fine Ruby. I think he actually got what was coming to him, in all honesty. Don't get me wrong, I didn't want to see him hurt but Adam is no longer any of my business. I'm merely the slightly concerned ex.' Frankie spoke in a monotone. She sounded devoid of emotion, and not at all how Ruby had expected her to react. She thought Frankie would sound a lot more shocked than she did; in fact, Frankie did not sound shocked at all. Her reaction was nonchalant, almost.

'Okay' Ruby said slowly. 'As long as you're sure you're okay? I can come over if you want, or if you need Brooke, or me just call, alright?

'Okay, thanks Rubes. I'm absolutely fine and pleased that the police visit was just routine. I have no feelings for Adam anymore, so there really is no reason for me to be any more upset about this than the next person.'

'Of course, of course. So pleased that the police didn't cause you any hassle. Guess you must be relieved that visit's over. Love you Angel. Speak soon.' With that, Ruby hung up, feeling a little confused by the conversation and less than convinced by Frankie's assurances. She had been almost certain Frankie would be in floods of tears and begging her and Brooke to go round. She decided she would call Brooke back later, when she had calmed down, or more to the point, when she herself had calmed down. Ruby picked out one of her grandpa's crystal tumblers and, with a shaking hand, poured herself a generous brandy.

***

Frankie sat in her kitchen, sipping the last dregs of a glass of wine. She had actually started to feel comfortable with this turn of events. The reaction from the police had been reassuring and she had unexpectedly started to feel quite proud of herself. She was not feeling a shred of emotion about Adam and she was not missing

Dexter at all. Frankie had been able to reassure Brooke that they could all get through this, when they had just spoken and she thought she had managed to get through to her and calm her down. Frankie silently congratulated herself and poured herself another large glass of Chardonnay.

***

The next day, the news had gone viral across Delvreton and even though none of the gang had particularly liked Adam, they were all stunned by what had happened and agreed even Adam did not deserve to be on life support in hospital. Of course, Bruce knew a hell of a lot more than anyone else about what a low life Adam could be, but much as he deplored Adam's lewd behaviour, he could not imagine why someone would beat him half to death.

Only on Thursday evening, Bruce had checked the camera focused on Adam's office. It was about eight thirty in the evening and the last parents and staff had left the building by eight o'clock. He had seen Adam inform the site manager, Malcolm, that it was fine for him to leave the site for a while, as Adam had a few chores to do, so would be in his office for at least another hour. Bruce had got bored watching Adam sending texts, and had switched off his screens, but something today told Bruce to re-visit the footage.

Ten minutes later and Bruce was scrolling through Thursday night's recordings once again. His hunch was right and he was not to be disappointed. Just a few minutes after Adam had put his mobile down, Suzie appeared in his doorway. Adam had also switched off the main lights so that his office was now dimly lit by only his desk light, the office blinds drawn. There was a wine bottle and two glasses on the small coffee table that sat next to a large tan leather sofa.

'You look hot,' Adam said, with a lascivious smile on his lips. 'Come and sit down over here and I'll pour you a glass of your favourite; I got it especially for you. We have a good hour before Malcolm gets back so, it's just you and me.'

Suzie smiled, characteristically flicking her mane of hair, knowing that all men responded well to this gesture. 'I can't wait for it,' she simpered much to Adam's delight. She meant the wine but also intended Adam to pick up on the double entendre. 'All that talking to all those parents.' Suzie loved the fact that Adam never took his eyes off her as she dropped her suit jacket on the back of his smart desk chair. She had unbuttoned several buttons on her tight fitting, striped blouse and she knew that her black pencil skirt, set off by her stilettoes, was working perfectly.

'What's your excuse to him indoors for being late back then?' Adam asked as he poured two glasses of wine before moving in to sit as close to Suzie as possible.

'Just a drink with the department so he won't be expecting me until ten at the earliest,' she smiled, licking her lips slightly and loving the effect she was having. Suzie had set up home with her fiancé just over a year ago and had been regretting the arrangement for some time now. She certainly found Adam more attractive, not in a

311

physical sense so much, as her fiancé was fit and a lot younger, but she was totally intoxicated by the kudos of Adam's position as headteacher and she had to admit that she was relishing the attention of this older man. She did not normally go for a sugar daddy type, but then Adam was very charming and she had observed the way many women doted on him, desperate to be the focus of a cheeky, flirtatious conversation. Suzie loved the fact that everyone had noticed that he had the hots for her and being his chosen one was definitely turning her on.

Within moments, Adam and Suzie were locked in a passionate embrace, a frenzy of luxurious kisses. Bruce wondered just how far they would go and could not help but be transfixed to the screen. He was slightly taken aback when he saw Suzie lift her skirt, revealing her black, lace hold ups as she sat astride Adam. His hands were all over her now, pulling her backside into him, before he gave it a hard slap and then moved to deftly unbutton her blouse. His mouth roamed voraciously down to her breasts. Bruce could clearly make out the bright red bra as he did so. This was steamy stuff indeed.

'Wait.' Adam said huskily. 'We need to be extra careful so let's move this to the bathroom – we don't want Malcom getting back early and spoiling our fun. God, I just want to fuck you so hard you'll want to scream but you mustn't, you dirty bitch.'

Suzie leered at Adam. 'Yes, I am your dirty bitch' she purred, pushing her hand down his trousers as Adam groaned loudly. 'You have no idea how dirty I can be,' Suzie said as Adam quickly stood up, shirt unbuttoned, trousers now beltless and carried Suzie into his bathroom, shutting the door firmly behind them.

**

Bruce sat back in his chair, totally stunned as he stared at the screen, now an empty office providing the only light as the image flickered on the monitor in his dark control room. He knew things had progressed with these two but had not expected to witness Adam's sex life while in the office of all places! More to the point, he was the head of their daughter Rosie's school and Iris' boss. Bruce was now feeling exceptionally uncomfortable with Adam in charge of this school. He just wished he could do something to expose Adam's unprofessionalism. Bruce zoned back into the room, suddenly realising Daisy was calling him and her footsteps were approaching. He slammed the screen shut.

'How long are you going to be in there? Daisy enquired. 'You said you'd definitely be free by nine and the takeaway's here a bit early.' Daisy was fed up of Bruce's long evenings in front of his PC screens.

'Sorry love. I just got caught up in that new hospital contract I won last week. With you right now.'

Bruce resolved to watch the rest of the footage as soon as he could get back to his office without arousing Daisy's disdain. She had been more touchy than usual recently and he did not want to rock the boat. Had he been able to watch the developments at Delvreton High that night, he would have seen Adam emerge from the bathroom in a far more composed state than he had

313

entered but grinning like a Cheshire cat. Like a finely tuned operation, he would have seen Suzie ushered out of the side fire door next to Adam's office, so that she could blend into the shadows while walking to her car and leave the site undetected by the site manager. Malcolm would once again check in on his boss at about nine forty five and berate Adam for the late hours he kept, urging him to look after himself and to get a better work/life balance.

If only Malcolm had seen what I've seen, Bruce thought to himself the next evening, when he watched the rest of the footage. Bruce mulled over the possibilities for how this new information could provide answers to Adam's beating. Had Suzie been involved? Or, more to the point had Suzie's fiancé found out about their sleazy affair? Still, Bruce was not going to get involved, for now at least. The last thing he wanted was anyone finding out about his secret surveillance project, especially now.

Chapter 29

11 February

Brooke was in floods of tears. The turn of events with Adam had shaken her to her core and she was still reeling. Furthermore, after finding out the police had visited Frankie, she had spiralled into a complete meltdown. She had paced her study for the last hour, trying desperately to use anxiety calming techniques she so routinely utilised with her therapy clients. This was to no avail.

Frantically trying to sooth herself with a bit of horseracing, Brooke was now staring at her William Lad's account in despair. How on earth had she managed to lose so much? She'd had near to thirty thousand just after Christmas, but the overindulgence at the races the month before had nearly wiped her out. She knew she was being frivolous at the time, but fuelled by Champagne and the excitement of the live race, she had been completely and utterly reckless with her bets. One thousand pounds, again and again, sometimes more. She knew she'd had a big win and had been certain she was at least breaking even, but it all become a bit of a blur after that and she had become overconfident and misjudged the amounts she could afford to bet.

After the race day, it had not stopped there. The excitement of the 'big win' had left her feeling invincible and she had been logging onto numerous online betting sites ever since, trying to recreate the adrenalin hit, but losing more and more. Then she had chased her losses to try to recoup. It was now a recurring pattern, almost every day. Brooke had signed up to so many sites that she did not even know what accounts she had anymore; in all honesty, she had totally lost track. She was just about to compose herself and go downstairs when, to her horror, Ronnie was suddenly right behind her.

'Brooke?' he said, with a concerned voice. 'What on earth is the matter?'

Before she could hide her tablet, he picked it up off her desk. Ronnie studied the screen, emblazoned with 'William Lad Betting' and the account detailing five thousand pounds in credit. On the face of it, this looked like a healthy amount, but Ronnie was no stranger to betting and he knew that for every big win, there were countless big losses.

'Oh bloody hell Brooke, you're gambling again. We talked about this!' Ronnie said with despair.

'I know, I know, and I stopped for a bit, but you know I like a flutter.'

'Well, yes I know you do, but how much have you lost?' Ronnie's voice was a little sterner, as anger began to rise within him, any tone of concern dissipating.

'Not that much.' Brooke's head was bowed.

'Brooke, how much? You'd better be honest with me, because I can check you know.'

'A lot,' she sheepishly replied.

'How *much* is a lot?' Ronnie's anger was fast becoming red hot.

'Over twenty thousand,' she whispered.

'What! Twenty bloody grand! For God's sake Brooke! Why? Just think what you could've done with that cash, what WE could've done! It's not like we're made of money. Jesus, Brooke, what's wrong with you?' Ronnie's tone was alien to Brooke, as his anger turned white hot.

Brooke did not like this, one bit. It was as if her whole world was crashing down around her.

'Well, it's my bloody money Ron. I don't need your permission to spend it! I can spend it, however I Goddam like!'

'Yes, Brooke, it IS your money, but this is OUR home, our lives. We both work hard and whether it's your money or not, I think we both know that shoving it on horses or roulette wheels is not a sensible way to spend it. You must get help.' Ronnie marched out of the room, without so much of a compassionate hand on Brooke's shoulder. She felt completely alone.

'Ronnie, I'm sorry!' she wailed after him.

He did not answer. Ronnie hated seeing Brooke so upset, but he just could not look at her right now. Anger eventually subsiding, he was left with a feeling of sheer disappointment.

Brooke crumbled into a sobbing wreck, head in her hands, slumped over the tablet with the glaring online betting casino still flashing lights of temptation, as if to mock her.

***

Two very frosty days later, both outside in the wintery weather, and inside at Ronnie and Brooke's place, the couple were sitting together. Brooke had experienced just about the worst day ever. Not only was she grappling with her mounting gambling problem, but she was worried sick about the attack on Adam. Would Blaze get

317

caught? If so, how long would it be before she and Ruby were exposed, as his accomplices? Ronnie had gone out on his own that evening and Brooke had sat alone, feeling sorry for herself with a box of Thorntons, but it had given her some time to think and she had made some big decisions.

'I've signed myself up for some therapy, Ron. I know I need to get my gambling into check and I know from my own psychotherapy training it's what I need. It's been hard to find a good therapist that I don't already know in a professional capacity, but I've found someone, who comes highly recommended on the other side of the city. Anyway, I'm starting group sessions on Saturday.'

Ronnie looked at Brooke, then slowly got up and hugged her. 'Bab, I'm so glad you're doing this. I don't want you, us even, to get into a mess with debt. Gambling should be fun, not stressful, and you know you can't ever chase your losses. Even if you're not in debt, you never really 'beat' the house. You must know that. That money could be used for all sorts of lovely things for us.'

'I know, and that's why I'm doing this. It'll be hard being the client, not the therapist, but at least I understand the process, so I know I'll get the most of out of this,' Brooke said looking into Ronnie's eyes.

Ronnie took her hands tenderly. 'Brooke, let's just get out of here. The last couple of days have been just vile. Come on, dinner's on me.'

Chapter 30

13 February

Two days later, on a sunny February morning, the day before Valentine's Day, Brooke stood looking up at the sign that read 'Banners Hill Counselling Suites', the red letters seeming to glare down at her reproachfully. She took a deep breath and entered the building. She had decided to be honest with the receptionist and told her that she was a qualified therapist herself, but that she had chosen to be here because she wanted a group support setting, rather than private counselling. Brooke had had her fill of one to one therapy during her training, not to mention all the supervision, and she needed a fresh approach.

Brooke tentatively stepped into the room. It was a fairly decent set up, if a bit clinical looking, but there had been some attempt to make it a little warm with plants dotted around and some calming artwork on the walls. There were seven function room style chairs arranged in a circle. They were the sort of chairs you might see at a wedding, but this was far from a celebration. There were two other people already sitting down. A woman, dressed in very bright colours with braided hair and kind eyes, welcomed Brooke and encouraged her to find a seat.

'Come in, come in. I'm Pauline. I'm the therapist for this group.'

Brooke sat down in an empty chair and looked at the other person across from her, a man, probably in his late fifties or early sixties, sporting a wax jacket and foppish hat. He had unfeasibly ruddy cheeks.

A couple more people entered the room and sat down: a young woman in her twenties, extremely overweight and very nervous and another slightly older woman, probably in her thirties with olive skin and jet black hair, wearing a beautiful turquoise and pink Kurti Kurta Indian style tunic. She sat down next to Brooke. Two more women joined the group and found themselves seats.

Pauline did a spiel on confidentiality and the 'safe space' to talk and then everyone was asked to introduce themselves and say why they were there. Each person spoke in turn: overeating, alcohol, gambling, drugs. They were all addicts from such different walks of life, but all together in this, their struggle to tame their demons.

It was Brooke's turn to speak and Pauline spoke softly, encouraging the new member of the group.

'Well... I gamble too much. I've... I've recently lost a lot of money and so I'm here because I want to get it under control.' Brooke's cheeks burnt red with embarrassment but that was nothing to the mortification burning into her soul. How on earth had she ended up here? However, her resolve would not be broken. She knew exactly how therapy worked and she was strong and determined to make it work for her. Brooke realised that she needed to put her excessive gambling to bed, once and for all.

That evening, Brooke logged onto her secret tablet. She withdrew what little was left in her various betting accounts, closed them down and unsubscribed from each site. She also blocked any pop ups for casinos and other games. She was not sure if it would be very last time or not. Every addict knows, once an addict always an addict; a person just has to take it a day at a time.

Brooke ambled downstairs, made Ronnie and herself a cup of tea and they chatted about music, DIY, art and travel plans, each fussing a Border terrier on their laps. Brooke momentarily felt a calming sense of ease in her relationship with Ronnie. They were the best of friends with shared values, hopes and dreams. A corner had been turned and Brooke suddenly felt like the luckiest woman on earth. Unfortunately, the moment was short lived. Intrusive thoughts filled her brain as she once again became aware of that awful, gnawing sensation in her stomach as visions of Blaze and the terrible attack on Adam assaulted her senses. She desperately wanted to blurt it all out. Be that as it may, she just could not bring herself to share this secret with Ronnie; that would just be too much for him to bear.

***

A little later that same day, Kerri stood outside Banner's Hill Counselling Suites. She looked up at the 1970s blue clad building and the clashing red lettering of the sign. She had been so desperate to get Poppy back home and had relentlessly contacted Arthur over and over, but to no avail. She had since been contacted by social services and had been told it was no longer in

Arthur's hands. Formal fostering procedures had been put in place, fuelled to some degree by the intervention of Poppy's school, when they had heard she was no longer living at Kerri's flat. Kerri's trembling hand was on the sliver entrance plate that said 'PUSH' in faded red letters. She hovered for a moment. A smartly dressed man bustled out of the exit door.

'Morning,' he said.

 Kerri did not answer. She looked at the man in his clean clothes with a smart briefcase and highly polished shoes. Every fibre of her being told her that she did not deserve to be here.

Kerri's lungs hurt as she breathed in the icy cold air. She lingered at the door for another moment, then, as suddenly as she had arrived, she decided. She was not going in and she definitely was not going to have any counselling. Kerri turned on her heels and walked back onto the misty high street, wind blowing through her thin coat. She tugged at the collar, drawing it to her neck to try to keep the chill at bay. Kerri's tiny frame disappeared into the mist and right into the nearest pub, a vodka calling out to her to thaw her frozen veins and numb her broken heart.

***

Ruby sat nervously, picking at her finger nails. It had been almost a month since Arthur had told her about Poppy and she had also since found out that Poppy was now formally in foster care, with his mate Barry's wife. Ruby knew Barry and his wife well and she knew the children in their care were treated like their own with some tough love but lots of compassion.

Barry's wife bustled into the homely sitting room. 'Can I get you a coffee, Ruby love?' she asked.

'Err, no I'm fine thanks. Maybe a glass of water, please?' Ruby replied nervously.

'Righto, I'll be right back. Poppy is dying to meet you,' she added.

Ruby was not 'dying' to meet Poppy, but she did care that this little girl had a decent chance in life and she also cared deeply for Arthur. She wanted to show him she was willing to, at least, give this a chance. They had discussed it repeatedly and it had been decided that, social services willing, Arthur would aim for full custody. Poppy would live with them full time and Kerri would have access rights, once she had completed compulsory counselling for alcohol abuse and demonstrated that she could provide adequate care for Poppy. It was not exactly a fairy tale ending, but Ruby was clear it was most definitely the right thing to do for this innocent little girl.

Poppy appeared at the door. She was sporting a trendy pair of trainers and cute, pink dungarees.

'Hello sweet pea,' Ruby said. 'I like your dolly; what's her name?'

'Her name is Annabella,' Poppy answered. 'Are you going to be my second Mommy?'

Ruby was taken aback by the directness of this six year old, but it was sort of true, she supposed. Yes, she was going to be a step mum, as she had already decided that she would support Arthur in whatever decision he made.

'Yes, I suppose I am because I am married to your daddy and I love him very much, which means that I can be your second mommy, if you'd like?' Ruby answered.

'Yes, I think I would,' Poppy said. 'Do you want to feed Annabella?'

The next thing she knew, Ruby was on the floor playing 'tea parties' with a motley crew of teddy bears, rag dolls, a plastic robot and a Barbie.

What had she got herself into? Ruby thought, despair suddenly washing over her.

***

Bruce was taking in the cosy, domestic scenes of his friends and he felt perturbed. His own life had drifted so far away from this and he could never have imagined feeling as distant from Daisy as he did right now. How had his life unravelled like this? Had his obsession to ensure all his family were safe actually begun to destroy them, as a unit?

It appeared that Brooke had decided to get her act together, and Ron was being the supportive husband. Arthur had also faced his past so that Poppy now had a good chance to be a part of his life. It also appeared that Ruby was being the supportive wife, despite her initial reaction and living at Bruce's place for nearly a week. Was it really as simple as 'honesty is the best policy?'

Bruce was reluctant to broach Daisy about her indiscretion of shoplifting and, although he internally congratulated his friends, who appeared to be working through their issues, he had not exactly been snow white himself, spying on his best mates and his family. Was it really time to come clean to his own wife?

Bruce pushed the feelings away and soothed himself by thinking about the fact that neither Ron nor Arthur knew about Ruby and Brooke's little plan to rough Adam up by hiring some dodgy hitman. So maybe it's okay that we all have our secrets, Bruce tried to convince himself as he decided that, for now at least, it was not the time for honesty. With a decision made to hold onto his secrets for now, he still had a hard time pushing away the overbearing feeling of pure dread that something terrible was going to happen.

Chapter 31

13 February

It had been exactly one week since Adam had been assaulted and things were looking critical for him. Patricia had tipped Frankie off that she had been informed that there was sadly, no hope for him. This had come as a huge shock, a complete lightning bolt. Everyone had assumed that Adam would be out of hospital in a few days, battered and bruised, and hopefully a lot less arrogant. No one had expected to hear otherwise, but Adam was on a life support machine and his parents and two children were by his bedside twenty- four hours a day, apparently. Frankie assumed the kids would have to go home to get some sleep but she knew that his parents would keep their devoted vigil at all times. That would be the case for anyone. She thought about her's and Ronnie's parents and how they would cope. Well, they simply would not be able to bear it; they would never be able to deal with something like that. As much as Frankie had come to hate Adam, she knew that there were many people who adored him, and his parents' love would always be unconditional. Furthermore, they had no idea what a total bastard he could be.

Frankie's phone suddenly cut through the silence of her office and she saw that it was Brooke calling her. Strange, she thought as Brooke hardly ever called her during the working day.

'Hi,' Frankie answered, sensing that something was wrong.

'Hi,' Brooke answered. 'Have you seen the news?' Brooke's voice had a desperate edge to it.

'I'm in the office, so no. Why?'

'It's just awful,' Brooke blurted out. 'God, Frankie, they are saying that Adam has deteriorated, seriously and,' Brooke faltered. 'They're saying that he is critical. He's been given only a few hours to live. Oh my God, Frankie. If Adam dies then, then that means he will have been murdered.'

Frankie's mind was whirring as Brooke spoke. The realisation that Adam could be a murder victim was certainly a harsh one. She shivered as unwelcome thoughts bounced around her mind again. Thoughts about the attacker. She could not help seeing Dexter's face and the pure hatred in his expression, when Adam had shoved him on that terrible Wednesday night, just over a week ago. She had not seen Dexter since then and she didn't want to. She was surprised that she had no sympathy whatsoever for Adam but she was worried about what her connection could mean for her, if Adam went and bloody died.

'Try to stay calm,' Frankie advised Brooke, a little surprised that Brooke was reacting like this. In the past, Brooke would have been cool and collected in a crisis; not so much lately. 'Patricia called me last night to warn me about this. Don't take this the wrong way, but Adam was, I mean, is a total bastard. Why are you so upset about the news?' Frankie was genuinely keen to hear Brooke's answer.

'I need to talk to you later,' Brooke said and Frankie thought she could hear real desperation in her voice. She sounded like she was crying, but why?

'Okay, I'll come to yours after work.'

'No! Don't come here. Let's meet at the Otter's at six.' Brooke sounded even more anxious.

'I'll be there. Now, try not to worry. It's all pretty shit but you don't need to go and get so upset by it all,' Frankie urged her friend. She had to admit she felt unnerved by Brooke's reaction and was very keen to hear why she sounded so desperately worried. It was going to be a very long day.

Frankie's day went quite quickly in fact as she went from meeting to meeting, made numerous decisions and checked in with various members of her team. Before she knew it, she was rushing out of the office, earlier than usual, at five thirty. Frankie just had to get to the Otter's to find out what had made Brooke so upset.

The news on the radio, as Frankie drove back to Delvreton, honed in on the brutal attack on the 'beloved headteacher, Adam Pearson.' Then there were the voices of a number of staff and students sending Adam their love, talking about everyone in the school community being devastated by the latest news about Adam's deteriorating condition. Frankie bit her lip, once again wondering whether Dexter could have attacked Adam. She shuddered. She did not want any part of this horrible mess but she was surprised by the complete lack of emotion she still felt when she thought of Adam. Her overriding response was clear: that he had deserved everything that had happened to him.

Hardly registering her drive back, Frankie found herself parking her car and walking to the main entrance of the Otter's. As she walked, she saw the card shop opposite, conveniently positioned next to the florist. Lights were on in both of the shop windows, subtly illuminating generous bouquets of luscious, deep red roses. Cards and red balloons were tastefully arranged in the card shop, announcing the imminence of the most romantic day of the year. Bloody hell, Frankie thought. It was just a few days to Valentine's Day. Only a year ago, Adam had been the man in her life and she had received the obligatory red roses, quite a small bunch, she recollected because he was such a cheapskate. Now, Adam was fighting for his life and Frankie did not care about him. What a difference a year could make.

The warmth and usual hubbub of the Otter's helped to offset Frankie's cold thoughts. She waved to Shane and Bonnie as she scoured the large lounge area. She soon spotted Brooke sitting at a corner table, probably the most discreet place to sit. Brooke was engrossed in what looked like an intense conversation with Ruby. Frankie had thought it was just her and Brooke but, no matter; Frankie always loved Ruby's company and she had not seen so much of her since Poppy had been on the scene. As she approached the table, Frankie was a little taken aback to see both friends looking so serious and downright worried sick.

329

Bruce knew that something had to give as the phone calls between Brooke and Ruby were becoming increasingly desperate. He had to admit that he had been beside himself too, wondering whether Blaze had gone too far or whether Dexter had taken his revenge, in a big way. Whatever, his close friends were far too close to what looked like an impending murder case. It was only a matter of time, according to all the news reports, before Adam's life support would be switched off. Bruce needed to hear the conversation at the Otter's, more than anything.

***

'Hi there,' Frankie said brightly as she gave both of her friends a hug. 'I can see you both have drinks, so I'll just get myself a wine. Back in two ticks.' As she went over to the bar, Frankie resolved to stay buoyant but could hardly ignore the haunted look in both her friends' eyes. What the hell was the matter with them both? Maybe it was Poppy, Frankie pondered as she waited for Shane to pour her wine.

'How you holding up then?' Shane asked as he put Frankie's glass down on the bar. For once, there was no banter from Shane. Like everyone in Delvreton, he seemed to have had any joy drained from him. It was as if the whole town was in some sort of strange limbo. Those balloons in the shop opposite the Otter's seemed incongruous and totally out of step with the mood of the close knit town. Maybe, their redness was completely in keeping with what was happening. Red did not only have connotations of love and passion but could also symbolise danger and death. How fitting.

'I'm okay, Shane. Thanks mate,' Frankie answered, picking up her glass. 'All pretty shit, isn't it?' Frankie knew she had to play the part of the sad ex, just to keep up appearances. She could not possibly admit her true feelings about Adam. Shane nodded morosely as Frankie smiled at him, before walking back to the table.

'What a day,' Frankie exclaimed with a sigh as she flopped onto the padded bench seat against the wall. 'How are you, Ruby? It's so good to see you.'

'Been better, Angel,' Ruby answered.

Frankie could not come to terms with how drained Brooke looked. What on earth was the matter with her?

'So, Brooke,' Frankie began, taking a sip of her wine. 'What do we need to talk about?' She thought she may as well cut to the chase.

Brooke leaned in to her. 'You need to know something,' her voice faltered, as she looked nervously around her.

'Know what?' Frankie asked, starting to feel that something was very wrong with all of this. Ruby looked so serious, her eyes downcast as Brooke spoke.

'We just can't believe that Adam's on life support and it doesn't look like he's going to make it.' Brooke's eyes were watering and a lone tear ran down her cheek. Ruby squeezed Brooke's hand and she nodded at her friend, encouraging her to continue.

'Well, yes, it's awful but none of us really gives a shit about him, do we?' Frankie asked, uncertainty creeping into her voice.

'Go on, just bloody tell her,' Ruby urged.

'Tell me what? You're worrying me now.' Frankie squirmed in her seat.

'Do you want to tell her?' Brooke looked at Ruby imploringly as Frankie became increasingly perturbed.

'Okay,' Ruby began, 'You're not going to find it easy to believe what we've done, but we really only did it for the right reasons,' Ruby paused.

'What on earth do you mean? You guys are really worrying me now. Just tell me.' Frankie said.

'I'll tell her,' Brooke continued. 'We have done something terrible, Frank and we just have to tell you.'

Frankie nodded for Brooke to continue.

'We all got so pissed off with how Adam was behaving, even after you dumped him. He wouldn't leave you alone and he was so bloody threatening. Always there in our lives. So,' Brooke looked over at Ruby, who nodded, signalling her support. 'Well, we wanted to teach Adam a lesson, that's all.'

'What?' Frankie asked. 'What do you mean?'

'We went to meet someone that Ruby managed to put us in touch with. I mean, me and Rubes couldn't frighten Adam off, could we?'

'You did what?' Frankie whispered, leaning across the table, a very troubled expression on her face.

Ruby took up the narrative. 'We hired someone to rough Adam up a bit. It was after he showed up at Brooke's, threatening her and we saw all those horrible texts he sent you too.'

Frankie paled as she listened to her friends. 'Oh my God. What have you both gone and done? Did this person you hired tell you that he went and attacked Adam? Cos he went way too far, didn't he? And...' Frankie paused again. 'You will be accomplices to fucking murder. You know Adam's going to die right?' Frankie sat back into her seat, shaking her head in disbelief and draining her wine.

Brooke was silently weeping and Ruby clutched her hand.

'Look bloody normal, both of you,' Frankie instructed. 'We need to think about all of this, very carefully.'

Brooke smiled weakly and Ruby sat up straight in her chair, forcing a smile and a chirpy voice, as she made small talk, just in case anyone happened to be watching them.

***

One person certainly was, just as he watched most things that took place in his friends' lives. Bruce had to admit that his two prime suspects for Adam's attack were Blaze and Dexter, but he was so worried that his closest friends had clear connections with both. They were undoubtedly in a very vulnerable position right now. Bruce continued to listen intently.

***

'We were thinking that, maybe we should make contact with Blaze; just find out once and for all what exactly happened,' Brooke said in a business like tone. She was clearly mustering every effort to compose herself and focus on solutions.

'But, maybe not,' countered Ruby. 'Maybe we should have no contact whatsoever. Surely, we need to distance ourselves from Blaze. I mean, we paid in cash and there's only the three of us that know we even met him.'

'Yes, that's got to be the right way to go,' Frankie nodded thoughtfully. 'It's just going to be hell, when Adam dies and a murder investigation is launched. But, even if Blaze did it, he needs to get caught, doesn't he? Before you are at any risk. How do we know he's the one? Dexter was pretty mad, after that Wednesday night and I wouldn't rule him out from going after Adam to teach him a lesson and it all going horribly wrong. That wouldn't be at all good for me. I could be viewed as an accessory, if the police suspect that I may have put Dexter up to it. Oh God!' Frankie went pale as she considered the possible scenarios.

'There's nothing we can do then but sit tight, is there?' Ruby concluded. 'We can't tell anyone about any of this. We just need to be there for each other, whatever happens.'

Ruby squeezed Brooke's and Frankie's hands as the three friends nodded in silence, the enormity of their predicament hitting them like a tanker careering out of control.

***

Bruce sat shaking his head, feeling utterly powerless to offer any help or solace. That low life Blaze was well capable of brutally attacking Adam. He would only pose a potential problem to Brooke and Ruby, if he was caught because they were clearly his motive. Dexter was equally capable of exacting his revenge. That would possibly put Frankie in a difficult position and mean that she would need to convince the police that she was not connected with Dexter's actions in any way. It was going to be a tense time ahead, for all of them.

Chapter 32

Valentine's Day

Valentine's Day arrived. It started as the flattest day ever, despite some rare, piercingly bright sunshine. All of the friends felt so low before the day spiralled out of control, as the most terrible, but inevitable news hit the headlines. Adam died at two minutes past nine that morning; there was nothing for it, but to turn off his life support machine. What a day to do it. The most romantic day of the year quickly became the most tragic of days as each of the friends dealt with the news. Brooke, Ruby and Frankie were beside themselves with worry, wondering when there might be a development in the police investigation, now a murder investigation. They were absolutely dreading the prospect of that knock on their door, should any new evidence come to light.

One thing sure, each one of them would remember, forever, where they were when the news of the 'Valentine's Day Murder' hit them. Apart from Daisy, who always started work at the crack of dawn on Saturdays, the others had nothing to get up for, but sleep had refused to offer them any much needed solace. None of them could stop torrents of unpleasant, frightening thoughts swarming round their heads like crazed wasps.

Ronnie was in his workshop, desperately trying not to dwell on the fact that he had encouraged Dexter to keep an 'eye' on Adam. Ronnie knew, only too well, the company that Dexter kept and he could easily have commissioned someone very unsavoury to do his watching for him, and who knows what else. Ronnie turned his attention to the wood he was sanding and resolved to let what would be, be. There was nothing else for it but when he heard the news on the radio, his heart skipped a beat.

Brooke had gone out for a run with Frankie and their three dogs, but had driven to the nature trail, a few miles away. Everyone was staying well away from Squirrel's Nook. When they got back to their cars, they cleaned up their dogs and it was then, at about ten thirty that Frankie saw the news alert on her phone. She looked at Brooke, who instantly knew what Frankie's shaking head meant. The two friends just stared at each other, the power of speech evading them for what seemed like hours, but was only moments.

'Shit!' Frankie said. 'It's a murder investigation, then. Let's hope Blaze left no evidence behind him. 'But,' she hesitated and then blurted out. 'What if it was Dexter?' As if rooted to the spot, the two desperately worried women continued to look at each other. Nothing they could say could make this any better. Reluctantly, they got into their cars and drove home, the weight of the world bearing down on them both.

Later that day, Ruby went to see Brooke, pleased that Ron was staying well out of the way in his workshop, which afforded them their much- needed privacy. They both pledged to stay true to the plan they had agreed a few days ago at the Otter's. Brooke reassured Ruby that

Frankie would do the same. They all had so very much to lose, after all.

Arthur knew Ruby had such a lot on her mind at the moment, trying to adjust to the prospect of her role as stepmother, but he knew that Adam's death had hit them all like a ton of bricks raining down on them. He had always tried to have as little to do with Adam as possible, even when he and Frankie were very much an item. Nevertheless, when someone you knew was a murder victim, it knocked your whole world off course. He kept himself busy playing with Poppy and her dolls' house, whilst he waited anxiously for Ruby to return to them both.

When Daisy walked in the front door of her home at about four o'clock, she smiled at the lavish bouquet of roses waiting for her on the kitchen island. Her smile soon slipped though, when the news headlines blared out from the TV screen on the wall, news of 'the Valentine's day murder'. Bruce was transfixed to the screen, watching intently as Daisy joined him. A middle aged woman, was recounting her experience of finding Adam's body at the heart of the woods, only a week ago but it seemed like an age. Then the camera swung over to an attractive fit looking chap who was clearly devastated. He was explaining how he had stayed with Adam, whilst they waited for the ambulance, but he had feared the worst from the outset. He was a medic, of some sort, apparently.

'Bloody hell, love,' Bruce said, pulling Daisy close to him.

She hugged him back, her steely blue eyes stuck to the screen as images of Adam bombarded them, followed by his grief stricken family leaving the hospital.

'Thank God we are all safe,' Daisy said and then picked up her beautiful bouquet and started to arrange her dozen roses in a stylish glass vase.

'I must call our Iris,' Bruce said as he told Daisy that Rosie had been on the phone to her friends all day. They were all in a terrible state, as any teenagers would be, dealing with news like this. He was proud of his Rosie, though, who was holding herself together really well and had taken up the role of providing support for her mates. He could not imagine what it would be like at school on Monday and wondered what sort of state Suzie Frazer would be in today.

Iris had seemed stunned, her voice monotone, when Bruce called her once again to check she was okay. Her headteacher, her boss, had just died, so she must be reeling from it, like all the staff in the school. He had spoken to her as soon as the news had broken earlier that day and she had been totally shocked, like all of them. He just needed to check on her again and suggested that she should stay with them tonight. Iris agreed. She just could not process what had happened and she certainly did not want to be alone, today of all days.

At the end of that life-changing day, Frankie could not get the conversation with Nancy out of her mind. Nancy had called round to see Frankie, to give her a massive hug and to offer any support she could possibly provide. That was what close friends did, of course.

As they both sipped their coffees, Nancy broached the subject of the night before Christmas at hers. There had been a similar conversation between Frankie and Nancy, when the news had broken about Adam's attack just a week ago. Nancy told her friend that she had felt decidedly 'spooked' when she had recalled the message spelt out on the Ouija board, so much so that she had gone to stay at Richard's place for a couple of nights. Now, though, the message had come true completely. Adam had been brutally attacked in Squirrel's Nook and he was dead! They all knew that he had been a 'bad' man but no one had ever imagined this could happen to him.

Frankie managed to calm Nancy. She said that, although they never thought they pushed the glass, they must have done. It was always a bit of drama to have a prediction of a death when anyone consulted the board, so there must have been some sort of subconscious desire that had moved the glass in that direction of the letters. All of them knew about Squirrel's Nook so one of them must have just made the letters fit.

By the time Nancy left, Frankie was satisfied that she had successfully allayed her friend's fears. But, as she closed the front door to the cold and darkness of the night air, Frankie shivered. It was a shame she had not managed to convince herself that there was nothing in that Ouija board message.

Chapter 33

15 February

Patricia slumped wearily onto the tan leather sofa in Adam's office. Still in a state of shock, no one in the school community or the wider community of Delvreton had come to terms with what had happened. Terrible events like this just did not happen round here - except that they had and everyone's world was spinning in some kind of free fall. This was especially true for Patricia. No, she had not liked Adam but she was his PA and she never in a million years would have wished this fate upon him. She looked at her watch and was surprised to see that it was already four o'clock. The day had passed in a complete blur as she had coordinated that terrible staff briefing, delivered by the Chair of Governors at the start of the day, all those awful assemblies for all seven year groups, the counselling team from the Local Authority and the media circus that had arrived in town. 'The Valentine's day murder' was dominating the news at local and national levels. Then the police officers had arrived, sending ripples of fear through the school as everyone knew that a killer was on the loose. The officers were given a discreet base room to conduct interviews with a long list of staff and students to see.

Patricia was shattered, totally spent as images of the sombre and tense day raced through her mind: Suzie screaming and running out of the staff briefing followed by concerned colleagues, who had made every attempt to soothe her, but to no avail. Suzie had to be sent home, advised to see her doctor, as a matter of urgency. All members of the senior team were completely devastated, of course, but they had to put on a brave face to support their staff and most importantly, so many students of all ages, who simply could not accept what had happened to their headteacher. A steady stream of young people, from the age of eleven to eighteen, had gone into the counsellors' offices and it was clear that the counselling team would need to stay at the school for some time. This sort of experience lasted, unfortunately. Young people who seemed alright one day would simply crumble the next as grief, like a tsunami, gathered in both its dreadful scale and momentum, sweeping through the school, the rubble and wreckage of emotion rising and falling as the giant wave wrought its destruction.

Something else was playing on Patricia's mind as she was becoming increasingly troubled. Jane, one of the deputies had confided in her that the police were following a key line of enquiry. Apparently, two very responsible sixth formers had some information about something that had taken place a few days before Adam had been attacked. It had been the Wednesday evening, when the snow had wiped out Delvreton. At about eight thirty that evening they had been out for a walk, to 'have some fun in the snow,' they had said. As they walked round the bend of Badgers Lane, they had seen Adam running ahead of them. They watched him get in his car parked further down the lane and saw him drive off quickly, given the hazardous conditions. Badgers Lane was where Frankie lived and the sixth formers knew that.

They had also reported a top of the range black Range Rover on her drive, which they had noticed when they walked past her house. Why on earth would Adam have been running away from Frankie's place? Patricia had guessed that the car must belong to Dexter and a bad feeling was growing, tightening her chest with increasing anxiety. Something was not right with all of this and she knew that she must alert Frankie, and quickly. She would wait, though until after six, when Frankie should be at home as she knew what she had to tell her would be hard to take in. She would rather Frankie was not driving, when she called her.

**

Bruce had checked in several times throughout that Monday on the activity taking place in Adam's office. He had such mixed feelings about the recent events. Adam had been a total shit and had definitely deserved a beating; there was a queue of likely candidates for that job, all keen to get some payback or just to teach the arrogant git a lesson he would not forget. However, Delvreton was now dealing with a murder and that was unthinkable. Patricia had done a sterling job, dealing with the grief stricken staff and students and she had efficiently managed the several news teams that had descended on the school. Bruce's attention really piqued though, when he heard the news about the two sixth form witnesses. He was so relieved that Patricia was calling Frankie to warn her, as it was clear that the police would soon be knocking on her door again.

**

After a fraught day, Frankie was home, pacing her sitting room as another news report on her large TV screen bombarded her with more images of Delvreton High. There were photographs of Adam smiling, surrounded by adoring students at various school events and the stark comments from several staff members, governors, parents, members of the community, as they were interviewed. Local and national news reporters seemed to be clamouring for the latest new snippet of information about Delvreton, about the school, about Adam, about speculations on the identity of his murderer and their motive. It was becoming unbearable. She pressed the button on the remote and relished the peace that came with the welcome silence, but that only served to highlight the sound of her breathing: quick agitated breaths, which she had to get under control, somehow. The sound of her mobile made her jump. Frankie reached for her phone and saw that it was Patricia. She must be having an awful time, Frankie mused as she considered what it must be like at the school right now, dealing with the shocking aftermath of the tragedy.

'Hi,' Frankie said, her lack lustre tone reflecting the dark mood of the day.

'Hi Frankie,' Patricia's tone was understandably flat.

'How are you? It must be awful for you all.' Frankie offered, by way of starting a conversation she did not want to have.

'I'm not good, not good at all,' Patricia replied. 'And I need to warn you that I think the police will be calling on you soon,' she said, an urgency in her voice.

Frankie felt her heart beat quickening again. 'Why? I've already spoken to them. What could they possibly want with me?' Frankie asked, unable to hide her desperation.

'Adam was seen at yours a few days before the attack. Frankie, two sixth formers saw him running away from your house, the night it was snowing. Why was he there? That just doesn't seem right, does it?' Patricia asked, not wanting to dwell on some of the possible explanations that had been coursing through her mind, ever since she had been aware of this information. Patricia thought a lot of Frankie and could not stand the idea of her being connected with Adam's attack, or much worse, Adam's murder. She waited for Frankie's response.

'Oh no!' Frankie answered as anxiety took hold again, twisting her insides so much that she let out a gasp. The police would know that she had lied to them and that would not look good at all. Her mind raced. She tried to work through her options – just how should she respond to the second visit from the officers.

'Frankie!' Patricia urged. 'Why was Adam at yours?' she repeated again.

'Oh Patricia,' Frankie crumbled. 'It's not what you're thinking but it's not good. Adam came face to face with Dexter that night and it was just awful.' Frankie let out an involuntary sob. 'But I didn't have anything to do with Adam's attack. God! You can't think that, can you?' Frankie implored her old friend.

'Of course not,' Patricia said. 'But something's not right here and you need to be ready for when those officers visit. I just had to warn you. We're in the middle of a bloody murder investigation and the victim is my boss.' Patricia started to weep quietly and Frankie's heart went out to her, as a dreadful sense of doom washed over her and she suddenly felt exhausted, defeated.

'Look, thanks for the warning. You just take care of yourself. It must be terrible in school at the moment,' Frankie said, steeling herself for her next conversation with the police officers. 'I'd better go. We'll meet up soon, bye, Patricia.'

'Bye Frankie. Please be careful,' Patricia said as she ended the call.

Talk about timing. Less than five minutes later, the doorbell rang and Charlie raced down the hallway, barking furiously. Frankie ushered him into the kitchen, before composing herself and opening the door.

'Hello again,' the female detective opened the conversation. 'We need another word please.' The tall, slim woman looked a lot sterner than last time, as did the young uniformed officer, who accompanied her.

'Of course,' Frankie said lightly. 'Come in.' She guided her visitors into the sitting room, signalling for them to take a seat on the sofa and offering drinks, which they declined.

After about twenty very uncomfortable minutes, the conversation, or grilling more like, was over. It had been difficult to have to admit that she had not been completely honest last time. Frankie had disclosed most of what happened but could not bring herself to recount all of the events of that fateful Wednesday evening. However, Frankie did not know that the forensic team would soon be scrutinising Adam's phone and she was completely unaware of the photographs Adam had taken. How could she be? Her eyes had been closed in ecstasy, just as Adam was peering through the kitchen window, capturing the evidence on his mobile.

Frankie had apologised unreservedly for not telling the officers that Adam had interrupted her supper with Dexter. She said that the reason she had not shared this information with them last time was because she was sure it had nothing to do with Adam's attack. She admitted that the encounter had been awkward and that Adam had only stood in the doorway, once he realised that she had company; she said she still did not know why Adam had decided to visit her that evening. Frankie just thought that she would save the police from wasting their precious time having to visit Dexter to interview him, when there was no point really. The reaction of the detective was not good and had made her feel like a naughty child; Frankie was left feeling ashamed by the whole ordeal. Now feeling desperately worried, she knew that the police would be heading for Dexter's and sharpish. She was worried because she could not be sure that Dexter had not gone after Adam. Surely, he had not attacked Adam that Saturday morning. The least she could do was warn Dexter, or should she? What allegiance did she have to him? She picked up her phone realising that her hand was shaking uncontrollably then she put it straight back down again.

***

Bruce was very troubled as he watched Frankie's latest interaction with the police. He knew, of course, that she was still withholding a lot of critical information, because Bruce had seen everything on that Wednesday evening. On the one hand, he was not surprised. Frankie would not have wanted to talk about what she had got up to with Dexter; it had been a pretty steamy alright. And there was no way she would want to admit that there had been class 'A' drugs in her home. Above all, if she had let on that there was any sort of altercation between Adam and Dexter, then she would have handed the police their prime suspect, on a plate. He knew that Dexter must be in the frame for the attack on Adam that had led to the fatality. He knew how desperate Frankie must feel right now but, as ever, there was nothing Bruce could do about any of it. He sighed heavily and sat back in his chair, feeling the intense pressure of a situation that was spiralling out of control, before his very eyes.

Chapter 34

17 February

Ruby and Arthur were sitting on their sofa in the extension that they loved so much. It was post dinner and the real log burner was blazing. A Disney film was on the TV and Poppy was squeezed in the middle of Arthur and Ruby. Murray sat at Poppy's feet, whilst she leant forward to gently stroke his velvet, spaniel ears.

'I like being here,' Poppy suddenly declared.

'Well, that's just great!' Arthur said encouragingly, nodding to Ruby to make an additional comment.

'Oh... yes, sweet pea. We love having you stay and did you know that your Daddy has arranged it so that you can stay here as much as you want to?' Ruby added.

Poppy looked at them, wide- eyed. 'Can I still see my mommy?' she asked, a little puzzled.

'Well, not for a little bit, but yes, you will be able to see her once a week, when she's better and then maybe even more after that,' Arthur explained.

'Mm, yes, when she's better, cause she's a bit poorly now,' Poppy echoed. Poppy seemed to accept this situation easily and asked if she could have a story.

'Your turn Ruby,' Arthur joked.

Ruby took Poppy's hand. 'Come on sweet pea, it's bedtime and I'll read to you, before you go to sleep.'

Ruby looked into Poppy's deep brown eyes and suddenly had a wave of maternal instinct for her. The poor lamb had had such a terrible experience so far. She must be overwhelmed being in a new house, with new people and Ruby was in awe of how much she seemed to be taking it in her stride.

'The Gruffalo' was selected, Poppy was clean and fresh after her bath, PJs were on and she was all tucked up in bed. Poppy's eyes soon became heavy and before Ruby had even finished the first page, she was fast asleep.

Ruby marvelled at this little being; she definitely possessed some of Arthur's features. This was not going to be easy though. Ruby was still coming to terms with the emotional aspects of the situation and there were all sorts of legal wrangles ahead. In addition, Kerri had not been seen for several days, so it was very unclear how much she would be permitted back into Poppy's life and when. For now, social services had agreed Poppy was best placed with the paternal parent and for some unexplained reason, Ruby suddenly felt at peace with it all. She could be a good step mum and she was going to do her very best to make sure Poppy had a better chance in life. She kissed the top of the little girl's head and went back downstairs to Arthur, who was waiting for her with a glass of wine.

'You know what Arthur,' Ruby said. 'Life is so short, isn't it? All this weirdness with Adam, well it just makes you realise life is so bloody fragile.'

'You're not wrong there', Arthur answered. 'I wonder if it was Dexter who killed Adam. I just can't see it somehow. We all know that he's a wide boy but surely he isn't capable of murder? Arthur stared into his glass.

'I know what you mean and God knows how Frankie has been able to hold herself together. Anyway, guess we need to leave it to the police now,' Ruby replied, counting her blessings once more that Blaze seemed to have disappeared into thin air. 'But I am sure of one thing. We've got a wonderful life, Arthur. Terrible events make you reflect and...well, I've reflected a lot lately and I know one thing for sure. I won't be shoplifting again,' she said, shame making her look at her feet. Arthur pulled her close and smiled dotingly at Ruby.

'Arthur, I know it's going to take me a while, but I do know I can love Poppy, like my own eventually. Who couldn't? She's adorable and it's not her fault her life got off to such a terrible start. I really feel like we can do a good thing here. I'd like to formally adopt her, if you and Poppy want me to that is.' Ruby looked intently at Arthur and waited for his response.

'Babes, I'd love that so much,' he beamed at Ruby.

'Love you,' she said.

'Love you more,' he replied. 'Thank you, you are truly an angel.'

Chapter 35

20 February

The weekend had been too terrible for words, following Adam's death on Valentine's Day, of all days. As the three friends had pledged, Brooke, Frankie and Ruby had forced themselves to carry on acting as normally as possible. They just had to stay strong and avoid any suspicion, given how precarious their lives were at present. So, they had done just that.

It was Tuesday and Frankie was driving back to the office, after visiting two very troubled teenagers in one of the secondary schools, when she heard the news and her heart missed a beat. She had to pull over into a side street, so that she could steady her breathing and try to steady her shaking hands too. The national news at one on her car radio led with the dramatic story of an arrest that morning. Apparently, the police had made a major breakthrough in the 'Valentine's day murder' investigation and a suspect was now in custody.

Frantically, Frankie's fingers scrolled through her contacts for Dexter's number. After a few moments, she heard Dexter's voice, leaving his answerphone message. Her heart seemed frozen, yet she also felt very hot. She told herself to stay calm. He was probably in a meeting at work. Ronnie would know if there was anything wrong. He did a lot of work with Dexter, after all. She decided to call him, her heart now beating so fast and loud.

'Hi Ronnie. Have you seen Dexter today?' Frankie blurted, trying to sound normal and failing.

'Hi Frank. God, haven't you heard?' Ronnie's voice was serious. 'Brooke's been trying to call you, all morning.'

Frankie glanced at her screen, seeing ten missed calls from Brooke. 'What's happened?' she asked tentatively.

'Dexter was arrested first thing this morning. The police came on to the apartment block building site, so me and Arthur saw it all. It's mad Frankie. We saw him being taken. You know, it was just like you see on the TV; they put their hands on his head as they put him in the back of the cop car and then they sped off.' Ronnie really did sound shocked. 'We can't believe it. Dex has some dodgy mates and he's hardly a choir boy but no one would think he could hurt anyone.' Ronnie was clearly still trying to come to terms with it all. Little did Frankie know, but Ron was feeling sick with worry, that he had played a part in setting Dexter up to do something so terrible. He was really regretting confiding in Dexter on that drunken night out in the Jewellery Quarter.

'Oh my God, Ronnie. This is a nightmare. I just can't believe it. It can't be happening. It must be a mistake,' Frankie said, her voice faltering and trailing off.

'Let's hope he's released later and there's nothing in it. You should phone Brooke. She really wants to talk to you. I'll see you later. Try not to worry too much.'

'Okay, later Ron,' Frankie replied, as the call ended.

She sat staring into the distance, becoming transfixed by the steady rhythm of the raindrops on her windscreen. She found herself scrutinising each droplet as it gradually lost its form and blended with the other, newer droplets to stream across the glass, completely blurring her view of the street ahead. How could a boyfriend go and attack her ex? That sort of thing happened in films, in dramas, not in her world. No, it must be a mistake. She had not seen Dexter since that awful night when she realised that yet another man was not who she thought he was. But how had she got him so wrong?

Frankie's tangled thoughts were stopped in their tracks by a call from Sam, her PA. She was concerned to hear Frankie sounding so vague in her responses and, once Frankie admitted to being struck down by a vicious migraine, Sam reassured her that the afternoon was clear of appointments, so she should go home and rest. That was a good thing as there was no way on earth that Frankie would be able to apply herself to anything. She had to get her head round all of this madness.

Somehow, she drove home, although Frankie could not recall any part of the journey. She used the migraine story with her parents to explain the untypical early finish and she collected Charlie. She needed her boy more than ever to curl up with on the sofa. By two o'clock, Frankie was in her pyjamas, large brandy in hand, staring into the flames of her minimal gas fire, Charlie nestling into her.

She had sent Brooke a text straight after talking to Ronnie, explaining that she was fine and would call from home that afternoon. That is exactly what she had done and the plan to meet up at the Otter's for tea at six made sense, as Frankie needed to get out and do something to escape the dark thoughts crowding her mind. 'Strength in numbers,' Brooke had said. Everyone would be there and they would support Frankie, every step of the way. At least, if Dexter was guilty, then Blaze had not got to Adam in time and Brooke's and Ruby's troubles would be over. That just left her, now then.

***

Dexter banged his hand down hard on the formica table in the brightly lit interview room, when the investigating officers left him, momentarily. That bitch of a detective was winding him up big time. Yes, so the photos he was shown from Adam's phone did not look good for him and he had to admit to being in possession of the coke. It looked like he was now the prime suspect for fucking murder. In the course of the latest interrogation, he had said nothing to suggest that Frankie hadn't also taken the cocaine with him. Let them give her some grief too. He was so mad with her, that her stupid fucking ex-boyfriend had walked in on them that night and put him in the frame. He hoped the pigs would pay a visit to Frankie and frighten the life out of her about her connection with class 'A' drugs, at the very least. He blamed her for his current predicament, big time. He was so angry at her, though it was not helping his case that the pigs could reel off a stream of names, his known contacts, who had been involved in all sorts of unsavoury activities in the underworld of Birmingham. It did not help that he had been done for assault several years ago. It was not looking good for him.

By the time Frankie walked through the door of the Otter's with Charlie, she was feeling a lot better. A third visit from the police had been totally degrading but she had managed to get everything in perspective now. She had been so embarrassed by those awful photographs, that were presented to her and she was sure that the detective looked smug as she did so. Frankie had squirmed when she had realised that the bastard Adam had photographed such intimate moments and he had also captured the image of that bag of cocaine on the kitchen table. After what had seemed like hours, it appeared that the detective was finally satisfied that Frankie was telling the truth about her relationship with Dexter. She had been so naïve and genuinely had not known the extent of his shady dealings, which meant that the events of that morning and his arrest were starting to make sense. The realisation that Dexter had a motive, and also had the track record to put him well into the frame for the assault on Adam was sinking in.

Frankie was also surprised that she was starting to find a sort of karma in what had happened. She hated Adam and the way he had behaved that night further deepened her hatred. She had been badly fooled by Dexter and she would never forgive him for bringing drugs into her home and pulling the wool over her eyes. How dare he. How dare both of them! These two men had manipulated her, well and truly. Maybe this was a simple case of natural justice. They had both just got exactly what they deserved.

It was only six o'clock but the Otter's was quite busy already, as the food was so good and many delicious dishes were already being served. Frankie smiled to herself as she acknowledged that she was hungry, famished in fact. Apart from a very light breakfast, she had only had a large brandy all day. She was first to arrive so she waved to Bonnie and a large table was quickly assigned to her. A brief exchange took place about the 'awful' events as Frankie ordered a large Chardonnay and Bonnie fussed Charlie, finding some doggy treats for him.

A few minutes later, the gang had arrived and were settling themselves at the table. Brooke was surprised but pleased by how positive Frankie was as she had been seriously worried about her. When the news of Dexter's arrest had broken, it had totally dominated all news channels and all of the conversations in the town of Delvreton. Nothing like this had ever happened before and the community's foundations were shaken. Brooke was aware that everyone in the Otter's knew about Frankie's connections with Adam, the murder victim of the 'Valentine's day murder' as everyone now referred to it. The average resident of Delvreton viewed Adam as a stalwart of the town so Brooke knew all eyes were surreptitiously on Frankie that evening and it was very important that she did not look as relaxed and happy as she did. She still could not believe that this turn of events also put herself and Ruby in the clear. The relief was palpable and only just starting to sink in.

After a quiet, whispered word in her ear from Brooke, Frankie composed herself and was careful to maintain a sombre demeanour. This came naturally as she quietly

357

talked through the events of her afternoon. The friends were transfixed, listening to Frankie's account of her latest ordeal with the stern female detective and her sidekick. She flushed slightly as she recalled her last evening with Dexter, the drugs, the sex and the final conflict between Dexter and Adam.

'Oh shit!' exclaimed Ruby. 'You poor thing. Thank God the police don't think you're into cocaine too!'

All of the friends nodded as Ronnie leaned across to give Frankie a much needed squeeze of her hand.

'The thing is,' Frankie continued, still in hushed tones. 'Dexter could be a bloody murderer. And I was seeing him.'

'You could have been in danger, yourself,' mused Daisy as Brooke nodded, the stark realisation dawning on her that the good time boy Dexter Croft was seriously bad news. Everyone was clear that he was not whiter than white because Arthur and Ronnie knew him well, but not that well it seemed.

'At least you're safe now,' Daisy continued. 'The fact that Dexter hasn't been released really does suggest that he did it, that he killed Adam so I guess we can all sleep a bit easier in our beds from now on.'

Frankie suddenly started to sob as the events of the last few days seemed to stampede through her mind reminding her of the danger she had been in. She was so grateful for the comfort as Daisy took her in her arms to soothe her distraught friend.

'Come on. You'll get through this. We are all by your side, every step of the way. Calm down now. You don't want people to see you like this in here. Have a big swig of that wine, mate,' Daisy advised gently.

Frankie followed instructions and started to feel a little better. Bruce observed all of this quietly from across the table, re-living the humiliating scene that afternoon, when the police had visited Frankie for the third time. He had watched her face go so pale when the photos Adam had taken were presented to her and he had heard her pleading with the officers to believe her, when she protested her innocence about never going near any drugs, let alone cocaine. He had also been slightly surprised, when Frankie had been so willing to throw Dexter right under the bus and to admit that, yes, Dexter had been outraged, when Adam had pushed him. Yes, she did have to admit that he definitely had a motive to go after Adam. Such was her level of shock and anxiety after that Wednesday evening, that Frankie had not even seen Dexter again, she had stated, desperate to distance herself from him. Surely, that said it all, she urged them to believe her. Finally, the detective seemed to be convinced and the two officers had thankfully left Frankie in peace.

She was very lucky, Bruce thought because Frankie herself had a motive to get her own back on Adam; she also had good reason to get her own back on Dexter. Just stay away from men from now on, Bruce silently gave his friend some very sound advice.

A couple of hours passed easily as the friends actually managed to enjoy their meal together and gradually moved onto more mundane topics of conversation than the dramatic events of the last few days. This was a most welcome interlude from the high octane, emotionally charged subject of Adam's death and Dexter's arrest. When they left together to start walking home at around eight thirty, there was a sense amongst them that life could, perhaps, get back to its normal rhythm again, one day.

Bruce made a mental note that he would let the dust lie for a while then he would return to Delvreton High. Under the pre-text of carrying out an interim service of the infrastructure he had installed, he would remove his spyware from Adam's office. He also planned to take the same approach to 'servicing' his friends' security systems, in each of their homes, so he could remove their cameras too. He felt that his work was done now. His friends, and especially his daughters were safe. Maybe, he could even try to get his own life back onto a more even keel, spend more time with Daisy and rekindle the flame a little. Bruce smiled to himself, comforted by his plan. He suddenly felt lighter than he had in months, especially knowing that the reprobate, Adam Pearson was well and truly out of their lives.

Epilogue

Friday evening and Bruce's computer screen flickered with the CCTV images of Adam's grandiose office. The regular school day was over but it was not unusual for Adam to be there well after hours. As unprofessional as ever, it was clearly visible that Adam intended to 'entertain' female company in there. Two empty Champagne flutes and a bottle of bubbles were carefully placed on his desk, the set-up like a lair to ensnare his prey. Bruce had been watching Suzie flitting in and out of his office all day. Patricia was clearly sick to death of Suzie's half-baked excuses to make appointments with her boss. His diary was already a nightmare to manage and the last thing she needed was his latest conquest taking up his precious time, for no good reason. The problem was that Adam insisted she make space and time for Suzie. Patricia had gritted her teeth and booked her in, yet again.

It was now well past home time. Patricia and most of the staff had left for the day. Bidding a hasty retreat, like a conformity of lemmings was the norm for Fridays. Adam always stayed until at least six in the evening. He certainly had no major desire to get home early to his brother's place, after all.

The slightly pixelated footage showed Adam looking up from his desk and smiling as his office door opened, but this time it was not Suzie who minced in, but another much younger woman.

As a relatively new member of staff, Iris felt a little nervous that she had been called to Adam's office but she had felt a lot closer to him recently through the text messages they often shared. The messages were always work based but undoubtedly tinged with flirtation. Meeting Adam, her boss, face-to-face and just the two of them was a different matter. Iris swallowed anxiously as she followed Adam's friendly direction to take a seat on the sofa and he sat opposite her on the matching tan leather armchair.

'Sit down Iris. It's great to finally get a private meeting with you. I need to officially congratulate you for landing that head of house job. We have lots to discuss and, since it's Friday, can I offer you a drink?' He glanced over to the two empty flutes and smiled, leaning towards Iris a little. She felt slightly uncomfortable with the idea of sharing a bottle of fizz with her boss, but was very keen to appease him and made every effort to appear at ease with the situation. After all, she had just managed to get a promotion and she had enjoyed the friendly banter over their text messages. Iris had reassured herself that all of the PE staff regularly messaged each other and Adam was just part of that group.

Adam smiled again, clearly taking his time to fully appraise the beautiful young woman opposite him.

Iris coughed slightly and replied. 'Err, just water please,' and she smiled back at Adam, her wide almond eyes making full eye contact as she seemed to grow in confidence a little.

As Adam turned his back momentarily to grab some bottled water, he rolled his eyes. He had been very much hoping he could 'loosen' Iris's inhibitions with a bit of Dutch courage. Still, not to worry; he had plenty more up his sleeve.

'So, you're rather special, aren't you Iris?' Adam looked at her intently. 'A great young teacher with so much potential and you've just got your first leadership role, so early in your career.' Iris felt herself inflate with pride.

He continued. 'Iris, you seem older than your years, more experienced than most young women your age. Well, at least that's the impression you certainly give me, judging from our secret text exchanges.' He paused, assessing her reaction. Iris sat still, like a startled rabbit in headlights.

'Err, thank you. I'm really keen to progress at Delvreton and I really do love working with...' Iris stammered.

Adam cut her off mid-sentence. 'Iris, you don't need to prove yourself at work. This isn't an interview,' he smirked. 'You know, I have enjoyed our texts so very, very much. If only you realised how much they brighten up my boring days... and nights.' Adam waited for Iris' reaction.

She was feeling unsure about how to respond. 'Well, I'm glad you like them,' Iris replied in an even tone. 'I was just trying to be friendly, after we had that great night in the Otter's, after the panto, you know. Well I want the boss to like me,' she laughed nervously.

'I do like you Iris, and you're such an asset to the school. This is why I want to see you again.' Adam sighed, looking into Iris' beautiful eyes 'I *really* want to see you again Iris, very much,' he paused, never taking his eyes off hers. 'What about we do that again, only this time, just you and me and maybe somewhere out of Delvreton, somewhere much quieter than the Otter's. Somewhere well away from the prying eyes of all the busy bodies round here. You see, it's better if no one else knows about more potential promotions, for the moment. Do you understand?'

Iris thought for a moment. This was starting to feel a little strange, but she was pleased that Adam clearly liked her and she thought that a business date wouldn't hurt if it could mean more progression opportunities. It was obvious he fancied her, but she didn't mind too much; it might even work in her favour. Iris sat up straight and leaned towards him slightly, smiling softly.

Yes, that sounds like it would be a good opportunity to discuss such things,' she replied.

Adam paused for a moment, drinking in the vision before him, almost revealing his thoughts as he considered the incredible possibilities this could lead to. Frankie ditching him had done him the best favour ever, as he was now free to sample younger women, younger flesh, and he was in charge of both of them. Suzie and now Iris. They were literally queuing up to be with him and he could not quite believe his luck.

'I'll text you,' Adam said with a dry laugh. 'I'm sure we can free up a few hours sometime this weekend, for starters anyway. Now, are you sure I can't tempt you with a glass of fizz?'

Iris controlled her breathing, despite her quickening heartbeat. Holding Adam's gaze, she slowly nodded her head.

'Yes, this weekend sounds fine. I'll look forward to it. You know, maybe I will have that glass of Champagne after all,' she beamed back at him.

Before Adam could pick up the bottle, a sudden knock at the door ended the liaison abruptly as Adam's deputy bustled in. Iris quickly excused herself, turning briefly to shoot a smile at Adam whilst she muttered her goodbyes. As she turned to leave the office, Iris' stunning face was fully captured by Bruce's cameras.

***

The lid on Bruce's laptop instantly slammed closed, followed by the desk chair being pushed so hard into the wall of the office that the windows shook in their frames. The door smashed shut as angry footsteps charged down the hallway. All of the screens in the control room were simply left flickering with static fuzz, accompanied only by a deathly silence.

***

As some of the friends knew, Daisy had suspected for a while that all was not well with Bruce. He had been spending more and more time in his office, checking his phone constantly and being generally distracted. She knew he had a very stressful job and at one point she had even worried he could be having an affair. So, out of concern for Bruce and her family she had just wandered into his 'control room' to see what he had been doing that was so important. What was it that had been constantly taking his attention away from their family life? Daisy had easily cracked his passwords and when the screens flickered to life, she was astounded at the camera set- ups and links to Arthur's, Ruby's, Brooke's, Ronnie's and Frankie's devices. Not to mention the reams of internet searches, echo requests, texts, video doorbell and drone footage and emails from all their friends. And all that unsavoury stuff on Adam, of course. No wonder Bruce had been so distant. He was too busy watching over everyone else's business. But Daisy had soon caught the bug too and could see how these little snippets of private information about their friends' lives could be so very intriguing.

Daisy had not planned to hurt Adam, let alone kill him. Fuelled with rage at what she had witnessed on the screen in Bruce's control room, she had been determined to stop Adam in his tracks, before Iris fell under his charm. There was no way on this earth she was going to let Adam take advantage of her beautiful daughter's naivety and Daisy certainly was not going to let him break her heart or worse.

Daisy knew only too well that Adam went for a regular morning run through Squirrel's Nook on Saturday mornings. He had been doing the run for some time, before he often spent the morning catching up in his office at Delvreton High. This was common knowledge from the days when he had been seeing Frankie. So, Daisy had scrambled into her track suit, and headed out at six o'clock, like she did most Saturday mornings. On this occasion though, her mind was filled with chaotic thoughts. What was she going to actually do? Would she even find him? What would she say if she saw him? Daisy did not have to wait long.   She had spent half an hour at the gym setting up for her clients, who she had booked in for later slots that morning. Then she jogged the short distance to Squirrel's Nook.

'Adam,' Daisy shouted as he pounded past her in the Nook's open fields. 'I want a word with you, you lowlife.'

'What the hell? What are you doing out here and how dare you address me like that!' Adam sneered as he came to a halt, breathing a little heavily. He could not help but notice the fierce expression on Daisy's attractive face. He could certainly see where Iris got her looks from.

'I know you're taking advantage of Iris and I'm here to demand that you leave my daughter alone. We all know your reputation with women. You can have your pick so pick someone else, you bastard. She's young and impressionable and I dare say you've made all sorts of empty promises to her about premature promotions.'

'You don't *know* anything Daisy,' Adam scoffed, still pretty shocked by this encounter. 'Iris knows her own mind. She is fully discrete about our little liaisons, as I've made it abundantly clear that it wouldn't be professional for her to kiss and tell. That could well affect her job security, if it were to come out. Anyway, it would just be my word against hers and I know who the Board of Governors would listen to.' Adam was getting well into his stride now and even starting to enjoy himself a little.

'You're such a bastard Adam. How dare you control Iris like this and threaten her job, so you can have your own way!' Daisy was seething.

Adam was suddenly confused. He was certain that he had enough of a hold over Iris for her to keep her mouth shut, but maybe she *had* told her mother after all. He was berating himself for admitting anything to Daisy. He could just have played dumb, made out it was a young woman's fantasy to date the headteacher. Anyway, it was too late; the cat was out of the bag. He definitely needed to act quickly now to shut Daisy down. He could not risk losing his bloody job over this.

'How *do* you know anyway? I presume Iris told you? Couldn't keep her mouth shut, just like a typical woman. Anyway, don't think I'm going to stand here and let you tell me what to do Daisy. Iris is a grown woman, with her own mind and she clearly has better taste than her mother. 'Adam knew he had gone too far, but he could not help himself. He loved seeing the reaction he was getting from Daisy. He sneered as he spat his words back at her. He had always felt like Daisy looked down her nose at him when he had been with Frankie.

'How dare you. You disrespectful piece of scum!' Daisy was now incandescent. She just could not get the smutty images out of her head of Adam with that slut Suzie. Yes, she had watched all of Bruce's camera footage and it had made her feel completely sick. There was no way this man would be allowed to corrupt her precious daughter.

Daisy stepped in Adam's way, but he shoved her aside and started to run away from her.

'This discussion isn't over!' she screamed after him.

'I think you'll find it is. Now go and crawl back to where you came from.' Adam's tone was venomous as he shouted back to Daisy, already sprinting off into the woods.

'Shit, shit, shit,' he chanted to himself, as he upped the pace. He would need to do some clever covering of his tracks to get out of this one. He just needed to get this run done and back to his office so he could make plans to protect his own back.

Daisy did not crawl back anywhere. In a frenzy of rage, she followed Adam into the woods. She was fit but she would never catch him up. However, she knew the route was circular and that Adam would come back to the concealed part of Squirrel's Nook. Waiting behind the majestic oak tree, Daisy steadied her breathing and she bided her time. The path was narrow here so Daisy knew exactly where Adam would run. Within a few moments, Daisy had carefully covered the exposed tree roots with moss and leaves. She then waited patiently, the grey mist mingling with her breath amongst the bare branches and bracken.

Moments passed, that seemed like hours. Eventually, Daisy heard Adam's footsteps and his panting breath approaching. As she had hoped, Adam's foot became entangled in the tree roots and Daisy seized her chance, as he completely lost his balance. Flinging herself at him from behind, Adam fell face down into the mud, as she pounced. Daisy was small in stature, but she was fit and her training had made her lean and strong. Kicking him over and over again, he couldn't get up, despite his muscular body far outweighing Daisy's. Daisy, however, had the advantage, as Adam had been taken by surprise. As he struggled to protect himself by holding his hands over the back of his head, she took the lump hammer and pounded it into his skull. Just one blow. Daisy heard the crack and saw Adam's body go completely limp. That was all it took.

Daisy could hardly believe what she had just done. She had never meant for this to happen. Adam had just been so hateful. Her protective instincts for Iris, coupled with his sheer disrespect and arrogance had simply spurred her on. She knew Adam was so much bigger and stronger than she was, so she had been ready with the lump hammer, the lump hammer she had taken from Ronnie's garage, just in case she might need it one day. She had hidden the small hammer in her underwear drawer and, on a whim, shoved it into her rucksack as she left the house that morning. The rush of adrenalin, when Adam had fallen had sent her into some sort of crazed frenzy and she had the hammer in her hand, mainly to defend herself if she had needed to. But events had not turned out like that. She had gone into some sort of out of body experience as she had carried out the frenzied attack. Daisy barely recognised the stranger she had become as she had kicked Adam, over and over and then hit him with the hammer. It had taken less than twenty seconds, but there Adam was, lying face down in the mud, his body totally still, blood staining the back of his bald head.

Daisy slowly retreated backwards, looking down on Adam's limp body. She started to shake, as the dawning realisation of what she had just done sank in. She panicked, then bent down to check that he was still breathing. Yes, but only just and he was clearly unconscious. Lump hammer still in hand, Daisy stuffed it into her rucksack and pounded away from the scene, heart and mind racing.

It was still only seven thirty in the morning when the dog walkers had started to emerge. Just getting light, it was not long before Adam's body was discovered.

Daisy knew exactly where she had to run, before heading back to the gym to start her day's work. She ran along the deserted canal path and she discarded the hammer in the murky, dark waters. It sank to the bottom instantly as Daisy's racing heart gradually regained its steady beat. As she jogged back to the gym, desperately trying to compose herself, Daisy recalled that mad moment when she had taken the small lump hammer from Ronnie's workshop just a few days ago. She had loved the feel of it and the experience of shop lifting with Ruby had made it so easy for her to slip the hammer into her rucksack, before going into the kitchen to enjoy a coffee and a chat with her mate. Who would have thought that her little 'snaffle', the hammer would be what she reached for that Saturday morning?

***

Blaze was in the Rockin' Robin Brew House Sunday lunchtime, nursing a JD and coke as usual. That was when his attention was drawn to the TV screen. The reporter's words instantly jumped out at him. A man had been found the previous morning in a local beauty spot in Delvreton. Blaze listened intently. The man's identity was confirmed. It was the headteacher of Delvreton High, Adam Pearson. He was found beaten in Squirrel's Nook, early Saturday morning and had sustained serious injuries from the assault. Then there was a photograph of Adam in happier times, dominating the TV screen.

'Jeez.' Blaze let out a long whistle. It was only that bloody geezer he had been paid to sort out. Oh well, saves a me job then, he chuckled to himself, with zero compassion. He had been planning to action his 'assignment' that coming weekend too but on the Sunday evening. Blaze could not help wondering who had done the deed though, then figured that maybe the two women had found someone else they preferred. Not that he cared. He still had the 2k. Well, what was left of it, after his latest cocaine spree. Onwards and upwards, he thought to himself. This was certainly his lucky day. Blaze smiled and headed back to the bar.

***

When Daisy had realised that Bruce had also been spying on her private conversations, she was horrified and had decided to keep her own record of what Bruce had been so obsessed with. At every opportunity, she had logged in to watch on the many screens in Bruce's office.

There had been so many opportunities, when Bruce was out pricing up potential new contracts or when he was at the Otter's, which was quite a lot.

What Daisy had not bargained for was seeing Adam with Iris and this had been the final straw, especially after she had seen the debauched scenes with Suzie. Worse still, Daisy had witnessed the scene in Frankie's kitchen before Christmas. Quite simply, she had watched just about everything. She had not had any other choice than to take some direct action and protect her daughter. By the time Bruce had tuned into the footage of Iris in Adam's office, Daisy had dealt with it. Bruce was just left thinking what they all thought – that Blaze or Dexter had sorted Adam out. There was still no definitive news about the perpetrator. Dexter was a prime suspect but had been released due to a lack of hard evidence. Nevertheless, Daisy was confident that no one would ever get near to suspecting her.

Bruce seemed much calmer these days and Daisy knew that he had tried to undo his misdeeds as a voyeur. He had taken out the surveillance cameras from his friends' houses and dismantled all of the other watching and listening devices. But, the thing was, Daisy was not at all happy with her husband. How dare he spy on everyone? How dare he spy on her? She would bide her time, just like she had done with Adam. When the time was right, she would make sure that Bruce paid the price for what he had done. He was not the man she thought he was and there had been a seismic shift in their relationship.

All things considered, Daisy felt a sense of natural justice that Adam had eventually died on Valentine's Day, of all days. The day of love. However, she knew one thing for certain. She had killed for one of her children and she would not hesitate to do it again, if she needed to. For now though, she sat quietly contemplating all that had happened. She recalled one of Bruce's late Grandma's sayings: 'a mother's love will conquer all.'

QUESTIONS FOR DISCUSSION

1. How far would you *really* go to protect your children?
2. If you had the power to watch over other people's private lives, would you?
3. How do you define addiction? What impact do you think addiction has, depending on your social and economic circumstances?
4. How does it feel to you that some of the characters are fortunate enough to be regularly eating in fine dining restaurants and adorning their dinner tables with feasts whilst others do not have enough money to put food on the table and are reliant on foodbanks?
5. Ruby and Brooke wanted to harm Adam, but did not have the nerve to do it themselves. If we have the desire to hurt someone, does that makes us as guilty as those who actually do the harm?
6. Is it ethical to take a child away from a loving mother, just because she lives in poverty and someone else can better provide for that child in a financial way?
7. Would you be able to love and accept a child of your partner, knowing this was the product of an affair?
8. Does Daisy have the right to be angry with Bruce, when, after all, she was also spying on her friends and family?

ACKNOWLEDGEMENTS

Thank you to parents, aunties, uncles and in-laws as well as many wonderful friends for their inspiration for some of the characters in this book. (You know who you are!)

If you enjoyed 'Privacy Settings' please tell your friends and family.

Privacy Settings is available on Amazon: Kindle or paperback

ABOUT THE AUTHOR

Privacy Settings was co-written under the pen name of Roanne Haskin. Both authors were born and raised in the West Midlands, UK. This is Roanne Haskin's debut novel. We hope you enjoyed it.

Printed in Great Britain
by Amazon